UNLEASHED

A SYDNEY RYE MYSTERY, BOOK 1

EMILY KIMELMAN

For Mette and David

I am a man, and therefore have all devils in my heart.
—Father Brown

CHAPTER ONE

BLUE

MY DOG once took a bullet that was intended for me. A bullet that ripped through his chest, narrowly missing his heart, and exited through his shoulder blade, effectively shattering it. This left him unconscious on the floor of my home. Amazingly, this bullet did not kill him.

Ten years ago I adopted Blue as a present to myself after I broke up with my boyfriend one hot, early summer night with the windows open and the neighborhood listening. The next morning I went straight to the pound in Bushwick, Brooklyn. Articles on buying your first dog tell you never to buy a dog on impulse. They want you to be prepared for this new member of your family, to understand the responsibilities and challenges of owning a dog. Going to the pound because you need something in your life that's worth holding onto is rarely, if ever, mentioned.

I asked the man at the pound to show me the biggest dogs they had. He showed me some seven-week-old Rottweiler-German shepherd puppies that he said would grow to be quite large. Then he showed me a six-month-old shepherd that would get pretty big. Then he showed me Blue, the largest dog they had. The man called him a Collie mix and he was stuffed into the biggest cage they had, but he didn't fit. He was as tall as a Great Dane but much skinnier, with the snout of a collie, the markings of a Siberian husky, the ears and tail of a shepherd and the

1

body of a wolf, with one blue eye and one brown. Crouched in a sitting position, unable to lie down, unable to sit all the way up, he looked at me from between the bars, and I fell in love.

"He's still underweight," the man in the blue scrubs told me as we looked at Blue. "I'll tell you, lady, he's pretty but he's skittish. He sheds, and I mean sheds. I don't think you want this dog." But I knew I wanted him. I knew I had to have him. He was the most beautiful thing I had ever seen.

Blue cost me $108. I brought him home, and we lived together for ten years. He was, for most of our relationship, my only companion. But when I first met Blue, a lifetime ago now, I had family and friends. I worked at a shitty coffeehouse. I was young and lost; I was normal. Back then, at the beginning of this story, before I'd ever seen a corpse, before Blue saved my life, before I felt what it was like to kill someone in cold blood, I was still Joy Humbolt. I'd never even heard the name Sydney Rye.

CHAPTER TWO

A HUGE FUCKING DOG

MY FOOT TAPPED against the spotted linoleum as the subway squealed over the Manhattan Bridge, and clacked up the East Side. I scolded myself for my constant tardiness and vowed that from that day forth I would change my life. I would get organized. I would become better.

Three hours later, a pastel-clad woman with bad hair asked if she could have a macchiato, which didn't make any sense. A woman wearing pastels, obviously from a place where they still wore scrunchies, asking for a shot of espresso with a touch of frothed milk on top. She should have been asking for a Frappuccino just like all the others who walked into the shop assuming that it was a Starbucks, because who could possibly imagine that there was coffee that was not Starbucks?

"Do you know what a macchiato is?" I asked.

The woman smiled benignly. "Yes, I want a caramel one." She obviously had no idea what she was talking about. You don't put caramel in a macchiato.

"So what you're saying is that you would like a shot of caramel and a shot of espresso with a touch of frothed milk on top."

"Why not? Let's give it a go." She smiled at me and I thought, this is amazing. She is willing to try a new drink--not only a new drink but a drink that she practically created for herself. Had anyone else ever

3

ordered this? I swear, in that moment, I was filled with a renewed sense of life. I had been wrong--not all dowdy women dressed in pastels were unadventurous lemmings.

"Oh, this isn't what I ordered," she said, looking down at my small cup of perfect caramel macchiato from above her two chins.

"Yes it is. It is a shot of caramel and a shot of espresso with a touch of frothed milk on top." I had been wrong. She was like all the rest of them.

"No, I've ordered this before at Starbucks and it's iced and in a very large plastic cup with a straw. It's not at all like this," she said as she waved her pudgy hand at my creation.

"Actually, this," I pointed at the little cup, "is exactly what you ordered. Exactly." I looked at the line of tourists that snaked out the door behind her onto 60th Street and continued, "I asked you if you wanted a shot of caramel and a shot of espresso with a touch of frothed milk. You said, 'Sure, let's give it a go.'" I used a high-pitched nasal voice to imitate her. "Now, I will make you a new drink," I said, "but it won't be any Starbucks knockoff and you won't get whatever it is you want unless you first admit that you are an idiot." The woman's face turned red and all her features made a mad dash to the center, leaving her with only cheek, forehead, and chin.

"That's right," I was really rolling now, "an idiot, a dumb-ass who has no idea what is in her coffee. I bet you don't know that Frappuccino is a Starbucks name, not the name of a real coffee drink. Frappuccino is a trademark, not a beverage." I was still explaining the finer points of coffee in an outdoor voice to the tourist when my manager, a guy named Brad who always seemed to be staring at my tits, came out from the back and fired me. Although the way I stormed out of there, you would think I had quit. I threw my apron on the floor and told Brad to fuck himself and stop masturbating in the coffee grounds. Yeah, the customers liked that one.

By the time I got home, I was crying.

It is not often that the weight of daily existence catches me in public. I usually have to be in bed, alone, in the dark. But this time I was standing outside my apartment crying so hard I could barely get my key in the door. The thing is, I wasn't crying because I got fired or because I'd broken up with my boyfriend, Marcus. My job was stupid, and Marcus was an ass. Breaking up with that dick-wad was something on the list of "shit I've done lately that I can be proud of," but it was pretty much the only thing.

I got the door open and Blue whined and circled me, desperately happy at my return. I sat down, my back against the door, crying. Blue nuzzled me and licked my face. I hugged him and he squirmed. "You've only known me less than a day and already you like me this much, huh?" I asked him, sniffling back my tears. He flopped onto his back, exposing his belly and warbled at me in answer.

Blue followed me down the hall and into the kitchen, where my answering machine sat blinking. "Five messages," I told Blue, wiping my face with the back of my hand. He leaned his weight against me and nuzzled my stomach.

I hit play and heard Marcus's voice. "Hey, listen." I heard Marcus's tongue slip out to wet his lips. My chest tightened. "I was thinking I'd come over later and we could...I don't know...talk or something. Call me back." Beep. "Hey, it's me again. Look, I'm in the neighborhood. I guess you're not home yet. I think I'm just going to head over...all right, um, bye." Beep. "What the fuck, Joy. I was just at your house and there was a huge fucking dog trying to kill me. I--" Beep. "Your fuckin' machine sucks, and where the fuck did you get that vicious dog? I mean, we just broke up last night and you already have a new dog. I don't know what that means, but I just don't know about you anymore." Beep. "Listen, just call me, OK?" Beep.

I exhaled. "Did you really attack him?" Blue wagged his tail and sat. "I suppose it would be your natural instinct," I hiccuped. "He was invading your home, right?" Blue looked at me blankly. "You don't look mean." He really didn't. He was tall and very skinny. I could see his ribs under his thick fur coat. With the snout of a collie, the markings of a Siberian husky, and the body of a wolf, with one blue eye and one brown, he was a very unique mutt. It occurred to me that I knew nothing about this dog. Our history was barely 12 hours long. I'd basically moved a large, hairy stranger into my house. The phone rang as I stared at my new dog, a little confused.

"Hey." It was my brother, James. "You want to get some drinks tonight?"

"Yeah sure, I have a lot to tell you."

"Anything good?"

"Not really. Well, I guess one thing." Blue had curled himself into a ball at my feet. "How about Nancy's at-- " I looked at the clock. It was 6:30. "How about a half hour?" I asked, planning a quick walk around the block for Blue.

"Perfect," James said.

The sun was slipping behind the brownstones across the street and turning the sky pink when I left for Nancy's. "Hey," said the guy on the corner who always said hey. I ignored him. "Hey, pretty lady, you got a beautiful ass," he tried again. I watched the concrete and power-walked away.

Ten minutes later I was at Nancy's, a low-key lesbian bar with a nice backyard. If you wanted to talk to a stranger you could, but there was no pressure. If you wanted to take someone home you could, but again there was no pressure.

I ordered a 'Tequila Gimlet, straight up'. The bartender, whose name I was pretty sure was Diane, nodded and moved off to make my drink. My face, reflected in the mirror behind the bar, peered from between a bottle of Blue Curacao and Midori. I needed a haircut. My fashionable bangs had grown out, and now I just pushed them behind my ears. Last night's fight with Marcus and my early-morning journey to the pound had left puffy, blue-tinted circles under my eyes. All those tears had left the white around my gray irises streaked with red and--I leaned forward a little to make sure--my upper eyelids a bizarre orange.

Diane placed a martini glass brimming with a sheer red liquid on the bar, and I handed her a ten. I moved toward the backyard, trying not to spill my drink all over my hand while spilling my drink all over my hand.

One overly cute couple sat in the soft candlelight cooing. I took a table close to the door and artificial lighting. As the tequila burned in my mouth, I wrangled with the memories of the past 24 hours. I usually shoved thoughts I didn't like to the back of my mind. But they never went away--they're always back there-- lurking right on the other side of my self-control.

James appeared in the doorway, smiling, holding a Tequila Gimlet, splash of cran (but his was on the rocks). He was a head taller than me at around six feet. We shared the same gray eyes and blond hair, though James's was short and styled while mine was reaching past my shoulder blades. Edging towards 30, James liked to talk about how his green-bean physique was morphing into eggplant. But the guy was still a pole.

"You look like shit," James said as he sat down. I smiled weakly and slurped my tequila. "Seriously, what the fuck happened to you?"

"Well, I broke up with Marcus"--this elicited a gasp--"and bought a dog."--an even bigger gasp--"Oh, and I got fired." I raised my glass in a mock toast to myself and polished it off.

"I talked to you yesterday! All this happened in one day?" I nodded, tried to finish my drink, then realized I already had. I went and brought back another.

"It's not really surprising," I said as I sat down. "We all knew it was coming."

James nodded. "Are you OK?" he asked.

"Well, I did lose my job because I went kinda crazy at work."

"Crazy?"

I told him about the plump tourist, her misorder, my insane reaction, and Brad's management decision. Then I told him about the masturbation comment.

James laughed. "I love it," he said. "I'm proud of you, Joy. That job sucked. Marcus was a tool. You've got a whole new fresh start."

"Easy for you to say. How exactly am I supposed to pay my rent?"

"You'll figure it out. Now, tell me about this dog. I can't believe you're such an asshole that you went out and got a dog because you broke up with your boyfriend. It's so pathetic."

"You're a real sweetheart."

"Somebody has to tell you."

"Jesus, I wanted a dog, so I went and got a dog."

"Oh, this was something planned?" James leaned his elbows on the table with mischief dancing in his eyes. "It's just a coincidence that you happened to break up with your boyfriend the night before." He smiled at me.

"Oh, just shut up. So what if I bought a dog to console myself?" He was right, of course. I had gone and bought a dog because I broke up with my boyfriend. And, yes, that was pathetic.

"So, what kind of dog?"

"He's really beautiful. He has one blue eye and one brown. Oh, oh, the best part is he attacked Marcus when he tried to come over." James laughed. "I know. Can you fucking believe it? He left me five messages today." I held up my hand with all five fingers extended.

"Your dog attacks people?"

"Not people, intruders," I said with more confidence than I felt. For all I knew Blue attacked all sorts of people. Maybe it wasn't that Marcus was breaking into the house. Maybe Blue would attack any douchebag we passed on the street. The thought made me laugh.

James smiled at me. "Not to talk badly about Marcus, Lord knows he was sexy as hell, but the guy is kind of an idiot. Not to mention that he tried to control you way too much. Low self-esteem fucks up a lot of men." James sat back, his hypothesis fully expressed.

I laughed. "I guess. Whatever, I'm over it." I sat up and scooped up my drink taking a long sip. "I'm so over it."

"Well, are you going to call him back? I don't think you should. Make a clean break."

I knew he was right, but I also knew that I had no control over myself whatsoever and would probably call him. "How's Hugh?" I asked, changing the subject. Hugh was James's boyfriend of four years.

"He's good," James smiled. "Actually, we're really good … Our offer was accepted." Hugh and James had spent the last eight months trying to find an apartment. Two months ago, they'd found it. A fifth-floor walk-up with a roof deck, two bedrooms (OK, a bedroom-and-a-half) and a kitchen that was recently renovated.

"Holy shit. That's awesome. How much?"

"It's a little out of our price range, but you always pay more than you want, right?"

Later, I stumbled into my building blind-drunk. I climbed the steps humming to myself, swinging my keys. I was feeling pretty good. Sure, I had no job, no boyfriend, and a weirdo of a dog, but life was not so bad, not so bad at all. I would make it; I could fix it. Everything was going to be just fine.

Blue greeted me at the door. "Hi, boy." I crouched and rubbed his ears. He nuzzled my chest, knocking me against the wall. Blue wrapped himself in my arms. I breathed into his neck, smelling the pound. "We're going to be OK," I said into his neck. "I'm going to take care of us. Starting tomorrow, I'm going to fix this mess of a life of ours." Then I passed out.

CHAPTER THREE

FIXING THIS LIFE

I OPENED my eyes and immediately closed them again. The sun rushing through the living room windows sent bolts of pain to the back of my head. Blue pushed his muzzle against my arm, encouraging me to get up. I squinted through my fingers at him. He tried to lick my eyeball. I laughed and then groaned.

Sitting up, my entire body rebelled. "Jesus fucking Christ," I muttered through sock-coated teeth. Groping the wall I struggled to stand. I could feel my brain floating on an ocean of tequila. Every movement crashing it into the walls of my skull.

Gently, I moved down the hall to the bathroom. In the mirror I saw I was wearing the same clothing as the morning before. I struggled with my jeans while the bathtub filled. Steam fogged the room, and I sank under the hot water, listening to my heart resound in my head.

Hair combed and teeth brushed, I checked the fridge hoping for fresh milk for my coffee, knowing that I hadn't bought any. I poured the coffee, scooped sugar in by the tablespoon, splashed in the milk (only one day late) and topped the whole thing off with a load of cinnamon.

After my second cup of coffee, I knew what to do. "First thing I'm gonna do today," I yelled to Blue from the bedroom as I got dressed, "is take you for a walk." I squeezed into a pair of freshly washed jeans, struggling to button the button. I found a T-shirt in a mound of clothing I kept on a chair in the corner of my room, smelled it, and put it on. "Then I'm going to find a job." I slipped on a flip-flop, glanced around for the other, got down on my knees and checked under the bed, found it and put that on, too. I walked back out to the hall where Blue waited. He smiled at me, clearly confident in me, and my plan.

Blue's body vibrated as I put the leash on him. We bounded down the stairs together and by the time we hit the street I was feeling pretty good. It was one of those gorgeous early-summer days when the temperature is just right, the sun is shining, and you get the distinct feeling that everything will be just fine.

I strutted down the street, admiring the way my wet hair looked in the sun, its many shades of white and gold catching the light. Blue trotted next to me, sniffing the warm air. Park slope in early summer was designed for dog walking. We wandered past boutiques, their windows filled with beautiful clothing. Well-dressed, good-looking people milled around the coffee shop. They all turned to look at us. Blue really did look like a creature from another land. His white and black fur glistening in the sunlight and his strangely beautiful eyes caught the attention of everyone we passed.

On our way back to my place we passed a school. Children flooded into the playground laughing and yelling, heading home. I smiled as the kids began to surround us, when suddenly Blue lunged and snapped at a passing teacher. The man, plump and freckled, jumped back, tripped over a piece of uneven pavement, and fell to the ground, his eyes wide and wet with fear. Blue strained against the leash, desperate to finish him off. His lips curled up to expose massive, razor-sharp teeth that snapped at the air, trying to sink into any part of the poor guy.

The children cowered and screamed for their mothers as my wolf dog strained to disembowel their instructor. Blue looked like a starved lunatic recently escaped from a mental hospital, spit whipping out of his mouth in long strings, his eyes rolling wildly in their sockets.

I gripped the leash with both hands and yanked it with such strength that Blue's body twisted backwards, lifting his front paws off the ground and landing them in the opposite direction. I used his momentary surprise to begin dragging him back toward the house. He didn't stop snarling until the sound of children's voices had dissipated.

As I was trying to find my keys, my next-door neighbor, Nona, opened her door. "I knew it," she said. "I knew you got a dog. Now, bring that little rapscallion over, and let's have some tea."

I first met Nona through my grandmother, who lived in my apartment before she passed away. Nona was a retired dancer in her early seventies. She'd been married three times to three men who all died within the first six months of marriage, leaving her with the full name of Nona Carvel Nevins Blatt, but she went with her maiden name, Jones.

Nona ruffled Blue's ears and cooed to him about how handsome he was, and so big. "Would you like a snack, you little rapscallion, you?" Blue answered by prancing behind her as she moved toward the kitchen, his massive tail swinging the width of the hallway. Photographs of Nona in front of the Eiffel Tower, the Mirage Hotel, an elephant, dotted the walls. Nona's hair, now a brilliant silver and cropped short, had once been long, silky, and black. In my favorite photograph, Nona is in the center of ten smiling women all crowded together. Behind them looms a large blimp.

Nona was half in the fridge with Blue by her side when I walked in. "How about a little chicken fricassee?" Nona asked as Blue's tail thumped against the cabinets. She had remodeled her kitchen, putting down cork floors, putting up blue cabinets, and laying butcher-block counter tops. Over the stove hung photographs of her three husbands, all beautifully framed with a slight layer of grease coating them. Nona stood up from behind the fridge door and smiled at me.

"So, you got a dog, broke up with Marcus--anything else dear?" she asked while feeding Blue from a Tupperware container. He sat quietly in front of her, licking his lips and tapping his tail.

"Yeah, I got fired."

Nona let out a laugh. "Isn't it all so exciting?" she said returning the

Tupperware to the fridge. Blue let out a low groan but didn't stop tapping his tail. Nona smiled at him before pulling down her teapot.

"I guess you could call it that."

"Oh, cheer up. You have a whole new fresh start," she said with a furrowed brow that quickly spread into an infectious smile. "You can do anything now." I smiled back at her, feeling slightly better.

We were soon settled in Nona's living room enjoying strong black tea and red velvet cake. Blue was curled up at my feet on the plush rug, snoring. "Now, about this job situation. Don't you think it's time you started thinking bigger?" Nona asked. I looked at her, my cheeks filled with cake. "I mean a career. Don't you want a career?"

I swallowed and then smiled. "Sure, but I don't know what I want to do."

"What did you go to school for again?" Nona asked and then refilled my teacup. I poured fresh milk in, enjoying the way it sank to the bottom and then rushed to the top in a delicious brown cloud.

"Undeclared," I said.

Nona nodded, her brow creased, as if I had said something important instead of a simple fact. "Why didn't you get a degree?" she asked.

I smiled at my mug. "I didn't want to be saddled with debt and no way of paying it off."

"But wouldn't going to college help you find a well-paying job?"

I just shrugged, in no mood to continue the conversation. We sat for a while listening to a clock tick on the mantel, the distant beeping of a truck's reverse warning, and the familiar sound of chewing in our heads.

"Do you think you will go back to school?" Nona asked, breaking the calm.

"I don't know. I'd like to, but financially it doesn't make sense."

"Isn't your mother's husband a wealthy man? Wouldn't they pay for it?"

Nona had brought this up before, and it made me angry that she was doing it again. "I don't want that, Nona," I said, trying to keep myself from snapping at her.

"But don't you think you should take advantage..." Her voice faded when she saw the look on my face. "Fine, then. What are you going to do?"

"Nona, I honestly have no idea, but I don't think I should be working in any kind of customer-service job anymore. My ability to deal with people has all but disappeared," I said jokingly, trying to break the tension in the room. Nona laughed for me.

"Well, if you're not going to college you'll have to go into business. I know of a woman who is selling a dog-walking business. She's a friend of Julia--you remember Julia, right? The one with the hip thing and the curly hair that looks permed but is natural?" I nodded, vaguely remembering a woman who used a cane and had strange curly hair. "Well, she has a friend, you know. She lives in Yorkville on East End Avenue-- nice area but no public transportation. I don't know how she does it with that hip. Anyway, this young woman, her friend, I can't remember her name, is selling her dog-walking business. It's good money, I understand, with room to grow. What do you think?"

"Well," I said. "I don't actually have much experience with businesses or walking dogs."

"What are you talking about? You have a dog. I assume you walk him."

"Yeah, but I wouldn't consider myself an expert." I flashed back to the all-too-recent attempted homicide of an unsuspecting elementary school teacher.

"You don't have to be an expert. You just have to know how to pretend to be an expert." Nona raised her eyebrows and smiled. "Look, here's what I'll do. I'll call Julia and get all the information, OK?"

"OK."

Two days after my vow to fix my life, I was sitting on Charlene Miller's overstuffed white couch with black-and-white photographs of flowers (suggestive flowers) above my head. Charlene Miller was the neighbor of Nona's friend Julia who was selling her dog-walking route. She was the type of woman you might see on the subway wearing a white suit--

the kind of woman who made you question how she managed to stay so clean in such a dirty place. "This is a really nice area," I said. Charlene smiled at me with big, clean, straight teeth.

"It's Manhattan's little secret." Charlene sounded as if she had expressed this opinion before.

"I can see that," I volleyed back.

"I remember the first time I walked around here; I wondered how it could be so quiet, especially with the highway right there." Charlene said, referring to the East River Drive which runs right next to, and slightly below, East End Avenue.

"I wondered the same thing," I said with enthusiasm. We smiled at each other and our shared ignorance about how a street next to a highway was so darn quiet.

"I'm trying to sell the route because I've got so many other things going on right now. Also, I might be getting out of town. I'm not sure yet," Charlene said. "It's really easy. You just feed and exercise the dogs. I only have three clients but the money's good." She smiled at me and pushed her auburn hair behind her adorably petite ears.

"Like how good?" I smiled trying to sound casual, not hungry.

She smiled. "I charge $40 an hour."

"Really? So that's..." I started to do the math when she finished it for me.

"$1,200 a week." She laughed at the look on my face.

"What kind of compensation are you looking for?" I asked.

"Well, you could either buy the route off me up front or give me a percentage of the profits for the first year."

"I don't have the capital to buy it up front but I think we could work out a payment plan that would make us both happy." I hoped I sounded responsible rather than broke.

"All right, that's fine. Everything here looks good," she gestured to my résumé and references on her coffee table. "I have a few other people I need to see, so would it be OK if I got back to you by the end of the week?"

"Oh, of course. I understand." She stood up and I followed. Charlene put her hand out and we shook. Her grip was strong. "Thank you for your time," I said.

Outside, the street was indeed quiet. East End Avenue runs between 79th and 93rd streets right next to and slightly above East River Drive, a four-lane highway that lets New Yorkers speed all the way from Battery Park City to the Triborough Bridge. I wandered up the avenue towards Carl Schurz Park which, in parts, is cantilevered over the highway. The FDR, in turn, is suspended above the East River. Makes you wonder what we are standing on.

Crossing East End Avenue, I walked into Carl Schurz Park. Big paving stones, neatly lined- up trees, and perfectly trimmed grass gave the place an air of formality appropriate for the only resident of the park- -the mayor of New York. Kurt Jessup lived in Gracie Mansion, a homestead built with a view of the river before there even was a city called New York, let alone a mayor to run it. The historic house is hidden in a corner of the park surrounded by its own gardens and very high fences.

I wasn't sure how I had performed during the interview. The fact that we both admired the relative silence of the neighborhood was good. But why would she give me the route instead of someone who could buy it off her? Did I even want it, I thought, as I looked over the dog run in the park.

A large shepherd was barking insistently at a cocker spaniel who'd stolen his ball and run under a bench, behind the protective calves of his owner. The shepherd's master, a guy in sweatpants and a windbreaker, was clearly annoyed at the cocker spaniel's owner, a man who was hidden behind the *New York Times*. The shepherd kept barking, and the cocker spaniel gnawed on the ball, pretending the shepherd wasn't barking.

I wandered past the dog runs (there was one for large dogs and one for little ones) to the esplanade that runs above the river. People sat on benches facing the rushing water, the sun glinting off its silver surface. Warehouses hugged the opposite bank. Downriver, the three Con Edison smokestacks painted red, white, and gray stood tall and alone, shaping the Queen's skyline.

I walked upriver, toward Hell's Gate, where the Harlem River meets the water from the Long Island Sound in a swirling, dangerous mess of tides and currents. A stone with a plaque atop memorializes 80 Revolutionary War soldiers who drowned there in 1780. Prisoners aboard the H.M.S. Hussar, they were shackled in her hold when she struck Pot Rock and slipped beneath the freezing, unforgiving waters of Hell's Gate. "They died for a nation they never saw born," reads the inscription.

I watched a train glide across Hell's Gate Bridge; a beautiful arch with bowstring trusses stretched over the treacherous water. In front of Hell's Gate Bridge, traffic moved slowly, in stops and starts, across the Triborough Bridge, a workman-like structure that connects Manhattan, Queens, and the Bronx.

My phone rang as I admired the urban landscape. "Hi, it's Charlene. Listen, I just thought about it and you can have the route."

"Oh, OK."

"Why don't you come back up, and we'll work out the details?"

Charlene was waiting at the door, looking paler than before. "I've got to get out of town for business, so the only type of payment I need right now from you is to take care of my cat, Oscar, until I get back." She walked through the living room into her kitchen. Oscar sat on the granite countertop, cleaning his face. He was a big tabby with white paws and a weight problem.

"Sure," I said.

Charlene walked over to her computer and grabbed pages out of her printer tray. "Here's a list of the clients and their dogs' info." I reached out to take them, but Charlene turned away and pushed the papers into a manila envelope. "The keys..." Her eyes wandered around the kitchen. "Where are the keys?" Charlene pushed past me and ran her hand over the empty granite counter. "I thought I...Oscar?" the cat meowed, and she gently moved him over to reveal a ring of keys. Charlene dropped them into the envelope with the papers and passed the whole thing off to me.

"We can deal with all the details when I get back, or I'll call you. Oh, and I'll leave a set of my keys at the front desk for you. You should come and see Oscar about every three days." The doorbell rang. She froze. The tension rippling off her was palpable. Charlene moved back into the living room slowly. I saw her hesitate, then, taking a deep breath, she checked the peephole. Her body relaxed and she opened the door.

"Hello, Carlos," Charlene said to a man in a custodial uniform standing in the hall. "Don't worry about it for now. I'm going on vacation and will call when I get back. Thanks for coming, though." He nodded and turned to leave as Charlene closed the door. She smiled at me, her lips tight and a mist of sweat at her hairline. "All right, so you have everything you need," she said, looking around the apartment.

"I guess," I said holding the envelope in my hand.

"Okay," she started moving me toward the door, "and I'll be in touch in a couple of days." She opened the door and I stepped through. "Thanks. Bye," Charlene said quickly and then closed the door. I heard the deadbolt click into place as I walked away.

That night I brought Blue over to James's place for dinner. Hugh answered the door. He is a big guy with a wide face, gapped teeth and an easy smile. His hair looks like his mother cut it by putting a bowl on his head. It works for him.

We hugged our hellos in the doorway. Blue put his snout between us and emitted a deep warble. Hugh pulled back, laughing. "Oh, my God, he's amazing." Blue stepped in front of me. Hugh laughed again and motioned for us to come in.

Boxes, some half-full, others overflowing, dotted James's one-bedroom garden-level apartment. Aurora, his cat, lay curled in a box on a pile of sweaters. She poked her head up when we came in, her yellow eyes bobbing at the edge of the cardboard and multicolored ears at attention. Blue walked toward the box. "I wouldn't do that if I were you," I warned him as he approached Aurora snout first.

Aurora sat up and hissed, drool spitting and splattering out of her. Blinded by the saliva, Blue stumbled back, but not before she had a chance to swipe out and lash him across the nose. He whimpered and scampered back to my side. The scratch beaded with drops of blood.

Kneading at the sweaters below her, Aurora moaned and settled back into the box.

"What a lovely creature," Hugh said as he headed for the kitchen to work on whatever was making the wonderful smell floating through the apartment. I walked back to the yard, where James waited with a pitcher of passion fruit margaritas. "Holy shit," he said when he saw Blue. "You weren't kidding when you said you got a dog. That thing is huge." Blue sat on James's foot and James laughed. "I like him." He filled a glass for me. The margarita was an opaque orange-red that glimmered in the soft candlelight.

"So, I acquired a business today." I sipped the margarita, a perfect mix of fresh juice and jaw-clenching tequila.

"Acquired a business, eh?" James poured Hugh a drink, then passed it through the kitchen window.

"A dog-walking business." James turned back to me, surprised. "What?"

I laughed. "I am telling you that this morning I went to the Upper East Side--Yorkville to be exact--and acquired myself a dog-walking business. But I think there's something weird about it." Hugh appeared in the window.

"What are you talking about? You got a what-walking business?"

"Dog-walking."

"What do you know about walking dogs?" James asked, "Or for that matter about business?"

"Well, I walk Blue." James stared at me. "And it's not really a business."

"Wait, wait. You have to start this story at the beginning because you are talking nonsense," James said. Hugh nodded.

"Wait a minute. Let's discuss it over the 'who's for'." Hugh disappeared into the kitchen. "Who's for" is what my family has always called hors d'oeuvres, as in "who's for some hors d'oeuvres?" According to my grandmother, it is an established expression, but I don't know anyone else who uses it.

Munching on Gruyère cheese puffs and mushrooms stuffed with

duck sausage, I explained about Charlene's drastic change, her quick decision, and the sweat on her hairline.

"Do you see what I mean by weird?" I asked them.

"The whole thing is weird," James said, then finished off the last of his drink. "I don't think you should do it. You know that means cleaning up dog shit all day."

"But," I argued, "it's good money and I don't have to deal with people, which we all know I'm not so good at."

"You're fine with people," James waved off my suggestion with a half-eaten mushroom cap. Hugh gave him a look.

"I've got an envelope that tells me what to do."

"An envelope?" James raised an eyebrow.

"Yes, an envelope that has all the information and keys I need." I pulled it out of my bag. "So I start tomorrow."

"You can't argue with that." Hugh admitted, refilling James's glass.

CHAPTER FOUR

MY FIRST DAY

IF JOANNE SANDERS passed me on the street, she would not recognize me as the person who ate seven of her cheddar-flavored Goldfish. Ms. Sanders wouldn't know that her Pomeranian, Snowball, welcomed me into their home by showing me exactly where she liked to pee under the kitchen table. Joanne Sanders would not know that I worked for her because Joanne Sanders had never met me.

Snowball, a ten-pound white puff ball with dark, almond-shaped eyes, was crated in a black cage with a leopard-print cover when I walked into apartment G5 on my first day as a dog-walker. Snowball looked like the recently imprisoned queen of a very small, safe jungle. Her subjects, in the shape of stuffed lions, tigers, and elephants littered the living room carpet.

Joanne Sanders, a broad woman in her forties, posed with friends, family, and Snowball in photographs displayed on the mantel of the fake fireplace. She had shoulder-length brown hair and bangs teased high above her brow. I could picture her behind ten inches of bulletproof glass sneering at me with gloss-encased lips for filling out my deposit slip incorrectly.

I fed Snowball half a cup of kibble and a spoonful of wet food as my envelope of information directed. She ate it quickly while making funny little squeaking noises. Once she had licked her bowl to a bright sheen, we headed out for my first walk as a dog-walker.

I steered us off East End Avenue and onto the esplanade that runs along the river. The water reflected the sun in bright silver glints. I smelled oil and brine. We reached Carl Schurz Park and turned into the run for small dogs. The gate leading into the run reached only to my knees, as did the rest of the fence designed to keep small dogs in and big ones out. A sign on the gate read, "Dogs over 25 pounds not permitted." Ten dogs under 25 pounds, and one who was probably a little over, played together in the pen. Their owners, in groups of three or four, sat on worn wooden benches and talked about dogs. Snowball ran to join a poodle growling at a puppy. They intimidated it behind its owner's calves. Then the poodle, a miniature gray curly thing with long ears, mounted Snowball. I turned to the river and watched a giant barge inch by.

"Hi." A woman wearing a fanny pack, pleated khaki shorts that started at her belly button and ended at her knees, black socks (pulled up), and clogs stood above me.

"Hi." I said back, raising my hand to shield my eyes from the sun.

"You're new." She wasn't asking a question.

"That's right."

"Taking over Charlene's route."

"Right again."

She sat next to me. "How long have you been walking dogs?"

"Not long."

"I didn't think so." I spotted two women on a bench on the other side of the run watching us. "You see, usually, when a dog you're responsible for is being a bully..." She raised her eyebrows at me, and I realized I was being lectured. "...You should intervene." I sat in silence, looking at her as she looked at me.

"OK," I finally said. I looked over to where Snowball and the poodle were playing happily. "Not now?" I asked.

"No, not now, now is too late. I'm talking about what they did to that puppy."

"So this is for my future reference."

She smiled, pleased with my grasp of the situation. "Exactly."

"Okay."

"I'm Marcia." She held her hand out. I put mine in it. We shook. Her hand was rough and her grip strong.

"Joy."

"Nice to meet you, Joy."

"You're a dog-walker." I wanted to see if her trick of stating facts worked both ways.

"Sure am." She didn't seem to notice. "And that's Elaine and Fiona." She motioned toward the bench down the yard. They waved. I waved back.

"You're all dog-walkers."

"That's right."

"You like it?" I asked.

She smiled. "Love it. I've been doing this for most my life."

"You know I didn't even realize it was a profession until recently." Marcia looked dumbfounded. "You know, I'd just never thought about it," I said, trying to make up for my obvious blunder. That made two in about as many minutes. Snowball jumped up onto the bench next to me, panting. I used it as an excuse to leave. "It was nice meeting you," I said as I stood.

"See you around," she said.

My next charge, Snaffles, a Jack Russell terrier owned by Mr. and Mrs. Saperstein, ran up and down the length of the kitchen, which was blocked off from the rest of the apartment by a child safety gate. He inhaled the three-fourths-of-a-cup of kibble I measured into his bowl and then continued his bounding and running while I tried to get the leash on him. Once the leash was attached, he stopped running and concentrated on killing it. Snaffles shook the leash with the gusto a wolf might use when taking out a bunny.

On the street he pissed on the trees, the parking meters, the trash bags, and when he ran out of pee, he kept raising his leg nonetheless. It took us the full 45 minutes just to get around the block. I returned him to his kitchen at two exactly, and, as I left, I heard the clicking of his claws while he raced back and forth and back and forth.

I left the Sapersteins' building and headed two doors down to walk the Maxims' golden retriever who, according to my notes, was named Toby. I nodded at the doorman. He was wearing a hunter-green jacket with puffed riding jodhpurs and knee-high boots. At the front desk, I was directed to a bank of elevators. A key from my envelope allowed me to push the button for the penthouse. When the golden doors of the elevator opened, I was standing in an ornate foyer. An elaborate flower arrangement stood on a pier table next to a large, imposing, dark, wooden door.

His whole body wagging, Toby welcomed me into the house. A wall of windows, with a view of the glittering river below and Queens in the distance, flooded the two-story room with light. It reflected off the polished wood floor and bathed three teal couches--one of which had the imprint of Toby's body in it--in bright, white sunlight. To the left, a spiral staircase curled up through the ceiling. Toby waited patiently, apparently used to the awe that the room inspired.

I found the kitchen when I walked through a door on the right side of the living room. The kitchen had floor-to-ceiling windows with the same view as the living room. Inside the enormous Subzero refrigerator, I found a Tupperware container labeled "Toby's lunch."

After he'd finished his mix of specialty frozen meats topped with several different powdered supplements, Toby pulled me through the lobby and out onto the street. He turned downtown, and I followed, hurrying to keep up. Toby pulled against the leash, tightening his collar and choking himself in the process. He coughed and made awful gagging noises until we reached a smell interesting enough to pause for. Toby sniffed intently for several seconds and then shot out to the end of the leash, hit it, and started the whole process all over again. My cell phone rang. I followed Toby to a fire hydrant, then answered it. It was James. "Hey," I said, then lost my balance as Toby lunged down the street. I landed on my right hip with a thud. The leash flew out of my hand and my cell phone bounced against a parked car and smashed onto the side-walk. Toby tore down an alley ten yards away.

I jumped up ignoring my throbbing hip, grabbed my phone and its disconnected battery, then gave chase. Toby's golden butt stuck out from behind a pair of dirty green Dumpsters. "Toby!" He ignored me, intent on whatever was hiding in the deep shade of the narrow alley. I picked my way through the littered dead end. After the relentless heat and bright sunshine of the street, the alley felt almost cold.

Toby poked his head out from behind the Dumpster. There was something hairy and black in his mouth. Oh Jesus, I thought, please don't let it be a rat. I stood in my tracks and called to him again. "Toby!" I yelled in a high-pitched, happy tone. He stood his ground and began shaking the hairy thing. A breeze blew through the alley and I smelled the putrid sweetness of garbage in June mixed with the rotten stench of decay. Toby looked at me, his eyes reflecting a shiny green in the darkness. I shivered in my thin T-shirt and wondered, for just a moment, if I could leave him here, go back to Brooklyn, take a nap, and pretend like none of this had ever happened.

Instead, I pulled my collar over my mouth and nose and took a tentative step toward him. He backed away. "Toby come." I took another step. He took another step away from me, holding the hairy, black mess tightly in his jaws. His leash--long, red, and nylon--curled off his choke collar onto the ground. With a swift move, I stomped it. Toby couldn't get away.

He whined through his stuffed mouth as I reached down to pick up the lead. It was in a puddle that I quickly realized I was standing in. The liquid was all over the leash, and when I looked at Toby, I saw that it covered his paws and dripped off the prize in his mouth.

"What the--" "Fuck" caught in my throat as I looked at the dark, thick, red fluid. I turned my head ever so slowly and looked at where Toby had found that black mass of wet hair. A hand--gray, limp, and lifeless--lay inches from my left foot.

Blood rushed in my ears. The hand was attached to a wrist that disappeared into a blue tracksuit jacket. Turning my head just the slightest bit more, I saw what had once been a face but was now a gaping red hole.

The top of the man's head had survived with its few pathetic strands of black hair. But his eyes, nose, mouth, chin--they were all gone. In their place was a mass of bloody pulp. The head lay in a pool of dark, clotted blood; I stood in that puddle and screamed.

CHAPTER FIVE

THE DISPATCHED UNITS

THE ONLY OTHER blood and gore I'd seen in real life was on the road. Animals, disemboweled, splayed on the cement, their blood ground into the pavement by a thousand tons of cars driving through it. Flies hovering above the carrion, buzzing away when a car came too close, but always resettling and continuing their work, turning the corpse into a nursery for their young.

When I first got my license, I would drive around because it was the only thing to do. I would smoke cigarettes and blast loud, angry music. Those carcasses on the side of the road in all states of decomposition, some fresh and red, others brown and sunken, would make my insides quiver.

As I sat there, with Toby at my feet, waiting for the police, all I could think about was this one decapitated cat whose insides were spread across the whole road, and there was nothing I could do but run over his fucking intestines. The doorman from the nearest building who'd responded to my screaming was chattering at me. There was blood on my hand, drying in the creases of my palm. And I just kept thinking about that poor cat.

The sound of clopping hooves preceded two mounted police officers rounding the corner. Toby shifted nervously and the doorman waved them over, desperately pointing to the alley. They stopped in front of us. Squinting against the sun, I looked up at the one closer to me. The light bounced off his helmet and badge.

"Hello," I said.

"Hi," he said back and removed his sunglasses. His eyes were the same color as the ocean in those ads on the subway for tropical vacations. His partner was talking to the doorman, who was shaking his head in a grotesque imitation of Toby's show with the mess of black hair. It turned out to be a toupee. I felt bile rise up in my throat. "I'm Officer O'Conner and that's my partner, Officer Doyle. Can you tell me what the problem is?" he asked.

"There's a dead body in the alley," I said, nodding toward the body. As Officer O'Conner climbed off his horse, the smell of leather wafted toward me. He entered the alley.

Officer Doyle dismounted and came over to where I stood. He asked me if I was all right. Doyle looked to be about 30. He had dark brown eyes and a nose that angled left. I nodded.

Officer O'Conner motioned from the mouth of the alley, and Doyle headed over to him. I examined the cracked brown tracks on my thigh. I thought about the dripping hair in Toby's mouth. The memory of that thing touching my leg as I pulled Toby out of the alley and back to the sanity of the street lurched up at me.

Sirens wailed and two patrol cars pulled up next to the horses. Officer Doyle explained that he would need a statement and to collect some evidence from me. I nodded. He went away and came back with a woman who was holding a camera and yelling at a young guy with glasses and adolescent acne to hurry up. She started snapping pictures of me and pulled my hands toward her. "Stay still," she commanded. Her assistant, his hands in tight latex gloves, scraped some of the dried blood from my legs into a plastic bag. Then the woman took Toby's leash from me.

"Hey," I said, but she ignored me. Her assistant smiled apologetically. His bone-white hands started on Toby's fur, trying to get the congealed blood into a bag while his boss's camera clicked away. He took off Toby's leash and collar. Doyle brought him a piece of rope, and they tied it around Toby's neck.

"OK, we're done here." The woman strode away, and her assistant hurried after her.

"Why don't you come with me?" Doyle said as I watched the photographer turn into the alley. Doyle pointed toward the end of the block. The light from a camera flash shot out of the alley as Doyle lead me away. I gripped the rope attached to Toby. The officer showed me around the corner and into the lobby of an apartment building.

Doyle spoke to a woman behind a large marble block that served as the front desk of the building. She turned and looked at me. Her eyes were a deep, warm brown and she'd painted her lashes thick with mascara. She clucked a couple of times and then took my arm. I handed Doyle Toby's rope and followed the woman into a small bathroom.

She turned on the tap. "Come on dear," she said, and gently pulled my hands toward the sink. The water spiraling down the drain turned from pink to clear. The woman wet a paper towel with warm water and handed it to me. I turned to my reflection.

I hardly recognized myself. Who was that thin, haggard woman in the mirror? When did I become this person? Did I ever brush my hair? Tears started down my cheeks, and I watched them as if the mirror was a TV screen--a big reflection of someone else's fantasy.

"Sweetheart?" it was Eyelashes looking at me with dilated pupils. This was the story she was going to tell for the rest of her life. I was her traumatic tale. The sweet blonde who found a dead body and went comatose in the bathroom while under my care.

I cleaned my face, rubbing my cheeks and then digging into my eye sockets. I cleaned the blood off my legs. My reflection now showed a face scrubbed clean, hair pulled back into a tight ponytail, and gray eyes rimmed with red.

Officer Doyle waited for me on a paisley-patterned couch, Toby sitting next to him, his face and paws washed. I sat down with them.

"Are you feeling OK?" Officer Doyle asked.

"I think so." I leaned back for a moment and closed my eyes, but the gaping hole that had been a face was waiting for me behind my eyelids. I snapped my head back up.

"I spoke with the doorman briefly, and he said that your dog found the body."

"No," I said. "He is not my dog."

"So how did you end up in the alley?"

I stared at him for a moment. "Oh, yes, Toby ran down there, but no, he is not my dog. He is a client's."

"You're a dog-walker?" Doyle asked, a small smile crossing his lips.

"Yes."

"If you give me his owner's contact information, I'll be happy to explain about the leash."

"OK." I found the Maxims' phone number in my purse and gave it to Doyle.

He looked down at the information for a moment. He pressed his lips together into a tight line. Then he looked up at me, smiled, and said: "I just need to ask you a couple of questions-- nothing big, just some basic stuff. It shouldn't take long. Do you feel up to it?"

"OK."

"What's your name?"

"Joy Humbolt."

"Occupation: dog-walker." He wrote it down as he said it. He got my address and all my contact information. "Now, please tell me in your own words what happened--how you came upon the victim?"

I told him about my falling down and Toby running into the alley. I told him how I thought he was killing a rat down there and how I had called to him but he hadn't come. I told him about how I had ventured down the alley, and then I started to get choked up.

"Take your time."

I started sobbing. Officer Doyle put a hand on my shoulder, and I grabbed on to him as if he were a floatation device, and I was in the middle of a big motherfucking storm. He sat there, letting me hold onto him without saying a word or moving a muscle.

"I'm sorry," I said, when I realized, quite suddenly, what an ass I was being. I moved away from him and lowered my eyes. He coughed something out about it being okay and reaching into one of his uniform's many pockets pulled out a tissue. I used it to wipe my eyes and face.

"Thanks," I said weakly.

"I know this is hard, but if you could just finish telling me what happened, I can let you go home."

I took a deep breath. "When I realized that there was a dead body, I started screaming." Doyle nodded. I sniffled. "Um, the doorman came, and when he saw the body, he threw up. I realized I had to get out of there. Toby fought me, but I managed to pull him out of the alley. He dropped the thing I thought was a rat, and it brushed against my legs." I looked down at my legs. They were clean.

"Go on."

"When he dropped it, that's when I saw it was a toupee." I looked up at Doyle. He nodded for me to keep going. "So I dragged Toby to the lobby where the doorman worked and used his phone to call the police. And then I went outside and waited for you guys to show up."

"OK," Doyle said. "I just want to double-check a couple of things." I nodded. "So you didn't touch anything in the alley besides the toupee touching your leg?"

"I might have put my hand on the Dumpster; I'm not sure. But the doorman--I know he touched the wall when he was throwing up. That's all I can think of."

"OK, and do you know if Toby touched anything besides the toupee?"

"I didn't see him."

"The detective in charge of the investigation may want to contact you again. Also, I'm going to give you my card in case you think of anything else." I put his business card in my pocket.

"Can I ask you something?" I said as he stood to leave.

"Sure."

"You ever see anything like that before?"

He nodded sadly and then gave me a crooked smile.

"But what kind of person would do that?"

"I don't know."

"But doesn't it seem awfully hateful to blow someone's--" I stopped to push a lump back down my throat, "--to just wipe away someone's face like that?"

"I would just try not to think about this anymore. Go home, take a nice hot bath, and forget about it." I nodded absently. "Work's another good way to forget."

"I don't think I'll be forgetting anything about this day anytime soon."

"It will probably stay with you for a while, but you'll figure out a way to cope. Everyone does."

He smiled at me. "You want me to walk you back to his place?" He pointed at Toby.

"I'll be fine. Thanks, though. I appreciate you being so nice." I picked myself up off the couch and was surprised to see how strong I actually felt. We started to leave the lobby together when O'Conner came in.

"Doyle, Detective Mulberry is here." O'Conner said the name Mulberry as if it were a dirty word.

Doyle turned back to me. "Ms. Humbolt, thank you for your help. I hope you feel better real soon."

"I already do, thank you."

CHAPTER SIX

HOME SWEET HOME

BLUE GREETED me at the door and danced around as I put down my bag and flipped off my shoes. Bending down I gave him a good petting, ruffling him behind the ears and scratching his chest. Then I noticed the feathers. There were a couple at my feet, but as my eyes moved down the hall, the number increased. I walked tentatively toward my living room, feathers swirling around my ankles. Blue's claws clicked on the floor as he followed.

Light from the street illuminated the front room. My red mohair down-cushion couch was leaking. One of the seat cushions was ripped open, and feathers spread onto my coffee table, across the floor to the tangled nest of wires below my TV, and over to where I stood. "Destroyed the couch, huh, boy?" I asked. Blue gave no response. "Well, it was a shitty couch, anyway."

I fed Blue his dinner, bypassing my blinking message machine, and took him out for a walk. We wandered down side streets, avoiding people and bright lights. My exhaustion turned into nervous energy, and soon I was craving a drink.

When we got back to my apartment, the door was open. Blue growled and raised his hackles. I felt the same. Marcus poked his head out. Blue let loose a barrage of barks and growls. I just stared.

"Jesus, Joy, can't you do something about that thing?" Marcus yelled over Blue.

"Fuck you," I responded, brushing past him into my apartment and dragging Blue with me.

"Did you get robbed, or did that darling creature destroy my couch?" Marcus asked.

"It was my couch, remember? You gave it to me. Quiet now, Blue. Would you just leave?" Blue's barking lowered to a deep growl.

"Have a drink with me. I want to talk."

"About your couch?" It sounded dumb the minute it came out of my mouth.

"Come on, one drink." He smiled, and I had a flash of him naked and on top of me. "Please." Marcus was tall, hard-bodied, and bad for me. He smiled with a twinkle in his eyes-- the same twinkle that mothers tell their children was in their dad's eyes. Marcus took a step toward me, and I wanted to wrap myself in his arms. I took a step back. We'd broken up for good reasons. Marcus didn't trust me. He thought I was cheating on him, which made me think he was cheating on me. A year and we couldn't trust each other. A year of his accusing me of being someone I wasn't. He took another step and I could smell him. Marcus smelled good. He might be a jealous, paranoid jerk, but he smelled damn good.

"Fine, one drink."

We had a drink. And then another. We fought, and then we laughed, and then I was drunk. I didn't tell him about the body until we had left the bar, and he was walking me home.

"You want to hear something fucked up?" I asked him.

"What, you gonna tell me about our relationship?" He snorted at his own joke.

"I found a dead body today." Marcus's drunk eyes swiveled in their sockets.

"What?" he asked.

"Yeah, a dead body. It was really fucking weird. His face was missing, and he was wearing a track suit." I stumbled and Marcus reached out and caught me.

"Wait, you found a dead body?" he asked, his voice quiet, eyes intent.

I looked up at him. "Yeah, I don't really want to talk about it anymore," I said looking down at his hand on my forearm. "I don't want to think about it. But I can't stop." I looked up at him. He licked his lips. And then I kissed him. He reacted quickly. Wrapping his arm around my waist, he moved me up against the closest building and pinned me. I let my hands wander from the back of his neck down his chest.

Marcus pulled away and hailed a taxi that was speeding by. He held me tight and kissed me so that I could barely breathe as the cab raced through empty streets to his apartment. Marcus threw money at the cabby and we rode in the elevator entangled. He smelled so good and he kissed so well. And dear Jesus did the man know what to do with his hands.

Marcus opened his door with one hand, keeping the other on the small of my back. Inside, I pushed him up against the wall and pressed myself against him. He lifted me up, and I wrapped my legs around him. I bit his lip, he pulled my hair, and then I was on the floor, on my back. I was right where I wanted to be--there wasn't a thought in my head. I was barely even human.

The moment it was over I knew I had made a massive mistake. We were on Marcus's floor, his arms wrapped around me. Usually when we lay like that, I felt that nothing could hurt me, that Marcus would protect me. But tonight I felt that he was holding me too tightly, that he was a danger to me, that I was a danger to myself. I had to get out of there. I needed to be alone. "I've missed you," Marcus said.

Crap. I tried to move away, but he pulled me into him tighter.

"Is something wrong?" Marcus asked, and then lightly kissed my ear. I cringed at the intimacy in his voice.

"Marcus," I paused, trying to figure out how to phrase it. "I need to go home."

"Hang out for a minute. Let's just lay here."

"I can't." I tried to get up again, but he held me close. I started to feel as if I couldn't breathe. "Marcus, let me up."

"Come on, just stay for a little while."

"No, Marcus. I have to go home." I wrenched myself free and started to look around for my clothes.

"What's your rush?" Marcus asked, watching me.

"I just need to get out of here. I need to go home."

"But why?"

"Because this was a mistake, Marcus," I said as I looked into his eyes trying to make him understand.

"A mistake? But it was great. Didn't you think it was great?"

"Yes, Marcus, it was great sex, but that's all it was." I found my underwear under his jeans and pulled them on.

"Just a great fuck? It didn't mean anything to you? What about us?" Marcus sat up and looked at me.

"There is no more us," I said, turning away from him.

"Then what the fuck was that?" Marcus gestured to his floor.

"That was sex. I needed to not think. Look, I'm sorry if you thought it was more, but do you really want to start seeing me again? We don't even like each other. You're constantly accusing me of cheating on you. You think I'm the kind of person who fucks strangers in bathrooms, which I'm not. You don't get me at all." I looked around for my jeans in the dark hallway.

"Well, you have to admit it was odd when you and Jeremy went to the bathroom at the same time at Mitch's barbecue."

"Jeremy! Jeremy!" I screamed at him. "You think I fucked your coworker in the bathroom of your friend's house. That is just fucking insane."

"I didn't say you fucked him. I just said it was strange. A strange coincidence."

"All right, I'm leaving now." I found my jeans flung into a corner.

"You know how you are Joy."

I paused in my clothes-gathering search to look at him. "What do you mean, how I am?"

"You know, how you are in bed."

"How *am* I Marcus?"

"You used me for sex. This is so like you." Marcus puffed out his chest. I pulled on my jeans, falling against the wall when my foot got stuck for just a second.

"Look, we can talk about this later, when we're not both still drunk." I spotted my T-shirt and grabbed it off the floor, my pants still undone. I did not want to deal with another conversation about how my being good in bed proved I was a psychopath. Just because I was a woman who didn't need to cry after every fucking orgasm.

"Oh sure, everything is on your schedule. Well, not this time." Marcus picked up my flip-flops and held them over his head. "We're going to talk about this now." He looked ridiculous--butt-ass naked holding a pair of bright green flip-flops above his head.

"I need to go home now. Please give me my flip-flops." I pulled my shirt on and held out a hand.

"No." His lips pursed and his eyebrows set against me.

"Stop being childish and give me the flip-flops."

Marcus faked a laugh, throwing his head back so I could see the hairs in his nostrils. He stopped abruptly and looked down at me. "No. Now, what're you gonna do about it?"

"Look, I had a really fucked-up day, and I just need to go home." I felt suddenly on the verge of tears.

"Right after you rip out my heart?" he screamed at me.

"You are acting like a child. I didn't rip out your heart. This is bull-shit. Give me my shoes." He just smiled, proud that he was taller and stronger and didn't have to give me my shoes if he didn't want to. "I'm the one who had the traumatic day and you are trying to make this whole thing all about you. Now can you see why maybe, just maybe, I want nothing to do with you, you asshole!" I stood in front of him, breathing heavily.

"No," was all he said.

"Fine! Just fine!" I screamed at him and then ran out the door, down the steps, and onto the street, leaving my flip-flops and Marcus behind. I started to cry as I stomped down the street. Big heaving sobs that made it hard to walk. I was angry and crying, and I didn't have any shoes.

I arrived home to my feather-covered house around four in the morning. "What a day," I told Blue as I sat on my bed, using a spoon to eat peanut butter directly from the jar. I jumped when the phone rang, and Blue took the opportunity to lick my peanut butter spoon. I didn't want to answer. It was probably Marcus. My machine picked up, and I heard James's voice.

"Where are you!" he yelled. I picked up. "Joy, Jesus. What happened to you? I've been calling your cell and it's been going straight to voice mail. The last thing I heard was you scream and your phone crash. I've been worried."

"Sorry I didn't call you back. My phone got slightly destroyed. Don't worry. I'm fine. I just had a really fucked-up day."

"What happened?"

"Listen, I'm exhausted. I'll come over tomorrow and tell you all about it."

"You're fine, though?" he asked.

"Yeah, I'm fine."

"Ok, I'll see you tomorrow?"

"Yes."

"Don't do that again," James said.

"I won't."

"OK, goodnight."

I hung up the phone, put my peanut butter aside, and slept.

I dreamed that my mother was drunk and hitting James with a dead hand covered in congealed blood. I woke up sweating and screaming.

CHAPTER SEVEN

THE WIDOW SAPERSTEIN

THE NEXT DAYS *Post* gave Page One coverage to the *Upper East Side Slaying*. They used a picture of the body bag, black and lumpy, being loaded into the coroner's van. I bought the paper and a cup of coffee at my corner bodega before getting on the subway.

On page three was a picture of the victim in happier days, his loving wife and devoted dog. I instantly recognized not only the dog but also the man and his wife, even the photo itself. I had seen it only yesterday hanging on an apartment wall. The caption, "Joseph Saperstein with his wife and dog at the Grand Canyon," confirmed what I had feared--the man whose dead body I had discovered was my client.

I couldn't believe it. Not only had I found a dead body, but I knew him. Well, not him so much as his dog, but I had been in the man's house. I devoured the rest of the article and learned that Mr. Saperstein was an accountant with the recently disgraced firm Pilfner & Brown. He and his wife had been married for ten years. He was 43 years old. The police had several leads but couldn't comment on them at this time. He had been shot in the face at close range. *The Post* hinted at the possibility that his marriage was rocky, that his job was more dangerous than it sounded, and that a serial killer could be on the loose. I vowed to pick up the *New York Times* as I approached my stop.

Everyone at the dog run was talking about the murder. Clustered into small groups, they gossiped away their fear. In one corner, the dog-walkers were huddled around Marcia and her fanny pack. A silence fell over the group when Snowball and I entered the run. It wasn't until the gate squeaked shut behind us and Snowball sprinted off to hump a pug that the buzz of conversation resumed.

A tall, thin woman with mousy brown hair in her mid-thirties, whom I recognized as Fiona, broke away from the pack and headed my way. "Have you heard the news?" she asked. I looked at her with my haggard, hungover eyes. She was wearing a floral-print, ankle-length skirt and a white tank top. She was smiling at me.

"Yeah, I heard."

"Isn't Snaffles one of yours?" I nodded. The woman furrowed her brow, clearly not satisfied with my one-word answer. "You're new, right?" She decided to try another tack.

"Yeah."

"How are you liking the job?" I could tell that the rest of the run was listening to us. Elaine and Marcia sat on a bench nearby, not even pretending to have their own conversation while a couple of women with big sunglasses wearing expensive sweatpants inched closer.

"Look, I don't really want to talk." My head was pounding from the night before and I couldn't get rid of the image of that faceless body, especially now that I had a face to go with it.

"There are rumors that you found the body," she whispered, leaning toward me, attempting to create an intimacy between us. Her breath smelled like she'd been chewing bubble gum. A strange scent on a full-grown woman.

"Oh, yeah?" I said.

She waited a moment for me to continue and then gave up. "All right, well, if you want to talk, we're all here for you." She gave me a big smile before returning to the bench where the other dog-walkers waited. I heard Marcia say something about shock and grief as she dropped a tiny bag of shit into the nearest trash can.

Left alone, my mind wandered in disturbing directions. I shuddered as I remembered the chill in the alley, the unnatural color of Joseph

Saperstein's skin, and the pool of congealed blood at my feet. Snowball and I left the run to the whispers of the crowd. All those people, enclosed in that little fence, were scared. You could smell it. I was the breathing, walking reminder that a respectable man's face had been blown away where they lived--where they did their grocery shopping, where they picked up their prescriptions, where their dogs played. The place where you couldn't even hear the highway.

When I got to Snaffles' door, I took a deep breath, inserted the key, and creaked the door open. "Who's there?" a clearly intoxicated female voice asked from another room. That's when I realized that I should have knocked.

"I'm sorry, I'm the dog-walker." A woman I recognized as Mrs. Saperstein stumbled out from the kitchen holding a nearly empty glass. I could smell the Scotch on her from the door.

"Well," she paused to regain her balance, "Isn't that nice? Life goes on. You want a drink?" She held her glass out toward me. Mrs. Saperstein was about my height with the lean body of a jogger. Her skin was tan and her hair bleached blond. If she hadn't been so drunk, I probably would have called her pretty.

"Um, well, I'm working, so maybe another time." Her eyes filled with tears. "Or right now would be fine," I said.

"Great," she replied as she started back to the kitchen. I heard her smash her shin on the dog gate and swear. I followed her over the gate and said hello to Snaffles. While she pulled out a clean glass and began filling it with ice, I prepared Snaffles food. "You know what happened?" she asked me. "It's all over the papers. You must know." She sloshed Scotch into my glass and then refilled her own.

"Yes, I do." I wondered if I should tell her I found the body.

"He was an asshole, you know," she said, leaning on the counter. "He was an asssshooollle."

I figured now was not the time to tell her anything. "Oh," was all I said.

"He loved that dog, though." She gestured her glass in Snaffles' direction. Scotch spilled over the lip. Snaffles abandoned his lunch and began licking it up. "He didn't love me. No, no, he did not."

"Oh." I sipped my Scotch. It burned my throat and helped a little with the shooting pains inside my head.

"I should have left him years ago. He was having an affair, you know."

"I didn't."

"Why would you? But I knew. I'm not a fool, you know."

"Of course not."

"Women know these things, you know. You can't pull the wool over my eyes. I can see through the wool."

"I understand." She leaned back and examined me.

"You look like you understand. I'm gonna tell you something that I probably shouldn't. But I don't care, not anymore. What's the point of caring, I ask you."

"Uh, the point of caring is--"

"Exactly. You don't know the point." I shook my head. "That's because there isn't one." I wondered if that is what she had planned to tell me that she thought she shouldn't. "I was having an affair, too," she whispered loudly and then laughed. "He deserved it, the fucker." She looked into her glass and became quiet. Then she asked, "Are you married?"

"No."

"You got a boyfriend?"

"Nope." She thought about that for a moment while she sipped her drink.

"You know, I thought when I got married everything would be wonderful." She released a snort of a laugh. "And now he's dead, and I don't know why. And Julen wants to marry me. He thinks this was fate." She laughed again. It was hollow and a little frightening.

"Julen?"

"The man I'm having...had...what tense should that be in?"

"You mean the man you had the affair with."

"Yes, but what tense should it be with?"

"I don't know."

"Me neither. Strange all the things you realize you don't know when your husband has been murdered." She refilled her glass again. "Julen wants us to run away together." She spilled more Scotch, this time down her shirt. She didn't notice.

"Hmm."

"Hmm is right, honey." She leaned toward me. The smell of Scotch was overwhelming. "He's the doorman," she said in a harsh whisper.

"Wow."

"He's Latin."

"Wow, a Latin lover."

She giggled. "I like you. You're nice."

"Thanks." Snaffles began to whine.

"That damn dog. He used that dog against me. He used him as an excuse to go to her house. That whore, that home-wrecking whore. Stupid dog." Her eyelids drooped.

"Do you think maybe you should lie down?"

Her glazed eyes met mine. They brimmed with tears and what looked a lot like sorrow.

"Sure. I'll lie down."

I helped her to the bedroom and laid her on her side.

"I'll walk Snaffles and then I'll be back," I told her, but she was already asleep.

When I returned Snaffles 45 minutes later, Mrs. Saperstein was still sleeping soundly. When I came back at seven to give Snaffles his evening walk, the apartment was dark and I could hear her snoring in the bedroom. I peeked in at her. The room was bathed in twilight, and she was lying on her back with her bleached-blond hair spread out on the pillow. Her jaw was slack, her arms flung wide at her sides. I felt a pang of sympathy for her. She was a widow now, a drunk, passed-out widow.

The doorbell rang. I jumped, and Mrs. Saperstein moaned, then turned over. I scurried quietly on tiptoes to the front door, and I looked through the peephole as the doorbell rang again. A handsome young Hispanic man in a blue and gray doorman's uniform stood outside with his hat in his hand. He looked nervously up and down the hallway, then reached for the bell again. I opened the door quickly, trying to stop him from waking Mrs. Saperstein. He took a step back when he saw me.

"Hi, I'm Joy, the Sapersteins' dog-walker," I said.

"Hello, I'm Julen, the doorman." He turned his hat in his hands and looked down the hall again.

"Can I help you with something?" He looked back at me, his eyes large, brown and tortured.

"I need to talk with Jacquelyn," he caught himself quickly, "Mrs. Saperstein."

"She's napping right now."

"Is she OK?" he asked.

"I believe so," I said.

"She is a very sensitive woman." He caught himself again and, realizing he had said too much, turned and headed back toward the elevator without another word.

"This is just shocking," James said, sitting across from me at the little table in his yard. Blue slept at our feet and Aurora was perched in the tree above us, pissed that Blue slept at our feet.

"Trust me, I know."

"I mean, you find a dead body, you know the guy, or at least his dog, then you find out the widow is having an affair, you meet the guy she is having the affair with."

"That sums it up." I sipped my mango margarita.

"Well, no, I forgot the part about you fucking Marcus. That was dumb." He shook his head at me.

"I know that," I said.

"Joy. I'm sorry. I can't imagine how you feel," he said, his tone softer.

"I feel weird. Really, fucking weird." I stared into my half-empty glass, hoping to find a better word than weird. None came.

"It's awful," James said.

"I feel--" I was trying to make him understand something I didn't understand myself. "--my whole life has changed in the last week."

"Is there anything I can do?" James asked, refilling my glass.

"Besides that? No, I don't think so. I just need to put this behind me."

"That seems to be the only option."

I wondered if that was true.

"James?"

"Hmm?"

"I'm thinking something crazy here."

"I like crazy. What's up?"

"I've spent my whole life putting things behind me, right? I mean I've jumped from crappy job to crappy job, from crappy boyfriend to crappy boyfriend."

"The crappy part is true, but I don't know if that's putting things behind you so much as moving forward."

I cocked my head at him and wrinkled my brow. "I would say it's more like standing still."

"I think you have made progress," James said.

"My point is, maybe I shouldn't put this behind me. Maybe I should do something about this."

"Like what?"

"I don't know, but something. I mean this guy is dead."

"That's true."

"And I knew him."

"You knew his dog."

"And maybe I could do something to help him."

"He's dead."

"But what about--I don' know. I just don't think I can put this behind me." I stopped talking and sipped my drink, my brain buzzing.

"I say you solve the murder, bring the killer to justice, and save the day in general." James clinked his glass against mine and smiled.

I laughed. "Look, right now my life is picking up dog shit and drinking. That's about all I got going on." He nodded. "The point is I don't want to stand still anymore. I want to do something. Something real."

"I don't know what you mean," James said.

"You know, like you. You do real stuff. And Hugh does real stuff."

"I create looks for TV advertising. I don't know if I would consider that real."

"But you do something. You contribute to society."

"What would those dogs do without you?"

"You're being sarcastic again."

"Look Joy, if you want to do something, then do it. You can do anything you put your mind to."

"I don't know if you could say anything cheesier if you tried."

"How about, I have faith in you." He smiled at me and I knew it true. He did have faith in me. "And one day you, too, will have faith in you."

"I was wrong. You can get cheesier." But I was touched and felt loved. And as I finished off the last of my margarita, I felt that I could do anything I put my mind to.

CHAPTER EIGHT

LEAVING IN A HURRY

OSCAR THE CAT met me at Charlene Miller's door and rubbed himself against my legs. I refilled his food and water dishes. Alone in the sink sat the glass Charlene had been drinking out of the last time I saw her.

"Is that strange?" I said to Oscar. He ignored me and concentrated on his food. Reaching into his bowl, he pulled out a piece of kibble with his paw, then another, followed by a third. He ate them off the floor, making loud crunching noises.

I wandered into her bedroom. It was a mess. The sheets and blankets were all twisted around. Clothing and shoes littered the floor. The bedside lamp was knocked over. I moved further into the room, careful not to touch anything. A book lay open on the floor next to a pot of moisturizer as if they had been pushed off her bedside table when the lamp fell. Small, dark-brown droplets fanned across the pillowcase. The apartment felt strangely still, and I suddenly wanted to leave.

Oscar took no notice of me on my way out. I closed and locked the door, then realized I was being silly. So she had left in a rush. That didn't mean anything. I was just being paranoid. She said she had business to take care of. It must have been urgent business. The cat could have knocked all that stuff off her nightstand. Was my room at home in any better shape? My clothing and shoes were all over the place. But I still felt anxious. I stood outside her door wondering what to do when my cell phone rang. I jumped and then chastised myself for being so jumpy.

"Hello, this is Detective Mulberry."

"Hi."

"This is Joy Humbolt, correct?"

"Yes."

"And you are the same Joy Humbolt who found Joseph Saperstein's body, correct?"

"Yes." I thought about what a glaring coincidence it would be if there were another Joy Humbolt with my phone number who had not found the body of Joseph Saperstein.

"I would like you to come by the precinct so that we can have a conversation," the detective continued.

"When?"

"As soon as possible. This is a murder investigation," he said.

I checked my watch, I didn't have time before my next walk, so I told him I could come by around eight that night or early the next morning. He made a sound like that wasn't good enough but said, "Tonight will be fine. I will see you around eight, correct?"

"Correct." He gave me directions to the precinct on 67th Street, then hung up without saying goodbye.

"Look, I'm trying to tell you what I know but you keep twisting my words around. I know what I saw and I know--"

"There's no need for that tone of voice, Missy," Detective Mulberry told me with what I suspected was a smile on the edge of his lips. He looked like he was in his late thirties. Crow's-feet radiated from his eyes, and deep lines around his mouth gave him a permanent scowl. Mulberry took up most of the other side of the desk. He wasn't fat but wide. The guy looked like he was made of boulders.

"If you don't stop calling me Missy, I'm going to--" I could feel my face flushing red.

"You won't do anything. All you will do is answer my questions." I had been sitting across from this machine of a man for over an hour already, answering the same questions. His voice remained even. His green eyes held onto me. I was pretty sure he hadn't blinked since my arrival. I pushed my thumbnail into my palm, trying to calm down. "You said that you met Mrs. Saperstein for the first time yesterday, and yet you are her dog-walker. How is this possible?"

"I told you already. I just started this job. I got it from a woman named Charlene Miller. Mrs. Saperstein is the only client I've met. I walk people's dogs because they are at work. Hence, them not being home and me not meeting them." I rolled my eyes and threw my hands in the air to point out how obvious an observation this really was.

"Tell me again about Charlene." The Detective looked down at a piece of paper in the center of his crowded desk.

"She was a friend of my friend Nona's friend, whose information I've given you. Charlene left town on business. I already gave you her address. What more do you want?"

"Mrs. Saperstein was distressed when you saw her, correct?" He didn't take his eyes off the paper under his face.

"Distressed and drunk," I told the top of his head, then stuck my tongue out at it.

"Did she mention her affair?" Mulberry made a quick mark with his pen and then looked up at me. I sucked my tongue back just in time.

"Yes. I already told you this."

"And do you know who she was having the affair with?" He asked.

"Yes."

"And could you tell me his name, please?"

"I already told you," I said.

"Yes, and I want you to tell me again." No anger, just fact.

"Julen," I answered.

"And his occupation?"

"He is the doorman at her building." I felt like I might start crying.

"You know Mr. Saperstein was having an affair, too."

"Yes."

"And how did you come to know this?"

"Mrs. Saperstein told me." I shifted in my chair. It was old, wooden, and creaked with my movement.

"Why would she tell you that if you just met her?"

"I already told you she was drunk."

"Do you know the name of the woman that Mr. Saperstein was seeing?"

"No."

"Don't you find it strange that she would mention her own lover's name and not her husband's?" the Detective looked back down at the paper.

"I already told you she was wasted. She probably doesn't even remember our conversation," I said.

"I guarantee you she does." He shuffled the paper around a little, then pulled out a pencil and erased something. I sighed loudly. Mulberry stopped erasing and asked: "How long have you had this job?"

"Three days."

"An exciting three days."

I wanted to hit him. "That's not how I would describe them," I said.

He looked up at me, his face blank and his eyes empty. "Do you like excitement?"

"What?"

"Did you know Charlene Miller socially or professionally?" he asked.

"Seriously, I meet her 15 minutes before I took over the dog route. I would hardly recognize her on the street."

"She was a beautiful woman. Recognizable for sure," Mulberry said.

"Oh yeah, did you know her?"

He sat back and cocked his head. "How long had you known Mr. Saperstein?" he asked.

"I told you I never met him."

"Yes, and I don't believe you."

"Well, it's the truth," I said.

"Did it occur to you that if you are mixed up in this, you could be next?"

"Whoa, what the fuck are you talking about?" I jumped out of my chair and backed up toward the wall. "I'm not mixed up in shit, OK? I just walk dogs."

"Did Mrs. Saperstein seem like a jealous woman to you? Please, sit down."

"What?" I looked around the office. Its glass walls were covered by dirty white Venetian blinds. The institutional gray filing cabinets piled with manila folders seemed close, and getting closer.

"I asked that you please sit down," Mulberry said.

"No," I put my hands out palms forward. "What are you talking about me being next? Are you just trying to scare me? Is that your thing? You like scaring young women." I was pressed up against the wall now, my weight bending the blinds, causing them to crackle and snap.

"Mrs. Saperstein was arrested for assaulting Mr. Saperstein not three months ago. Did you know that?" I had a flash of Mrs. Saperstein hurling a pot of something boiling at Mr. Saperstein, him ducking and the pot smashing onto the wall behind where his head had just been.

"Why don't you answer my question?" I asked.

"I think if you would sit down and think for a moment you might understand my point."

I didn't sit down. "I get your point. You're implying that Mrs. Saperstein killed her husband and is going to kill me next. But that's bullshit. I don't even know these people."

"I'm just letting you know that Mrs. Saperstein is not the woman you think she is."

"You have no idea what I think of her. You don't know anything about me."

"I know you have a short temper. You have proved that this evening."

"Yeah, well, I learned you're a dick." Fuck, I should not have said that. But the detective just smiled and looked down at his paperwork.

"You are free to go, Ms. Humbolt. Get home safe."

I grabbed my bag off the chair and flew out of his office onto the street and into the subway. My adrenaline was pumping hard as I waited for the train. This guy was clearly insane. I mean, what kind of psycho implies that a woman you only just met is plotting your death? He obviously had no leads and was lashing out at whatever made a remote amount of sense according to his deluded understanding of the case. Then it occurred to me that I had forgotten to clean Oscar's litter. "Dammit," I said out loud. No one even glanced at me. The glassy stares of my fellow passengers continued to deny their surroundings. "Fuck," I said a little louder. Nothing. I love this city, I thought to myself as the train clacked and squealed me back to Brooklyn.

CHAPTER NINE

GOSSIP IS A POWERFUL DRUG

I WAS RUNNING LATE when I got to Charlene's apartment the next day. Snowball had escaped the dog run through a hole in the fence and then evaded me by hiding in some shrubbery. At Charlene's, Oscar followed me into the bathroom where his litter was and meowed purposefully as I cleaned it out. "What, boy? You want more food or water?" He released a meow, arched his back, and puffed his tail. I rubbed his head. He took the pettings gladly and encouraged me by flopping onto his back. "I'd love to hang out and scratch your belly all day, but I've got to get back to work." He just purred with his eyes closed. When I stood up, Oscar's eyes opened, and he rolled back onto his paws.

I left the bathroom. He got under my feet, moving between my legs in a figure eight, purring, and tripping me. "Oscar, come on, I've got to go." He just rubbed himself against my leg, begging for a little more attention. "Poor guy, you must be lonely here all by yourself." He meowed in agreement. "Listen, buddy, I'll come back later, all right? I have to go now." I passed the open bedroom door and about ten steps later realized I was almost positive there had been a man in there. I stopped mid-stride, filled instantly with fear, the same kind I get at night when I'm alone, and I can't sleep, and I swear I hear something, or someone, creak outside my bedroom door. Oscar took my pause to mean that I wanted to pet him, so flopped onto his back, wiggling his belly and stretching his paw toward me.

My ears fought through the buzzing sound of my fear to hear. My brain told me to move toward the door--it screamed for me to walk out the door. But my ears didn't want the distraction. I held my breath and listened to the beating of my heart, Oscar's purr, and the undeniable sound of a footfall on the carpet behind me.

"Hello, Ms. Humbolt." I spun around. Detective Mulberry was standing in the hallway behind me, looking amused. He was shorter than I remembered, only about three or four inches taller than me, but he was stocky.

"What are you doing here?" I felt relieved, but adrenaline was still pumping through me. He pulled off a pair of white rubber gloves, the latex snapping in the air.

"Just looking into a lead."

"Have you gotten ahold of Charlene yet?"

"No, I have not." He shook his head looking at the inside-out gloves in his hands.

"Do you have a warrant to be here?"

His green eyes flashed yellow with anger. "Your little friend could be dead, and you want to know about a warrant." He moved down the hallway at me. I stood my ground, fighting against a powerful urge to flee. He stopped six inches from my face. "Do you understand the gravity of the situation here?" Intense green eyes was all I could think.

"What?" I said straining to keep eye contact.

Mulberry shook his head then brushed past me to the front door. "Try not to touch anything in here. This could be an official crime scene before too long." He left, using his sleeve to protect the doorknob from his fingerprints.

Oscar, unfazed by the stranger, curled his body around my left leg and purred. Could Charlene really be dead? Why was he convinced that I was involved in this mess? I found myself wandering through Charlene's place. The bedroom was a mess, but there was no sign that a person had been murdered there. I opened her closet. It was jammed full of clothing. But so was mine at home. For all I knew, she had packed half her wardrobe and left with it. Or she had been forced out of her apartment with nothing. Could Detective Mulberry know any differently?

I walked into her bathroom and opened the medicine cabinet. Day face cream, night face cream, makeup remover, body lotion, hand cream all sat neatly next to each other. But there was no toothbrush, so she must have packed to leave. Or maybe she needed a new toothbrush and had thrown the old one away. I looked in the trash. It was empty. So maybe she had taken the trash out when she left. Then she definitely would have been leaving of her own free will. Kidnappers do not allow you to pack a toothbrush and take out the trash--unless they don't want it to look like you've been kidnapped. I noticed the clock on Charlene's bedroom wall. I was officially late.

I picked up Snowball for his afternoon walk and headed over to the dog run. The regular crowd was there, milling around the pen. I nodded to them and sat on a bench in the far corner facing the river. Why would Detective Mulberry insinuate that Charlene was dead? How was she connected to this case? What did he know that I didn't? I found myself wanting to go back to her apartment. What was he looking for? Or what had he found?

I was surprised to see the detective striding purposefully along the esplanade talking on his cell phone. His thick arms pushed against his summer-weight suit jacket with each step. His brow was furrowed and his face red. The sun caught glints of gray in his short, dark hair. I watched him walk into the park toward Gracie Mansion and out of my sight.

"Hi."

I looked up and saw Marcia standing over me. "Hi," I said.

"You know him?" she asked.

"Who?"

"I know him, you know. I know everyone in this neighborhood."

"You do?"

"Of course. I've been walking this neighborhood for 25 years. I know everything that happens around here," she said.

"Really?"

The other dog-walkers started to move toward us. "This is Fiona," she gestured to the mousey-haired women who had approached me the other day. "And this is Elaine." A young woman with long chestnut hair and thick glasses smiled at me shyly.

"Hi," I said, nodding at them.

Marcia turned to me. "You're all mixed up in this case now, huh?"

"Yeah. Well, no. Wait, what are you talking about?"

"You know what I'm talking about."

"You are certainly more mixed up in this case than most people," Fiona said. They had formed a circle around me now.

"Were you scared when you found the body? I would have been really scared," Elaine said. She looked like the type of girl who was scared of squirrels.

"Yeah, I guess."

They all nodded.

"That makes sense," Fiona said. "I could see how that could be scary." She picked at a hangnail on her left index finger, digging into it absently.

"Did you throw up?" Elaine asked, her eyelids fluttering in a series of blinks that had to be a tic. "I'm sure that I would have thrown up."

"I didn't throw up, but the doorman did."

"Willy threw up! We didn't know that," Marcia said, delighted with the new detail. "He said that you threw up. But then again, you can never quite trust Willy for the truth." The other dog-walkers murmured their agreement. "Philip said that he thought Willy was the one who threw up." Marcia stated proudly.

"Who's Philip?" I asked.

"You don't know who Philip is?" Elaine asked, her eyes wide.

"Philip is the manager of Ten House," Marcia boasted.

"Oh, where the Maxims live?" I asked.

Fiona snickered.

"Am I missing something?" I asked.

"Stop it," Marcia silenced Fiona. "The Ten house is more than just where the Maxims live. It is a very well-known building. It is a GB," she said, her tone the same as my kindergarten teacher's when she explained to me what story time was.

"A GB?"

"A Good Building," Marcia told me patiently.

"Oh."

"Only certain types of people are allowed to live there," Fiona said, her hazel eyes following an unattractive mutt as it raced past us.

"Wealthy families with the right last names," Marcia finished.

"Oh. I see," I said.

"Eighty-Eight is a GB, too," Elaine told me, trying to be helpful. I nodded and smiled so she'd know that I appreciated her gesture.

"Julen, Mrs. Saperstein's--" I trailed off.

"Mrs. Saperstein's lover," Marcia said. "Don't worry; it's not a secret. Everyone in the neighborhood knows that Jackie was using him to get back at Joseph."

"Do you guys know who Mr. Saperstein was sleeping with?"

"Only rumors," Fiona told me.

"What kind of rumors?" I asked.

"Well, I'm not one to gossip," Marcia started, "but I've heard from several people it was a man," she paused for dramatic effect, "and that his name was Charlie."

"Has anyone told the detective this?" I wanted to know.

"He has not come to speak with me," Marcia said. "A foolish mistake."

"What can you tell me about Detective Mulberry?" I asked the group.

"I think he lives in the neighborhood," Fiona said.

"Is he a good detective? I mean, does he have a good reputation?" I asked.

"He gets the job done. But he does it dirty," Marcia said. "He has been reprimanded more than once for breaking procedure." She looked around and continued in a whisper as loud as her speaking voice, "In other words, he has no problem with beating confessions out of people."

"How is he still on the force then?" I asked.

Marcia snorted out a laugh, which caused Elaine to giggle. "You don't have much experience with cops, do you?" Marcia asked me.

"I've never been arrested, if that's what you mean," I said.

"You ever hung out with cops?"

"No."

"There are some really good ones. That Officer Doyle, he is a true gentleman," Marcia said, all of the women nodded.

"I met him," I said. "He was really nice. He took my statement when--" I trailed off.

"We know dear, we know," Marcia comforted me. I looked past the dogs wrestling in the pen to the river.

"Who do you think killed him?" I asked.

A silence fell over the group. "I wouldn't know about that," Elaine finally said and then made a show of looking at her watch. "I have to go." She hurried over to pick up a dachshund, a miniature pinscher, and a small mutt. Their leashes became tangled as she moved toward the exit.

"I think it must have been his lover," Fiona stated boldly.

"Men can make you crazy," Marcia said with a smile. Fiona blushed.

"Do you guys know if anyone saw anything? Like one of the doormen on the block or something?" The two women shook their heads. Elaine hurried down the esplanade away from us. "Someone must have seen something," I practically whined.

"Oh, I'm sure someone did, but no one has said anything to us," Marcia told me. "You should talk to Michael. He was the last person to see Mr. Saperstein alive."

"Who's Michael?"

"You don't know him? He's one of the doormen at the Sapersteins' building," Fiona said.

"Why would I know who Michael is?" I asked

They smiled at me.

"You'll know why when you meet him," Fiona said.

Julen opened the door at the Sapersteins' building and pretended I was a complete stranger. "Hi, Julen," I said. He coughed and nodded. "I was wondering if you could help me with something?" He scanned the lobby.

"I don't think so," he said, trying to get rid of me.

"I need to speak to Michael."

Julen smiled with relief. "Of course. He comes on at midnight and gets off at eight in the morning."

"Do you have his number? I don't exactly work those hours."

Julen shook his head. "Michael does not have a phone. You will have to see him at work."

"He doesn't have a phone?"

"No. He does not believe in them." Julen, looking amused, smiled widely, showing off clean, charmingly crooked teeth.

"Doesn't believe in them?"

"Michael is an artist," Julen said in explanation.

"OK... thanks."

"You are welcome."

I knocked on Mrs. Saperstein's door. There was no response, so I let myself in. The house was empty. No Mrs. Saperstein and no Snaffles. The living room was neatly put together, the cushions on the couches puffed, the lamps dusted, and the floor vacuumed. In the kitchen, the dishes were washed, the sink spotless and the counters uncluttered. It did not look like the house of someone who had been brutally murdered.

The photographs in an album I found on their bookshelf showed the Sapersteins as a happy family. Joseph and Jackie at their wedding. She had long dark hair then. He had a bushy mustache. They had gone on vacation to somewhere tropical, when her hair was cut short. He had worn a Speedo. In the autumn of another year, they had gone to a bed-and-breakfast. Joseph had his arm wrapped tight around Jackie and she smiled with her whole body. Nothing foreshadowed that he would have his face blown away and she would be the prime suspect.

In the kitchen, there was leftover Chinese food in the fridge and three apples. In the closet, Joseph's coat hung above his briefcase. I pulled out the obviously expensive brown leather case and opened it. A gold wedding band and a silver Rolex sat on top of a stack of papers with the letterhead Pilfner and Brown.

Someone was putting a key in the door. I snapped the briefcase shut and shoved it back into the closet. Mrs. Saperstein, wearing loose jeans and a pink T-shirt, walked through the door holding Snaffles on a leash. She jumped and screamed when she saw me. "Jesus, you scared me." She held her hand over her heart. "What are you doing here?"

"I came to walk the dog, but he wasn't here, so I figured I would wait a while to see if you came back so I could walk him," I sort of lied.

"Oh. OK." She took a breath. "I just gave him a walk, so I guess you don't need to worry about it today."

"All right. Do you want me to come back for his evening walk?"

"No, I can do it." She sighed and looked past me at something not in the room.

"I'll get going then."

"Sure." I walked past her and out of the house. That was close. Why did I do that? Did those papers say something about life insurance?

CHAPTER TEN

CREEPY

THE NEXT MORNING, on the subway, leaning over a man reading the *New York Times*, I learned that the police were looking for Charlene Miller. She was not a suspect. They just needed her to answer a couple of questions. The article also said that a search of the victim's home had turned up some interesting leads.

The dog run was buzzing when I arrived. All the ladies came hurrying over to me. "Did you see the paper?" Fiona asked.

"Yeah. It's crazy."

"Do you know where Charlene is?" Marcia asked.

"I wish. I only met her right before I took over the route. I don't know anything about her. Have you guys heard from her?" I asked.

"None of us were that close to her," Marcia said. Fiona nodded. I turned to Elaine but she just shrugged.

"What's her deal? Charlene's I mean. None of you knew her at all?" I asked.

"She didn't really hang out with the likes of us," Fiona said.

"What do you mean?" I asked.

"All I'm going to say is that I guess membership in the Biltmore Club can't protect you from everything," Fiona said.

"What is that supposed to mean?" I asked.

"Being the newest member of the Biltmore Club didn't do her much good, did it?" Fiona said.

"I didn't know she was the 'newest member.' Are you a member?" I asked.

Fiona cast her eyes away. "I wouldn't join them if they begged me. They are all snobs, think they run the city don't they?"

"Oh stop it Fiona," Marcia said.

"I'm really lost, what is the Biltmore Club?" I asked.

Fiona opened her mouth to answer, but Marcia cut her off. "It's a private New York Club with some very influential members."

"They only let women become members in the mid-90s," Elaine said.

"Another reason I would never join," Fiona interjected.

"You know that gorgeous townhouse in the Mews covered in ivy?" Elaine asked, her eyes wide with admiration.

I thought for a moment and remembered a townhouse right across from the park that was coated in a large green vine. The plant looked like some giant green muppet that was eating the roof and would eventually get at all the inhabitants. "Yeah, I know what you're talking about."

"It's beautiful isn't it?" Elaine asked.

"Easily impressed," Fiona muttered.

"Charlene was a member?" I asked.

Marcia answered me, "She must have friends in some pretty high up places. You have to be sponsored by a member and then voted in or some such nonsense."

I left the run, thoughts of the Biltmore Club floating in my mind. The Sapersteins door flew open as soon as I knocked. "Where is Charlene, and what does she have to do with this?" Jackie demanded. Her hair looked like it had been slept on wet and her cheeks were flushed.

"I don't know."

"What do you mean you don't know? How could you not know?" she demanded.

"You'd be surprised how much I don't know." She glared at my attempt at a joke. I laughed uncomfortably. It echoed in the hall. "Would you like me to walk Snaffles?" I smiled.

"Come in." She moved aside, and I walked into the apartment. The dark blue drapes were drawn, but the sunlight managed to shoot through creating shafts of bright light in the otherwise dark room. Mrs. Saperstein walked to the kitchen. Snaffles was curled up in a ball in the corner, asleep.

"He looks tired," I said because I didn't know what else to say.

"I've been walking him a lot. We've been walking a lot." Her eyes shone through the half-light.

"Have you given him his lunch?"

She smiled. "Yes."

"OK, then I'll take him out."

"OK."

"Come on, Snaffles. Come." He didn't move. I walked over to him. The corner was dark, and I stepped on a squeaky toy. The sound made me jump. Snaffles didn't even twitch.

"Maybe you should just go," Mrs. Saperstein said.

"Whatever you want." I started to back away from Snaffles.

Mrs. Saperstein stood in the doorway of the kitchen silhouetted against the strange light of the living room. I walked toward her, but she didn't move. "Tell your friend Charlene I'm on to her," she hissed at me.

"She's not my friend," I protested. A tense silence bulged in the space between us. Finally, she moved aside, and I squeezed past her. What the f was that, I wondered as the elevator took me back down to street level. Snaffles had looked really dead. I mean really dead. Did she kill her dog? Excuse me--her cheating husband's dog? As I stepped out into the warm light of the day I felt goose bumps rise on my flesh.

At the Maxims' I gave Toby his lunch, and then we headed out for a walk. Halfway through the marble-encased lobby, a tall gentleman with jet-black hair that turned silver at his temples, wearing a tailored pinstriped suit, intercepted us.

"Ms. Joy?" he asked with a raised eyebrow.

"Yes."

"I am a friend of Marcia's."

This must be the famous Philip, I thought. "How do you do?" I said.

"Marcia told me that you were wondering if anyone had seen anything on the early morning of your former employer's departure from this world and his unpleasant ascent to the next."

"That's one way of putting it."

"May I suggest that you talk to Gregory Chamers? He works at Eighty-Eight East End Avenue."

"Why?" Instead of answering me, he floated off to the front desk, where a woman in her early sixties wearing a pink velour jumpsuit and carrying a gold lamé purse was talking in increasingly higher-pitched tones to a distressed-looking bellboy. I watched Philip soothe the woman, place his hand on her elbow, and lead her to the elevator banks.

Toby and I left the building and turned uptown. The clip-clop of horses' hooves caused Toby to turn. When he saw the giant beasts approaching, Toby ran to me and squeezed himself between my legs. I raised a hand to shield my eyes from the sun and looked up at Doyle and O'Conner. "Hello, officers."

"Hello Ms. Humbolt," they said in unison, which I thought was pretty darn cute. Two strapping police officers on horseback was really quite a sight, I decided.

"How's the investigation going?" I asked.

Doyle frowned. "I'm sorry I don't know. Unfortunately, I knew the victim personally so have no access to the case." He saw the look on my face and continued. "It's fine," he said. "I didn't know him well. We just belong to the same social club." He threw a glance at O'Conner who tipped his helmet at me and rode off down the street. Doyle shifted in his saddle and leaned down toward me.

"Is something wrong?" I asked.

"No, no," he smiled. "I just wanted to know if you'd be interested in going out with me some time." He smiled with big white, straight teeth. "I'm not involved in the case in any way so there is no ethical reason why I shouldn't ask you out."

I laughed. Doyle leaned back and touched his hand to his heart. "She laughs at me?" he said in mock shock.

"No, I'm sorry. I just never had a guy mention ethics while asking me out."

"Maybe the wrong kinda guy's been asking you out."

I laughed. "Maybe."

"Are you free Saturday night?"

I thought about fake checking my phone to see if I was booked but instead I answered, "Yeah, I'm free."

"Great," he grinned at me. "I'll call you tomorrow."

"Perfect," I said. He trotted to catch up with his partner. I watched them as they turned toward the park, a huge grin on my face. What fun, I thought. Toby stayed cowering between my legs.

I did not give Snaffles his evening walk. I paced outside his building and decided the whole thing was too creepy. It was Friday, and Mrs. Saperstein owed me for the week. My other clients had paid--cash in white envelopes with my name on them--so I decided I was justified in waiting until Monday. But looking up at the 20-story building as the sun was just starting to slip down the west side of the world, I worried about Snaffles and his mistress.

A soft orange glow lit the building's brick facade. Lamplight glowed from several apartments. In others, I could see the eerie blue flicker of the TV. A warm breeze blew my hair around my face. I left, walking toward the subway, feeling sick to my stomach and alone.

CHAPTER ELEVEN

NIGHT WALK

BLUE WAITED for me on the other side of my door. He jumped around, desperate to be petted but too excited to stay still. I rubbed his back and he tapped his feet. I moved down the hall, and he followed, bumping his long snout into my hand. "No, Blue," I said, and lifted my hand out of his reach. He whined, spun in a circle and sat. I laughed and couldn't help but rub his ears. He leaned into me and looked up with eyes so filled with devotion it seemed unreasonable.

After taking him out for a quick walk, I ordered General Tso's chicken and settled myself on what was left of my couch (I'd duct- taped it together as best I could). I turned on the TV and watched 30 seconds of *Seinfeld*, then clicked over to *Friends*, click, *Everybody Loves Raymond*, click, *Pastor Bill Tells It Like It Is*. I watched my stepfather behind a podium, his hair big and full.

"Life's trials," Bill was saying, "especially poverty, are a result of sin." He licked his lips and slapped the podium in front of him. "Do you hear me, Lord!" His voice quieted. "Can you hear me, Lord? Because, you know, He's speaking to you every day."

He moved from behind the podium and out onto the stage in front of his attentive choir. His voice rose up again. "The good man brings good things out of the good stored in his heart, and the evil man brings evil things out of the evil stored in his heart. For out of the overflow of his heart, his mouth speaks. Luke 6:45."

Bill nodded, and the camera showed an audience of thousands nodding back at him. As the camera panned the crowd, I could see some of their faces wet with tears. Other people held their arms in the air, their eyes closed.

"Now, I want you all to make a vow." Bill's voice spoke over the image of all those people undulating, weeping, and shaking for salvation. "A vow to yourselves, to God, to Faith Foundation. A vow that you will not be poor anymore." His voice rose. "That you will not be a sinner anymore. That you will give, from your own pocket, from your sinful earnings, $1,000."

The camera cut back to him. He was standing at the edge of his stage, sweat shining on his face. As he walked along the edge, his tone turned conversational. "Now, I know what you're thinking: 'Bill, that's a lot of money.' But if poverty comes from sin, then how do we free ourselves from poverty?" He paused and looked out at his audience. "We atone. We make a vow. We free ourselves." A phone number and Internet address appeared at the bottom of the screen. I changed the channel, the taste of bile in my mouth.

The last time I saw my mom she was alone. I had lunch with her near Madison Square Garden where Bill was preaching later that evening. We fought viciously about my lack of direction, churchgoing, and general usefulness to the world. I called her a drunk (which she hasn't been for years), and she called me a sinner (which if you believe the Bible, most people are). I left, and neither of us called.

I picked at my takeout chicken, and in the time it took me to go pee, Blue had scarfed up the rest. I laughed at the sight of him sitting bolt upright on the deflated couch with the cardboard cartons licked to a sparkle, pretending he didn't know what had happened to all that food.

Laughing, I said, "All right, boy, time for your walk." He bounded off the couch and bolted for the door.

A dense fog hung in the dark sky. The mist dulled the glare of the streetlights. Beads of dew covered the parked cars and sparkled in the soft yellow light. Blue led the way into Prospect Park.

As soon as I let him off leash, he bounced down the paved path. The gently rolling lawn glowed a silver green. The man-made forest was a wall of blackness. The fog hung low above us. We wandered onto smaller trails and roamed through the trees, up steps to the top of the biggest hill, then down and around the lake that glimmered in the night's light.

Three men sat on a bench. They wore rags and suckled on bottles in brown paper bags. One stood up, unsteady. He opened his mouth to speak, a naughty smile playing in his rummy eyes. Blue stepped out of the shadows, where he had been investigating an interesting smell, and moved to my side, falling in step with me. Fear twisted the man's smirk into a grimace. He stumbled back to his friends, whispering, "Devil." The three men cowered on the bench as Blue and I passed. We walked home with our heads held high, afraid of nothing and nobody.

The next morning Blue and I headed to the bodega for a cup of coffee and the paper. I tied Blue up out front (hoping that he would not attack anyone while I was inside) and walked through the flaps of plastic that keep the cool air in and the hot air out. "Morning," I said to the woman behind the counter. She smiled and waved, her long nails were painted in glitter and shone under the fluorescent lights. Making my way over to the coffee machine, I poured a fresh cup, added two creamers and a packet of sugar, then yawned.

The headline of the *Post*: *Black Widow Arrested in Upper East Side Slaying* was a slap in my sleepy face. I grabbed up the paper dumbfounded. There was a photograph of Jacquelyn being escorted by Mulberry out of her building, her eyes down, her hair falling in strings around her face. I could make out a blurry Julen in the background looking, well, he looked fucking broken.

The Detective's jaw was set in a hard line and he wasn't looking at the camera either. He seemed to be concentrating real hard on where his feet were headed. I paid for the paper, the coffee, and one of the slices of banana bread they keep by the register for suckers like me.

I read the paper walking down the street. Blue barked, and I looked up to see that I was about to walk gut first into a parking meter. "Good dog," I said and ruffled his ears. I folded the paper under my arm until I got back to my stoop.

According to the *Post*, a woman matching Mrs. Saperstein's description was seen leaving the scene of the crime during the early hours that the murder occurred. Mrs. Saperstein was the only beneficiary on his life insurance. She did not have an alibi and her husband's infidelity gave her a classic motive. They didn't even mention the possibility of the dead dog. But somehow, some way, I just didn't think she did it.

CHAPTER TWELVE

THAT'S SEXY

THERE ARE two mirrors at my place. Both came with the apartment. One's full-length and can be found in any dollar store throughout the city. The other's in my bathroom; it shows only from my waist up and is very high quality. The full-length mirror's closest light source is an exposed bulb that once had a shade but now just sticks out of the wall. The bathroom mirror is lit by vanity lights all the way around it. I looked completely different in these two mirrors.

The full length makes my hips look funny, and I often find myself contemplating what not to eat while examining my reflected image. The other makes my face look great, but I constantly wonder if my shoes *really* match my outfit. Sometimes I try and lift my foot up to my waist to see if they match but it never helps. Before going out, I usually run between these two mirrors attempting to decide whether I am presentable to the world. But I always look great in one and ridiculous in the other. That's exactly what I was doing when James called.

"Did you see the paper," he asked.

"Yeah, crazy right?" I walked into my kitchen and poured myself a glass of water.

"Do you think she did it?"

"No," I said without hesitation.

"Really? Because she looks awfully guilty. Did you read the *Post*?"

"Come on, you don't believe the *Post* do you?" I said.

James laughed. "No, I do like fucking with you though. But seriously, why don't you think she did it?"

"I don't know. I get that she looks really guilty, but I just don't think she did it." I finished my water and put the empty glass in the sink.

"What are you up to tonight?" James asked.

"I'm going out on a date."

"Oooh, with who?"

"That cop, Officer Doyle."

"Shut up!"

I walked back into my bedroom and examined my closet. It was a mess. "I know, but I don't have anything to wear."

"What's his first name?" James asked.

"Ha, you know what? I don't know."

"You don't know his first name?"

"Nope," I said.

"How mysterious."

I laughed. "It's pretty funny."

"Funny and sexy," James said.

"Shut up."

"Where are you guys going?"

"I don't know yet." I pulled a pair of jeans out of my closet, then threw them back because I knew they made my thighs look wide.

"What about that seafood place you love?"

"I'm waiting to see if he has any ideas." I looked in the full-length mirror at me wearing a T-Shirt and my underwear. "Will you come over and help me pick out an outfit."

James laughed. "I'd love to, but I've got to get work done."

"But it's Saturday," I whined.

"I know that. Hugh is out to brunch with Pat and Chris, and here I am surrounded by moving boxes, trying to figure out how to convince people to buy more shit."

"When will you be done?"

"Never."

"Come on, I need your help. I hate all my clothes." I pulled out a pair of shorts I hadn't worn in years. "I should really throw some of this stuff away."

"What time is your date?"

"I don't know yet, but I'm guessing around seven." I picked up a black shirt. It was covered in Blue's hair. "Shit."

"What?"

"This damn dog has covered everything I own in hair." I looked over at Blue snoring on my bed.

"Welcome to the wonderful world of animal companionship."

"Come over," I said.

"I'll try to get there by six."

"But--"

"Have several outfits ready, so I just have to choose. I am not rooting through your closet. That is your job."

"Fine." I hung up the phone and returned to the disaster I lovingly called my wardrobe.

Doyle texted that he'd pick me up at 7:15. At 6:15 James showed up. He took one look at the outfits I'd laid out on the bed and sighed. "Will you never learn," he muttered and then headed to the closet. He pulled out a blue and white sundress that made me look just sweet as pie. "Put this on," he said.

"You don't think it's too cutesy for a first date?"

James rolled his eyes. "No such thing."

He was right. The dress looked perfect; it pushed up my boobs and stayed tight to my waist, where it flared out into a full and bouncy skirt that fell a couple inches above my knees. And it was covered in little white flowers. Who doesn't like small white flowers? By the time we managed to duct tape all of Blue's hair off me and do my hair and makeup, we had 15 minutes to spare.

"OK, you have to leave now," I said to James. "Before he gets here."

James laughed. "The only reason I agreed to come over was to meet this cute cop."

"But I don't want him to think that--"

"What is he going to think?"

"That you're here to check him out."

"That *is* why I'm here. You got anything to drink?" James asked moving toward the kitchen. Blue hopped off the bed and followed him.

"I'm not giving you a drink. I want you to leave," I said following them.

James found a half bottle of wine on the counter. "How old is this?"

"Too old. You don't want it. Now leave."

He pulled out the cork and smelled it. "Oh, this is fine. Joy, you should not lie." He clucked his tongue and pulled two glasses out of the cabinet. I gave up and accepted the glass of wine he offered me. "To your date," James said, then clinked his glass against mine. I took a sip, and the doorbell rang. I jumped and spilled wine on the floor as Blue started barking and scampered out of the kitchen. "I'll get it," James said and dashed into the hall before I had a chance to recover.

"Hi, I'm Joy's brother, James," I heard him yell over the barking. "Shut up Blue."

"Declan Doyle. That's a big dog."

I took a deep breath and came out from the kitchen. James was bent over using his free hand to hold Blue back. Doyle was looking down at my dog, concern resting above his eyebrows. Blue was no longer barking, but a deep rumble was emanating through his closed mouth. A mouth that it appeared James was holding shut.

"Hi," I said.

Doyle looked up and smiled. "You look gorgeous," he said. His big warm eyes were making me melt just a little bit.

"Please come in," James said, moving aside and dragging Blue with him. Declan didn't move as he watched Blue's hackles raise.

"We should really go," I said.

"Well, if you must," James said, struggling to keep his wine from spilling and at the same time look casual holding Blue's muzzle shut. I grabbed my purse off the hall table and moved past them.

"Don't worry, I'll take care of him," James said motioning toward Blue.

"Thanks," I said. James mouthed "He is super cute," as the door closed. I turned to Declan and we both smiled.

We went to a bar named Sun-deck, a short walk from my apartment. It does not have a sun-deck, but it has a backyard and excellent Sangria. Declan opened the door for me and ordered a pitcher of white sangria (without asking my opinion), then led me to a quiet table in the garden.

As we walked through the room women swiveled their heads to look at the man walking with me. It wasn't that he was so good looking; there was just something about the way that he moved. It was almost like watching a tiger or some other large creature with no natural enemies walk through his stomping grounds.

Declan paid no mind to his admirers. He kept his eyes on me and his hand in the small of my back, steering me through the space. When we sat down, he pulled out my chair for me. I could not help but smile.

The yard was strung with colorful lanterns. Declan's creamy white shirt glowed softly against his tan skin. The waitress arrived with our pitcher and filled our glasses, smiling at Declan the whole time. When he took his glass from her, I saw a beautiful gold watch peek out from under his cuff.

When I looked at his face, he was smiling at me. The waitress left and Declan pulled up his sleeve to show me the watch. "It was my great-grandfather's."

"It's beautiful," I said, then sipped my drink. The sangria was delicate and not too sweet. I could just make out the flavor of brandy.

"Thanks," he smiled. "He was a bootlegger."

"Really?" I laughed. "How did he feel about you becoming a cop?"

"He passed away before that. But he would have been fine with it. I have enough brothers and cousins to run the family business."

"They're still bootleggers?" I joked.

"Close. We have liquor stores all over the region."

"Sounds like a fun family."

Declan laughed. "I guess we know how to have a good time."

"So how did you become a cop?"

Declan smiled. "How'd you become a dog walker?"

77

"Ah, I see, it's my turn." He bit his lip and nodded. "A friend of a friend knew of a friend with a dog-walking business for sale."

"It's that simple?"

"I guess," I shrugged. "Walking dogs is something I'm naturally good at. You should see me walk Blue. I'm excellent."

Declan laughed. He bit his lip again but didn't say anything. He was dead sexy, which raised alarm bells. Nice boys are not this sexy. "What about you? Coppery your life's passion?" I asked.

He laughed, a deep rumble. "Coppery, I like that."

"I like making up words."

"I bet. I'm very passionate about my work," he said, lowering his voice. "I absolutely love what I do."

"Wow. I don't know anyone who loves what they do." I leaned toward him, interested.

He closed the gap between us further. "It started out that I really wanted to help people. You know, step between the abusive husband and his wife, stop the burglary in progress. I pictured returning purses to pretty young ladies like you all day." He laughed softly and reached his hand out casually taking mine in his. He played with my fingers as he continued. "But, as you might suspect, there is a lot more paperwork than that." I laughed. "Now, what I love about it is working with my brothers and sisters in blue--the camaraderie, the collective will to do good. I really like working in that environment."

"Even working with guys like Mulberry?" I asked, remembering what Marcia had told me about his rumored violent behavior.

"Girl, you're going to get me in trouble."

"Why?" I asked.

"You really are gorgeous." He reached out and pushed a strand of my hair behind my ear and then left his hand resting on my cheek.

"Trying to change the subject?" I teased.

He sat back laughing and picked up his drink. I took a slug of mine too. It was cold but did little to cool me off. "Mulberry and I were partners," he said.

"Really?"

"Until the incident." He raised his eyebrows.

"I've heard rumors," I said.

"This was years ago, when I first joined the force. Mulberry was my senior officer. We shared a car. His father was a decorated officer, you know. He died a hero. A lot of people in the department give Mulberry leeway because of his dad. But I regret to say the son is nothing like the father."

"Did you know his dad?"

Declan shook his head. "Before my time. I was really excited to be working with his son though. But it didn't take long for me to see that Mulberry was crooked."

"Crooked? How?"

Declan leaned toward me and quieted his voice. "I never saw him take money from anyone, but the guy had a lot nicer things than his salary would afford."

"Said the man wearing the gold watch."

Doyle laughed and smiled at me. "The only difference is Mulberry's grandfather was a penniless immigrant, and mine was a multimillionaire who built a big, legitimate business."

"Oh," I said.

"But it wasn't the extravagant lifestyle that concerned me. I was young enough to ignore it. The thing is he wanted to be as great as his Dad, and sometimes that drove him to 'create a break' in a case."

"What does that mean?"

"I don't want to go into details. It's just a fact that the guy can be really rough on suspects. Eventually he did something so fucked-up I demanded that they move me. And that's how I became a mounted police officer."

"Was that a punishment?"

He smiled. "No, a reward. For protecting him."

"Jesus."

The waitress arrived with another pitcher of sangria. She filled both our glasses. Declan looked up to say thank you and then looked right back to me. "When I complained to my superiors, they offered me my present situation, which is pretty awesome." He reached out for my hand again. "I get to meet lovely ladies like you. And Mulberry is under much closer supervision."

"Oh, you meet a lot of ladies on the job?"

He laughed. "You're the first witness I've ever asked out."

"I bet."

Declan wound his free hand into my hair and, leaning forward, placed his smooth, warm lips on mine. He backed off an inch and then pulled me toward him. I did not protest. His tongue darted out and wet our lips. I pulled away, my heart banging in my chest.

He smiled at me. "Sorry, I just wanted to kiss you." He opened the space between us to pour some more sangria. As the waitress passed, he asked her for a charcuterie platter and two glasses of water.

CHAPTER THIRTEEN

SUNDAY, SUNDAY, SUNDAY

I'M A FAN OF SUNDAYS. Usually there is not much to do, and I laze around in bed for at least an hour reading whatever happens to be on my side table. I was going through an old *New York Magazine* when Blue, sick of my Sunday style, started whining by the door.

I ignored him at first, but I swear the dog pitched his whine to the exact note necessary to explode little pockets in my brain. I finally got out of bed with an exasperated, "Fine."

I took Blue over to the coffee shop and ordered an iced latte, then we wandered the neighborhood. I looked in at store windows sipping my deliciously creamy beverage while Blue sniffed the cornucopia of scents littering the sidewalk. He managed to find an abandoned half slice of pizza and scarfed it down. I figured it was time for real breakfast.

As I chewed a piece of toast and looked out my window, I thought about Declan. He was not like other guys I'd dated. First of all, he was a police officer and dedicated to his job. He ordered things for me, while I was very used to ordering my own drinks. There was a part of me that liked it though. Maybe I could be the kind of woman who enjoyed being taken care of. He certainly took care of me last night, I thought with a sly little smile.

We went back to his place after dinner and enjoyed each other like only people who barely know each other can. I'm not saying I screw every stranger who crosses my path, but the fun thing about such quick sex is you can be whoever you want to be in bed. They have no idea who you really are. That first night with Doyle, I was a lamb to his tiger, and I liked it.

I caught a cab home just as the bars were letting out. He wanted me to stay (or at least he said he did), but I needed to get back to Blue (or at least I said I did). I like catching a town car home late. I like sitting back in the leather and watching drunken people fill the streets after final call is over. They are all looking for a fight or a fuck. And, Lord Jesus, they are not going home until they get it. The late night crowd knows what they are living for. Sometimes I wish I had their clarity.

The rush to find an outfit the night before left my bedroom in a state of disarray. I had not gone through my closet since moving into the apartment a year-and-a-half before. I decided this was the perfect Sunday to take it on.

I put on NPR and listened to the news while I pulled out all of my clothing and started dividing it into piles. I heard an interesting story about a large private corporation that owned tons of supermarkets under all different brand names. That made me wonder what it would be like to come from a family of supermarket magnates. I was picturing myself on a large yacht with servants to clean out my closet (and bring me fresh produce from my very own supermarkets) when my attention was again drawn to the radio.

"The mayor is hosting a party for the Biltmore Club tomorrow evening at Gracie Mansion. This is the second gala event the mayor has hosted since coming into office. It raises money for underprivileged New Yorkers. Joining me is Laura Piper, the events coordinator for Gracie Mansion since 1995. Thanks for joining us..."

That was the second time this week I'd heard about the Biltmore Club. Weird I'd never heard of them before. I picked up the phone and called James. "Hey, you ever hear of the Biltmore Club?" I asked when he picked up.

"No, but let me ask Hugh." I heard James calling out to Hugh but didn't hear his response. "Hold on, he's coming over."

"Hey Joy," Hugh said.

I asked him about the Biltmore Club.

"I don't know a lot about them, but when I did that stint with that private chef agency a couple of years ago, I heard some rumors."

"Rumors?"

"Yeah, crazy shit."

"Really?"

"The only thing I know for sure is membership is coveted. All the major power brokers are into it."

"Really?"

"A shit-ton of the people who could afford our services were members of the society."

"What? Seriously? How have I not heard of these people?" I asked.

"They don't want you to hear about them."

"Hugh, come on."

"Joy, I'm serious. The world has little resemblance to what most people believe."

"How can you say that?"

Hugh laughed. "Come on Joy, you don't see things the way most people do. You know you can make yourself invisible. We all can."

"What are you talking about?"

"Think about when you're on the subway. No one looks at you, right?"

"Yeah?"

"If you do something crazy like, I don't know, scream 'fuck' at the top of your lungs, does anyone look?"

"No, but that's not me making myself invisible. That's those other passengers ignoring me. I'm sure they see me."

"Really? How do you know they just plain never see you?"

"I see people on the subway do crazy shit, and I don't say anything."

"Sure, but you turn your eyes to look at them. You have a reaction. I'm telling you Joy, there is all sorts of shit happening around you all the time that you don't want to see, so you don't. Here, try this tomorrow. When you get on the subway, sit down and really look at everyone in your car. I mean check out the creases of their skin, the sleep in their eyes. Do your best to make eye contact. See how much more becomes visible to you."

"You're blowing my mind, Hugh."

He laughed. "Just try it."

"How do you know these Biltmore Club people are into crazy shit?"

"I was single at the time, Joy."

I laughed. "So?"

"These people like to party. And I mean party."

"Crazy?"

"Seriously."

I heard James in the background saying something. "Hey Joy, I've got to go. We're headed to the farmers' market to pick up dinner."

"OK, thanks."

"Sure, we can talk more later."

James got back on just to say his good-byes, and then I was alone in my bedroom surrounded by piles of clothing, no closer to a clean bedroom or a solution to the mystery before me.

I spent another hour on my closet and managed to get almost everything I wanted to keep put away. That left two bags of donations. I hefted them a couple of blocks to the clothing drop-off box. It was a painfully hot day, and by the time I got back to my place, I was drenched with sweat.

I took a shower and spent the rest of the day on my couch watching TV, doing my nails, and generally being a good-for-nothing. I ordered take-out Chinese. When the guy came to the door, he handed me my food, and I passed over a twenty. After he left, I realized that if you put that guy in a lineup, I wouldn't be able to point him out. I ordered food from the same two places most days of my life, and there was no way I could pick out the different men who brought it to my door. Maybe Hugh was right.

I ate my food watching bad Sunday-night TV. There was a show about some vampires who lived in a gated community and were constantly pulling guns on each other. Why they needed the guns was the most burning question of the whole series, at least that's what I thought.

CHAPTER FOURTEEN

MAD DRAMA AT THE OFFICE

MONDAY MORNING it felt like everyone in Yorkville was talking about the arrest. The name Jacquelyn Saperstein permeated the air. I passed a pair of women, hunched with age, wearing hats appropriate at church or a horse race, as one said, "I never liked her. You can't trust a woman that thin." The other nodded sagely.

There was no one to hold the door for me at the Sapersteins' building. A worried-looking maintenance man stood behind the concierge desk. "What's going on?" I asked. He motioned with his head to a door behind him marked Employees Only. I could hear soft weeping inside. "Who's in there?" I asked.

"Julen," he said.

I tried the knob, but it was locked. "Julen," I called. "Open the door."

"Go away!" he yelled, his voice thick with tears.

"Julen, if a resident of the building walks through the lobby, you are going to be in some deep shit."

"I have nothing left to live for," he cried back.

"That's a little dramatic, don't you think?"

Julen let out a highly dramatic wail. My friend of few words held up a key. "Skeleton," he said. Inside, we found Julen huddled in the corner of a very small employee lounge. When he saw me, he scrambled to his feet.

"Leave me alone. I want to be alone," he said wiping at his face with the back of his hand.

"Then you shouldn't have shown up for work. You need to pull yourself together and get back out there."

"But they have accused my one true love. The only woman I have ever or will ever care for." He fell back against the wall and slid down it with a moan.

"Julen, you are going to lose your job," I said. My skeleton-key-holding friend nodded behind me vigorously. Julen covered his face with his hands. "Locking yourself away in an employee lounge is not going to help her," I said.

"You are right," Julen said looking up at me with red-rimmed eyes. "I must help her." He paused and stared down at the floor. "I will confess," he said in a small voice. "Yes," he said louder. "I will go to the police and tell them." He started to stand up. "I'll tell them that it was me. I wanted him dead."

"Julen, that is a really bad idea," I said. More vigorous nodding from the maintenance man. "The police will not believe you, and it will only make her look more guilty."

Ignoring me, Julen started for the door. My new friend and I blocked his path. "Let me out," Julen demanded.

"You are acting totally insane," I said.

"Loco," added the other man.

"First you tell me that I cannot stay in here, and now you tell me I cannot leave. What do you want from me?" He turned back into the lounge and threw his hands in the air.

"Where was Jacquelyn when her husband was killed?"

The question caught him off guard. "Why do you want to know that?"

"Because I want to help her."

"Why? Why do you want to help her?" I didn't have a ready answer. I hadn't even known that I wanted to help her until I said it. Why did I want to help a woman who very well could be guilty? Was, in fact, more than likely guilty?

"I don't know, but I do. Do you know where she was?"

"She was with me." He hung his head in either exhaustion or shame or maybe both.

"Where?"

"At my house, in Queens. I already told the police this. But, of course, they don't believe me."

"Did anyone see you two together?"

"No, we were very careful. Careful." He laughed a mirthless laugh and sat down, more like collapsed, onto a small, battered love seat. "Nothing matters now...now that I have lost her."

"What do you mean, lost her?"

"She ended it with me." His eyes filled with tears.

"She dumped you?"

"She told me--" A lump rose in his throat and cut off communication. "She told me that she didn't want to see me anymore, that she didn't love me, that she never had." A tear ran down his smooth cheek. I realized how young he was. No more than 22.

"I'm sorry, Julen." He let his head fall into his hands again. Soft sobbing rocked his frame. "Why are you so desperate to help her if she has hurt you so much?"

His head sprang up. "Just because she no longer loves me does not mean that I will abandon her."

All of our heads turned at the sound of the revolving door.

"Julen, get out there," I whispered sharply. He jumped up and hurried into the lobby, wiping his face with his sleeve. I closed the lounge door most of the way.

"Hello, Julen." It was Detective Mulberry. All I could see was the back of Julen. "I just have a couple more things to clear up with you."

"Of course, Detective, but I am working now. Could we talk later?"

"I think we should talk now." The door revolved again. "I think you should come for a chat at the station."

"Sir, I could lose my job."

"Come on, let's go." I heard the sound of two men wearing hard-soled shoes walk toward Julen. A hand wrapped itself around Julen's arm and moved him. I was suddenly facing the detective. Ducking behind the door, I hoped he hadn't seen me. I heard the door revolve several more times, then silence. The maintenance man sharing my hiding place shook his head and clucked his tongue against his teeth.

I waited a couple of seconds, holding my breath, listening. When I was sure the lobby was empty, I walked out of the lounge. Mulberry was waiting for me. He smiled, enjoying the mix of fear and surprise on my face.

"What are you doing here?" he said.

"None of your business." It was his turn to be surprised. I walked past him toward the elevators.

"I asked you a question." Mulberry ran a couple of steps to catch up.

"And I gave you an answer." I pushed the up button and prayed for the doors to open.

"I'll ask you again. What are you doing here?"

The doors opened and I saw myself reflected in the mirrored walls of the elevator as I said, "none of your business." I stepped inside.

"Don't push it, Miss Humbolt."

I turned to face him, then pushed the button for the Sapersteins' floor. The detective didn't try to stop the doors from closing, nor did he take his eyes off mine.

A short, plump, clean-faced woman opened Jacquelyn Saperstein's door. "Hi, I'm--"

"Who is it?" came a voice from inside; it was strong with an accent born out of shit loads of money. The woman in front of me winced.

"Hi, I'm Joy, the dog-walker." I held my hand out to the woman in front of me. Tentatively, she laid her soft hand in mine. I squeezed and shook. She watched. I let go and her hand slipped out of my grip and back down to her side.

"I'm Cecelia."

"Nice to meet you," I said. "I know this is a difficult time and--" A rail-like woman, her face encased in cosmetics, brushed Cecelia aside and started talking over me.

"You must be the dog-walker. Cecelia, why do you have her standing in the doorway? Please excuse my sister. She forgets herself," the woman said, looking at a point above my head. Cecelia melted away from the door and onto the couch in the living room with her eyes downcast and her hands clasped in front of her.

"That's all right. As I was saying to your sister, this is--"

"Come inside," she said, cutting me off again. She closed the door behind me. "There is no reason for us all to be standing around like a bunch of idle ninnies," she said in the direction of her sister, who flinched.

Snaffles was in the kitchen. He was awake, but he looked much older. His snout sported gray hairs, and he walked with the air of an animal that had lived too long, dragging his left back leg and wheezing with each labored step. "What happened to Snaffles?" I asked the thin sister.

"I'm sure I don't know what you mean. You just have to walk him. I think just about anyone could handle that responsibility." She lit up a very long, white cigarette and looked down her sharp nose at me. "I mean, even a trained monkey can walk a dog." She laughed at her own joke, and gray smoke plumed past her perfectly white capped teeth and into the air.

"I'm sorry. I didn't catch your name."

"Mrs. Point."

"I understand that this is a hard time for your family, but there is no reason to talk to me like that."

"I'm sure I don't know what you mean." She blew a long stream of smoke in my direction.

"I just want to know if Snaffles is ill."

"Just shut up and walk the dog." She started to leave the room.

"Excuse me?" I said.

She whirled around and glared at me. "Who do you think you are? You are my employee, and you will do as I say."

"I'm not your employee, and I feel bad for anyone who is."

"Then I guess you will find other employment."

"I guess I already have it." I started to leave but couldn't help myself. "This was a young and healthy dog only days ago, and now he looks like he is in death's doorway. I asked what happened to him, because I care about the well-being of the animal-- something any person would do. Perhaps even a trained monkey would have the heart to find out what happened to a defenseless creature." Mrs. Point looked down at me, her cigarette gripped tightly between long, claw-like fingers.

"How dare you speak to me this way," she sputtered. "Get out." She stamped out her cigarette into an ashtray and pointed to the door. Cecelia walked into the kitchen.

"What's going on here?" she asked with a tremor in her voice.

"I fired the dog-walker."

"Mildred, we need someone to walk the dog," Cecelia said.

"Do you think she is the only dog-walker in New York City? Now get out," she said to me.

"No," Cecelia said. Her hands balled into fists at her side. "You stay right where you are."

Oh Jesus, I thought, these bitches are crazy.

"Mildred," Cecelia started, "this young woman is right. You're heartless."

Mildred's jaw dropped, but she picked herself up quickly. "Where would you all be without Harold and our money? Where?" Mildred almost screeched.

"Maybe we would be happy. Maybe we would all get along," Cecelia said, her words harder than her voice.

"You live in a fucking fairy tale, Cecelia, and I'm sick of looking after you." She lit another one of her long cigarettes, leaning against the kitchen counter, positive she would win this one.

"Sick of looking after me? Who was there when you got kicked out of Elexer Prep School? Who convinced father not to throw you out of the house?" Cecelia's face flushed pink.

"That's ancient history. I've been saving your ass for years," Mildred said.

"You are an embarrassment. The way you treat people is horrific and disgusting." Cecelia took a step into the room. She was looking up at her sister with eyes as hot as the ember at the tip of Mildred's cigarette.

"Whatever, Cecelia, I don't need this shit from you or anybody else." Mildred stormed past her sister. I heard the front door slam behind her. Cecelia stood in the kitchen doorway.

"I'm sorry you had to see that." She pulled a handkerchief out of her skirt pocket and wiped at her eyes. "She is the youngest, you know. They are always--well, never mind."

"Would you like me to walk Snaffles for you?"

"Very much so. I'm going to lie down for a nap."

I put Snaffles' leash on. He looked up at me with unfocused eyes. Outside, he peed on the closest tree, then sat. "Come on, boy," I said in a high, happy tone. He stood up and followed me around the block, wheezing and panting. After only 20 minutes of exercise, I took him home.

The house was quiet. I put Snaffles in the kitchen. He slumped onto his bed and began snoring softly. I took a moment to thank a God I don't believe in for my brother and his kindness, then let myself out of the apartment, locking the door behind me.

I headed over to Eighty-Eight East End Avenue to find George Chamers who, according to Philip, had some information about the morning of the murder. The lobby of Eighty-Eight East End seemed vaguely familiar, like something out of a dream. I walked up to the block of marble that served as the front desk and asked a white-haired, deeply lined man if George Chamers was around.

"Well, now, I'll have to check." He brought out a large binder from under the desk filled with phone numbers, which he muttered over. "Here it is." He dialed, checking the binder several times. "Hello, Chamers? Is that you? Oh, Wilson," he laughed. "Yes, you two do sound alike. Listen, Wilson, I have a lovely young lady up here"--he smiled at me, I smiled back--"who wants to speak to Chamers." He listened for a moment. "Uh-huh, I see. OK. Thank you." He hung up. "Sorry dear, but he is not in today. Tomorrow he goes on at 7 a.m."

"Thanks. I'll come back."

"You're welcome." As I turned to leave, I noticed a paisley couch and realized I was in the lobby that Declan had brought me to. I tried to take a step, but my foot didn't want to listen to me. The room whirled. The paisley was everywhere. The marble looked cold and foreboding and was getting closer. I hit the ground hard. I stayed there.

When I woke up I was back on that paisley couch, and the white-haired man was leaning over me, his brow wrinkled. A woman dressed all in black with burgundy lipstick watched me from over his shoulder. "An ambulance is on the way," she told me.

"I don't want an ambulance." She looked surprised. "I'm fine. I just, I don't know, but I don't need an ambulance."

"But you had a spell. You should go to the hospital to find out what's wrong with you."

"I don't need to go to the hospital." I sat up and felt my brain swimming inside my cranium. It felt light and delicate. "I'm fine. I just need to go home." I stood up. My feet felt very far away. I put my arms out to steady myself. The woman touched my elbow. I pulled away from her and fell back onto the couch. I tried to get up again, but the white-haired man put a hand on my shoulder and told me to wait. "Wait for what?" I asked stupidly. He was nice enough to just smile at me.

"Everything will be fine," he told me.

"I don't have insurance," I said. He didn't let this worry him. He just smiled at me sweetly.

"I can't afford this," I tried to explain.

"Just rest." But I couldn't do that, so I pulled myself up again. They both moved out of my way as I put one foot in front of the other. Carefully, deliberately, I made it out onto the street. The warmth of the sun felt good on my bruised face. I stood for a moment with my eyes closed, collecting my thoughts. The long walk to the subway seemed unbearable. I wished for a "beam me up, Scotty" machine to zap me into my bed. Instead, I climbed onto a cross-town bus.

I'd never fainted before. I hardly thought that women of my generation did such things. I mean, sure, if I wore a corset and was prone to hysterics like women who wore hoop skirts and became overwhelmed by short walks and loud bangs, then I could explain the episode, but this was a new millennium. My mother's generation burned their bras and freed us from, among other things, the need to faint from emotional distress.

Later, on the phone, James was adamant that I should go to a doctor. "I fainted. You don't have to go to a doctor about fainting."

"Yes, you do. What if you have a tumor?" he insisted.

"It's not a tumor," I replied in my best imitation of Arnold Schwarzenegger from Kindergarten Cop.

"I can't believe you still quote that movie. You should see a doctor about that."

"That one I will give you." I flicked on the TV. "I'm going to watch the news now."

"To see if your case is on?"

"Mhmm."

"I'll watch with you."

I heard his TV zap to life. Betty Tong smiled out at us, then quickly frowned when an image of a darkened New York skyline appeared above her right shoulder. "Our top story tonight: Does New York City have enough power to survive the summer? John." The camera cut to John Schoop, Betty's co-anchor.

"Also, new developments in the Saperstein slaying. Betty." Back to Betty.

"And what kind of park has the mayor singing its praises? All that and more after the break."

"Do you think the city has enough power?" I asked James.

"Probably not." The news came back. Betty introduced us to an expert who assured us that if we had a heat wave, we would have a blackout.

"That's not good," James said.

"That's bad," I agreed.

"Mayor Jessup returned from a visit to Long Island today with praise for a new park-- an underwater park, the first of its kind," John Schoop announced. The screen showed the mayor on a boat, leaning over the edge, shaking hands with a man who bobbed in the water. "The main attraction in this Shipwreck Park is the H.M.S. Culloden, a 74-gun frigate that sank over 200 years ago." The screen cut to the mayor in his press conference room.

"I was very impressed by the park," the mayor stated. "I love to dive-- the adventure, the freedom to breathe underwater. And not only do I think it's great to be introducing more people to the sport of scuba diving, but this park is also providing protection for the artifacts resting at the bottom of Fort Pond Bay. People I've spoken to joke that everyone with a boat and a wet suit has some part of her history." His face turned serious. "And that has got to stop. We can't have people looting our history. I am overjoyed by Albany's decision to fund this park."

John Schoop appeared again. "The Culloden sank in 1781 while in pursuit of French vessels assisting the American colonists. Betty."

Betty was laughing when the camera cut back to her. "Mayor Jessup does love to dive."

"Do you think he's running for governor?" James asked.

"I don't know."

"I wouldn't want to face him. Scary." Kurt Jessup won the mayoral election three years earlier after his opponent, the incumbent, lost his mind. He ended up in an upstate facility so drugged up that all he does is drool. After Jessup's landslide, rumors of poisoning spread. But most people agree the guy just snapped, that Jessup got a lucky break.

Mrs. Saperstein's mug shot filled the screen. She looked exhausted and dumbstruck. "A new development in the Upper East Side slaying of Joseph Saperstein," Schoop told us. The screen cut to footage of Mrs. Saperstein being led out of her apartment building. "A doorman at the victim's building claims to have spent the morning with the accused widow on the day of the murder." Jackie was shown stepping into an unmarked black car. "Police say that his claim is unsubstantiated, and they have witnesses who saw Jacquelyn Saperstein leaving the scene of the crime."

Back to Betty Tong. "Action News Live Alert: Now Channel 7 has learned that the doorman was having an affair with the widow, and this is one of the reasons the police find his story suspect."

Mulberry, in front of a bunch of microphones, said, "I believe that Julen Valquez would say anything to help Mrs. Saperstein, and therefore I am not taking his statements seriously." Mulberry turned to leave as the crowd of reporters yelled unintelligible questions at him.

"We will have more on this story as it progresses," Betty said. I turned off my TV.

"Joy, I have to admit. She looks really guilty," James said.

"I don't know. I just don't think she did it."

"Then who?"

"I don't know yet." I chewed on my lip and stared at the blank TV screen.

"Joy, you there?"

"Yeah, yeah, just thinking."

"You're not going to faint are you?" James asked with a note of fear in his voice.

"No. I'm fine. I just, I need to figure this out."

We didn't say anything for a while, but I could hear James breathing on the other end.

"I'll figure it out," I said.

"I bet you will," James said.

CHAPTER FIFTEEN

GEORGE AND MICHAEL

I WOKE up early the next day. There was a bruise on my cheek from where I'd hit the marble. It was sore and slightly puffy but not too color-ful. I applied some concealer and headed uptown. If I hurried, I would have time to see both Michael, the mysterious man without a phone, and George Chamers, the man Philip at Ten House said I should talk to.

I usually avoided the hours when the majority of humanity squeezed onto the subway. It's hot, it's too tight, and it makes me feel like a sheep, like one of them. I don't like being "one of them."

As I stood holding onto the bar, there was a man wearing a suit with a bluetooth in his ear on the one side, and a pregnant woman with sweat dripping into her eyes on the other. I thought about what Hugh said. Directly across from me, her hand gripping less than an inch below mine on the center pole, was a woman in her fifties dressed in a busi-ness suit. I looked directly into her face. She wore a glazed expression, and, though I stared into her eyes, she did not react.

I shook my head, whipping my ponytail against the bluetooth-wearing male and the pregnant female. They both gave me more space, but neither of them looked my way. I took a breath of humid air and sighed. Could Hugh be right? Did humans just see what they wanted? Were we really blind? "FUCK!" I yelled.

The woman across from me jumped a little but did not glance in my direction. "Excuse me," I said to her. She did not respond. I touched her arm, and she just backed away. "Excuse me, can you see me right now?" I asked. She squeezed back into the crowd behind her--a mass of people who I didn't really see, just the colors of their shirts and the difference in their heights.

I gave up and spent the rest of the subway ride looking at my shoes.

At Eighty-Eight East End Avenue, a heavyset woman with a unibrow had replaced the white-haired man from the day before. She phoned Chamers for me, and several minutes later, the freight elevator arrived carrying a good-looking man in his late forties.

"I'm George," he said offering a calloused hand.

"I'm Joy. Philip suggested I talk to you. Is there anywhere we can speak in private?"

"Yes, Philip said you'd be stopping by. It's your friend Charlene who is missing. I don't know if I can help you but I'm happy to try." I didn't bother correcting him. If Charlene being my friend helped him talk to me, then so be it. George led the way to the freight elevator. It was quilted in blue fabric meant to protect the walls. George inserted a key, and the doors closed with a well-oiled swoosh.

"Philip said that you saw something the morning Joseph Saperstein was killed."

The elevator carried us past the basement to the sub-basement. George sighed. "Yes. I did."

The doors opened onto a clean, white hallway lit by fluorescent lights. Our steps echoed around us as we followed the hall to where it ended in a T and took a left, followed by a right and then another left, which brought us to an unmarked door that George opened with a key that hung on a ring with about a hundred others. He motioned me inside and pointed out a chair facing an old wooden desk. He sat behind the desk and ran a large hand through his dark hair. "Why do you want to know about this?" he asked.

"I'll be honest," I said, and then bit my lip. "I found his body, my friend is missing, and I don't know what else to do but try and figure out what happened."

"Really?" He frowned. "I guess this is kind of a mess, and maybe you should just leave it alone."

"What do you know about it?"

He looked up quickly, "Nothing. I just know what I saw, and I barely know that."

"Will you please tell me?"

He sighed again then studied me with deep brown eyes set in a lean and handsome face. "It was around 7:30 in the morning," he started. "I was in here when I heard the emergency exit alarm go off. I hurried to hallway N11. It's a bit of a hike, and it probably took me five or seven minutes. I was very surprised to see a woman standing in the exit. I called out to her, and she ran down the hall. I followed, but she was quicker than me. I've got a bad knee." He reached under the desk and rubbed the knee, his eyes unfocused. "She could have gone in so many different directions."

"Where does the emergency exit lead to? The one you saw her standing in."

George shook his head. "It's where the body was."

"You didn't look out the door?"

"No." He shook his head again. "I called the police. They took my statement over the phone."

I wondered for just a flash how different my life would be if George had opened that door. If someone else had found him lying there in his own blood, missing his face. "What did the woman look like?" I asked.

"Blond hair under a blue baseball cap. She was wearing jeans and a black T-shirt."

"Do you think her hair was dyed or natural?"

He smiled and cast his eyes to the floor. "I'd say it was bleached."

"Did you see her face?"

"Only for a second, and it was dark. Because of the energy crisis, we've only been keeping every third light on in certain sectors."

"Was she carrying a gun?"

"Not that I saw."

I thought about how Joseph's face was obliterated. It must have been a big fucking gun. "Do you think it was Jacquelyn Saperstein?" I asked.

He didn't look at me but instead concentrated on a spot above my head. "I've spent many hours trying to reconstruct her face in my mind. It was only a flash you understand?" He looked at me, and I nodded. "I can't for sure say it wasn't, but I'm not going to testify in court that I saw her there. I told the police that."

"Did they try to pressure you?"

He laughed. "Not in so many words. Of course, they want it to be all buttoned up, but I just can't say I saw someone I didn't. She had a similar build, and the hair was about the same I guess. But she got away from me, and I'll never know without her confession that it was Mrs. Saperstein."

"How big is this place?" I asked.

He smiled again. His teeth were crooked in a charming way. "It's the biggest place I've ever worked. I mean, these passages lead all over the place--to the parking garage, other exits to the street, deeper sub-basements. Before the Second World War, this place extended straight to the river. It had a yacht club. People used to sail right off the back of the building."

"Wow."

"Sure. Before the East River Drive was built, these buildings went right up to the water. There are so many different hallways around here, and because of all the construction and changes over the years it's not easy to find your way around. I even heard rumors there are secret passages leading to the park." He laughed easily. "William Franklin is probably the only man in this city who knows the whole building."

"William Franklin?"

"He's the manager here at Eighty-Eight East End Avenue, has been for 30-some-odd years."

I made a mental note of the man's name and thought I'd try to get ahold of him later. "How do you think the woman got in through the emergency exit?" I asked. "Would she need a key?"

"She would, and I don't know how she got it. I've got a copy, Franklin's got one, and there is one kept at the front desk."

"What about a skeleton key?"

"There is one, but it wouldn't work for that door. The skeleton is only for the apartments and the tenants' storage rooms."

"Would you show me where you saw the woman?"

"Sure." He used the arms of the chair to push himself into a standing position. As we moved down the hallway, I noticed the limp his bad knee gave him.

"What happened to your knee?" I asked. "If you don't mind me asking," I added.

"Not at all," he smiled. "I played football in high school." He laughed louder when he saw my expression. "I know, I'm not a big guy. I was the quarterback. And one day I just got hit wrong. Happens all the time."

"I'm sorry."

He laughed again. "I'm not. I had some of the best days of my life out there on that field. And it's not so bad. Gives me an excuse to talk about the old days."

We walked through a maze of corridors and up a short flight of concrete stairs to a door marked in red "Emergency Exit" with yellow crime-scene tape stretched across it. The bright colors looked alien in the stark white hallway. "Can I open it," I asked.

"I don't think so. That's why they put the tape across it."

I laughed. George was looking down at me, smiling. "Right. I guess so."

"You always like this?" he asked.

"What do you mean?"

"So persistent?"

"Ha, no," I said. "I don't think so."

"I guess I understand."

"Yeah?"

"When your life is changed in an instant, you want to understand it. You want to pick it apart and find out what happened. How did this all happen so quickly?"

"Yeah, that is it." I cocked my head. "How did you know?"

"My knee," he patted the injured joint. "I watched that tape, God, I don't know how many times. I wanted so badly to know what went wrong. Where was the mistake?"

"Did you figure it out?" I leaned toward him eager for a positive answer, but George just laughed. "What?" I asked confused.

"No, because there is no answer. That's just how life decided to go that day. You can't figure out why it decided to do that."

"But this is different." I pointed at the door. "Someone killed Joseph Saperstein in that alley. There is an answer to this mystery."

"Sure there is," George shrugged. "But it's not going to change what happened to you. Nothing is going to take back the instant you found that body. It is unchangeable. No matter what you do now, that is over."

"I know that."

"I hope so, because the only closure you can find is in yourself."

"You a Buddhist or something?" I asked smiling at him.

He laughed again. I liked the way it sounded--warm and happy in such a cold and lonely place. "No, I'm not a Buddhist. I've just been through enough to know that the only thing you can change is yourself. And that ain't easy."

"All right, philosopher," I said. George laughed again. "Where were you and where was she?"

"I was coming the way we just came, and when I turned the corner, I saw her back and the door closing. I called out to her."

"What did you say?"

"I think I said 'hey' or something like that. I was real surprised to see her. She was standing right here," he said as he stood close to the door, his back to me, under a dead light fixture. Looking down the hall, I saw that every third florescent light was out. Conservation can be a bitch, I thought. "When I called out to her she turned like this," George demonstrated as he turned his head just enough to glance at me. "And then she took off down the hall." He pointed to where the hall extended for what seemed like an endless distance. The final wall was cloaked in a velvet blackness. "She took a left up there." George and I walked to where the mysterious woman had turned. Another long and poorly lit hall extended before us. "I chased her, but by the time I got to here she'd ducked into another corridor and was gone."

"What is down there?"

"Storage rooms and other hallways."

"Could we explore a little?" George looked down at his watch. "I understand I've taken up a lot of your time. I really appreciate the help you've given me already, and if you need me to go, I will."

He shook his head with a smile. "I guess I have a few more minutes." We walked side by side down the hall. Most of the doors were locked. Those that were open revealed small rooms filled with a mix of boxes and old dusty furniture.

"Most of these locked doors are tenants' storage," Chamers told me.

"So tenants have access?"

"Sure, they pick up the elevator key at the front desk."

"But there is no skeleton for the emergency exit?"

"That's right."

"Could she have come from inside the building? I mean who's to say she was coming in the emergency exit?"

"No one at the front desk saw a woman of her description come in."

"There must be a woman who lives in the building who would fit the description. Couldn't she have come down from her apartment?"

"We checked the elevator footage. The woman did not come down it." George's cell phone rang. He answered it. "I'll be right there," he said, then hung up. "That was the front desk. I've got to go."

George escorted me back through the maze of hallways to the lobby. "Thanks again, George," I said. "It was really great of you to talk to me."

George smiled. "Anytime." I nodded to the woman behind the desk and walked back out into the sunlight. Michael would be getting off work in five minutes, so I hurried over to the Sapersteins' building. A ridiculously hot guy stood behind the front desk.

"Hi, are you Michael?"

"Yes, I am." He smiled a perfect smile at me.

"My name's Joy. I--"

"I know who you are. Nice bruise. How'd you get it?"

"I fell down." I felt myself blushing. The makeup must have worn off, I thought, as I reached up to touch my cheek.

He smiled. "That's what they all say."

"How did you know who I was?"

"Julen told me all about you. Before he got hauled off to the pen."

"He's in jail?"

"You didn't know?" He started to take off his uniform jacket. Michael was wearing only a white T-shirt underneath. I could see that his body was one that should be sculpted for posterity. Michael must have noticed the look on my face. "Do you mind if I change? I get off work in about two minutes, and I want to get out of here."

"Sure, change away." I giggled. He smiled his movie-star smile at me and excused himself into the employee lounge where I had found Julen the day before. I stood by the desk trying to figure out how to recover some dignity. I decided I would ask him if I could buy him a cup of coffee and have a chat. But I wouldn't say chat. I would say something cool. Before I could come up with a replacement for chat, he came out of the lounge dressed in worn jeans covered in paint stains, his white T-shirt and a leather jacket. "Isn't it a little warm for leather?" I asked without thinking.

"Not when you're doing 70 over the bridge." I giggled again. *Pull yourself together*, I screamed in my head. "So you want to talk to me about Joseph, right?" Michael asked.

"Maybe I could buy you a cup of chat and we could coffee."

"I know a great place a couple blocks from here."

"I meant a cup of coffee and a chat."

"I know."

He motioned for me to walk ahead out the door, which I did with images of his uniform draped across my floor dancing in my head.

Ten minutes later I was sitting across from him in a Starbucks, his idea of a great little place. I would have lost all attraction for him right then and there if his eyes hadn't been the same color as sweet green grapes. "I'll tell you the same thing I told the cops. He left at six for his jog."

"Was that his normal time?"

"No, he usually left around eight, right as I'm leaving."

"Did he say anything?"

"He said, 'Good morning.' "

"Did he look scared?"

"I wasn't really paying attention to him. I was working on a collage."

"A collage?"

"Yeah, I'm a mixed-media artist." He leaned back in his chair, his crotch angled toward me. I sipped my burnt coffee, trying really hard not to imagine him naked.

"Did you notice if he was wearing his wedding ring and watch?" I asked.

"Not a clue." He crunched down on a piece of biscotti. "You want to get out of here?" he asked, his mouth full.

"I have to go to work soon."

"Blow it off. Let's take a ride." He leaned his elbows on the table, which tensed his incredible biceps, and winked at me.

"I really can't."

He leaned back again and looked around the coffee house. "You got any other questions for me?"

"What was he wearing?"

"A jogging suit."

"Blue?"

He nodded.

"What about his toupee?"

"Nah, he never wore that jogging."

"What?" But he was smiling at a woman behind the counter. "Did you say he was not wearing his toupee?"

"That's right. He never wore his toupee when he jogged."

"But his toupee was found with the body. Do you think he could have had it in his pocket or something?"

He looked at me and laughed. "You ever heard of anyone keeping a toupee in their jogging suit pocket?"

"But how did it get with the body then?"

"I don't know." He sipped his low-fat vanilla latte. It left a small mustache of foam on his lip. He licked it off with an incredible pink tongue. "Are you sure you don't want to go someplace with me?"

"Maybe some other time. Thanks, though. I need to go."

"Come see me anytime." I left him in the Starbucks making the girl behind the counter giggle.

CHAPTER SIXTEEN

A WALK UPTOWN

THE REST of the day went by without me. I was in my head wondering how a toupee joins a dead body after the fact. I wanted to talk to Jacquelyn. I wondered if she could remember if Joseph wore his toupee jogging. Maybe he went back to the house, and Michael didn't notice. Or maybe, like this morning, Michael left his post before his replacement arrived. And what about the blond woman in the emergency exit? Was it Jacquelyn? I needed to ask Julen what time they left his house. These questions continued to roam through my head all the way home, through my take-out Chinese and the laugh-tracked sitcoms, right into Blue's walk.

I found us wandering not to the park but toward the Brooklyn Bridge. The night, sticky from the day's heat, made me sweat as I walked through Carroll Gardens. The windows of brownstones flickered with the reassuring light of the television. Walking down Brooklyn Bridge Avenue we passed Family Court, a hideous building with a flat facade and barred windows. Across the street an ancient-looking armory sat dark and deserted.

We walked over the Brooklyn Bridge on the wooden pedestrian path that hangs above the roaring traffic. We followed the thick steel cables under the massive granite towers. To my left, glass skyscrapers mixed with smaller turn-of-the-century stone buildings perched on the tiniest tip of Manhattan. A gaping hole in the sky where the towers used to be made the island look off- balance. The Statue of Liberty glowed small but still impressively in the distance.

City Hall, white and large-windowed, stood at the end of the bridge. I turned us uptown, and we passed more courthouses. People stood outside fiendishly smoking in doorways, even at this late hour. Most were women who had come to watch their husbands, sons, and boyfriends be arraigned. To cry in the bathroom, to plead with the judge, to yell at the officer behind the bullet-proof glass, to smoke cigarettes outside.

Heading uptown, we passed Canal Street, its storefronts covered in pull-down metal gates in every shade of gray, deserted by pedestrians, at least human ones. The entrance to the Manhattan Bridge was still active with cars honking at each other as they tried to make the turn. A police officer watched from his parked cruiser.

In Soho we passed the flagship stores for Prada and Apple, and art galleries with photographs of Bob Dylan and Audrey Hepburn. Above us, giant windows of fabulous lofts glowed. The occasional cobblestone street, the uniquely dressed, the tall, the skinny--here was the center of deciding what we want to be, how we want to live, what will make us belong. Giant billboards of young girls caressing bare-chested, glistening men in expensive jeans loomed over us.

Crossing Houston with its four lanes of traffic into Greenwich Village, we watched drunken coeds pour out of loud, stinking bars. "That's a really cute dog," a perky brunette, illegally drunk, told me from between the supporting arms of two friends.

I turned east toward First Avenue to avoid the congestion of Union Square. An ambulance, sirens singing, lights flashing, barreled down First and turned into the emergency entrance of Bellevue Hospital. I watched as two men in jackets that stated "Paramedic" lowered a person out of the back of the vehicle. Two nurses in light-pink scrubs joined them, and they all hurried toward the fluorescent white of the emergency entrance. The ambulance, its back doors open and lights revolving, waited in the abandoned drive.

My calves were burning, and my feet ached as we headed through Midtown up into the Upper East Side, but I just kept going, something urging me forward. Blue kept right at my heels as we passed through the neighborhoods housing the white-collar workers of New York City, quiet and calm. At 79th Street, I turned east again until it met with the river and the bottom of East End Avenue.

We walked past Charlene's building. I looked up at her window. It was dark. I kept going until I was standing at the bottom of the drive leading to Gracie Mansion watching a fancy dress party come to a close.

The mansion--with its yellow exterior, tall windows accented by green shutters, and wraparound porch--is a country estate in an urban landscape. Women in long gowns and men in tuxedos dripped down the steps into waiting limousines. The mayor waved from the porch with one arm around his wife's slim waist.

CHAPTER SEVENTEEN

THIS SITUATION IS EXTREME

THE NEXT DAY A MAN ASKED, "Haven't I seen you before?" as I waited for the elevator with Snowball. He was tall and good-looking in that stockbroker, American Psycho kind of way.

"I don't think so." The elevator dinged, and we stepped in. "What floor?" I asked him as I pushed my button.

"Seventeen." The elevator doors closed, and we rose skyward.

"Wait. I know. You were outside of Gracie Mansion last night with that incredible creature."

"Yeah, that was me." I smiled and felt my face color.

"So you have two dogs?" He pointed to Snowball.

"This one isn't mine. I'm a dog-walker."

"Ah, the oldest profession." He smiled at me with big teeth too white for his age.

"I don't think so," I said.

"I have a dog you could walk." His smile made me feel like meat.

"You have a dog?" I tried to make it sound as if I were really talking about a dog, as in the four-legged, furry creature.

"I most certainly do." He moved closer to me. The elevator dinged and opened on my floor. I stepped quickly out. "Do you have a card? I really would like to continue our conversation." The elevator tried to close, but he stuck out a loafer-clad foot and stopped it.

"I don't think so."

"You're not looking for new clients? How do you expect your business to grow?" The elevator dinged impatiently.

"Sorry. I have to go." I turned and hurried away.

"I'll see you around," he called to me.

The next day, that guy was dead. His name was Tate Hausman, but now he was dead (found hanging from his coveted exposed beams), and I was having another awful conversation with Detective Mulberry.

"You were one of the last people to see him alive."

"That makes me the killer? Then I guess Michael killed Joseph Saperstein."

"What do you know about that?"

"Everyone knows that."

"Who's everyone?"

"Everyone who lives or works in this neighborhood."

Mulberry wrote something angrily on a piece of paper. "Have you spoken to Michael?" he asked.

"Sure, he's the doorman at a building I work in." I tried to make it sound casual.

"You two don't work the same shift, do you?"

"Not exactly. But I've been coming in early to walk Snaffles, since Mrs. Saperstein's arrest." He tapped his pen against his palm.

"Do you think she did it?"

"Jackie? No, I don't think so."

"So who do you think it was?" he asked.

"I have no idea."

"But you're interested?"

"Is there anyone around here who isn't interested?"

"Let's go for a walk."

"A walk?" He stood up from behind his desk and came around to where I was sitting. I stared up at him.

"Come on, let's go."

I stood up and let him lead me out of the police station and onto the street. The sun had set, and a cloud cover moved in. The sky hung low and red above us. I followed the detective away from the station.

"You need to be careful," he told me, gripping my arm more than was necessary.

"What?"

"You don't know what you are getting into."

"I'm not getting into anything."

"You weren't in anything, but now I get the feeling you have put yourself in it. I know that you spoke to Julen and Michael, and, yes, I even know about Chamers. I don't know why you are talking to all these people. This has nothing to do with you."

"A minute ago I was the killer. Now it has nothing to do with me."

"Look." He spun me around to face him.

"Ow," I yelled, a shooting pain vibrating down my arm and back, but he ignored me as did the people passing us on the street.

"You need to stop what you're doing." I struggled against his grip, but it was like struggling against an iron shackle. He shook my arm, sending new pain through it. "Are you listening to me?"

"It's hard with all the pain," I said through clenched teeth. He loosened his grip, and I took a breath. "I don't know what you're talking about."

"Yes, you do." He shoved his face up into mine. "You have to stop, or you are going to get yourself and those around you hurt or even killed."

"What are you talking about?"

"This is bigger than you. Bigger than me. I can't protect you. No one can protect you if you figure anything out."

"Figure what out?"

"This is what I'm talking about. You have to stop asking questions. Do you understand?"

"OK, OK."

He looked at me. "Do you mean it?"

"Yes."

"OK." He started to let go and then pulled me back toward him again and whispered, "Get a weapon." He let go of me, turned on his heel, and melted into the crowd.

I went straight to James's and Hugh's house. They oohed and ahhed over my bruised face. We sat in the yard, and I told them about my completely deranged conversation with Mulberry.

"So the two killings are related?" James asked.

"I mean, the police have not said that officially, but obviously they are. Right?"

"I guess so," James said.

"You need a weapon," Hugh said. "I happen to have a weapon."

James and I both turned to stare at him. "What? Like one of your kitchen knives?" James asked, trying not to laugh.

"Actually, it's a state-of-the-art Taser."

I nearly choked on my wine.

"You have a state-of-the-art Taser? How did I not know that?" James asked.

"Oh, I've had it forever."

"Then I guess it's not that state-of-the-art," James muttered. Hugh ignored him.

"My mother gave it to me when I told her I was moving to Brooklyn." James and I both laughed. "I think you should start carrying it," he said to me.

"You guys don't think this is just some ploy to try and get me to leave the whole thing alone?" I asked.

"Whether it's a ploy or not, you should leave the whole thing alone and start carrying the Taser," James said.

"That's extreme."

"And this situation is--" James said with his eyebrows raised and his palms up, leaving me to fill in the blank.

"Two people are dead," Hugh pointed out.

"What time is it?" I looked around for a clock.

"Almost ten," Hugh replied.

"I want to watch the news. See if there's anything on about it."

A Live Action News Alert opened with a digital American flag waving across the screen. Betty Tong, wearing garish red lipstick and a bright-pink suit, told us, in her best impression of a news anchor, that there was a serious terrorist threat against the subway system of New York City. They cut to a clip of the mayor giving a statement. His thinning blond hair was plastered to his scalp, his tie, a brilliant blue, brought out his eyes.

"We are taking this threat with all seriousness. We will be doing random searches of bags at major subway stations. There will be an increase in uniformed and plain-clothed officers on the trains and plat-forms." It cut back to Betty, who told us that federal officials had received intelligence about an attack over the next few days, but they did not think it was credible. The mayor, however, was taking no chances.

"I don't understand how searching random bags at subway stops is going to help. I mean, if you were carrying a bomb, and you saw the cops searching bags, wouldn't you just leave and go to the next stop where they weren't searching bags?" I asked. Hugh and James nodded and made agreeing noises.

The news cut to a "man on the street" piece where a young blond woman asked subway riders how they felt about the searches. A heavyset black woman told the camera that she was sick and tired of terrorism. A young white guy at Union Square station said he was just going on with his life and wasn't taking the threat too seriously.

"Only a week after Joseph Saperstein's brutal murder, another death in Yorkville," said Betty, setting up the next story.

"This is it," I said, leaning toward the television. Hugh turned up the volume. A young, clean-shaven reporter stood in front of Tate Haus-man's building.

"Tate Hausman, a successful investment banker, an avid scuba diver, a well-liked man, took his own life late Tuesday night. He hanged himself in his home."

"What? His own life?" I said.

"A close friend of the mayor's, Hausman had struggled with depres-sion for years." The screen showed the mayor and Tate in wet suits, face masks pushed up on their foreheads, wind playing with their hair, smiling as their boat pulled away from the shore. "His body was found this morning by his cleaning woman. The police refuse to comment on the existence of a note but say that there is no doubt it was suicide." The news cut back to the mayor.

"Tate was a good friend of mine. He introduced me to scuba diving. He helped me through law school," the mayor sighed. "I just wish I could have helped him through this. Depression is a horrible disease but treatable. I urge depressed New Yorkers with suicidal thoughts to call for help." He looked straight into the camera. "There is help for you. You just have to ask."

"He's good," James said.

"Yeah," Hugh agreed.

"His own life?" I said.

"I'm gonna roll a joint. I can't watch this shit sober," Hugh said. James and I nodded and made agreeing noises. By the time we were smoking, a man named Storm Jenkins was telling us about the heat wave on its way to the tri-state area.

"Great," James said, lungs full of smoke. He exhaled. "That should just about blow out the power grid." Hugh started laughing, then I started laughing, then James started laughing. As Storm finished off the five-day forecast, we were all laughing so hard we weren't making any sound. We just rocked back and forth trying to breathe.

CHAPTER EIGHTEEN

QUESTIONS, DECLAN, AND CHINESE FOOD

"WHAT HAPPENED TO YOUR FACE?" Marcia stared at me as I entered the run.

"Oh," I brought a hand up to the bruise, touching it lightly. It hurt. "I fell down."

"Are you OK?" Elaine asked.

"Yeah, I'm fine. Better than Tate Hausman, anyway."

Fiona picked up the ball that a French bulldog named Chompers had dropped at her feet, and threw it. Chompers flew after the ball.

"Do you really think he killed himself?" I asked.

"I seriously doubt that," Fiona told me. "The man was a complete egomaniac. As far as I know, egomaniacs aren't exactly the suicidal types."

"Maybe he was confident on the outside but really scared and sad on the inside," Elaine suggested. Chompers got hold of the ball, despite its best efforts to bounce off his nose.

"If you ask me, he was murdered," Fiona said.

"What makes you think that?" I asked. Chompers, tail high, ears perked, made the rounds of the run showing off his ball.

"I think he was killed by one of his many women," Fiona said, turning to me. "He was a total slut." Snowball noticed Chomper's satis-fied look and launched herself at him, trying to wrest the ball away. "The way he treated women, he deserved what he got."

"That's harsh," Elaine said.

"Not everyone is as sweet as you, Elaine."

"And not everyone holds onto a grudge as long as you, Fiona," Marcia said.

"What did he do to you?" I asked Fiona.

Chompers was not giving up the ball, and Snowball began to bark in an attempt to intimidate him.

"I dumped him," Fiona said.

"You two dated?"

"Hardly," Fiona forced a laugh. "We hooked up one night, but that was it. He was too much of a slut for me."

I looked over at Marcia who turned her attention to the dogs. Chompers returned with his ball and dropped it at Fiona's feet.

"Was he sleeping with Charlene?" I asked.

"I don't know," Marcia said. "But he was also a member of the Biltmore Club."

"Seems like it's a dangerous group to be a part of all of a sudden," Fiona said with an unattractive smile.

"What about you, Elaine? Do you know?" I asked.

Fiona threw the ball again, and Chompers hurried after it.

"I...I think. I don't know." She started to twist a strand of her hair around her finger. No one said anything. It took only about ten seconds for her to become overwhelmed by the silence. "I hate to guess at something like that. But," she stopped and looked out to the river, "I think Charlene was sleeping with a lot of people."

"What makes you think that?" Marcia asked.

"One time when I was at her house, the phone rang and she went into the bedroom to talk. Her address book was sitting on the kitchen counter, and I was getting a glass of water, which she told me I could get, and I knocked it over," Elaine said speaking very fast, "and the water spilled onto her address book, and I had to put paper towels on it to stop the ink from dissolving, and I saw--"

Chompers returned. We ignored him. "Go on," Marcia encouraged.

"There were lots of men's names. Men from the neighborhood. And their numbers and all these little symbols next to the names."

"What kind of symbols?" I asked.

"Like smiley faces and dollar signs and Xs and Ys. I don't know. It looked complicated."

"Was Joseph Saperstein's name there?" Chompers began to whine, gesturing to the ball.

"I only saw the 'H' page and Tate Hausman was there."

"What did his name have next to it?"

Elaine swallowed and looked around the run nervously, then said in barely a whisper, "A hangman's rope."

A hangman's rope, a hangman's rope, I thought over and over again as I opened Charlene's door. Oscar meowed at me. He needed to be fed, his litter needed to be changed, and I wanted to take a look around for a certain black book.

Stepping into Charlene's living room, I knew I would never find it. Someone had searched the place before me. The books were off the shelves, the couch torn apart. Pots and pans spilled out of the kitchen cabinets. I walked into the bedroom. The bed was stripped, the pillows punctured, the closets emptied. Oscar pushed himself up against my leg, arched his back, and cried. I scratched the top of his head. He squeezed his eyes shut and purred.

A battered photo album lay open on the floor. I sat on the carpet and pulled it to me. Oscar climbed into my lap, pushing himself up against the album, insistent that I pay attention to him and not it. "Come on, Oscar," I said, trying to push him away. He pushed back, his purr turning into a rumble. "Fine." I held the album up, making room for him on my lap.

The album started at the beginning of Charlene's life. Charlene slept in her exhausted, smiling mother's arms at the hospital. Charlene took her first step on brown carpeting next to a big blue chair. Her hair came in red and curly soon after she got out of diapers. A picture of her parents showed her father as an older man, his collar turned up against a wind that played with her mother's hair and pushed autumn leaves around the frame. By the time Charlene was starting kindergarten, the first in a series of school photographs, her father was gone. He was there for the vacation on the beach, and the Christmas Charlene got a stuffed pony, but he was out of her album soon after. Oscar's paw reached up and played with the edge of the book as the years of Charlene's life passed.

Discolored rectangles marked the places of missing photographs. The album ended with Charlene in braces, her hand by her face. It was a posed photograph, probably taken for school. I flipped back through the book noticing that there were no family portraits. No signs of brothers, sisters, aunts, or uncles. Only Charlene and her parents. I wondered who had been removed.

I changed Oscar's litter and filled his bowls. He followed me around the house begging for love. He looked desperate. I bent down and gave his head one more firm ruffling before letting myself out. I could hear him wailing as I walked down the hall.

There was a new doorman at the Sapersteins' building. He was tall and black and wrinkled. "What happened to Julen?" I asked.

"I don't know, ma'am."

"Uh, you don't need to call me ma'am."

"Miss, then," he said.

"Just Joy will do. I don't live here or anything. I walk the Sapersteins' dog."

"The Sapersteins?" He was curious.

"You really don't know what happened to Julen?"

"I heard he was fired."

"For what?"

"Sleeping with Mrs. Saperstein."

"Right. That is the kind of thing that gets you fired."

"It certainly is."

"Do you have his phone number?"

"I don't, but you could ask in the office."

"Where's that?"

"Third floor. Apartment 302."

"I'll try that. Thanks."

Inside apartment 302, a slightly overweight woman sat with her ankles crossed behind a large, dark, wooden desk. "Can I help you?"

"I was hoping to get some contact information for Julen, the doorman." At the mention of Julen's name, the woman stiffened.

"He is no longer employed by this building."

"I know that. I was just thinking that you might have his phone number on record."

"Why do you want it?"

"I just wanted to see how he's doing, what with losing his job and all. That kind of thing can be rough."

She looked me up and down. I smiled my nice-girl smile.

"It's not policy to give out employee information," she said.

"But he's not an employee anymore."

That stumped her.

"But he was," she said, uncertain.

"But you fired him."

"I didn't fire him."

"Right, but the building did."

"Yes, the building did."

"So you could give me his phone number then." She stared at me for one more long second and then turned to a wall of filing cabinets made of the same dark wood as her desk.

She wrote the number down on a sticky and handed it over.

"Thank you so much. I really appreciate this," I said.

She smiled for the first time. "Tell him Jessica says hi?"

"I'd be happy to."

When I went to walk Toby, he greeted me at the door and so did Mrs. Maxim. She was tall, blond, leggy and only a year or two older than me. "Hi, it's great to meet you," she said, her voice full of bubbles. "My little Toby-Woby has told me all about you, haven't you, boy? Yes you have." She reached down and mushed Toby's face while she talked. He appeared to love it.

"It's nice to meet you too, Mrs. Maxim."

She giggled. "Call me Pammy. Everyone else does."

"It's nice to meet you, Pammy."

"Are you OK?" she asked, pointing to the bruise on my face.

"Yeah, I'm fine. I fell down is all." She shrugged, then turned and walked toward the kitchen. I followed. The bottom of her butt cheeks crested her shorts with each step.

"Do you miss Charlene?"

"Miss her?" I questioned her butt cheeks. She twirled around, her hair flaring out in a perfect, highlighted arch.

"I thought you two were good friends." She seemed surprised that I didn't know that.

"I'm sorry but that's just not true. I only met her right before I took over the route."

She pouted her pink, gloss-covered lips. "But the E-mail that Charlene sent me said that a good friend of hers was taking over the route. I'll have to talk to her about this."

"Good luck. She's kinda missing."

"Oh. I know." Her eyes lit up. "You know, I knew Tate and Joseph. It's very sad." She frowned.

"What does Charlene have to do with Tate Hausman?"

"Oh, just from around. You know how it is."

"Not really, how is it?" She opened up the fridge and stuck her head in.

"From the neighborhood. You know." Her voice came from behind the giant stainless-steel door of her Sub-Zero. "Did you hear his maid found him?" She brought her head out and popped a baby carrot into her mouth. "We have the same maid." She crunched the carrot between her straight white teeth.

"Oh, yeah?"

"Yes, but she won't talk to me about it." She pouted again. I could see the lines around her mouth where the wrinkles would form.

"How did you know Tate and Joseph?" I asked.

She laughed and hopped up onto the kitchen counter, letting her long, bare legs swing back and forth. "Tate I've known for years; Joseph, too. They were friends, you know."

"Really?"

"Sure, they went way back. Like, forever back."

"So they were close?"

Pammy hopped off the counter and moved back to the fridge. "I don't know. I think they saw each other every once in a while. And, of course, Joseph was Tate's CPA." Pammy stopped to think. She turned toward me. "Now that I think about it, I'd seen them out together more in the last couple of months. Really since Joseph lost his job." She shrugged and got herself another carrot and one for Toby, too. "You know who else Tate was friends with?" I shook my head. Pammy smiled and raised her eyebrows, "The mayor."

"Oh, yeah. I think I heard about that on the news."

Pammy lowered her eyebrows. "They met in law school."

"Yeah, it mentioned that."

"They used to scuba together," she tried.

"Are you friends with the mayor?" I asked

"No, but my husband Bobby knows him." I gave her the look of surprise she'd been searching for, and she smiled. "I've met him a couple times."

"Wow."

"Yeah, he's nice." Pammy pulled her hair back into a ponytail and then let it go. Her hair fell back around her shoulders. "You're pretty," she said.

"Thanks," I said.

Pammy stepped closer to me and pushed a strand of hair out of my face.

"Very pretty," she said. I took a step back and lowered my eyes. "How was it finding the body?" She leaned against the fridge, her pale blue eyes examining me. I decided she probably wasn't as dumb as she looked.

"Bad."

"I just can't believe my little Toby was involved in that." She reached down and smushed his face against her, then gave him a carrot. Toby crunched it loudly. "Do you think the police will give us back our leash?"

"I don't know." I said.

She smiled. "Do you like to go out?" she asked.

"What do you mean?"

"Party, you know."

I shrugged. "Well, I guess I better take Toby for his walk."

Pammy pulled out a piece of paper and a pen from a drawer and wrote a number on it. "This is my cell--if you want to talk about finding the body or anything. You know, go out and take your mind off things. I'm here for you."

"Wow. That's really nice," I lied. She smiled.

When I got home, I left a message asking Julen to call me, ordered a General Tso's from my local Chinese place, and settled myself in front of the TV with Blue by my side. But I couldn't sit still. I wanted to talk to the maid who had found Tate Hausman's body. I wanted to know why Mulberry was telling me to back off if it was a suicide.

The phone rang me out of my head. It was Declan. "Hi," I said a little too enthusiastically.

"Hi. How are you?"

"Eh, same old, same old. What about you?" I muted the TV and lay back on my couch.

"I'm doing all right." He had a sexy phone voice. I like a sexy phone voice.

"I met Mrs. Maxim today," I told him.

"Oh, yeah."

"You ever met her?"

"I almost arrested her once."

"What?" I sat straight up.

"Drunk and disorderly."

I laughed. "When?"

"Before she was Mrs. Maxim, when she was still Pamela," he paused.

"What?"

"Mistress Pamela."

"Excuse me?"

"She was a dominatrix."

"You're kidding!" I had an image of Pammy with her long hair pulled back into a bun, bright red fingernails, narrowed eyes, and a whip.

"Dead serious."

"What does this Mr. Maxim do that he is having run-ins with dominatrices?"

"He owns Fortress Global Investigations."

I laughed. "You know that sounds like an evil organization with an underground fortress where the guy pets white cats."

Doyle laughed. "It's not nearly that interesting. They do due diligence and provide security for corporations. Robert is an old family friend. He is not evil, nor does he have a cat."

"Ok, well the cat-petting evil mastermind sounds more likely to have a dominatrix wife than this upstanding businessman you're describing. How did they meet?"

"At the Biltmore Club."

"You're telling me the Biltmore Club is an S&M thing?"

Declan laughed. "Do you want to find out?"

"How?"

"Come with me Saturday night."

"You're a member?"

"Born into it baby. The whole Doyle clan has been members since prohibition. If they wanted liquor, they had to let us in." He laughed again.

"And it's an S&M club? I thought it was like a stodgy, old person thing."

"There is only one way to find out."

"Wait, are you inviting me to tie you up?"

"Or maybe I'll tie you up," he said quietly.

My heart almost stopped beating. "What?" I whispered.

"Are you in?"

I smiled. "So you won't tell me what I'm in for."

He laughed. "Where would the fun be in that?"

"Ok, fine. I'm in."

"Meet me at my place at seven."

"What should I wear?"

"I'll take care of that."

"Really?"

"It would be my pleasure."

CHAPTER NINETEEN

POISON

JACQUELYN SAPERSTEIN WAS RELEASED on bail in a flourish of camera flashes. Her lawyer made a statement on the courthouse steps proclaiming her innocence and bashing the police for not releasing her sooner. A picture of Jacquelyn with a coat over her face climbing into a limo filled the front page of the *Post*.

When I arrived at Mrs. Saperstein's door that day, I heard muffled yelling. I knocked, but the yelling continued. I knocked louder. The yelling started moving in my direction. "...don't. Just shut up. I...I just don't know what I'll do."

"Oh, that's rich. Rich I say."

The door flew open, and I was face to face with Jacquelyn Saperstein. She was flushed and breathing heavily. The lines on her face had deepened, and dark, menacing circles hung under her eyes. Mildred Point stood in the living room, arms tightly crossed against her chest. When she saw me, she made a horse-like sound meant to show disgust and walked purposefully out of the room.

"Hi," I said with a smile.

"Oh, hello." Jacquelyn motioned for me to come in. "Thank you for taking such good care of Snaffles for me," she mumbled.

"Actually, I wanted to talk to you about Snaffles."

"Yes?" She looked a little confused.

"He seems a lot older. Like he's sick or something."

"Didn't anyone tell you?"

"No."

"He ate rat poison in the park." I recalled signs on the fences surrounding the shrubbery in the park warning that rat poison had been set out in the area.

"Is he going to be OK?"

"The vet said he would never completely recover but that he wouldn't die, either."

"Good. I'm glad I know."

"What? Did you think I had done something to him?" She laughed a high-pitched laugh.

"No, of course not!"

"Well, I would kill my own husband. Why not his dog? Right?" She laughed again, and I took a step back from her. She saw my reaction and stifled her cackles. Jacquelyn lowered her head. "I'm sorry. I've had a hard week," she told her bare, unpedicured toes.

"This must be very difficult for you."

"Difficult doesn't start to describe it."

"Can I ask you a question?"

"OK." I wanted to ask her about her husband's toupee but it suddenly seemed so inappropriate.

"Do you know that I am the one who found your husband's body?" She became very pale quite suddenly. I walked her to the couch, and we sat down.

"Of course, they told me it was a dog-walker. But I didn't think it was *my* dog-walker."

"I thought they told you. Mulberry made me think that you knew who I was and that--" I paused trying to figure out how to tell her that the detective insinuated that she might come after me next.

"What?" She looked up at me.

"That you might try and kill me."

"That man," she said, her voice filled with rage.

"Did you know Joseph's toupee was found with his body?"

"I only knew it wasn't here. What does that have to do with anything?"

"Did you see him leave that morning?"

"No, I wasn't here."

"When did you get back from Julen's?"

"You know I was at Julen's house?"

"He told me. Have you talked to him?"

"I've been avoiding his phone calls." She started to finger the fringe on a couch pillow.

"He was fired because of your affair, you know?"

"I know."

"He is your alibi."

"A lot of good it's doing me. I swear they're after me. It's a conspiracy." She punched the pillow softly.

"I don't know about conspiracies, but the last witness to see your husband alive says he was not wearing his toupee. But when I discovered his body, it was there." It took a couple of seconds for this to register with her.

"What does that mean?"

"I don't know, but somehow his toupee got from here to there. He only had the one wig?"

She nodded. "He got it last year. It was the beginning of the end." Her eyes got a little misty.

"What do you mean the beginning of the end?"

She sighed. "He started losing his hair three years ago, but it didn't bother him until last year. He wanted everyone to find him attractive. Especially younger women. At first I thought it was just a phase. Maybe he would buy a fancy car and then that would be it." She laughed at her own ignorance. "But then he lost his job. That hit him really hard. And it wasn't like he got fired. The company went under. He would have found something else." She pulled at the pillow, running the fringe through her fingers.

"I think it took him a month of unemployment to start having an affair," she went on. "He was so weak. I thought he was strong, you know? I thought the man I married was strong. But he wasn't. He was weak. Weak like every other man. Why is that?" She looked up at me but didn't wait for an answer. "What is it with men being so weak? They're supposed to be the strong ones, but it's the women, isn't it? It's the women that hold this godforsaken world together."

I opened my mouth, but before I had a chance to speak, Mildred stomped into the room. "I would like to speak to my sister alone," she told me through gritted teeth.

"I'll just take Snaffles for his walk," I said. As I was closing the door behind me, I heard the yelling start again.

As Toby demolished his lunch, the Maxims' phone rang. I listened to the message being left on the machine. Manhattan Maids would be arriving at three that afternoon instead of two due to unavoidable delays. Two hours later, I was waiting with Toby for Manhattan Maids to arrive. A tall, slim black woman in her early twenties wearing a blue uniform and white apron opened the door at exactly three.

"Hello," I said.

She jumped and let out a little yelp. "You scared me," she said with a smile.

"Sorry. I didn't mean to. I'm Joy, the dog-walker." I held out my hand. She shook it and smiled.

"Karen, the maid."

"We don't usually run into each other," I said.

"Yeah, I'm running late today."

"Oh yeah?" She walked back into the hall and brought in a carryall filled with cleaning products.

"Yeah, I had a meeting I couldn't refuse."

"Detective Mulberry." She put down the cleaning products and looked at me with her head cocked. "I've been there," I explained. "I found Joseph Saperstein's body."

"Right. Yeah. I think Mrs. Maxim, I mean Pammy--" She rolled her eyes, I smiled to let her know I thought Pammy as ridiculous as she did. " --mentioned that. I guess she told you I found Tate Hausman."

"Yeah. I'm sorry. I know it's hard."

"Yeah." She looked down at nothing for a moment. Then her eyes hardened against whatever images filled her mind. "He was an asshole."

"I met him once." I told her. "He acted like an ass."

"Come on to you in some foul way?"

"He told me he had a dog I could walk."

"Aw. That's disgusting," she said.

"You're telling me."

"He always told me about how much he liked chocolate."

"Gross. I can't believe women fall for that shit."

"Some girls are clueless." Karen pulled out a cloth and spray bottle and began to clean the glass coffee table. "That guy was a real sicko. You know how I found him?" My heart started pounding, and I shook my head. "He wasn't just hanging, you know. He was beat up. There was blood everywhere." She shivered at the memory.

"How does that make him sick?"

"That's not everything." She leaned toward me. "He was wearing a thing, like a bar that kept his ankles apart, like from pulp fiction or something--and he had a ball gag in his mouth." She nodded at the shock on my face.

"Do you think he hanged himself?"

"I don't know." She started cleaning the table again, working on the brass legs. I waited for her to continue. "He was badly beaten. I mean, his face was really swollen. I don't think he did it to himself or asked to have it done."

"Do you think he was beat up in his place or somewhere else?"

"His place. The house was trashed. It looked like there'd been a fight. But you never know."

"Do you think he was into rough stuff?"

"I don't know, but the way I found him--" she stared off into nothing. "I don't know." She started to clean the table again.

"Did you see a note?" She put down the cloth and spray bottle and pulled out a duster from her box of tools. She shook her head, then began to dust the lamps beside the couches. "So then, there's no way it's suicide."

"I'm sure he wouldn't be the first person to not leave a note."

"That's true."

"Besides, it could have been a mistake," she said.

"How do you mean?"

"If he was playing some sex game and hanged himself by accident."

"I think I've heard about that. What's it called?"

"I don't know."

"Do you think he was into that kind of stuff?"

"He always struck me as the kinda guy who would want to be in control. But, then again you can't ever tell, like Ralphie on Sopranos."

"What about him?"

"You know, he was all tough, but he liked to be--"She made a motion with her duster to signify penetration. "--in the butt while Tony's sister told him she was gonna pimp him out."

"Right." I nodded, and Karen went back to dusting. "So, what do you think happened?"

"I don't know. But I do know that I don't want to think about it anymore," she said with her back to me.

"I understand."

"Finding a body isn't like on TV," she said.

"No, it's not," I agreed.

While rummaging through my newly cleaned clothes trying to find something to wear to James's housewarming party, I heard, "In an exclusive report, we have learned that Detective Mulberry has been removed from the Upper East Side Black Widow investigation due to inappropriate behavior." I tripped over a pair of sneakers racing into the living room and fell, landing on my funny bone.

Through the blinding, not in the least bit funny pain, I heard, "According to sources, Detective Mulberry is under investigation for the suspected mistreatment of a witness who apparently found the mutilated body of Joseph Saperstein." A picture of Mulberry grabbing my arm on the street flashed up on the screen.

"Holy shit." My phone rang.

"Is that how you got that bruise on your cheek? Is this detective really hurting you?" James blurted out before I even had the chance to say hello.

"No! I don't know what the hell is going on."

"The police are not releasing the young woman's information," the reporter continued.

"Well, that's a relief," I said to James.

"Yeah, except your picture's on the news," he pointed out.

"We have learned that she is a dog-walker employed by the Sapersteins. We will bring you more information as soon as it is available. Betty."

"Shit," I said.

"You're taking that Taser. I'm calling Hugh right now and telling him to bring it tonight." Before I could protest, my doorbell rang. Blue barked wildly and barreled to the door. He threw himself against it, barking and growling uncontrollably. "What the hell is going on?"

"I don't know," I yelled over Blue. "Hold on a minute. Blue shut up." I grabbed him by the collar and pulled him off the door. He continued to bark and bark and bark. "Shut up!" I screamed at him. But he just kept barking at the door, his hackles raised, his nostrils flared. I was a bit nervous myself as I peeked through the peephole. In the rounded, distorted view of my hall I saw Detective Mulberry staring back at me.

"Come on, open up," he yelled over Blue.

"It's Mulberry," I whispered to James.

"What? I can't hear you. Speak up."

"It's Mulberry," I said, cupping my hand over the phone to block Blue out.

"What? Did you say it's Mulberry?"

"Come on, I can hear you," the detective yelled.

"Should I open it?" I asked James.

"Are you crazy? He's probably crazed with rage. It's your fault he got kicked off the case," James said.

"No, it's not and you know it."

"But does he know it?"

I heard Nona's door open. "Can I help you?" she asked Mulberry, raising her voice above Blue's barking. I grabbed Blue's collar and shook him, trying to make him shut up, but he kept on barking.

"I'm here to see Ms. Humbolt. Detective Mulberry."

"She doesn't appear to be opening her door, which means either she's not home--"

"She's home, ma'am. I can see the shadow of her feet under the door."

"--or she doesn't want to talk to you. You're not arresting her, are you?"

"No, but I am investigating a murder."

"I just heard you were off the case." I could see Mulberry's face flush red through the peephole.

"That's part of what I need to talk to her about."

"Apparently, you're off the case for abusing her, so I think you should leave before I am forced to call the police, the ones who are still on the case," Nona said. Mulberry opened his mouth to protest but nothing came out. Then he turned to my door.

"I just need to talk to you for a minute," he yelled at the peephole. "I'm going to slip my number under your door. Please call me."

"What's happening?" James asked as Mulberry bent over and shoved a business card under the door. Blue stopped his barking and attacked the card. I had to drop the phone to wrestle it away from him. "Joy. Joy. What's happening?" I heard James's voice from the phone. Blue let go of the card--well, three quarters of the card. I picked up the phone and looked out my peephole. Nona was standing in front of my door.

"James, he's gone. I'll call you back."

"Wait, what happened?"

"I'll call you right back." I hung up and opened the door. Nona's breath caught in her throat when she saw the bruise on my face.

"Did he do this to you?" she asked.

"No. I fainted," I said as we moved into the living room. She sat down on the couch, and I sat next to her.

"I saw on the news."

"I know."

"He was grabbing your arm."

"Oh, I know. But he didn't hit me. He was trying to warn me that I should stop doing what I was doing."

"What were you doing?"

"Still am doing," I corrected her. "I'm investigating Joseph Saperstein's death."

"But why?"

"I wish people would stop asking me that question."

"I think it's a pretty obvious one."

"Well, I don't know, but I'll tell you something isn't right." I leaned toward her. "A lot of things don't make sense. His toupee was not on him when he left his house and then it was when I found the body. Charlene has been missing ever since I took this job, and she left her place in a hurry, if not by force. Chamers saw a woman wearing a wig or with bleached-blond hair, leaving the scene of the crime. And now Tate Hausman, Joseph's old friend, is dead and I don't think it was suicide I think--"

"Slow down," Nona interrupted me. "I still don't understand how you got the bruise on your face." I reached my hand up to the fading yellow on my cheekbone.

"I fell down on some marble."

"How?"

"I fainted."

"Why?"

"I became overwhelmed. It's never happened to me before, and I don't think it will happen to me again."

"What overwhelmed you?"

"It was in the lobby of the building that I went to after I found the body. I didn't recognize it at first and then when I did, I fell down."

"It sounds like you should see someone."

"For fainting? Come on."

"Not for just fainting. You have had a very stressful experience, and a psychologist could give you some tools for dealing with it," Nona said.

"I'm fine."

"Fine? You think collapsing onto marble makes you fine?"

"I feel fine. That kind of stuff happens all the time."

Nona laughed. "I fainted once."

"Really? When?"

"When Mr. Nevins died. You know how he died?"

"No."

"We were on our honeymoon in Paris. We went to the amusement park next to the Louvre after dinner on our third night. We were both a bit drunk, I suppose, him more than me as was usual, and we went into the haunted house. It was very scary, not because they had convincing monsters or anything like that. It was scary because you might die." She laughed again, although I was having trouble seeing the humor in her story.

"It was so dark in there. You really couldn't see a thing, and the floor was covered in spinning disks that you could easily break an ankle on, and there were creepy things hanging from the ceiling. We linked arms and laughed and fell down in the dark. It was so much fun. We even did a little kissing." She laughed gently, her eyes unfocused.

"But then we walked out onto the balcony area where the ground shifted beneath you, and we had to grab at the railing to keep from falling on our faces. Well, poor Mr. Nevins, the railing broke at his touch, and he fell face-first onto the ground below. When I saw the pool of blood that was forming around his head, I fainted."

"That's horrible, Nona."

"Yes, it was dear, but I got over it with the help of a psychologist."

"Oh."

"Just think about it. It could help you."

I promised to think about it. After Nona left, I called James back.

"Why do you think he showed up at your door? Do you think he's mad? You need to start carrying that Taser of Hugh's," James said.

"I don't think they're legal in New York."

"Oh, and I suppose it's legal for detectives accused of beating you up to show up at your door."

"That might be legal."

"Are you going to call him?" James asked.

"I want to hear what he has to say. I mean, it seems to me that something is wrong here. We know he didn't hit me, so why is he off the case?" I said.

"Maybe you should ask Declan," James suggested.

"I don't know if I want to talk to him about this stuff. He would probably tell me to leave it alone. Everyone else has."

"Well, I changed my mind about you leaving it alone. I support whatever you want to do. Just don't get hurt, OK?"

"I'll do my best."

"That's not funny."

"It wasn't meant to be."

"Just be smart. Don't go running off half-cocked."

"Will do, captain."

"Oh, shut up. I've got to go get ready for the party. I'll see you at 9:30."

After we hung up, I fidgeted with what was left of Mulberry's card. Without too much thought, I dialed the number.

"Mulberry." His voice came across the line gruff and assertive. He was definitely Mulberry, and he knew it.

"This is Joy Humbolt."

"I'm glad you called." His voice softened. "Could we meet? I don't want to talk over the phone."

"When?"

"As soon as possible."

"How about tomorrow morning?"

"You can't do it tonight?"

"No. I have plans."

He sighed. "OK. How about eight?"

"How about ten?"

"Fine. Where? "

"There's a diner called Snow White on Chambers. That's kind of in between our two houses." And a public place, I thought to myself.

"I'll meet you there at ten."

"OK."

CHAPTER TWENTY

MULBERRY'S NEW LINE

I WOKE up Saturday morning with a nasty hangover. My alarm just would not shut up, and Blue was whining because he had to pee. I pulled on a pair of shorts and a T-shirt, took Blue out, and squinted at the morning light.

Leaving Blue in my apartment, I walked to the subway. In the summer, packed trains are even worse than in the winter because of all the exposed skin. You have to be careful what you push up against. I had positioned myself against a door, which is a really good spot as long as it's on the side of the train that doesn't open, which this door was until we got into Manhattan. At Brooklyn Bridge a million people pushed me into the middle of the car, and exposed body parts surrounded me as I held onto the greasy center pole.

The train rumbled along, and I tried to see the stops, but the crush of people blocked my view. I thought we had just passed 42nd street when I felt the tip of something hard press into my back. "Don't fucking move," a hot voice said into my ear. "You're a really stupid little girl," the voice continued, "and if you're not more careful, you're going to die." The train lurched to a stop, and the crowd shifted to allow people to exit and enter. An overweight woman wearing a giant floral-print dress pushed me back against the man in my ear. He put his arm around my waist and held me tightly.

"If you don't let go of me I will scream," I told him.

"I wouldn't if I were you."

I screamed a high-pitched, echoing, can't-ignore-it scream. The shifting crowd stopped to look at us. The man immediately let go of me and barreled a path through the crowd, out of the car, and into the 59th Street Station. I never saw his face.

"What did that guy look like?" I yelled at the car full of people. The ding-dong announcing the closing of the doors sounded, and people hurried to be on the right side of them. "What the fuck did that guy look like?" No one looked at me. "Someone must have seen his face. He threatened my life. Hello!" A circle of space opened up around me as the mass of commuters pretended I didn't exist.

I waited for Mulberry in a red vinyl booth at the diner, shaking. I stirred my coffee aggressively just to give my hands something to do. Mulberry showed up ten minutes late. "Where have you been?" I asked.

"Sorry I'm late."

"Yeah, well, someone just threatened my life on the subway in front of half the fucking city. But, of course, no one saw shit." I gestured wildly and knocked over my coffee cup. Mulberry leaped up, avoiding the hot liquid racing across the table toward his lap. "Sorry, shit, I'm sorry." I tried to soak up the spill with our napkins but they just turned limp and brown. The waitress came over with a wet towel and wiped the table down. "I'm sorry," I told her.

"It happens all the time," she said without looking at me. Mulberry sat back down, and the waitress brought me another cup of coffee.

"Sorry," I said again.

"It's all right," Mulberry said. "Tell me what happened."

"I was on the subway because I was hurrying to meet you, who was late." My anger about his tardiness seemed childish after tossing a cup of coffee at him, but I wasn't about to give it up. I told him the rest of the story without any more dramatics. Mulberry's eyes widened when I told him about the screaming, but he let me continue. "He ran out of the car.

I never saw his face, and everyone on the train pretended like I didn't exist when I asked them."

Mulberry snorted. "No one saw nothing. That's how it always is."

"That's all you have to say? I tell you someone threatened my life, and you're disgusted by the subway riders."

"Hey. You got yourself into this."

"So it's my fault?"

"I'm just saying I warned you."

"Thanks. Thanks a lot." I slumped down in the seat and fell silent. Mulberry sipped his coffee and looked across the table at me. "So, what's up?" I asked. "Why are we even here?"

"You know what's happened?"

"They kicked you off the case for beating me up," I said. He grunted. "I suppose you want me to go to the media, and tell them that it never happened. That you are an exemplary officer, and the whole thing is a big misunderstanding."

"I think that would be a very bad idea."

"What?"

"I warned you that this was something you should not become involved in, but now you are, and I need your help."

"What?" This was not at all how I had pictured this meeting. I was thinking there would be some level of groveling on his part while I toyed with him until finally calling the *Post* and telling them the whole thing was shit. But Mulberry asking for my help with the case?

"You have no idea how deep this thing runs. I need your help. I need to know who killed Joseph Saperstein and Tate Hausman."

"But according to the news, their deaths were unrelated and Hausman's was a suicide," I said, hearing how dumb the words sounded.

"Not unless he beat the shit out of himself first."

"His maid said something about Ralphie and the Sopranos and how you never know." Mulberry looked at me, mystified.

"I highly doubt it. I would think your experience on the subway this morning would convince you."

"What do you want from me?"

"I want to know what you know." He took a sip from his cup.

"I doubt I know anything you don't know."

"I want to make sure."

"OK."

"You can start with Joseph Saperstein," Mulberry said.

"What about him?"

"What bothers you most?"

"Bothers me?"

"What's the wrongest thing about it?" He said.

I thought about that alley, colder and darker and more shadowed by my memory. The empty face at my feet, the details of the wound--crisper, brighter than they could possibly be. "Someone put his toupee with him," I started. Most likely a blond woman or one wearing a blond wig. I think it was put there after he was killed, because otherwise it would have been burned by the gunshot, right? I mean it's made of plastic, isn't it? Or at least part plastic. So it would have been singed at least. But I have no idea why someone would want to put his toupee on him after he was dead."

Mulberry watched me with his green eyes and nodded. "What else?"

I told Mulberry about the hangman's rope that Elaine saw next to Tate Hausman's name in Charlene's address book. He didn't seem shocked. "Do you have her notebook?" I asked him.

"No address book was found with her personal belongings. I just don't find it that surprising that they knew each other."

"Is there something you're not telling me?" I asked.

Mulberry sighed and ran a hand through his hair. "Charlene wasn't just a dog-walker." He didn't look at me.

"What do you mean?"

"I'm not sure I should be telling you this," he said.

"Just spit it out."

"You're not taking this seriously enough." He leaned forward, his elbows on the table.

"Listen, either I'm in this, or I'm not. There's no sort-of being in it, right? So which side of the in-it line would you say I'm on?" He looked confused. "I mean, I'm already in this deep, right? So how could going deeper hurt me?"

"You can still get out, you know. If you leave it alone, you'll be safe." I stared out the window at the street beyond. "I don't even know why you're doing this in the first place," he said.

"Why are *you* doing it?" I asked him.

"It's what I get paid for."

"But you're on suspension."

Mulberry laughed. "I might as well tell you." He shifted in his seat and pulled out his wallet. The brown leather was worn away at the edges. Mulberry pulled out a folded photograph. He opened it and stared down into the world it contained, then slid it picture-side-down across the table to me. I turned it over and found a family portrait. Mulberry, young and scrawny, his ears sticking far out from the side of his head, stood next to his father or uncle or somebody who looked a hell of a lot like him. This older, paunchier version of Mulberry had his arm around a beautiful red-headed woman. She held, barely visible in its cocoon of blankets, a sleeping baby. I recognized the couple from Charlene Miller's family album. They were her parents.

"Charlene's your sister?" I asked, looking across the table at Mulberry.

"Half-sister." Mulberry coughed, clearing his throat. "Same father, different mother."

"What happened to your mother?"

His jaw clenched. "She died."

"And your father?"

"Him, too. When Charlene was four. He was killed in the line of duty." Mulberry sipped his coffee and looked out the window. I followed his gaze and watched a bus wheeze to a stop on the adjacent corner.

"I'm sorry," I said, watching men and women hurry off the bus and others clamber on. Mulberry turned back to his coffee.

"I didn't stay in such good touch with my stepmother and Charlene. I hadn't even seen her since she moved here."

"Why?"

He looked back out the window, his face in a grimace. "I guess I just didn't call and neither did she and--" he strayed off. "We were mad at each other. Charlene and her mom thought my father was selfish. Charlene's mom was not cut out to be a policeman's wife. She wasn't strong enough. She just didn't get it, why he did it." He looked back at me. "My mother understood how important his work was, but Charlene's mom, she thought he should leave the force. She thought if he really loved her and Charlene, he would have gone into the private sector." Mulberry sighed. "And I thought my father was a hero. He risked his life to protect his community. I wanted to be just like him."

Mulberry sipped his almost empty cup of coffee, then examined the dregs. "I don't know anything about her. I didn't even know where she lived until I started this investigation. I hadn't seen her since she graduated from high school." He leaned back against the cushioned booth and rubbed his eyes, pushing them back into his skull. "I just don't want to see her get hurt." He reached out and took the photograph off the table, then pushed it back into his wallet. "Listen, you don't have to do this. In fact, you probably shouldn't." Our waitress came over and refilled our coffees.

"I'm not going to let that asshole on the subway think he scared me," I said. The waitress pretended like she was alone.

"He did scare you," Mulberry pointed out after the waitress walked away.

"That's besides the point. He doesn't know that he scared me. I'm not the one who ran off that subway car. He was. He's the one running. Not me."

Mulberry smiled. "You got balls, kid."

That felt nice to hear. "Thanks."

"You ever thought about going into law enforcement? I think you could be a real success."

"I'm not really the cop type."

"What type would that be?"

"I didn't mean to imply anything. But I'm not that into laws and their enforcement."

Mulberry smiled. "Then why are you doing this?"

"Not because of the law. That much I know."

"You're doing it for some kind of law, maybe not man's or God's, but you've got to have a pretty strong conviction to be sitting here with me." I didn't answer him. He smiled again.

"You said you thought your dad was a hero. Do you still?" I asked, changing the subject.

He sighed. "Sure. He was a good man. To be honest, I don't know what a hero is anymore," he smiled. "I used to think being a cop was the most noble thing you could be, but with almost 20 years behind me I don't feel noble."

"What do you feel?"

Mulberry laughed. "You're not gonna get me talkin' about my feelings."

I laughed. "Well, if you don't like being a cop, why try to convince me to be one?"

"Eh," he waved a hand through the air. "Just because you'd be good at it. The truth is you are a detective."

"What?" I laughed.

"You can't let a wrong go without trying to right it." I looked at him in silence, and he looked back at me. "You're like a Sam Spade or a Philip Marlowe. You get knocked down for your effort, but you keep doing it. You, kid, are a regular fictional character." I sat stunned. Mulberry waved over the waitress, who refilled our nearly full cups. When she went away Mulberry said, "You really want to know everything?"

"Yes."

"Charlene was a --" His cheeks pinked "--dominatrix."

"What?"

"She worked as a dominatrix. And when I started to pursue that lead, it got me thrown off the case."

"Wow." I felt a chill run down my spine.

"Looks like Tate Hausman died while participating in erotic asphyxiation or 'breath play.' At least that's what it was supposed to look like," Mulberry continued.

"So you're saying someone in this 'S&M' scene killed Tate and Joseph?" Mulberry shrugged. "Wouldn't it just be really stupid if you were his partner in this 'erotic asphyxiation' and then he dies like that? The finger would point directly at you," I said.

"Unless it was a warning."

"To who?"

"Other members of the community."

"I don't understand."

"Me, neither."

"So what do you want to do?"

"This is where you come in. I think that you could go to these parties without being suspicious."

I laughed. "Funny you should say that."

"You wouldn't have to participate. I could probably arrange to send you in undercover as a monitor or coat-check girl or something--"

"Mulberry--"

"Wait, just hear me out. I'd just need you to identify some people." He leaned forward, so earnest I almost laughed.

"I've already been invited."

"What?" He sat back into the booth.

"I've been seeing Declan Doyle." Mulberry's face flushed. "And he invited me to the Biltmore Club for some kind of party. He implied S&M was involved, but I kind of thought it was a joke."

Mulberry straightened himself. "Declan Doyle, huh?"

"I know you guys have a history."

"Yeah." Mulberry looked away from me.

"He said--"

"He lies." Mulberry turned back to me, his eyes cold.

"He said something much worse about you."

"Look," Mulberry slid a folder across the table to me. "In here are pictures of the men who I think are trying to stop this investigation. Please let me know if you see them there." He stood to leave but hovered above me. "Did you get a weapon?" he asked.

"Actually, I did. A stun gun."

He looked surprised. "Those are illegal in this state."

"So is what you're proposing."

"No, it's not."

"I'm pretty sure it is."

"Listen, just be careful, OK? Stun guns are not toys."

"Thanks, Dad."

He didn't like that. "Let me see it." I sighed loudly and pulled it out of my purse. It was black and looked like an evil flashlight. A big, thick shaft with one button on it led to a wide head with two metal prongs facing each other. I hadn't pushed the button yet, but I imagined a string of electricity would light up between them. Hugh had handed it to me, whispering something about safety first, as I climbed into a cab last night. "Where did you get this?" Mulberry asked.

"I have my sources." Hugh's paranoid mother in the South.

"Just read the directions. And try not to stun yourself." He handed me back the gun. I watched him go up to the counter and pay for our coffees. The crowd watched him. He was different. Mulberry did not carry an iPod or push a baby stroller. People could tell he was a cop, and that made them uncomfortable. His presence was an unwelcome reminder that men like him existed--that his outdated suit and strong back were all that was between them and people who wanted to take away what they had.

CHAPTER TWENTY-ONE

DATING DECLAN DOYLE

DECLAN WAS WEARING A TUXEDO.

The bruise on my cheek was almost gone, and I'd covered it with concealer but he noticed as soon as he opened the door. "My god," he said, reaching his hand out and placing it lightly on my cheek. "Did Mulberry do this to you?"

"No, no. I fell," I answered, turning my face away from his touch.

"Are you OK?"

"I'm great." I smiled at him. "I'm excited to see what I'll be wearing this evening."

"I'd like to talk--" he said as I walked into the apartment.

"Let's not do that, OK?" I said turning to him and laying a hand against his silk lapel.

"What?" he said, raising his eyebrows.

"The whole getting involved in each other's lives thing," I said with a smile. "I'd just like to have some fun. Does that work for you?"

He cocked his head. "If that's what you want." Doyle smiled but there was a tightness around his eyes.

"At least for now," I said stepping further into the apartment

Doyle closed the door. Last time I'd visited his place I was drunk, and he was all over me, so I'd missed the details. It was very nice, masculine.

I entered into a large living room with two brown leather couches and a tv. Everything was beige, distressed, or patinated. Doyle took my hand and led me into the bedroom. I recognized the king-sized bed. He passed it and I watched his reflection in the wall of mirrors that lined the far side of the room. His movements were elegant and filled with confidence. His power frightened me and reassured me at the same time. Pushing one of the mirrors aside, Doyle opened up his closet. He pulled out a full length black, strapless gown.

"My God," I said when he held it out for me to see.

"You'll look gorgeous," he promised, bringing it over and laying it on the cream-colored bedspread.

"You really had me believing we were going to an S&M party," I laughed reaching out to touch the fine fabric. I'd never worn anything so beautiful in my life.

He smiled at me. "I don't disappoint." Declan returned to the closet and pulled out a large gift box wrapped with a silver bow. He handed it to me. I untied the knot, anticipation turning to an almost nauseous excitement. Pushing aside black tissue paper, I found a corset, thigh high stockings, a garter belt, and a pair of fur-lined handcuffs. They were all black to match the dress.

Declan stood behind me as I stared down into the box. He brushed my hair aside, and the scent of shampoo wafted between us. He kissed my neck. "I'll help you get it on," he whispered into my ear. I turned to face him, and he wrapped me into his arms and kissed me so that I could barely breathe. His hands moved down my back unzipping the dress I wore. Wrapping one of his big hands into my hair he used the other to unsnap my bra. Doyle moved his lips down to my neck and pulled the dress with him. I slipped out of my bra. How many times had he done this? Did I really care?

I studied his profile as he leaned away from me, reaching into the box. Declan's jaw was strong and his lips soft. The man's crooked nose saved him from being too good looking. His hair fell around his eyes as he looked down at me. Who was this guy? What was I doing here?

"Scared?" he asked.

I shot my chin into the air. "Nothing scares me," I said.

Then Declan dressed me, slowly, carefully, beautifully. Like a man who knew what he was doing.

"Go ahead and take a look at yourself," he said once he was done.

I crossed to the wall of mirrors watching the way the dress's full skirt moved around me. My breasts were pushed up and my waist never looked so tiny. The corset was tight but I could still breath deeply. Doyle stood next to me in his tuxedo, and I couldn't believe *that* was me. He put a hand around my slim waist and I took a deep breath. "I don't look like myself," I said. But I felt very much alive. I don't know if it was the corset, or the feel of the garter against my thighs, the knowledge that those handcuffs were in Declan's pocket or what, but while I hardly recognized myself in the mirror, I knew that woman looking back at me. My gray eyes flashed silver and for a brief moment I saw something in my eyes I'd never seen before. Something darker than I'd ever admitted lurked there.

"Let me fix your hair," Declan said. He disappeared into his bathroom and came back out with a brush and bobby pins. Within minutes he'd put my hair up into some kind of loose, sexy knot. With the bruise, I almost looked like I'd just been in a fight. A sexy fight.

A heavyset African American woman wearing an ankle-length black dress and a white apron opened the door. "Master Doyle," she said. "Welcome back."

"Thank you Gertrude. This is Joy Humbolt. She is my guest this evening."

"Welcome to the Biltmore Club." Gertrude said as she stepped aside. We entered a large foyer. Gertrude's small heels clicked against the black and white tile floor, and she opened a second set of doors. With Doyle's hand in the small of my back, I stepped into the Biltmore Club. A chandelier hung from a domed ceiling bathing the men in tuxedoes and women in gowns as glam as my own who filled the elegant room.

"Can I take your wrap?" A young woman wearing the same outfit as

Gertrude asked, her hand held out and an expectant expression on her face.

"Yes, thank you," I said. Doyle slipped the silk wrap that matched the dress off my shoulders and passed it to her. As I scanned the room, I felt out of place.

Doyle leaned down and whispered into my ear. "You look ravishing." He placed his hand into the small of my back. Doyle's touch reminded me that this was an adventure not an audition. He steered me into the crowd toward the bar.

"Declan!" We turned as a tall man with salt-and-pepper hair and a clean-shaven face approached us with a grin. "How are you? It's been too long."

They shook hands heartily, both smiling. "Good to see you Brian." Doyle turned to me. "This is Joy Humbolt. Brian Cordelver. Brian is a good friend of mine. He is the head of due diligence at Fortress Global."

"It's nice to meet you," I said.

We shook hands and Brian turned back to Doyle. "How's the force treating you?"

"Fine, thanks. That's how I met this lovely lady."

I smiled.

"Robert's here," Brian said looking around. "I know he wants to talk to you. And I'm sure he'd love to meet your," he cleared his throat and let his eyes settle on me, "companion," he finished with a smile.

"I'm more a fuck buddy than a companion," I said.

He started and I smiled. Prick, I thought. Doyle laughed.

Brian cleared his throat and smiled, recovering from the shock of my words, and turned his attention back to Doyle. "Well, I'm sure Robert will find you."

"Trying to get me to come over to the other side," Declan said with a smile.

"Always man," Brian slapped Doyle on the back. "This guy," he said turning to me, "is destined for great things at Fortress Global."

I smiled.

"In a couple of years Brian," Doyle said.

"Nonsense. We want you now. With all you've already done for the firm. Come on, Declan, due diligence has never been so hot."

Doyle looked over at me and licked his lips. "I'm going to get this beauty a drink," he said.

He steered me away, and Brian turned back into the crowd of tuxedoes to find his next conversational victim. "I've heard hot things about due diligence," I joked.

Doyle laughed. "Yeah, I'm sure you have." He moved his hand off my back and squarely onto my ass as we moved through the room. I watched the faces we passed, vaguely looking for the men Mulberry had asked me to search for. I saw one and let my eyes linger on him, allowing Doyle to navigate me through the room. A waiter passed us with champagne flutes on a silver tray. Doyle saw the way I watched the elixir go by and called after the server. He grabbed me a flute, and we continued on to the bar where Doyle ordered a bourbon on the rocks. I love the taste of bourbon on a man's lips.

But how was I going to taste him? There was just no way all these people were about to strip down, pull their handcuffs out, and start fucking. There were old ladies with their hunched husbands. They were all dressed the same, but there was no way they were all down with the get down. Impossible.

As I scanned the crowd I saw another of Mulberry's men. The only way to find out why they were here was to wait. More people came up to Doyle, and we made small talk with them. I'd finished my first glass of champagne and was halfway through my second when I saw Pammy Maxim across the room. She was smiling and talking to a good-looking older man. Pammy laughed and rested her hand on the man's arm.

Her dress was full length like my own, but tighter. Or maybe she just filled it out better. She must have sensed my stare because she suddenly looked right at me. I blushed and turned away, but I knew she was going to head over.

Doyle, who'd been talking with a gentleman in a tux I would have struggled to pick out of a lineup from other middle-aged white guys, sensed my discomfort and looked down at me. I just smiled and bit my lip. He cocked his head and smiled back.

"Hey there," I heard Pammy say behind me.

Doyle looked over my head at her. "Pamela, always a pleasure to see you," he said.

I took a deep breath and turned to her. "Mrs. Maxim, you look lovely this evening."

She really did. Pamela was a couple of inches taller than me. Her bright silk blue dress was obviously expensive, as was the diamond choker that hugged her throat. "May I speak with you alone?" she asked me.

Doyle looked down at me. I shrugged. "No problem," I said.

She took my arm like we were good girlfriends on our way to the ladies room. "I'm so glad you came," she said. "I've been thinking about you ever since we met at my place." She guided me through the crowd, or did it part for us?

We arrived at the coat check, and Pammy walked behind the young woman there, who just smiled and nodded. Why was Pammy, former (perhaps still present) Mistress Pamela, taking me into the coat room? We stepped into the tight space, surrounded by the summer-weight outerwear of the wealthy. We could not help but stand close. She smelled like expensive perfume. "I just want you to give her a message for me," Pammy said, leaning even closer to me.

"What?"

"Please, just tell her that I miss her." Pammy bit her lip and looked down.

"You two were together?" I asked, guessing we were talking about Charlene.

"Did she say that?" Her eyes shot up to mine.

"Not to me. I really didn't know her that well."

Ignoring this, Pammy forged ahead. "I just--I just want her to know that I miss her. Oh God," she turned away from me and reached out, playing with the soft silk of a burgundy wrap hanging nearby. "I know she was in love with someone else. I'm not a fool." She laughed softly. "At least I never thought I was."

"Who was she in love with?"

"You didn't know either?" she asked.

UNLEASHED

I shook my head. "I don't even know if it was a man or a woman," I said.

Pammy smiled. "With Charlie you could never tell."

"Charlie?" I knew I'd heard that name before but couldn't remember where.

"Charlene's nickname," Pammy said, taking a step closer to me. There was barely an inch between us. "You really didn't know her, did you?"

"No." I could smell bourbon on her breath, and I leaned toward her. Apparently, I liked the smell of bourbon on a woman, too. That's when it hit me--Charlie was the name of the man that Joseph was rumored to be having the affair with.

"You're here to play?" Pammy asked.

"I guess," I said.

"Better decide soon," she said licking her lips before stepping away from me. Her dress swished across the polished floor as she left the coat room. I took a deep breath before following her.

I began to work my way back through the crowd to Declan when I heard my name. "Joy?" I turned around and was face to face with Elaine. Mousey, scared of squirrels, dog- walking Elaine.

"What are you doing here?" I asked, then immediately noticed the tray of champagne flutes. "Working," I said, answering my own question.

"Yeah, Charlene got me the gig."

"You guys were pretty close huh?"

"Still are," she said with a small smile.

"You've spoken with her?" A man came up, and Elaine offered him the tray. He took two flutes and then melted back into the crowd. "If you've spoken to Charlene, you should really tell me," I said keeping my voice low.

"What? You said you hardly knew her."

"Yeah, but she is in deep shit," I said.

An older woman who was reaching for one of Elaine's glasses of champagne turned to look at me. "Watch your language young lady," she said before turning her back on me with a harrumph.

Elaine blushed. "I can't talk now. I'm working."

"Wait, Elaine, have you talked to her?" I asked.

She started to walk away, but I reached out and grabbed her free arm.

"What are you doing?" Elaine said looking down at my hand.

"Have you spoken with her?"

Elaine glanced around. "Yes," she whispered.

"When?"

"She's fine. We've been e-mailing. I'm helping her."

"How?"

Elaine smiled. "Spreading rumors," she whispered and glanced around the room. "She wants me to make everyone believe she was with Tate Hausman."

"Why?"

She shrugged. "I don't know."

"So that thing about the hangman's rope was made up?" Elaine shrugged. "Does Tate Hausman even play?" I raised my eyebrows so she was sure to understand what kind of "play" I meant.

"I've never seen him. He's not really that fun, you know."

"Wasn't that fun, Elaine. He *is* dead."

"Right." She bit her lip and glanced around again.

"Elaine, do you realize that rumor makes Charlene look guilty of killing him?" She ground down on her lip and seemed to go pale. "When did you get this e-mail?" I asked.

"I thought it would keep people from knowing about her and Joseph--" She stared at me, her eyes wide with shock at her slip.

"Charlene and Joseph were together?" She didn't answer. I wanted to shake her. "Elaine!" I said through clenched teeth.

"I have to get back to work. It's almost time," she said and pulled away from me.

I watch her blend into the crowd. Jumping to conclusions, I decided Charlene and Joseph were in love, planning on running away together until someone killed him and either kidnapped Charlene or sent her running for her life. Whoever that person was, they could very well be in the room tonight. I headed over to the bar. "A Tequila Gimlet, straight up, splash of cranberry juice, please."

The bartender needed some coaching, but he got me my drink just as

Gertrude, the woman who'd met us at the door, approached me. "Miss Joy."

"Hi Gertrude." I sipped off the top of my martini glass.

"Will you please join Master Doyle in the library?"

"Sure. Where is it?"

Gertrude led me behind the bar and through a door into a hallway lit by antique wall sconces. The carpet was intricate and plush. I sipped a little more off the top of my drink ,trying not to spill it all over myself.

Gertrude opened another door and motioned for me to step through. The room was dark and I hesitated. Gertrude waved her hand at the darkness and encouraged me with a nod to enter. I stepped through. She closed the door behind me. I felt dizzy and off balance. It was pitch black. I reached my free hand out searching for the wall, and hopefully a light switch, but found only empty space.

I felt a presence, and suddenly there was an arm around my waist. "Wait," I said, but then he was kissing me. I felt tequila spill out of my glass onto my hand. A handcuff clicked around my free wrist and then he took my gimlet away. I heard the glass break on the hard wood floor.

He pushed my hands behind my back and locked them together. "Declan," I said. My eyes were starting to adjust to the darkness. I could just make out his figure in front of me. He pulled me further into the room. There were large windows to our left covered in dark curtains. In the dim light I saw shelves filled with books, several reading chairs and a couch sitting in the center of the room. Declan pushed me up against a shelf, the books pressed against my bare arms and I felt the leather of their spines.

"Declan wait," I said.

He leaned down and whispered into my ear. "The safe word is doppelgänger. Don't use it unless you really want me to stop."

I closed my eyes and let the darkness take me. It enveloped me, letting me feel pain and lust as one dangerous cocktail. I wanted it to stop and couldn't bear to have the moment end. The handcuffs, despite their fur lining, rubbed my wrists raw. I wanted them in front of me instead of behind my back. Declan tried to stop me but I pushed him away, using one heeled foot. He stumbled back from me and I squatted down, rolling onto my back and brought my bound hands around my feet.

Declan grabbed my arm roughly and pulled me to my feet. I felt him with my hands. "That's not how I want you," he said.

"I don't care," I answered before biting his lip hard enough to make him groan. He pushed me back against the stacks and I heard books land on the hard wood floor, their pages flopping to one side.

"You're not good at being submissive," he said against my throat as I ran my bound hands through his hair.

"You're observant," I joked.

He pinched me hard and I yelped. "I'm not kidding," he said as he grabbed my hair, pulling my neck back painfully. His lips against mine. "Do you want to learn?"

"Never," I answered.

He laughed. "Good."

Bruised, battered, and beyond satisfied I rested against Declan's chest, curled up on his lap in one of the large leather chairs. He unlocked the cuffs and kissed my wrists. "Do you want to go back to the party," he asked.

"You ripped my stockings," I said.

He laughed, a deep rumble I felt run through my body. "I don't think anyone will notice," he said.

"Do we have to?" I asked.

"No," he said shaking his head. "Lord knows I wouldn't be able to make you."

I laughed and shook my head, my loose hair brushed against my bare shoulders. "I'd like another drink," I said remembering that I still didn't have any useful information to give Mulberry.

"I suppose I owe you one," Declan said, shifting so that he could get up. I waited in the leather chair and watched his form move through the darkness. Moments later the room lit up. Doyle returned, his pants back on, his hair every which way. I smiled at him before standing up and attempting to flatten it down for him as he buttoned his shirt. "I'll get you a drink. Sorry about the last one." He said with a smile that made it clear he was *not* sorry about the last one. "Stay here," he said kissing me quickly. "I'll be right back."

"Wait. Help me get this thing on first," I said, crossing the room to where the corset lay crumpled next to the bookcase. He smiled and obliged, tying the ribbons a little tighter than before.

Declan left to replace my gimlet, and I stepped into my dress. It was a little wrinkled, but I didn't think anyone would notice. I was zipping it when someone said, "Hello Miss Humbolt." I swirled around holding the dress to my breast. I didn't see anyone.

"Hello," I called out. "Who's there?"

A man I'd never seen before stepped out from between the stacks. "I'm sorry. I didn't mean to startle you," he said.

"How long have you been here?"

The man was a little taller than Doyle, which made him quite a bit taller than me. He was wearing a tuxedo and what looked like real diamond cufflinks that twinkled in the low lighting. "I swear I've only been watching a moment. I'm disappointed Declan didn't want to share." I held my dress tighter and took a step back. The man smiled. "I don't mean to frighten you." He came toward me. I shuffled away from him.

"How about you keep your distance," I suggested.

He laughed at that. The man was probably in his fifties. His hair was brown, with silver at the temples. "I'm sorry. I should have introduced myself. I'm Bobby Maxim. You work for me."

"Well that makes this even more awkward," I said.

He laughed. "Won't you come into the main room?" Bobby held out his hand to me, but I shook my head no.

"I'm not dressed," I said.

"You'd be considered overdressed where I want to take you."

"Then I don't want to go."

I heard the door open, and Doyle was back. When he saw Bobby, he almost dropped my Tequila Gimlet. "Robert," Declan said and cleared his throat. "Good to see you."

"Can you zip my dress?" I asked Declan.

Doyle handed me my drink and zipped me up. Robert didn't take his eyes off me. "I was just admiring your date. I invited her to the main room, but she seems frightened."

"I'm not scared," I said. "Just totally satisfied."

Doyle suppressed a laugh and Bobby nodded. "I like a lady who is not afraid to share her thoughts. I also like a little bruising." He motioned to my cheek. "Did Doyle do that?"

"No," I said.

"Your lips are swollen too, I bet he did that."

"Sir--" Doyle started, but Robert stopped him with a wave of his hand. He approached me, and when I took a step back I bumped into Doyle's chest.

"I'd like to show you something, if you don't mind?" Maxim said to me. "I promise not to touch you unless you ask."

I took a sip of the tequila and watched him over the rim of the glass. His eyes were bright and intelligent. They didn't leave my gaze. "Fine," I said.

We walked through the stacks until we came to a large fireplace. "Declan, will you please?" Maxim said.

Declan scurried forward into the fireplace. It was as tall as he was, made of pale gray stone, blackened by years of smoke. Declan pushed against the back wall, and it opened. I took a deep breath, feeling the restraint of the corset.

Robert offered me his hand but I shook my head. He shrugged and led the way into a narrow room. The ceiling was only about eight feet high. Shackles lined one wall, and on the other hung whips, chains, paddles, and ball gags--everything an S&M club might need.

I felt drawn to the instruments and walked over to the display. I ran a hand over one of the whips feeling the cool leather that I knew would sting hot. That was the attraction, the dichotomy, the hot and the cold, the pain and the pleasure. All the roughest, toughest, softest, hottest feelings could be elicited right here, with these tools, among these people.

A couple entered the room from a different entrance. They were clearly intoxicated. I recognized the man almost immediately as one of the people Mulberry wanted me to find. And here he was in an S&M dungeon in the most elite club in New York City.

"Are you all playing?" he asked. The woman by his side was small and plump and very much his junior. Her eyes were glassy, and I'd have bet good money she was high.

"No, we were just leaving," I said. I led the way out of the room, my skirt swishing across the stone floor. Maxim followed closely behind me. I spilled a little of my drink onto my dress and stopped to wipe at it.

Robert was suddenly there with a pocket square. He slowly reached out. "May I?" he asked.

I shook my head. He smiled and turned to Doyle. "A woman who knows what she wants."

"And is in the room," I said. "Didn't your mother teach you that's it's rude to pretend like a lady isn't in the room when she is?"

"Rude?" Maxim said. "You wouldn't believe how *rude* I can be." He slipped the kerchief back into his jacket pocket.

I smiled knowing that I was here to spy on him and his kind. That he wanted me but I had him right where I wanted him.

"I dare you to touch me," I said.

He didn't wait, grabbing my wrist he yanked me against his chest. But I twisted free and slapped him hard so that my palm burned. Maxim licked at a small bead of blood pooling on his lower lip and then smiled. Declan stared at me and then Maxim.

I turned on my heel and marched out of the library. Doyle chased me down and grabbed my arm before I could get back into the front hall. "Joy, wait," he said.

"I'm fine," I said, pulling free from him.

"This is usually a shared experience. I told you why we were coming here," he said, following me down the hall.

"I don't think I like it."

"You did a minute ago. Robert doesn't mean anything. He just likes a good fight."

He was right. I had put myself in this situation. Why wouldn't that man think he could touch me? I just fucked a guy in a library. It was a joke to be acting like I was a lady. We reached the door to the main room and I turned around. "I'm sorry," I said. "You're right. I don't know why I did that."

Doyle nodded. "Well, he liked it."

"I think it's time to go," I said turning and opening the door. As we moved through the main hall, I saw that most of the older crowd had left. Elaine was cornered by a balding man in a red vest, but she did not seem to mind. There was an electric charge in the air. I stopped for a moment and turned around, surveying the whole space. Doyle looked at me, questioning.

"Are they all going to fuck each other?" I asked.

Doyle laughed. "Not all of them, but yeah, a lot of them."

"Do you do this all the time?"

He shook his head. "Not all the time."

"But a lot?"

"Enough so that I know what I'm doing."

I suddenly realized I was in way over my head.

CHAPTER TWENTY-TWO

NEVER DO IMPORTANT THINGS WHILE DRUNK

MY PHONE WOKE me the next day. I rolled over and tried to ignore it. I heard myself on my answering machine encouraging the caller to leave a name, number, and a brief message after the beep. "Hi, this is Julen. I am calling you back."

"Well, Blue, I guess it's time to get out of bed." He snorted softly and tucked his head farther under his back leg. I watched him breathing slowly at the foot of my bed and decided that I loved my dog. He had gained weight since moving in with me, and there was something about his soft, rhythmic breathing, his lightly closed eyelids, and the sound of air passing through his nose that overwhelmed me.

"Come on, boy. Let's get up." He ignored me. "Blue, it's time to get up." I prodded him with my foot. He grumbled but didn't move. "Fine. I'll get up." As soon as I pulled the blanket off myself, his head popped out. I slipped on a robe and made for the kitchen. My body was sore but not in a bad way. It felt like I'd spent some time at the gym working out (yeah, like that ever happened).

I turned on the radio and the coffeemaker, both of which sputtered to life. Blue followed me around the small space of the kitchen as I gathered coffee, sugar, and milk. I spooned a cup of dog food into Blue's bowl, which he crunched on as the coffee machine filled the house with the irresistible smell of fresh-brewed French roast.

After enjoying most of the pot of coffee and listening to the news of the day while staring out my living room window, I went to get dressed. I had slight bruising on my wrists, and there was no way I was putting on any tight pants. I found a long, loose skirt and a pile of bangles that made me look like a hippy but covered up the evidence of the previous night's "play."

I took Blue for his morning business. Blue inspected a nearby tree, a somewhat fascinating piece of newspaper, and the tire of a Vespa. When I got back upstairs, my message machine blinked two. I listened to Julen's message again. The second message was from Mulberry. He sounded sad or something. He wanted me to call.

When I called Julen back he didn't sound happy to hear from me. "Why are you calling me?" he asked.

"I'm sorry. I didn't mean to upset you. I just had a couple of questions."

"Are you a cop?"

"What?"

"Don't call me anymore. I told your friends I would do what they asked. Just leave me alone. Leave me alone." He sounded on the verge of tears. Julen slammed the phone down, missed the receiver, cursed, and then another bang, and the line was dead.

"What the fuck was that about?" I asked out loud. My friends? Who would my friends be? Cops? He thinks I'm a cop. So maybe the cops asked him to do something. But what? I immediately called Mulberry.

"Hey, it's Joy."

"I'm glad you called. How did it go last night?"

I didn't want to get into that. At the moment I wasn't sure how much I wanted to tell him. I rubbed at my wrist. "Fine. I saw some of the guys you asked me to look for."

"Great, great. Can we meet?"

"How about happy hour at Flannigan's on the West Side," I suggested.

"Sure, that'd be great. Thanks again."

"It was my pleasure."

When I went to meet Mulberry, the place was filled with smoke despite the statewide ban. Looking around the dim, wood-paneled space, I saw him at the bar talking with an older man over pints of amber beer. Not wanting to interrupt them, I walked over to the jukebox.

Four quarters bought me two songs. "Oney" by Johnny Cash--the song of a man who after 29 years of "buildin' muscles puts his point across with a right hand full of knuckles."--followed by "How Long Has This Been Going On?" sung by the one and only Judy Garland. I've never really understood that song. I couldn't tell if she has been cheated on and wants to pretend it didn't happen or if she just found out her man was cheating on her and wants to know how long it's been going on. But that had nothing to do with why I put it on. She belts out, "kiss me once, then once more" in a way that makes me tingle.

My two songs came and went. The detective's drinking partner left, and I moved around the bar to sit with Mulberry.

"Hey, how long have you been here?" he asked.

"Long enough to drink most of this pint. I'm ready for another. You?" He called over the bartender, an Irish guy with bulging muscles and piercing blue eyes, who you could just tell was a rabid rugby fan. "Another round," I told him. He moved off to pour our pints.

"I've got some pretty fascinating information for you," Mulberry said.

"And I for you," I said, still unsure of how I was going to tell him about what happened the night before.

"That man who just walked out," he said, pointing at the door with his almost empty glass, "He's the pathologist assigned to Tate Hausman's case, and--" The bartender came back with our pints and a shot of whiskey for Mulberry. He downed the shot, paid, and the bartender went away. "He did the autopsy on Tate, and he says that he died of strangulation but not from being hung up the way he was. Tate was strangled while lying face down." I sipped my beer and listened. "He thinks he had a fight with the killer. The murderer managed to knock

Tate to the ground then choked him using the same line he hung him up with. Tate was already dead when the perp suspended him from the ceiling."

"That makes sense." His eyebrows rose. "As far as I could tell, Tate Hausman was not a part of the scene I attended last night."

"Really?"

"Elaine was there, and she said that, get this, Charlene e-mailed her and asked her to start a rumor about the two of them."

"What?"

"She thinks it was to throw people off the truth that Charlene was having an affair with Joseph Saperstein.

"I suspected as much." he said sighing.

"Why didn't you tell me?"

He shook his head. "Doesn't matter."

"I thought we were working on this thing together!"

"Keep your voice down," Mulberry whispered.

"Sorry, but really."

"You're right. I'm sorry."

"Is there anything else I don't know?"

"No."

"OK then." I sulked for a moment. "I don't think the message was from Charlene."

"Of course not. She's not an idiot. Tell me, did you see anyone there? Anyone I asked you to look out for?"

"Yes." I'd gotten home late last night, but I'd made sure to check the photographs before passing out. "The Commissioner of Police, Harold Faultner."

Mulberry banged his fist on the bar. "I knew it! Faultner is pushing too hard on this thing. That guy," he said, pointing to the door referencing the pathologist, "told me he was being asked to rule Tate's death a suicide."

"Is he going to do it?"

"Yeah, I think so." Mulberry shook his head. "He's close to retirement. I mean he's got too much to lose."

"I think someone is leaning on Faultner. I don't think it's his idea."

"Yeah? What makes you say that?"

"I don't know." I thought back to the drunken man and the pudgy girl we'd left behind at the fireplace. "He didn't seem like a killer. And what would his motive be? I could believe he is being blackmailed but not that he is the killer."

"Look," he leaned towards me. "There is someone with a hell of a lot of clout trying to make Tate suicidal and Mrs. Saperstein a black widow." He leaned back and picked up his beer. "It's not just the Commissioner. When I tried to get a warrant for Charlene's place I was refused. Do you know how ridiculous that is?" He looked up at me, and I shrugged my shoulders.

"But I thought you did search her place."

He smiled. "Yeah, I got a different judge and myself off the case."

"All right, so someone is manipulating the pathologist, judges, and the police commissioner." We sat in silence for a while draining our beers and thinking. "You know Robert Maxim?" I asked.

Mulberry turned slowly toward me. "Yeah. Everyone knows Robert Maxim."

"It was his dog who found the body."

"You're saying maybe it wasn't a coincidence?"

"Maybe the dog knew the body was there." Mulberry narrowed his eyes. "He was at the party--playing," I continued. "I saw him talking to the police commissioner, and he is obviously a powerful guy."

"Powerful is an understatement. He basically runs this city. I mean Fortress Global provides security for half the corporations based out of New York, both overseas and in the States. He is up to his neck in this city."

"But look, I'm telling you the guy is deep into S&M. He married a dominatrix."

Mulberry choked on his sip of beer. "What?"

"Yeah." And she's kind of hot I thought to myself. "My point is if you're this all- powerful guy-, why would you kill someone not as impor-tant as you, using a method that would make it look like you did it? That's almost as dumb as Charlene writing an e-mail to Elaine asking her to spread rumors that make her look guilty of murder."

"Someone else must have written it," Mulberry said, his half-intoxi-cated tongue fumbling over the word written, making it sound like witten.

"What?

"The e-mail to Elaine from Charlene. Someone else must have written it."

"What do you mean?" I asked.

"Hacking into someone's e-mail account isn't exactly brain surgery. I mean, if this person can turn murder into suicide and a grieving widow into a murderess, then a bogus e-mail would be child's play."

"Good point."

"It's someone who knows about the parties and is powerful enough to control the most important people in the city. Possibly even Robert Maxim." Mulberry contemplated his beer and then, with a smile on his lips, continued, "The only person more powerful than the people we're talking about is the mayor, and I don't think he's running around killing stockbrokers and accountants."

We both sipped our beers. "That is crazy. Right?"

"Yes," Mulberry said without looking at me.

"There's no way."

"None."

"He was friends with Tate."

"Even more of a reason not to murder him."

"They were scuba buddies, you know?" I said.

"Yeah, I watch TV."

We sat in silence for a moment.

"Another round?" the bartender offered. The beers arrived dripping with condensation. Mulberry threw back his shot, slamming the small glass onto the bar.

"I got a really weird phone call from Julen this morning," I said. "He told me not to call him anymore and said he did what my friends asked. Any idea?"

Mulberry nodded. "He changed his statement yesterday afternoon. He now says that Mrs. Saperstein was not with him. That she wanted to kill her husband."

"Jesus." My phone rang. "Excuse me." It was James, and he was almost drunk.

"You have to come out here," he yelled over the background noise.

"Where?"

"I'm on the Lower East Side at Meow Mix and there's the greatest band playing. They're called 'The Pussy.'"

"What?"

"The Pussy. You'll love it. Get over here."

"I'll see you in a bit." I walked back to Mulberry.

"I was just thinking," Mulberry said as I sat back down on my stool. "The woman in the doorway--the blonde that Chamers saw."

"Yeah?

"You know, we never figured out where she went. We combed the place. We opened every locked door, went down every passage. We even had the head of the building, William Franklin, helping us. We found all sorts of shit. Boxes of records" he said as he ticked off a finger, "old wet suits," another finger, "dust, a lot of dust," he looked at his third finger for a while then continued, "but no unsecured or surveillanced exit."

"Is there surveillance in the halls?"

"I wish. Only on the parking entrances, and all the other doors have alarms, like the alley exit."

"Maybe she was disguised and changed before she entered one of the parking lots."

"No. No women at all during that period."

"Maybe she hid in the building."

Mulberry waved his hand, "There is no way. We searched the whole place. Trust me. She did not leave through any of the exits that we know about, and unless she is down there right now crouching in a corner, the woman is a ghost."

"What's your point?"

"I think there's an exit we don't know about. There has to be." His cheeks were flushed.

"So you want to try and find it?"

"I want *you* to try and find it."

"What? Come on. How am I supposed to do that?"

"Talk to Chamers. He liked you."

"He's not going to tell me anything he didn't already tell you."

"You have to." He slammed his drink down, and beer sloshed over the rim of the mug.

"Whoa, I don't have to do anything." I stood up. "I'll talk to you when you're a bit more sober."

"What? You're leaving? Come on," he whined.

"You're drunk and I'm outta here." I turned to leave. He grabbed my arm, and I ripped it away from him. "Back off," I hissed at him.

"I'm sorry. I'm sorry. Please sit down." I turned and left.

I found James drunk, leaning on a dirty bar, sipping from the lip of a Corona bottle. "Hey," I yelled over the music.

"You made it," he shouted. "Let's get you a drink." James waved to the bartender, a woman with a shaved head and an 'I heart Mom' tattoo on her neck. On stage, four girls in short skirts with dark eye makeup jiggled. The lead singer, her faux hawk dyed midnight blue, held the mike right up to her full lips and screamed while shaking her thin legs. The guitarist moved to the edge of the stage and rubbed her instrument between her thighs to the wild cheers of the crowd. "Here." James pushed a shot of tequila into my hand.

"Oh, so this is how it's gonna be?" I yelled at him.

"What?"

"So this is how it's gonna be!"

"What?"

"Never mind." I poured the salt onto my hand, licked it, quickly shot the tequila which made me feel like I was going to throw up, sucked aggressively on the lime, and felt a shiver. "Argh. Beer," I yelled to James. He passed me a Corona. I took a nice, cold slug and felt better. "Argh. I hate that."

"The first one's always the worst." It was already relaxing me. Mulberry's outburst had me worried. I was starting to think that he was crazier than I thought, which made me crazier than I thought. The next shot of tequila lessened these worries even more. By the third I had forgotten I had a problem and was in the middle of the dance floor with James, bouncing to the music.

"I have to pee," I yelled to James, and he nodded. I moved through the crowd toward the bathroom. The line made me groan out loud. "Is this the back of the line?" I asked a woman leaning against the wall behind ten other women.

"Yup.

"Thanks." I stared absently into the surging crowd. A woman broke free of the mass and passed me heading for a door marked "Employees Only, Stay the Fuck Out." Her hair was chopped almost to her scalp and dyed Pepto-Bismol pink. Her face was in shadow, but I could make out strong features in a grimace. I inched forward with the line. Where had I seen her before? The door opened, she turned to look over her shoulder, and a light illuminated her eyes for just a moment. My heart started beating really fast. Charlene Miller. Charlene fucking Miller. She wasn't dead; she wasn't kidnapped; she was in the back room of a lesbian club on the Lower East Side.

I dragged James out to the street. "What are you doing?" he protested as I marched him down the deserted block and away from the crowd of smokers outside the club.

"I don't want anyone to hear us," I whispered.

He looked back at the crowd of drunken people. "I don't think you have to worry about them."

"Just shut up."

"Hey, what's going on?"

I stopped on the corner. "I just saw Charlene."

"Who?" He looked confused and intoxicated.

"Charlene," I enunciated as clearly as possible. "The woman I got the dog-walking route from who mysteriously disappeared."

He gasped. "Where?" he whispered and peered around us.

"Inside. She walked right past me and went into a room for employees only."

"Holy shit. What are you going to do?"

"I guess I should call Mulberry."

"Right. That's a good idea."

"But, he's drunk."

"Oh."

"Do you think we need another drunk person around?"

"Probably not. Wait. I have an idea," James said.

"Great."

"Let's follow her." He smiled wildly.

"Right. That way we will know where she's hiding out," I said.

"That's right. And then when Mulberry's sober, we can tell him."

"OK. We should have coffee."

"Right. Coffee." We looked around the empty streets. Nothing was open but a tired-looking bodega on the adjacent corner. The fluorescent lights made us look like the drunk, sweaty fools we were. "God, this is not the lighting for us," James said, looking at me as I poured thick, brown sludge into a Styrofoam cup. His skin, hair, and teeth were all the same unpleasant yellow. We paid for our coffees and walked back out into the night. The coffee had been burnt in the original brewing and then sat for most of a day.

"Well, we have to sober up somehow." I shrugged.

"Right. We are on a mission," James said and we smiled at each other.

"Let's finish these and join the smoking crowd. That way we'll see her leave, and we won't look suspicious," I suggested.

"Don't you think she might recognize you?"

"Good point. And what if there is a back entrance?" I said.

"I think we should finish our coffees," James said. I nodded. "And then go back inside," James continued. "Have some water." I nodded again. "Then blend with the crowd until we see her leave," he finished.

"I agree," I agreed.

But before our plan could be put into action, I saw her bright pink head exit the bar.

"There she is," I said grabbing James's arm.

"All right, all right. This is it. Stealth."

"Stealth." She started toward us. "Crap, hide me."

"Don't be so obvious," James whispered. I was turning in circles and trying to cover my face with my coffee cup. "Pull yourself together, Joy. Stealth, man, stealth." Then he started laughing. She was on the other side of the street, and as I watched her head turn toward us, I spun my back to her. James leaned on me, laughing.

"Pull yourself together," I whispered harshly at him.

"No, you idiot, start laughing." He was right. Being drunk was the perfect cover. I started to laugh along with him. "She turned down Pitt Street. Let's go," James said. We both straightened up and turned serious. During the day, Pitt would have been bustling with shoppers and commuters, but at three in the morning it was just her and us. "Where do you think she's going?" James asked.

"I don't know."

"Are we obviously following her?"

"She hasn't turned around yet."

"True." And just then she looked back at us.

"Act natural," James said through his teeth. She was standing under a streetlight, and we weren't. I prayed that was enough to keep her from recognizing me. She started walking a little faster. "I think she saw us."

"Shit." We picked up our pace. She took a left onto Stanton Street. We followed, but there was no one there. "Where'd she go?" I asked. James and I looked around. Cars lined one side of the block. Street lights formed pools of yellow that illuminated every third car. On the other side, a grove of trees marked the corner of Hamilton Fish Park.

"She could be hiding behind one of the cars," James whispered.

"You think she saw us?" I whispered back.

"Uh, yeah."

"Who the fuck are you?" came a voice from behind us. We turned around to face an angry looking Charlene Miller with a shiny new pistol in her hand. James and I both reached for the sky in what would have been a comic reaction if the gun hadn't been so real.

"Sorry," James said.

"Yeah, sorry." She looked closely at me, and I saw the recognition flicker in her eyes.

"Oh, my God. You're--" I smiled and laughed a nervous snort. "How did you find me? Who sent you?" Her surprise had turned to suspicion.

"No one. Really. It was a coincidence. I just happened to be at the club. James," I motioned toward him with one of my raised arms, "called me and told me a great band was playing and that I should come and check it out, and then when I went to pee, I saw you." My explanation spilled out of me.

"Then why are you following me?"

"If I may," James cut in. "We don't want to hurt you." She stayed quiet. "We just thought you had gone missing. Joy's been really worried about you. Mulberry's worried about you, too. But we didn't want to approach you in case we scared you."

She laughed. "You two scare me? I'm the one with the gun."

"I'll admit our logic was flawed," James said. "But we don't want to blow your cover or anything. We'd like to help."

"Help? Why would you want to help me?"

"Because you seem to be in some kind of trouble," I jumped in. "Forces are working against you. Powerful forces."

"What do you know about it?" she said harshly.

"I think someone is after you."

"Just leave me alone." She started to back away. She reached the end of the block. "Don't follow me." Then she darted out of sight. James and I lowered our arms.

"We just had a gun pulled on us," James said.

"I know."

"Ten years in New York, that's the first gun I've had pulled on me," James said.

"Last call's in a half-hour and I need a drink."

There was still a crowd outside of Meow Mix. Inside, the speakers piped in music I didn't recognize, and the crowd simmered around the bar. We got beers and moved to the quietest, darkest corner. The beer calmed our nerves quickly, and soon the whole thing seemed really funny.

"You looked like an idiot with your hands in the air," I laughed at James.

"You're the one who put your hands up first."

"Are you crazy? You totally were the one. And you're the one who said we should be stealth." We both burst out laughing again. "Stealth." I wiped a tear from my eye. "That's funny."

"Power--" James laughed.

"What?" He held his hand up and laughed so hard that no noise came out. His face turned red.

"Powerful," he lost it again. "Powerful forces," he finally squeaked out. "You said there were powerful forces working against her." I almost squirted beer out my nose. I stamped my foot and James slapped his thigh.

CHAPTER TWENTY-THREE

DRAGGED DOWN, BEATEN TO HELL, AND ALL ALONE

WHEN I WOKE up the next morning, a film lined the inside of my mouth, and my head throbbed. It took me a couple of minutes to remember my name and then a couple more to grasp the events of the night before. When I walked out of my bedroom, I heard soft snoring coming from my living room. I was surprised to find James passed out on my sofa next to a nearly empty bottle of tequila.

I quietly made coffee and took Blue out. When we came back upstairs, James was sitting up on the couch, his blond hair flattened to one side of his head and sticking out of the other. "My head hurts," he said.

"Yeah, look at that bottle of tequila." His bloodshot eyes roamed to where the bottle lay on its side on the coffee table. He groaned. "Coffee?" I offered.

"Please."

I poured him a cup and joined him in the living room. "I can't believe we drank that much last night."

"Me, neither. We've never done *that* before."

"Shut up."

"What I can't believe is that we had a gun drawn on us," James said.

"The missing Charlene Miller."

He sipped his coffee. "What are you going to do?"

"Call Mulberry, I guess. The bigger question is if we can find her again. I can't imagine she'll stick around after last night." The doorbell rang. Blue flew down the hall and started barking as loudly and deeply as he could. James covered his ears and groaned.

"Blue, shut up!" I yelled, following him down the hall. He was growling with his nose pressed against the crack at the bottom of the door. "All right, all right." I dragged him out of the way and looked through the peephole. It was Charlene Miller. Holding Blue back, I opened the door.

"I want to apologize for last night," Charlene blurted out, her hands clasped at waist height and her shoulders rounded.

I wrestled Blue into a sitting position. "It's OK, really. Please come in."

"Who is it?" James yelled from the living room.

Panic spread across Charlene's face. "It's my brother," I reassured her. "You met him last night." She released her breath. I followed her into the living room, holding Blue by the collar. He struggled, rearing up on his hind legs and whining. James made room for Charlene on the couch. She repeated her apology to James.

"You're scared. We understand," James told her.

"Yeah. It's fine," I agreed.

She looked at me. "I think someone is trying to hurt me. I don't really understand what's going on, but I know I'm in trouble." James and I stayed quiet. "I just don't know what to do." Her chin wobbled. James put a hand on her shoulder.

"Do you want me to call your brother?" I asked her.

"Joseph told me to stay away from the police. To not trust anyone."

"Mulberry is really worried about you," I said. She stared past me at the blank ceiling above my head. "I think he can protect you."

"I guess." I let go of Blue, and he flew to Charlene's side. He licked her hand. She looked down at him, unmoved.

"I'll call Mulberry. Do you want a cup of coffee?"

"Sure." I went into the kitchen. Mulberry answered on the fifth ring. "I found Charlene," I said pouring a cup of coffee.

"What?" I heard him knock something over. He sounded as hung over as me. "Shit."

"I found Charlene last night, and now she's in my house."

"In your house?"

"Yeah, get over here."

"I'm on my way." I hung up and went back to the living room. It was filled with silence. I handed her the cup of coffee. Blue sat on her foot.

"Thanks," Charlene said.

"He's on his way."

"Good. I guess." She looked at the coffee without tasting it.

"I think he can help you," I said.

"I hope so."

"Can you tell me what happened? How did you know you had to hide?"

"Joseph called me." She stopped, her eye rims pinking. "Joseph and I were in love, you know? He was leaving his wife. We were going to be together."

"But I thought he lost his job. What were you going to do for money?"

"He said he was working on something big. Joseph said he was going to have enough money for us to live like royalty for the rest of our lives." The memory of this promise shone in her eyes.

"What happened?"

"I don't really understand. Joseph said we would be leaving soon, which is why I wanted to sell the dog route. But then he called me the day I met you and said we had to leave the next day. He said something had gone wrong. We were supposed to meet at Penn Station to catch a 9:15 train to Florida. He told me that if he didn't show, I should hide-- from the police, from everyone I knew. He said they would be looking for me." She sniffed back tears.

"Who're they?"

"I don't know, but when he didn't show up, when I saw that the train was gone, I started to head for the exit, and a man, a very large man, tried to force me to go with him. He said Joseph needed to see me, but I could tell he was lying. I ran away from him, he pursued me. I made it onto the subway moments before he did." The coffee cup in her hands shook. "He was very scary," she whispered.

"Where did you go?"

"I went to the only person I knew I could trust. She took me in and helped me disguise myself." Charlene reached up and ran a hand along her mutilated hair. "You don't need to know anything about her."

"What do you think Joseph was involved in?"

"I don't know." Her eyes, unfocused, wandered the room.

"Can I ask what your relationship was with Tate Hausman?"

"I didn't know him that well. He was friends with Joseph. They grew up together."

"What about your work at the Biltmore Club?" Charlene's eyes focused on me.

"You know about that?" I nodded.

"Does my brother?"

"Yeah."

James looked at me, and I waved him off. I'd have to explain the whole thing later.

"Shit," she looked down at her feet and laughed. "What did he say?"

"He's just worried about you," I said. "Do you think your work at the Biltmore was connected in any way to Joseph and Tate's deaths?"

"Tate's death? But I thought he committed suicide." Looking at her, I was struck by the difference between the woman sitting on my couch and the one I had first met. That woman, with her beautiful green eyes and shining auburn hair, had seemed almost mythical in her beauty, her style, her New Yorkness. She was everything a strong woman of today should be, with her own business and expensive apartment. The woman sitting on my couch was the picture of desperation. Her hair had been chopped off and dyed by amateur hands, the pink still marked the tip of one ear and the very edge of her forehead. Charlene's eyes, which I'd found so intoxicating on our first meeting, were bloodshot and sunken inside dark circles of exhaustion.

"Tate Hausman did not kill himself," I said. Charlene's chin trembled with terror. "It was made to look like suicide or a breath play accident, but it wasn't. It was murder. I think someone is trying to make it look like one of the members of the Biltmore killed him in order to manipulate them."

"I don't know. But--" she paused, bit her lip and then continued, "Joseph and Tate were always friends, but a couple of months ago they started spending a lot more time together." She paused, then said, "I think they were doing something illegal."

"Like what?"

"I don't know--" She rummaged through her bag and pulled out a blue and silver scarf wrapped around something. "Joseph gave this to me the last time I saw him." She unwrapped the scarf, her lower lip shaking, to reveal three gold coins. Charlene held them out to me. They were stamped on one side with a crowned shield and on the other with the profile bust of a man with long curly hair and a serene expression. "They're from George II's reign, Joseph told me. He said they were used to pay British troops. He said he had lots more." James and I stared down at the softly glowing gold. The doorbell broke the silence.

"It's probably Mulberry. But put that away," I said over Blue's renewed barking. He skittered down the hall. I opened the door and Mulberry stood on the threshold. I got Blue to sit down, and he came into the apartment. He moved down the hall slowly and then stopped once Charlene was in view. She looked up at him.

James and I stayed quiet. This was something we didn't understand, not knowing if your sibling was there for you. I just couldn't imagine how you'd go on. The awkward silence stretched into an awkward minute. Then Blue pushed his way into the living room, laid down on the floor, and, as if things couldn't get any weirder, Blue began to clean himself (if you know what I mean).

"OK Blue, that's enough." I shoved him out of the room and, turning to Mulberry, said. "How about you give your sister a hug?"

Mulberry moved to his sister's side and enveloped Charlene in a hug. She started to cry. "It's going to be OK. I'm here now," Mulberry said. He looked over her pink head at me. "Thank you for finding her."

"You're welcome."

"We've got to get you some place safe," he said.

"I don't know where we can go," Charlene said.

"I've got a friend who can look after you. He's a retired cop, so he knows what he's doing. The guy lives upstate. I'll get you there myself." He stood up.

"Wait." She held out her hands.

"Look, I'm guessing that Joy's place is being watched, so we need to get you out of here now. I promise you, I'm going to take care of this."

"How do I know I can trust you?"

"I'm your brother! Do you think I would hurt you for anything."

"Where have you been?" She started crying harder. "I haven't heard from you in years."

Mulberry bit his lip, and for a second I thought he was going to start crying, too. "I'm sorry Charlene. I can't tell you how sorry. Please let me help you."

She shook her head.

"Charlene," I placed my hand on her knee. "I think you should go with him. I certainly can't keep you safe, and the way you're living now is not sustainable. Mulberry can help you."

She started to cry more. Charlene bent over herself and sobbed. It was James who finally had enough.

"Charlene," he said gently. "You need to go with Mulberry now because I'm starting to get paranoid that someone is going to break down my sister's door looking for you. So I'd like you to leave." He smiled at her, but he meant it.

"OK, OK," she said. "I guess I don't have a choice."

"You have a couple of choices, but only one of them is any good." James stood and so did Charlene. I held Blue back as Mulberry led her slowly past us.

At the door Mulberry turned to me. "We'll talk later?"

"OK." I closed the door behind them.

"This is insanity," James said.

"I've got to go."

"Where are you going?"

"Uptown. I want to talk to George Chamers' boss." I started gathering my stuff.

"What? Why?" I found my cell phone on the kitchen counter.

"I had been kind of assuming that the blond woman that Chamers spotted was Charlene, or she knew who it was, but obviously she has no idea. All we know is that whoever it was, knew her way around that basement, so who knows that? The man who knows who knows is George Chamers' boss." I grabbed my bag off my bedroom floor.

"Who knows who knows?"

"What?" I scanned the living room for my keys.

"Exactly."

"Where the hell are my keys?

CHAPTER TWENTY-FOUR

DROPPING INTO DARKNESS

SPOTTING ME, the white-haired man behind the front desk of Eighty-Eight East End Avenue began to smile, then recognizing me, frowned. "Hi," I said, trying to sound like someone who was not going to faint.

"Welcome back." He attempted a welcoming smile but failed.

"Thanks. I was hoping to see William Franklin."

"He is working in the park today."

"Really?"

"Yes, he volunteers. I'm guessing you'll find him on the esplanade."

William Franklin was kneeling on the ground next to several wooden stakes and a group of black-eyed Susans that had tilted over. His white hair fluttered in the river's breeze, and there was a smudge of dirt on the tip of his dignified nose. He smiled up at me. "Hello dear, can I help you?"

"My name is Joy, and I'm a student at NYU. I'm taking an urban planning class and thought that you would be the perfect person to speak to about 88 East End Avenue."

"I'd be happy to tell you about her," he said, his voice filled with a father's pride. "Just give me a couple of minutes."

I sat on a bench nearby and watched as he finished propping up the black-eyed Susans, using string to tie the long stems to the wooden stakes he'd beat into the ground. Franklin stood up and stretched, then reached down and grabbed a vine with white flowers with both hands. He ripped it out of the earth and dragged it over to a trash can. The flowers were pretty, and I didn't understand why he was destroying them.

"Datura," he said when he saw my face. "It's poisonous. Just one of their seeds can make you crazy, three will kill you."

"Scary," I said.

Franklin wiped his hands on the seat of his work pants and then smiled at me. "How can I help you?"

"First let me buy you a cup of coffee."

"That sounds nice." William Franklin walked with the ease of man who knew his way around. He led the way to a quiet coffee shop I hadn't noticed on 80th Street, all the time pointing out buildings and telling me little bits of history. He smiled the whole time, clearly enjoying his guided tour. We both ordered iced coffees, and Franklin joked with the young woman behind the counter that soon he would see her at the debutante ball. She smiled at him, humoring an old man's ancient notions about what girls like her dreamed of.

"Would you like to walk with these?" he asked, signaling with his bushy eyebrows toward the park.

"Sounds great."

"I worry we will have a heat wave soon," William said as we strolled down 80th toward the river.

"I hope the city doesn't lose power," I said.

"Luckily for the residents of Eighty-Eight, we have a generator."

"That's helpful."

"Yes. We have used it during several emergencies."

"I guess there's plenty of room for a generator in that giant basement of yours." Franklin nodded. "George Chamers said it was one of the largest in the area." We entered the park and turned onto the esplanade.

"Do you know George personally?" William asked as he nodded at a woman making her way using a walker. She smiled back at him.

"No, I was just doing research. How is it that the basement is so large and uncharted?"

"There are several reasons the basement is so hard to navigate. Firstly, the original blueprints were lost in a fire in the late '30s. Then, as the years passed, there have been many additions and subtractions to the basement of Eighty Eight. The building used to have a yacht club. It extended directly to the water. But now, of course, there is the F.D.R." He looked out to Hell's Gate, his eyes squinting against the sun. "Lots of changes."

"Chamers joked that there are passages directly to the park." Franklin smiled and shook his head. "Are the rumors true?" I asked.

"There are lots of rumors in this world," William said. "Some people say that there are passages that lead right into Gracie Mansion. The land was originally owned by the Walton Family. Scared of increased conflict with the British, they built tunnels under their house for an easy escape. This proved unnecessary since George Washington and his troops appropriated the estate in 1776."

Franklin laughed softly at the Walton's bad luck. We were approaching the memorial for the soldiers who drowned aboard the H.M.S. Hussar when William Franklin stopped. "There are rumors that the Hussar was carrying the British payroll when she sank," he said. "That millions upon millions of dollars' worth of gold bullion rests a mere 80 feet beneath the surface, lying within easy reach of common scuba."

I felt a tingling all over. Gold. Scuba. Was it possible that the coins Joseph gave Charlene came from the Hussar?

"Men much smarter than you and I have gone looking for it," he continued. "Simon Lake, the famous submarine inventor, spent many years and much of his fortune groping around in those murky waters looking for the Hussar. In 1985, Barry Clifford, the well-known aquatic salvager, claimed he'd found the wreck but nothing came of it."

"Do you think there's gold down there?"

Franklin shook his head and laughed. "I doubt it, and even if there was, it would be under rubble. Pot Rock, the rock the Hussar struck, was demolished, along with the rest of the reefs that helped earn this stretch of water its name."

I looked out at Hell's Gate, the waters churning under the hot sun.

"What about tunnels into Gracie Mansion? Do you believe those rumors?"

He smiled and shrugged. "Who knows? There are supposed to be tunnels leading in and out of the White House. Why not Gracie Mansion?"

"Are there tunnels that lead into the park?"

"You ask a lot of questions."

"You have a lot of knowledge."

He laughed. "Was it your mother who taught you flattering old men would get you what you wanted?"

I laughed but didn't answer. We strolled on, circling Gracie Mansion, in silence.

William Franklin went back to work and I called Mulberry. "Hey," I said. "I'm in the park, and I just learned something amazing. Did you know there were secret passages built under Carl Schurz Park before the revolutionary war?"

"What?"

"There was a passageway, a secret passageway." I was pacing under the shade of a cherry tree. "I mean, there have to be. The blond woman either knows the building well, or someone in the building taught her how to go. The thing is there can't be that many people who know about this."

"Slow down, Joy."

"Are you listening to me? We're almost there. I can feel it."

"OK. OK. I need you to start over."

I watched a squirrel chase another down a tree. "Mulberry, Jesus. Don't you understand what I'm saying? Secret passageways. Tunnels, underground, leading from one place to another. Ways to travel underground without anyone knowing."

"Where?"

"Are you serious? In the goddamned park." The squirrels stopped near a fence and chattered at each other. They waved their little arms around and bobbed their heads.

"William Franklin didn't mention this to the police," Mulberry said.

"That doesn't mean it's not true."

"But why would he hide it?"

"You're joking, right?" One squirrel started chasing the second. They ran into the bushes.

"Sorry. I'm just tired."

"All right," I exhaled loudly. "Look, is Charlene safe now?"

"Yes, she is."

"OK, so you need to look forward. You need to understand that this isn't over."

I could hear him bristle over the phone. "I'm on my way," he said gruffly.

"Fine."

"Fine." I flipped my phone shut loud enough that I hoped he could hear it. The squirrels started making some serious noise--loud squeaking and thumping. My prurient interest overcame my decorum, and I peered through the bushes. They were doing it on top of a square hatch marked *Drainage*. The squirrels finished up and scurried off. I was still staring at the drainage hatch. I cocked my head. "That's a hatch," I said out loud.

Before thinking about it too much, I climbed over the wrought-iron fence into the bushes. Ducking down, I was invisible from the pedestrian path as long as no one was looking for a young woman crouching in the foliage. The hatch hinges looked well-oiled, but when I tried to lift the metal top, it didn't move. I pulled with all my strength against the solid edge, but nothing. Sweat dripped into my eyes. There had to be some kind of trick to the thing. But all I saw around me were dirt, branches, and sprinkler heads. Digging my fingers into the dirt, under the edge of the hatch, I pulled up. Nothing happened.

I sat back on my haunches. Dirt, branches, and sprinkler heads. Then I saw it. One of the sprinkler heads was not like the others. While most of them were silver and modern-looking, the one closest to the hatch was bronze and stained green from age. I pushed on it, I pulled on it, and then I kicked it. The head shifted slightly, and the hatch opened silently.

I peered into the dark hole, now exposed. Cool air scented by the river hit my face. I opened my cell phone and lowered it into the hole. In the dim, gray light of my cell phone's face, wooden steps glowed. "Holy shit." I glanced around me: branches, dirt, and sprinkler heads. I stepped down into the cool air. Goose bumps spread from my ankles up to my nose as I descended.

Sunlight streamed down from the opening and cast my shadow over where I was stepping. The space below me was filled with murky dark-ness. At the tenth step, the metal hatch began to close. I held my breath and squeezed my eyes shut. It must be an automatic door, I told myself. The metal thunked into place above me, and I was left alone with the cold, packed-dirt walls, the solid wooden steps, and the reassuring light of my phone. I kept moving down.

About 30 steps later, I reached the bottom. A hallway faded into blackness in front of me. The ceiling was strung with light bulbs in yellow plastic cages. There was no obvious switch to turn them on. Two steps later, the bulbs brightened with a whirr of electric current. The hall ended 40 feet in front of me at a gray door with a chrome knob.

The knob turned easily, and the door opened into a dark, cramped space. I felt my way forward and quickly found another doorknob. Turning this one got me into a larger dark space. I found a light switch on the wall to my right, and when I flicked it on, I discovered I'd come out of a closet. The room I was standing in was empty, and there was a door to my left. I lingered on the threshold peering out onto a hallway that had the telltale white walls and sporadic lighting of Eighty-Eight East End Avenue. The hall ended in a T. I decided to go left because it was as good as going right, but before venturing beyond my doorway, I turned to study it.

There was nothing that would distinguish it from any other door in any hall. I took a pen out of my shoulder bag and made the smallest of blue marks by the middle hinge. Then I started left. I reached the hallway at the end of the first hall and realized I didn't have a plan. Should I try every door? Should I wait for Mulberry to arrive and then try every door?

I was suddenly paralyzed with indecision, and that turned into fear faster than squirrels copulate. I broke out in a sweat. As the fear was hitting its peak, and all I could hear was the rushing of the blood through my veins, a door behind me opened and voices and footsteps echoed.

The halls I could see were empty. The acoustics made it impossible to tell where the footsteps were coming from. I went to take a step and stopped, my foot hanging in the air. They would hear me. There was a door only a few feet away, and I wracked my brain over how to get to it without making a sound. Then again, maybe they already knew I was here. If there were sensors to close the hatch and turn the lights on, why wouldn't those same sensors notify someone in a room somewhere filled with security monitors that an intruder had entered the building? Maybe it didn't matter if I made any noise.

"Christ, you're such an idiot," a man's voice said. "Betting on the Mets is like betting on the fat guy in an eating contest."

"You just can't understand that the Mets are the greatest team in the world," said another man. I pictured potbellies and easy laughter. I took as soft a step as I knew how. The slightest of taps echoed through the hall. I took another quiet step and was standing in front of the door. "If you refuse to acknowledge the greatness of the Yankees, there's no help for you," came the predictable retort.

I wrapped my sweaty palm around the knob. It opened nice and quiet. I went in and closed the door behind me. Leaning against it, trying not to breathe or let my heart beat, I listened. Through the door, I could still hear the muffled voices of the men. I was pretty sure they were getting closer. Light leaked in under the door and lit my sneakers. I took two steps back, just in case they were looking under doors for shoes. Their shadows passed by, blocking the light for a second. "All right, I'll bet you $500."

"You know what? Make it a thou--" The rest was muffled. Their voices gone, I peeked out the door. What was I doing down here? I shook my head trying to physically remove my doubt. I started trying doorknobs. The first room was filled with, as far as I could tell, a tenant's storage. A milk crate of vinyl records sat next to a turntable. A puffy, black-leather couch covered in plastic was pushed up against the far wall. A glass coffee table with chrome legs was next to the couch. Two wet suits spilled out of an open box. A married man's bachelor's belongings, I guessed.

The next room held sealed wooden crates. "Fragile" was stenciled in red across them. I tapped on the crate closest to me. A hollow echo told me it was empty. So was the next and the one after that. I tried opening one, but it was as sealed as it appeared. "Strange," I told the empty room. By one of the crates, I found a flashlight. "The Expedition 1900 Aluminum Limited Edition L.E.D." was inscribed into the handle. When I turned it on, a burst of light filled the room. The beam was wide and exceptionally strong. I took that baby with me.

While searching my third room, an apparent dumping ground for old lobby furniture, it occurred to me that I should be looking for closets. The tunnel I'd just come out of originated in a closet so maybe other tunnels started in closets. There was no closet in the bachelor's room or the wooden-crate room. The third room had a closet, but it was empty, and no amount of tapping on the back wall revealed a secret passageway. I looked at the paisley couches piled around me. There was no way I would ever find anything using this method. I sat down on a couch. A puff of dust rose around me. It stung my eyes and made me sneeze. I had to resist the urge to start crying.

"What am I doing here?" I whispered to the paisley. I got no response and got angry. "Someone is killing people and getting away with it, and I'm the only one who cares." My voice was rising, but I didn't care who heard. I punched a cushion, and dust flew back at me. "Stupid dust," I coughed. "What is wrong with this world? Dammit." I stood up and paced. "You know it shouldn't be up to people like me to deal with this. The police should be down here looking for tunnels. Why aren't they looking for them? Oh, because some old man likes to get his rocks off in a kinky way. So stupid. This whole thing is so fucking stupid." I threw myself back onto the couch. I dropped my new super flashlight on the ground and covered my face.

Frustrated I threw my hands aside and lay looking up at the ceiling. Directly above me was a fire sprinkler-head. I sat up and looked around. There were three, all linked to the same pipe. I stood on the couch and reached for the closest one. I pushed up, I pulled left, then right, I pulled down. Nothing. I moved one of the chairs under the next one and tried again, but nothing. The third sprinkler brought the same results. I went back to the first and tried twisting it. The couch began to sink. I sat down quickly. The couch was definitely being lowered into the ground; a whole section of the floor was dropping into darkness.

The trap door clinked and clanked down into a small room with a very low ceiling. Standing up, I scanned for an exit. A single exposed bulb flickered and then glowed steadily from a socket in the ceiling. I stepped off the platform, and it immediately began to thunk and click and rise. I watched it go. As the floor from above became the ceiling again with a sickening click, I reminded myself that there was a way out of this room. Even though there was no obvious exit, that didn't mean there wasn't one--unless this was a trap to catch nosy dog-walkers who wandered around in basements they weren't supposed to be in.

I wrestled with fear for a couple of minutes, staring blankly at the long column that rose out of the floor and supported the platform. Made of dark metal it appeared to be smeared with oil. Maybe they would release gas into the room to knock me out, I thought. "Shut up," I told myself. "Take a deep breath, and find the exit. OK. Good idea."

I moved around the tight space, running my hands over the concrete walls, trying to find anything that could be a lever or pressure point. I knocked on the walls and stamped on the floor but heard only solid thunks. Panic rose again, but I pushed it down. There had to be a way out. This place was just a foyer to something bigger. It had to be. I went over the whole room once. Then again. And again. After about a half an hour, the room was becoming stuffy. There was no air coming from anywhere. "I'm going to die here. No you're not. Shut up. Don't be dramatic. Don't be dramatic. I'm in a fucking coffin. Shut up. OK. OK. You're going to be OK."

I sat down on the floor and concentrated on calming myself down. Deep breaths in...and out...and in...and out. I took a yoga class once on one of my I'm-going-to-get-in-shape kicks, and the instructor taught us some breathing techniques that I tried to remember. The teacher was this elastic, dark-haired beauty who kept saying, "Good. That's good, guys," Even when she was demonstrating something, she would tell us we were doing great. In...and out...and in...and out.

I opened my eyes to the small, dark room. "I'm going to get out of here," I told it. I stood up and walked the perimeter again. There had to be something. I looked at where the column entered the floor. I touched it. My fingers came back covered in oil. Someone had to oil it. Oil didn't just get on columns by itself, right? A machine like this had to be maintained. There was no point in having a complicated platform-lowering machine unless it led somewhere. I put my hand back on the column. I felt around the base. There was a slight draft. I breathed in deeply. There was a way out. I just had to find it.

Another walk around the room. The walls, the floor, and the ceiling were all rough concrete. I ran my hands along the uneven surfaces. I closed my eyes and put both hands on a wall. I pushed. Nothing. I pushed harder, still nothing. I went to the next wall and tried it again. Nothing. The third wall I pushed moved back with a lurch. I snapped my eyes open. A breeze hit my face and I filled my lungs with the air. It smelled of mold, dirt, and damp. I pushed harder. The whole wall moved back another foot. A string of bulbs illuminated a long hall that ended in what looked like elevator doors.

CHAPTER TWENTY-FIVE

THERE IS ONLY ONE RESIDENCE IN THE PARK

I WALKED DOWN THE HALL, occasionally turning back to make sure that my wall was still open. I reached the elevator doors and pushed an unmarked button next to them. The doors opened. Inside was a silver room that had to be an elevator. I stepped in. There was no panel of buttons, but after the doors slid shut, I felt it move up. Moments later I was standing at the entrance to a study. A large, dark, wooden desk faced me. On the walls hung paintings of Revolutionary War battles. Ships cannoned each other in the dark night, illuminated by orange bursts of ammunition. I stepped into the room, the elevator doors closed behind me, then two bookcases moved to cover the doors.

I walked to the window. A manicured lawn dotted with statues, and in the distance, Hell's Gate. As far as I could tell, the building was in the park. So I wasn't in Eighty-Eight East End anymore. But what building was in the park? There is only one building in the park--Gracie Mother-fucking Mansion. The door opened behind me, and the mayor of New York City walked into the room.

He stared stock-still, the door open behind him, one foot in the room, one out. He looked shorter than on TV, but there was no mistaking his stocky frame, his thinning blond hair and his famous blue eyes. "Books move," I said and pointed at the bookcases hiding the entrance to the elevator. His eyebrows moved together to form a confused expression. "The books move," I tried again and pointed enthusiastically at the shelves. His eyebrows got closer.

"There's an elevator," I managed. His face broke into the most wonderful, charming smile, and I suddenly wished I had a baby so that he could kiss it.

"I don't know how you got in here," he laughed a conspiratorial laugh, "or why, but I like you." He nodded, agreeing with himself.

"I voted for you."

"Thank you." He looked genuine when he said it.

"I'm sorry. I didn't know I was breaking into your house. There's an elevator behind those books." He walked over to his desk and opened a drawer, then closed it.

"I don't know about that." He laughed again. "But one thing I do know is that you are very creative." Two security men--huge, hulking men in dark, ill-fitting suits--burst through the door. They didn't pause; they didn't talk; they rushed me. I hit the ground hard. One was on my chest, and I could barely breathe. The other pointed a gun at me.

"Don't move!" the one on my chest yelled in my face. His breath huffed and puffed onto my cheeks. I gasped for air.

"You're under arrest," the one with the gun told me. I gasped for breath.

"Don't hurt her," I heard the mayor say. I squeaked. I saw spots. "You're crushing her."

"Sir, we need to evacuate you," I heard a woman's voice say.

"Don't be ridiculous. She's just a confused girl."

"Don't move."

"Can't breathe."

"Dammit, she can't breathe."

"Sir, we need to evacuate you."

"Get off her."

"Sir. I must insist."

"Get off her." The large man was suddenly off me, and I coughed, desperate for air. I felt bruised and unable to breathe. "Are you OK?" Those famous blue eyes searched my face. He was down on his knees, holding my shoulders. "You're going to be OK. Breathe slowly. Slow." I tried to take my time, but panic seized my lungs and I couldn't breathe. "You got the wind knocked out of you. It will pass," he told me, but it was not the blow that was constricting my breath. It was fear. I knew that hot breath. I recognized the man who had bowled me over. He was that faceless, hulking figure who barreled off the train away from me, and now I was on the floor in front of him without my breath. "Slowly," Kurt Jessup told me again, "slowly." The big man watched me watch him. Did he know I knew who he was? Gasp. "Slowly." Jessup massaged my shoulder. Gasp. And what about this guy? He was the big man's boss. Gasp. He had to be involved. Breathe, breathe, breathe.

The mayor stood up and offered me his hand. I took it, and he pulled me off the floor. A woman with a pinched face and an expensive red suit stood next to the desk, trying to hide her indignation. The mayor turned to his bodyguards.

"Thank you, gentlemen. You can wait outside." They left without a word, but my attacker scowled as he followed his partner out the door. His retreating back was hauntingly familiar. "Samantha, you can go, too. Thank you for responding so quickly." Her nostrils flared, but she left, leaving us alone again. "Now, what's this about an elevator?" he asked, smiling.

"Um. There's an elevator behind the bookcase," I said, unsure how to act or what was happening.

"Who told you that?"

"No one. I found it. It connects to the basement of Eighty-Eight East End Avenue."

"Really?"

"Yes."

"Will you show me?"

"I don't know how to open it."

"I think if you opened it once, you can open it again." He smiled at me.

"I can try."

"That's all anyone could ask." I walked over to the bookcases and stared. Did he really not know how to open the thing? Was there any doubt that he was involved in this? He'd known both victims; he had a secret tunnel leading from his office to the basement of Eighty-Eight East End. Was there any way he was innocent?

"As you can tell, I'm a little obsessed with the Revolutionary War," the mayor said behind me. I scanned the books, *Great Ships of the Revolutionary War*, *The Turning Point of the War for Freedom*, *A Guide to Revolutionary War Battle Sites*.

"I see."

"I am especially interested in the ships of the period. I'm an avid sailor and diver, you know."

"I've heard that," I said, pretending I didn't know about him and Tate being scuba buddies. As if I didn't suspect they'd found the Hussar.

"You know, this area, the whole Hudson Valley, was crucial to the Revolutionary War," he said. I turned to see him looking at me expectantly, leaning lazily against his giant desk.

"I remember something like that from school, I guess." He took this to mean I was interested.

"You know, the H.M.S. Hussar sank right there." I was looking at a wall sconce to the left of the bookcase, wondering if it was a lever that would reveal the elevator, so didn't see where he was pointing, but I knew he meant Hell's Gate. "She was a British ship. Part of a Cork fleet. They were privateers, which is pretty much the military version of pirate ships." I pulled on the sconce, then pushed on it. "The Hussar is not famous for any great battle she was in or her effect on the outcome of the Revolutionary War, but rather for the amount of gold and treasures that were on board when she sank." I moved to the other side of the bookcases to the sconce's twin. I said nothing, but my mind was racing.

"It is said that the Hussar went down with not only the payroll for the British troops on board, but also commandeered treasure from several American ships. Some say one-and-a-half billion dollars' worth of treasure rests at the bottom of Hell's Gate." Why was he telling me this, I wondered. The sconce had a brass base from which an elegant arm curved toward the ceiling. On top, a white shade rested on a low-wattage bulb.

"Of course, with all of the changes made to the East River since

1780, it is highly unlikely that the wreck is still there." I pulled on the sconce. "The rock the ship struck that caused its sinking doesn't even exist anymore." I pushed on the base. "It was destroyed when Hell's Gate was cleared in the mid-1800s. You know, it was the largest man-made explosion prior to the atomic era. It sent a 150-foot tower of rock and foam into the air. It's really quite a fascinating event in New York history. Do you have much interest in the city's history?" I was taking the shade off the lamp when I realized that he wanted a response. I turned to see him standing next to the giant windows framing Hell's Gate. The water swirled brown and silver behind him. He was smiling at me, waiting for an answer. He did not look like a killer, a monster who strung up his good friend and demolished the face of another. He looked like a history buff excited by his topic.

"I guess, as much as anyone else," I answered.

"You seem like a very curious person to find your way in here."

"I wouldn't describe myself as curious." I blushed and turned away. I didn't know what to do. Was he a madman toying with me, or a political figure trying to understand how I'd snuck into his office?

"I have always found this city's history fascinating," he continued. "History in general, of course, but New York's in particular. It is, after all, the greatest city in the world." I scanned the space between the bookcase and the wall. The cases had slid into place, so there must be some kind of track. I couldn't see one, but that didn't mean it wasn't there. I looked at the wall, the path the case would have to travel to reveal the elevator. It looked like a normal wall, white with a high base-board and crown molding.

"Wouldn't you agree? Don't you think this is the greatest city in the world?"

"Yes. That's why I live here."

"Were you born here?"

"I moved here five years ago," I said without turning around. There was something discolored on the baseboard to the right of the book-cases. It looked like a shoe scuff, but I wasn't sure. I bent over to look at it more closely.

"That's one of the things I love about New York--everyone is from somewhere else. Even me," he chuckled. "My parents brought me here from Germany when I was only six months old." The scuff was indeed a scuff. "Where are you from?"

"Beacon."

"That's on the Hudson, right?"

"Yes, about an hour north of the city."

"Are your parents still there?"

"No." I took a couple of steps back, trying to figure out what to look at next. The two bookcases and the two wall sconces were the only things on the wall. Paintings hung on all the other walls, but this one had large empty spaces on either side of the lamps.

"So where are--"

"Why are there no paintings on the walls?" I asked, interrupting him.

"There are lots of paintings on the walls." I turned to look at him. He was smiling at me as if I were a small and amusing child who had just mispronounced a word.

"There aren't any paintings on that wall." I pointed at the empty wall.

"I don't know. I don't do my own decorating." He shrugged his large shoulders and looked around the room as if he'd never been in it before. I looked at the other paintings of Revolutionary War ships blowing the shit out of each other.

"You picked the paintings, didn't you?"

"No. I have a decorator."

"Did she put in the bookcases?"

"No. He didn't."

"Anything else that came with the room?"

"Those lights," he pointed at the lights I had been toying with, "and let's see. Oh, this." He walked over to a bust of George Washington that sat on a pillar next to an overstuffed armchair. I walked over to it and pushed on Washington's forehead. His head flipped back and the bookcases slid apart to reveal the stainless steel doors of the elevator. The doors opened, and the small cubed space of the mysterious elevator was exposed.

"Oh, my God." The mayor was staring at the elevator, his mouth agape. I watched his face. Was this really the first time he'd seen the elevator? He took a step toward it, then stopped and looked some more.

"Would you like to go for a ride?" I asked.

"Yes. Yes, I would," he answered. We stepped inside. He looked around us as the doors closed. "Where are the buttons?" he asked.

"There aren't any." The elevator started down.

"How deep does it go?"

"Not that deep." The elevator stopped and the doors opened. The long, dim hall stretched before us. I wanted to keep him in front of me, just in case.

"After you." The mayor stepped into the hall, and I followed. "This leads to a small and rather claustrophobic room up ahead. And then we catch a couch up one flight." The mayor turned around, he looked confused. "You'll see," I assured him. We walked down the hall in silence. The wall was still open and we stepped into the anteroom. The exit began to close behind us. I took a deep breath and reminded myself that there was a way out.

"What's going on?" the mayor asked with panic in his voice.

"It's OK. This happened to me before." The door thunked into place.

"I don't like this." The mayor looked around the stuffy space, his eyes open wide.

"There's got to be some way of calling the couch down. See, this is the pole it will come down on. It's a whole section of the floor, really." Just then the couch began to descend. "Or maybe it's automatic," I said. He nodded but didn't speak as the couch clunked into place. "Have a seat." I motioned to the dusty paisley couch and the mayor looked at me. "It's all right," I told him.

"I'm sorry. This is just a lot for me to take in all at once." He sat down. A dust cloud poofed up around him. "How long have you known about this?" he asked. I sat down on the couch next to him.

"I found it like an hour ago. I wonder who built it," I said. He nodded but didn't answer me. The couch began to rise. "I can think of a million reasons a person might want to get into Gracie Mansion, but who could build this kind of thing without it being noticed?" I asked.

Jessup looked up as we approached the room above. I tried to spy a glint of recognition in his eye but there was nothing. It seemed this was all new to him. The floor locked back into place, and we were in the room of abandoned furniture.

"This is a serious matter of security," the mayor said. "You haven't told anyone about this, have you?" he asked, looking at me as if I were a security risk.

"No. I'd just arrived into your office when you walked in."

"This is very serious." He stood up and walked around the room.

"I know."

"You can't tell anyone about this." He was pacing, head down, lips pursed.

"Do you want to see the path up to the street?" I asked.

"Definitely. Lead the way." He motioned toward the door. I stood up and headed for the exit. The mayor followed. I heard him stop, and then I heard a scrape on the floor. As I turned back, a sign telling me that all visitors had to be announced connected with the side of my head. I flew into a high-backed chair. There was blood in my left eye. I tried to scramble up but couldn't control my legs. I looked down at my feet and didn't understand.

The mayor strode over to me in two swift, determined steps and picked me up by my throat. I clawed at his hands, digging my nails in deep, but his grip tightened. I choked for breath. His blue eyes glittered two inches from my face. I kicked at his knees and his shins. He stood his ground, a slow smile changing the shape of his face. I kicked harder, and his hands tightened. I felt my windpipe close. I struggled, but I just couldn't breathe.

It was as if I were in a horrible dream, one of the ones where you can't muster the strength to hit hard enough or scream loud enough, where you are paralyzed and there is nothing you can do. I let my hands fall from his. I could feel myself giving up, hoping to wake up. I closed my eyes and listened to his labored breathing as he struggled to hold me and squeeze me enough to kill me. That's what he was doing--he was murdering me right here with all this paisley. Kurt Jessup, the mayor of New York, was trying to end me. In that moment, something clicked.

My body, drained of energy and oxygen, made one last attempt to keep breathing, keep going, not die. I brought my knee up into his balls.

He cried out the way men will when you knee them in the balls. I pulled away from him. He dropped me, and I hit the ground gasping. Backing away from him on my hands and knees, my brain moving more slowly than my body, I grabbed at my bag. He recovered quickly and came at me again.

His fist connected with my cheek, sending me reeling with spots of light in my eyes, but it didn't hurt. Nothing hurt. I found the Taser in my bag and turned back on him as he grabbed my arm and began to haul me up. I fixed the device on his stomach and pressed the button. He went rigid. His eyes bulged from his tan face. I pulled the Taser back and stuck it to where I thought his heart would be and pressed the button again. I felt his shaking. He fell onto his face on the floor. I put the prongs to the back of his neck and zapped him one more time.

CHAPTER TWENTY-SIX

WHEN SHIT HITS THE FAN, THE FAN GETS DIRTY

PANTING HARD, I opened the door. The hallway was empty, and I ran. My throat felt bruised and tight, which was making it hard to breathe. Blood was on my hands and leaking into my eye. I wiped it away with my shirt as I looked for my blue mark. I felt the world spinning, and it was getting hard to concentrate. All the doors looked the same, the hallways never-ending. My shoes squeaked on the floor. I stumbled from door to door, leaving a trail of blood, until there it was--my door.

It wouldn't open. Groaning, I pulled on the knob harder. Tears stung a cut on my cheek. "Come on," I wheezed. But the door didn't care that I was bruised and bleeding. I hit the door and collapsed onto the ground. The Taser was still in my hand, and I held it tight to my breast. This wasn't over. I had to get out.

I reached up and turned the knob. It opened easily. Right, turning the knob, should have tried that first. Gathering my strength, I hauled myself up and through the door. I stumbled through the room, into the closet, and through the passage out. The lights came on, and I hurried down the passageway. I just had to get to the surface, to the park, and everything would be fine. I climbed toward the drainage hatch on all fours.

Several steps before I reached it, the door opened, and the sunlight hit my face. I pulled myself up into the bushes. I fell over the iron fence and onto the paving stones. I rolled onto my back and let the sun beat down on me. Hearing footsteps, I turned my head. A woman walking her Pomeranian stopped when she saw me. Her mouth formed into a little O. "Snowball?" I whispered. The woman turned and hurried back the way she came. I closed my eyes.

"Joy. Jesus Christ. Joy?" I opened my eyes. Mulberry stood above me, silhouetted against the setting sun. "What happened to you? My God. Are you OK?" I smiled with parched lips.

"I'm alive. And I found the killer." I closed my eyes again, enjoying the orange-tinted darkness.

"You need a doctor. Jesus, who did this to you?" He reached down and took my arm. I opened my eyes and looked at him. His face was very close, an expression of concern tinged with fear on it. Mulberry smelled like clean laundry and greasy food. He helped me up. "I'm going to take you to the hospital."

"I think that's a bad idea." My head was beginning to clear. "I can't explain what happened to me."

"You don't know?"

"Oh. I know." I swallowed, trying to dull the pain in my throat but only made it worse. "But I can't tell anyone."

"Even me?"

"I mean doctors. I'll tell you when we get back to your place."

"I really think you need to go to the hospital. You may need stitches."

"I'll be all right," I told him as we left the park. "Let's just go to your place. It's close, right?"

Mulberry lived in a converted tenement. It had an antique elevator with big push buttons and a gate you had to pull closed yourself. His apartment was warm, small, and cozy. Mulberry cleaned my wounds. I tried to push him away, but he hushed me and continued to wipe the dried blood off my face. When he was done, he put an ice pack on my swollen cheek. I slept between clean sheets with a fan cooling the air around me. I slept all night until the sun peeked over the horizon and turned the sky outside a dusty blue.

My throat was swollen and painful. The left side of my face shot a pain through my head and down my neck when I touched it. I got out of bed and found a bathroom. My reflection was shocking.

The entire left side of my face was deep purple. An angry scab sliced across my cheekbone. A smaller abrasion sat just above my eyebrow. On my neck, in dark blue, with green edges, was the imprint of the hands that had tried to choke the life out me. When I climbed into the shower, I found a bruise the size of my fist on my hip and a welt on my elbow.

I let the hot water pound the back of my neck and rush over my chest and down my legs. I breathed the steam and tried not to think about anything except the rushing sound of the water. The room was filled with swirls of white, and the walls were coated in condensation when I got out. I found a towel hanging next to a silk robe. The robe was black with small white dots and smelled like a man. It felt good against my damaged body.

Mulberry was asleep on a tan, overstuffed leather love seat that faced a large television. He was snoring under a blanket, his mouth open, his eyes fluttering. The dawn light filled the room, filtered through sheer white blinds. His feet, bare and hairy, stuck out over the armrest. He was too big for the little couch.

I wandered into the kitchen and looked at the pictures on the fridge-- one was of Charlene and Mulberry at Charlene's high school graduation. They smiled at the camera, their arms wrapped around each other's shoulders. They looked young. Another picture showed Mulberry as a kid with his father, who wore a full-dress uniform. His father's hand rested on Mulberry's shoulder.

I found coffee in the freezer, and filters in with the mugs. Mulberry's machine was a classic drip. I made a big pot of thick and serious coffee, hoping it would help clear the fog from my mind. I found fresh milk in the fridge next to a nearly empty six-pack of Newcastle. My whole body hurt, but here I was doing what I did every morning... except today I had fresh milk.

As I poured myself a cup of coffee, Mulberry walked in, his eyes puffy and his hair sticking out in odd, though not unflattering, angles. He wore a white undershirt over a pair of Christmas boxers. Santa rode, in an overstuffed sleigh, across his thighs, over his crotch and around to his butt. "Mornin,'," he said in a scratchy voice.

"You want a cup?" I asked. He grunted. I filled a mug and passed it over to him. Mulberry leaned against the counter and sipped it with his eyes closed. The whole thing was surprisingly comfortable considering that we didn't really know each other at all. "How old are you?" I asked. Surprise showed through his puffed lids.

"I'll be 40 in a month," he answered.

"Congratulations."

"Thanks." He sipped his coffee loudly. "Nice robe, by the way."

"I like it."

"Me, too." He smiled. "Nice shiner." I reached my hand up to the bruises and stopped just short of touching them.

"Thanks."

"How does your throat feel?"

"Like someone tried to choke me to death."

"You want to talk about who that someone was?"

"I don't know." He raised his eyebrows. "It's gonna sound insane," I said. "I can't even really believe it." He waited. "All right. It was the mayor."

He smiled. "Come on, Joy. You can tell me. I'm on your side, remember?"

"I'm not kidding." I turned my back to him and refilled my coffee. "He tried to kill me after I found a secret passage that led directly into his office from the basement of Eighty-Eight East End. I know it sounds insane, but it's the truth." I turned back around and saw that Mulberry was starting to believe me.

"You're not kidding."

I looked him straight in the eyes and watched his face fill with fear. "I know," I said. "I don't know what to do. I think the mayor killed Joseph Saperstein and Tate Hausman, and here's the really crazy part--I think he killed them over long-lost treasure."

"I'm sorry, back up. The mayor really tried to kill you." Mulberry was looking at the finger marks on my neck.

"Definitely."

"How did you escape?"

"I Tasered the shit out of him." Mulberry choked on his coffee.

"What?"

"What? He was trying to kill me."

"Is he OK?" Mulberry asked.

It suddenly occurred to me that I had left a man in his late forties lying in a basement, gurgling. I felt my blood make a mad dash to my toes. "Oh, my God," I whispered.

"What?"

"I didn't even think about it."

"What?" Mulberry looked scared.

"I just left him there. I just wanted to get away. I couldn't have killed him, could I have? No. Is it possible?"

"Yes. There's a reason those things are illegal here. I mean, if he has heart problems and you shocked him near his heart, it could kill him." He put down his mug and walked toward me. "Where did you shock him?"

"In his stomach."

"That should be OK."

"And his heart." His face fell. "And when he was on the ground, I zapped him in the back of the neck."

"Holy shit." Mulberry took a step back from me. "Um. I." He wiped his mouth with his palm and rubbed his stubbled chin. "I have to pee." He turned and left the kitchen.

"Mulberry?" I called after him, but he didn't respond. The bathroom door closed and the shower turned on. "Fuck." I finished off the cold coffee at the bottom of my cup and walked into the living room. I flopped onto the couch and rested my head against the back. Closing my eyes, I tried to squeeze the image of the mayor on the floor out of my head. It didn't work. I snapped my eyes opened and looked around for something, anything to fix this mess. But all I saw was a big TV, a coffee table, and a bookcase.

I scanned the books neatly lined up on Mulberry's shelves. *Leviathan* by Thomas Hobbes sat next to Sir Francis Bacon's *The Great Instauration*. I found Caesar Beccaria's treatise *Of Crime and Punishment* next to Dostoyevsky's *Crime and Punishment*. I smiled at his selection.

In a framed photograph on top of the TV, Mulberry smiled with his arm around a pretty blond lady holding a dog's leash. The dog, a chocolate lab, sat between them with his tongue hanging out. It occurred to me that I owned a dog. I ran back into the bedroom and found my phone in my bag, but it was dead. I hurried to the kitchen and used the phone on the wall to call Nona.

"Nona. Thank God. Can you go over and take care of Blue for me? I'm--" I didn't know how to finish the sentence.

"Done and done dear. I heard him in there alone yesterday and took him out and fed him. Are you OK? I was worried about you. Why didn't you come home?"

"I got beat up."

"My God. Are you OK? You sound hoarse."

"I'm all right. Nothing permanent, but I have some pretty gruesome bruises."

"Did you go to the hospital?"

"Yes," I lied.

"And you filed a report with the police? Do you know who it was who hurt you?"

"I never saw his face."

"Where were you?"

"In the park."

"Carl Schurz? I thought that park was so safe, what with Gracie Mansion there and everything."

"I was surprised."

"I'm glad to hear you're OK. Strange James didn't mention this to me."

"Huh?"

"Didn't you call him?"

"Not yet."

"He's in your apartment."

"He is?"

"Yes. He and a friend arrived about an hour ago. I saw them in the hall, and James said that he was taking care of the house for you. I asked if you were OK, and he said that he couldn't talk and ran inside."

My heart started beating faster. "What did the friend look like?"

"I only saw the back of him, but he was shorter then James and stocky. Blond hair."

"Did James look OK?" I asked barely above a whisper.

"I guess so. He was a little out of breath. I guess, now that I think about it he looked-- scared. Joy is everything OK?"

"Scared?"

"Yes. Joy?"

"All right, Nona. Thanks. I'll call you soon."

"If you need anything, don't hesitate."

I hung up. My whole body tingled. James was in my apartment with a blond man. I dialed James's cell phone with a badly shaking hand.

"Joy Humbolt. How nice of you to call." A lump constricted my throat, and I couldn't respond to the syrupy-sweet voice. He laughed at the other end of the line, a low and menacing rumble.

"Don't you hurt him," I growled through the fear.

He laughed harder. This time he was really amused. "Too late."

"Fuck you."

"Those are big words for such a little girl."

"Yeah, how's your neck?"

"I bet it's feeling better than your delicate little throat. You sound like shit."

"What do you want?"

"A fair trade. You for your brother."

"OK."

"Come to your apartment."

"Let me speak to James. I have to make sure he's OK."

He laughed again. "Don't worry, he's alive."

"Put him on the phone or no deal."

He laughed again. "Why not?" he said, and I heard the phone changing hands.

"Joy?"

"James, are you OK?" Tears welled in my eyes. "I'm so sorry. I'm going to get you out of this."

"Hey. I'm OK. Just a little bruised." He lowered his voice to a whisper. "I think the mayor is crazy." I heard a slapping sound and James say, "Ah, fuck" over the sound of the phone clattering to the floor.

"James! James, are you there?"

"You two are a real laugh riot." The mayor was back. "I don't like to be kept waiting."

"I'll hurry."

"Come alone. If I see one cop, or even the hint of a cop." He laughed low and menacing. "Come alone."

"I'm on my way." He hung up. I placed the phone back on the cradle and stared at it for a couple of seconds. I heard the shower turn off.

"The mayor's alive," I yelled to Mulberry through the bathroom door on my way to the bedroom. I pulled my jeans over the bruise on my hip and put my head through the hole of my T-shirt with extreme care. Mulberry came out of the bathroom wearing just a towel. His torso surprised me. It was rock-solid. Water glistened in his chest hair. He caught me looking.

"You took my robe." He walked past me into the bedroom and grabbed it off the chair I had thrown it over. He wrapped it around himself and let the towel underneath fall.

"I have to go," I said and went into the bathroom to check myself in the mirror. "Do you have a scarf and a giant pair of sunglasses?" Funny how the accessories for being fabulous in a convertible are identical to the ones used for covering up severe facial bruising.

"What?"

"I can't go out looking like this."

"Where are you going?"

"I need to go home."

"We need to talk. You assaulted the mayor of New York City."

I turned on him. "He tried to kill me. Do you get that?"

"But if you killed him you're going to be in serious trouble."

"He's not dead."

"How do you know?"

"Trust me." I picked up my bag, felt around inside, and made sure I had my keys, wallet, phone, and Taser.

"Where are you going?"

"Home." He followed me into the hall.

"If you wait five minutes, I'll come with you."

"No." I turned back to him. "I need to rest. I'll call you later."

"I don't think you should be alone."

"You really can't follow me. Just don't, OK? I need to be alone."

"All right," he said, his voice hesitant.

"I'll call you later."

"All right," he said again. I left him in the hallway in his funny silk robe, and I wished to God that he would follow me, and I prayed that he wouldn't.

CHAPTER TWENTY-SEVEN

DEATH

I OPENED MY DOOR, and Blue greeted me. He pranced in the hallway, his claws clicking on the wood. "Hello," I called to the living room, adrenaline coursing through me, making me feel strong and out of control.

"In here," the mayor answered. Blue followed me to the front room. James was tied to a chair. We'd bought it together at a flea market when I first moved to the city. It was covered in a deep-pink upholstery. I used it to throw my clothes on when I was too lazy to put them away. Now James, a dark bruise on his chin and a bright red hand print on his cheek, sat on it with his hands behind him and his ankles tied to the legs. A scarf I wore in my hair at the beach filled his mouth. His eyes were big and he blinked at me, making a small noise through the fabric.

Blue picked up a bone that sat near James's feet and brought it over to me. The bone was large, and bits of whatever animal it came from still clung to it. "I got that for him," the mayor told me. "He likes me." Blue wagged his tail and encouraged me to take the bone. I ignored him, keeping my eyes locked on the mayor's face. He looked gray. His neck was bandaged, and I imagined the burn marks my weapon must have left on his neck.

"OK. You can let James go now. I'm here."

The mayor laughed and raised a black pistol with a silencer screwed to the end. He aimed it at my chest. "No one is going anywhere." A cigar smoldered on my coffee table. He picked it up. "Not until I get what I came for." The smoke caught the light pouring in through the windows. "Don't you know you should never trust a politician?" He bit the cigar and smiled largely, showing me his teeth.

"I don't know why you're doing this. I don't think I am who you think I am. I'm not a threat to you. I'm just a dog-walker," I tried to sound small. It wasn't that hard.

"Don't be silly Joy. You and I both know what you know. You know all about Joseph and Tate, those imbeciles." His knuckles turned white gripping the cigar. He lowered it from his face.

"All I know about them is that they're dead, and I don't want to be."

"That's a good attitude to have. Joseph and Tate could have learned something from you." He looked at the tip of his cigar with narrowed eyes. "That Joseph. He had a real future if only he had known how to be faithful. You know, loyalty, faithfulness," he said as he brought the cigar to his lips and took a long puff, "they are very hard qualities to find."

Smoke seeped out of his mouth, rose above his head, and dissipated into the air. "Especially in men." He stood for a moment, the pistol trained on my face. "That's why my closest associates are women--my deputy mayor, my wife," he smiled at me, "my secretary. These women would not abandon me for anything. They are loyal. Joseph Saperstein was not loyal; he was not faithful. He wasn't even interesting," Kurt snickered at his joke. "I let him in on it. I didn't need him. I could have sold the stuff myself. I don't need an accountant to tell me how to hide things." His eyes turned cold. "I was willing to make him a rich man. But he wanted to run off with some hooker half his age. And that wife of his, Jesus. She didn't do anything to stop him," he lowered his voice. "That's OK, though. She'll get what she deserves." He looked out the window to Mrs. Saperstein's dismal future and smiled.

Kurt Jessup turned back to me and continued his monologue. "You know, it's OK to leave your wife. If he wanted to marry this--" he paused to find the right word, "this girl, that's fine. He just should have done it without my gold." His eyes glistened with a nervous excitement, and his cheeks flushed a deep red. "Nobody steals from Kurt Jessup. Nobody." He looked like a man with a bad fever. "But you know all of this already, don't you?"

"I know that Joseph and Charlene were having an affair. I don't know anything about gold or stealing." I tried to sound reasonable, like this was a normal conversation, like he wasn't a gun-toting, cigar-smoking, gold-loving maniac.

"Charlene didn't show you the gold?" He raised his eyebrows and watched my face intently. "I can tell that you're lying, Joy. If there is one thing I can't stand, it's a liar."

"I'm sorry," I said.

He liked that, and a smile spread across his face. "That's all right. Just don't do it again." He sat down on my couch and motioned for me to sit next to him. I moved around James's bound body and sat. He put his cigar-holding hand around my shoulder and spoke softly, intimately into my ear. "Tate was a liar." His breath was hot. "He lied to women to make them sleep with him. He lied to men to make them like him. And he lied to me to make me trust him. But I don't trust anyone." He squeezed my shoulder, being careful not to burn me with the hot ember of his cigar. "Do you want to know why I killed Tate?" he asked in a whisper. Goose bumps spread over my skin, and I was stunned into silence. The mayor stood up. "Don't act so shocked, Joy!"

"I'm not shocked," I said recovering myself.

"Don't lie!" he yelled.

"I'm sorry."

He took a step back and turned away from me. "I'm getting sick of your apologies," he snarled with his back to me.

"OK."

"Do you want to know why I killed him or not?"

"I don't know how to answer that."

"Honestly. Just answer it honestly." He turned back to face me. "All I ever ask for is honesty."

"Tell me."

He smiled. "He got greedy." Kurt did not continue. I sat on the couch with my knees together trying to figure out how to survive. The silence lasted a long time. Blue chewed on his bone, I stared at the floor, and the mayor watched me. "Don't you want more details?"

"Yes." I felt as if I were standing outside myself, watching. I noticed the way my eyes were fluttering around the room, like a scared little bunny rabbit caught in a trap, struggling against the metal talons holding me, fighting toward my death.

"He tried to take more than his share," the mayor started. "There was plenty to go around. The H.M.S. Hussar is one of the greatest finds in history. Not only is she a piece of Revolutionary era history, a veritable time capsule of the late 1700s, but she also carried millions upon millions of dollars' worth of treasure." He liked watching my face when he said treasure. "It was right after law school when I started looking," his eyes unfocused and appeared to drift back to that period in his life. "It wasn't on purpose, you know. I wasn't thinking about the Hussar when I found the map. I'd heard of the wreck, of course, every diver has, but the map was misfiled. I was looking for the blueprints of a recently demolished building in the Rare Books Room when I found it. Joy, you have no idea how I felt when I realized what it was, what I had."

"Why all the secrecy? Why not tell the world what you'd found?"

Kurt glared at me. "Do you know the number of regulations involved in something like that? We are saddled with endless rules, ordinances, mandates, and acts of Congress that it makes me wonder if this country is even a democracy at all or just a bureaucratic artifice." He was spitting with every word. "Since the late 1800s, Congress has slowly strangled the ability of American's enterprise. Why shouldn't a person just be able to do what he dreams? Why must he plead with the government to let him make an attempt?" His face was red and his eyes wide with fury.

"But aren't you a member of the government?"

"You are so naive, Joy. You think that I am a representative of the people, eh? That I am a law-abiding public servant, that I am your leader." He moved close to me, and I concentrated on not squirming.

"I just was thinking that if you hate government so much, why be a part of it?"

"What else would I be? On the other side with the likes of you? Unable to do anything? A sheep. You think I'm a sheep?"

"Absolutely not."

"Of course not."

"I just don't understand why you're doing all this. I just don't get it."

"Don't you see? Being the mayor means nothing. You think I don't owe people for the power I have? It's not like you get to the top and you're free. There are a lot of people who I owe, Joy." He paused and then in a quieter voice he continued, "But the Hussar is mine, all mine. I can take her treasure and it will make me free." He was looking at me with his eyes wide and wet. For a brief moment, I felt bad for him. Here was a man who believed treasure would make him free, when clearly nothing in the world could grant him liberty, not with a mind like that.

"I found her, Joy. And she is mine. I found the map. I found the first chest of gold. I almost missed it." He laughed, looking at something far away. "It's almost impossible to see down there, you know? The East River has some of the lowest visibility in the world, but I've got a nose for these things." He tapped his gun to his nose, just in case I didn't know where it was. "We found more than I ever could have hoped for-- jewelry and coins, raw gems. Fantastic!"

"That's a lot of treasure," I said.

"Yes, it is." The mayor became thoughtful. "But Tate didn't think his half would be enough. It wasn't even all to the surface, and he tried to steal it. Can you believe the man?"

"What a fool."

His face lit up. "That is exactly what I thought when I realized what he was doing. Wasn't there enough for everyone? Especially after I killed Joseph. Wasn't half enough? Wasn't it enough to warrant a little loyalty?"

"You would think."

"You would, wouldn't you?" He was pacing, gesturing first with his gun and then with his cigar. "But Tate was not a loyal man. He was a greedy liar and now," he stopped pacing and looked directly at me, "he's dead."

"Good riddance. Sounds to me like he deserved it."

"You're smart, Joy. It's too bad about you." He was smiling down at me.

"What do you mean?" My skin felt hot and my gut frozen.

"I mean that it's too bad we didn't meet under different circumstances. I think you could have worked for me."

"Well, I did vote for you."

He laughed. "Indeed you did, and I appreciate that." He sat back down next to me and sniffed my hair, then stood up again.

"You know what I need, don't you?"

"What?"

"I need Charlene Miller and the coins she's got."

"I don't know where she is."

"Wrong answer," he raised his gun and aimed it at James's foot.

"No!" I yelled, but with a silent thwap, a bullet raced through space. James's foot began to pump out blood. He screamed through the scarf. James's eyes filled with tears and turned red. "Stop! Stop!" I ran toward James, but the mayor knocked me back. Blue jumped to his feet and let out a warning growl. The mayor laughed.

"I can shoot you too, you know," he told Blue and then looked at me. "And you. Now, Charlene."

"OK. I'll find her. I just need to make a phone call. Give me a minute." I looked over at James. His eyes were wide and he was pleading with me. "I'll get her."

The mayor motioned to my phone on the coffee table. My mind was racing. I had no way of reaching Charlene. Mulberry would never tell me where she was, and I didn't have a clue. "Her number's in my purse," I said, buying myself a few more precious moments to think. The mayor nodded and waved at my purse. Picking it up, I rifled through it. My Taser was in there, but I had no way of pulling it out in time. James was already shot, and I could never make it to Kurt without getting a bullet wound myself. I pulled out my wallet and picked through the business cards.

"Hurry it up. Your brother is bleeding. I wouldn't want to have to put another hole in him." My hands were shaking as I stared at a business card for a fish restaurant in Baltimore I'd been to about a year ago. I dialed the number quickly forming a plan, hoping that a woman would pick up.

"Charlie's Fish Shake," a woman said.

"Charlene, I'm glad I caught you. I really need you to come over." The woman tried to say something, but I kept talking. "It's really important. It's for your own safety." Kurt smiled at that. I let the woman tell me I had the wrong number and then said, "Good, I'll see you soon."

"She'll be here as soon as she can," I lied.

"Where is she now?" he asked, sitting on the couch, just behind James.

"On the Lower East Side. That's where she's been living." He frowned. "Can I please bandage my brother's foot?" The blood was slowly forming a puddle of red on the floor. Beads of sweat dotted James's pale face.

"Sure, go ahead." Kurt waved his gun at the injured foot. I went into the kitchen and gathered all the dishrags I owned. In the bathroom, I found an ancient bottle of hydrogen peroxide under the sink. I carried it back into the living room and tried to remember any first aid I could. The yellowed Heimlich maneuver poster from my first waitressing job wouldn't leave my brain.

"I'm going to pour peroxide on it now." James looked down at where I crouched near his foot. "OK?" He nodded and closed his eyes. I poured the liquid over the wound. It bubbled white and red. James moaned against his gag. "All right, that part's done," I told him. "Now I'm going to wrap some towels around it. I'm going to wrap it really tight to try and stop the bleeding a little." James nodded. I lifted his foot gently and put one of the rags underneath and then brought the two ends around. I tied it as tight as I could.

"I feel like there was something about a pencil and making a tourniquet. Do you remember anything like that?" James nodded. I turned to the mayor. "Can I take his gag off so that he can tell me how to make a tourniquet?"

"No." The mayor chewed on the end of his cigar and watched me. I wrapped another rag around the foot and then another. I didn't know if it was doing any good. When I was done, I sat on the floor near James's foot.

"You're good," Kurt said. "That whole thing about it being for her safety, that was smart. I really do wish we could have been on the same team."

"Me, too. Yours is obviously the winning one."

"That's true." He smiled.

"You've probably been a winner your whole life."

"Not my whole life, but most of it. You know, I'm just willing to go further than the next guy."

"Is that how you do it?"

"It's part of the reason I'm successful." You would have thought he was a college professor and I, an eager coed. "But it's also just a lot of hard work."

"And quick thinking."

"Of course, quick thinking." He puffed on his cigar, then realized it was dead. The mayor put down his gun, reached into his pants pocket, and pulled out a silver lighter with gold edges.

"You're going to kill us both, aren't you?"

He looked over his cigar at me, puffing hard, getting the thing burning. "I'm afraid that I have to. But, Joy, before you get upset, let me say that I really like you. I respect you and your brother. He put up a real fight, you know. It was not easy to get him here. And that cat of his, what's her name?" Kurt put the lighter back in his pocket and picked up his gun.

"Aurora."

"Aurora fought for him. Look what she did to my ankle." He pulled his pant leg up to reveal deep, angry scratches all along his Achilles. I couldn't resist a smile for Aurora's loyalty. "It was a shame I had to kill her." My face fell.

"You killed her?"

"Joy, you know, I'm not really like this. If Tate and Joseph had stuck to the plan, if you had kept your nose out of it, if Charlene hadn't tried to run, no one would have gotten hurt." I looked up at him. He was serious. Not a hint of irony played across his face.

"All right. I get it. Go ahead. I don't want to drag it out anymore. Just kill me." I spread my arms out, exposing my chest.

"Joy, don't be like this."

"How would you like me to be?" I stood up and walked to the windows. "Do you want me to beg for my life?" I heard him stand up.

"No, of course not. Just wait until it's time. Come on. Sit down." I turned around. He was pointing at the couch with his cigar, his gun arm hung by his side. When I didn't answer him, he moved a step closer. "It's just what has to happen," he explained from only an arm's length away.

"Do you want me to beg for my life?" A red blush started to spread up his neck.

"Stop it." He came even closer. Adrenaline rushed through me, pushing my heart to pump faster, sharpening my vision, filling me with strength.

"How about I fight for it?" I grabbed for the arm with the gun in it and caught his hand as he tried to pull it away. He tried to point the gun at me, but I had both my hands on it. I twisted so my back was up against his chest, and the gun was in front of us where he couldn't see it. He put the burning ember of his cigar into my shoulder. It was a white heat, and I screamed. He twisted the ember, and my skin burned. The smell of it filled the air.

I lifted his gun hand up to my mouth and bit the soft flesh between his thumb and forefinger. He grunted behind me and dropped the cigar. He tried to get some distance between us, but I kept my back pushed up against his chest. I felt his body's shape and heat as he struggled to be free of me. Blue was barking and circling us. The mayor punched me in the kidneys but didn't have enough room to put much strength behind it. My mouth filled with warm, salty blood when I broke through his skin.

He dropped the gun, and I followed it to the ground. It was slippery with blood and I struggled to gain control of it. Holding it with both hands, my finger on the trigger, I turned to face the mayor. He was aiming a small gun at my head. I watched as if in slow motion. He began to pull the trigger.

Blue, mouth open, fangs bared, catapulted himself at the mayor. Blue twisted in the air when the mayor fired, and an inconceivable bang ripped through the room. Blood exploded out of Blue's shoulder and splattered my face, arms, and chest. His injured body landed on top of Kurt Jessup, knocking him back onto the couch. The mayor pushed Blue off him onto the floor. A large red stain marked where Blue's wound had met with the mayor's white shirt. Kurt stood up, as did I.

"Just leave," I told him the gun steady on his chest.

"You haven't won yet. I still have a gun." He leveled it at my chest.

My heart was pumping so loud I could barely hear. "Just leave," I tried again.

"You can't pull that trigger."

"Don't tempt me." He took a step toward me, and I took a step back. I felt I could see the life rushing through him. I watched his chest rise and fall with each breath. He took another step toward me. I fired a warning shot above his head that sank into my molding. He stopped.

"Get out now."

"I can't leave without Charlene."

"You're going to have to."

"Do you think you can go far enough?"

"I can go as far as I need to." He turned quickly and fired a shot into James's chest. My heart stopped beating, and the floor fell out from under me. My vision tunneled. I didn't even notice the gun slipping away from me as I watched the blood drain out of James's face.

"Tempted?" The mayor was smiling at me, a smattering of James's blood on his cheek. I ran to my brother's side and pulled the gag from his mouth.

"You're going to be OK."

"I know." His breath was coming in gurgles. I ripped my shirt over my head and pressed it against the wound.

"James, you hold on! Do you hear me?" My vision became blurred with tears. "Nona!" I screamed. "Nona call the police! An ambulance! Call an ambulance!"

The mayor was watching us, the small gun held loosely in his hand. I looked over at him, then down at my brother. James smiled at me and said, "I love you, Joy."

UNLEASHED

"Stop it. You're fine. You're fine." I pushed some hair off his forehead. "I love you, James."

I was filled with something I can't even describe as rage or sorrow because it was so much more than that. I could feel the mayor watching us, and I wanted to shoot him, but not just shoot him. I wanted to destroy him. I wanted more than his death. I wanted him to have never existed. I could see that my brother was going to die right here. He was going to die.

"Now it's your turn," he said, his gun aimed at me. Before I thought, or he blinked, I was on top of him. I flew on him, slamming us to the ground. The gun clattered to the floor. My eyes blind with tears, I wrapped my legs around him, pinning him to the floor. I threw my fist at his face, connecting as often as not.

He tried to wriggle away, out of my grip, I held him between my thighs. He kicked at me but I was sitting too high on his chest for him to touch me. I kept striking at his face. His skin was warm. Its life, its color, made me insane. I tore at it with my nails, trying to make him bleed.

I pushed my thumb into his eye socket. His face contorted and he fought harder. I put my other thumb in his other socket and pushed. "Stop!" he yelled, but I kept going. He shook his head, so I gripped it with both my hands and slammed his skull against the floor, then I held on tight while I pushed his eyes. I could feel their shape, his pulse running through them. I was breathing hard. I was about to push his eyes all the way to the back of his skull. I wanted to blind him. I wanted to hurt him. I needed to kill him. But then something inside me balked, and for just a moment, a millisecond, I didn't want to be a murderer.

He sensed my hesitation, and planting his feet on the ground, bucked me off him. I flew forward, landing on my face, and he scrambled to his feet. He whirled around, searching for the gun, his face swollen. He looked over at me, and I saw that he was scared.

"Leave," I told him from the ground. He was breathing hard. Sirens wailed in the distance. "The police are coming. You better just leave."

"Not without Charlene." I stood up. He scanned the floor for the gun.

I saw one under my bookshelf far out of his vision. The other was behind his left foot under the couch.

"She's not coming." His head shot up, and his eyes narrowed. I practically saw the decision happen. It was like the change in a person's eye when they see someone they know--the look of recognition. He'd lost this one. Kurt Jessup didn't waste any time. He turned and left, not bothering to close the door.

CHAPTER TWENTY-EIGHT

WASTEFUL

WHEN THE PARAMEDICS ARRIVED, I'd untied James and was holding him in my arms. They pushed me aside and started to work on him in a flurry. Nona followed closely behind them. She wrapped me in an embrace and covered my face so I couldn't see anything. She whispered in my ear that it would all be OK. But I knew she was wrong. I knew that James was going to die, and I knew that it was my fault. Even in the dark warmth of Nona's assurance, I knew.

I rode in the back of the ambulance. It bumped and shook as we raced, sirens blaring, through the streets of Brooklyn. A siren sounds different when you're in it. It's not the usual approach and retreat, where you hear the siren coming, then you listen as it keeps going, away from you to someone else. When you're in it, the siren is squatting on top of you. It's wailing for you.

At the hospital, nurses and doctors in blue and pink scrubs loaded James onto a gurney and wheeled him away from me through large double doors that flapped back and forth. A well-intentioned nurse in her late fifties tried to take a look at me--maybe give me some stitches for the cuts on my face, X-rays for my injured neck. But I pushed her off and watched the doors flap. Someone wrapped a blanket around my bare shoulders.

Hugh arrived, eyes wide, face drained. "Joy. My God, what happened?" But I couldn't tell him. I couldn't speak. I just stared at him. It was all my fault. I opened my mouth and closed it. "Is he going to be OK?" Hugh asked. Seeing the answer on my face, his eyes started to shine. "Joy, what's going on?"

"I'm sorry," I whispered and began to cry. My throat constricted painfully. I squeezed my eyes shut until the blackness was dotted with white spots. I felt Hugh hugging me and shaking.

A police officer in uniform tried to ask me questions. I didn't turn to look at him. He squatted next to me and kept talking until he stopped. He stood back up and sighed. Then he walked into my vision and through the flapping doors.

Nona arrived. She hustled and bustled around us, getting us coffee and Danishes that sat untouched. She talked to the nurse about insurance and held paperwork under my nose to sign. "They are going to perform surgery." She rubbed my back in a circular motion. "He has a chance." Nona was playing the part of pillar of strength, but her red eyes gave her away.

"Joy, you need to see a doctor yourself," Hugh told me after a while of waiting.

"After."

"After what?"

"After we find out about James, I'll let them take care of me. Let them take care of him now."

"Joy, they can look after both of you at the same time."

"No." I pulled my knees up to my chest and hugged them.

After a time, a doctor came out from behind the doors that led to the part of the hospital we weren't allowed in and introduced himself as Dr. Mufflin. "I was one of the physicians working on your brother. We did everything we could, but I'm afraid he didn't make it. He fought hard, but his wounds were just too severe." My vision darkened at the edges and I lowered my head, letting myself fall into the abyss.

I woke up between clean sheets with my head supported by two fluffy pillows. I blinked in the darkness and saw Hugh asleep, his head at an awkward angle, in a chair next to my bed. A curtain surrounded us, providing the illusion of privacy. I could hear a roommate snoring.

I tried to sit up and realized there were tubes going into my arm. I looked at the machines next to me. Little green lights glowed in the dark. I fumbled around trying to see what was attached to me. I found a small round thing with a button on it. I pushed the button and felt instantly more relaxed. I pushed it again and floated into a deep sleep.

Sun was streaming through a large window when I opened my eyes for the second time. The curtain was gone, along with Hugh and my snoring roommate. I knew I was in the hospital. I knew my brother was dead.

I started crying. It hurt my throat and burned the cut on my cheek, but it felt better than not crying. I cried so hard that I couldn't see, I couldn't breathe, I couldn't think. I felt I was caught in a wave, and it was spinning me around. I didn't know which way was up and which was down. I became afraid that I would drown.

Hugh was suddenly at my side. "It's OK. I'm here," he said, holding my face against his chest. His love only made me feel more lost. I didn't deserve his comfort or friendship. I had taken away the man he was supposed to spend the rest of his life with. It was my fault.

I couldn't breathe, and I felt pressure building inside me. Hugh reached over, and pushed that little button. I forgot where I was, another click, why I was there, another click, who I was, one last click, what I had lost.

When I woke up, the sun was setting, filling my room with a soft orange glow. Hugh and a doctor were talking in hushed tones, and one of Nona's blankets warmed my feet. Hugh saw that I was awake and hurried to my side. The doctor left the room. "Hey, how do you feel?" My throat was dry, and I told him as much. He picked up a plastic cup from the bedside table and held its straw to my face. I sipped up water and felt it travel down my throat into my belly. I felt foggy and wobbly. I let my head fall back onto the pillow.

"I thought you might like to know that Blue is going to be OK."

"He saved my life."

"I don't know if you're up for this, but there are some police here." I didn't respond. "They want to talk to you about what happened. You know, the longer we wait, the less we have a chance of catching whoever did this. Nona gave them a description of the guy she saw going into your house with James, but she only saw the back of his head. You're really the one they want to talk to. Did you know the guy, Joy?" My brain was in too thick of a haze to figure out what to say, so I just didn't say anything. Hugh looked up and out the window.

"There's something else I need to talk to you about." He cleared his throat. "Your mother is on her way with Bill." It almost upset me. "I don't think I'll be allowed to visit you once she gets here, and I'm afraid she's going to try and mess with the funeral plans." Hugh choked up. I put my hand on top of his.

"I'll talk to her. Don't worry. We won't let her ruin his memory." Hugh swallowed and attempted a smile.

"James had a will, so it shouldn't be a problem, but I just don't trust your mother."

"Me, neither."

"She should be here by tomorrow morning."

"OK, I'll prepare myself. I've got to lay off whatever is in that clicky thing."

Hugh smiled. "Morphine."

"It's good stuff."

The door opened, and Nona walked in. "You're awake. Wonderful. All right, Hugh, she's awake, not in a fit of tears, so now you can go home for a while."

"I can wait a little more," he said.

"No you can't. Joy, this young man has to go home, because he has been here for over 24 hours."

"Hugh, go home and take a shower, get a change of clothes. I'll be fine." I smiled at him hoping he would go.

He inspected my face. "I'm fine. I can stay."

"Hugh, it would make me feel bad."

"Well, I can't go home." His face tightened. "It's a crime scene."

Nona's mouth dropped at her own insensitivity. "I don't know if I can ever go back there." Hugh hung his head. Nona crossed the room and put her arms around him. He leaned into her, and I saw him grasp at her blouse, squeezing it in his fingers.

"You can go to my house," she told him. Hugh's breath caught in his throat, and he began to cry. He sobbed into her shoulder. I held back my own tears with what strength I had left. "I have to bury Aurora," he cried. Tears sneaked out of my eyes.

"I'm so sorry," I said to his back. He turned to me, big, wet tears streaming down his face.

"It's not your fault," he said and sat down on the bed next to me. Nona put her arms around us both, and soon all three of us were sobbing. We cried for James, for Aurora, for ourselves, and for each other.

CHAPTER TWENTY-NINE

HARD CONVERSATIONS

HOURS LATER, Nona was knitting in the chair next to me, Hugh was showering in a nearby hotel, and I floated in a comforting morphine sea. Each time I began to think, started to feel pain, I clicked on my button, and away I would go.

My mother was arriving the next morning. I needed to figure out what to say to the police. The gentle click of knitting needles and the warm fuzz in my brain kept me, if not happy, at least unaware.

It was dark and quiet in the hospital when I reached for my button and didn't find it. I blinked in the darkness and saw Nona's frame silhouetted in the light leaking under the door.

"That's enough now," she said softly.

"That's up to the doctor, Nona," I argued.

"You've had enough."

"I'm in pain," I whispered. My whole body felt sour. I needed my medicine.

"You have to deal with it."

"The doctor knows how much pain I'm in. The doctor gave it to me. You can't take it away."

"My second husband died because of this." She held the controller out to her side, and I saw its shape in the darkness. I reached out for it but didn't even get close. "He was hurt in the Korean war. He had shrapnel in his hip and posterior. It made walking painful. But more than that, it made him afraid. The doctors gave him little blue pills," she swallowed loudly and continued, her voice heavy with emotion. "They took away the pain in his body, and they blotted out the memories that haunted him. He had been to hell and back, and those little blue pills let him hide from that. You can't hide from hell, Joy. It came for him as it always will, and he wasn't ready. Accidentally or on purpose I'll never know, but what I do know is that I'm not letting you march into this thing dulled on painkillers." She leaned over and kissed my forehead. "One day you'll thank me."

"Nona, please. It hurts."

"It's bound to." She sat back down, taking my button with her.

"Nona. I won't be able to sleep without it. How will I face tomorrow without a good night's sleep?" The clicking of the knitting needles started again. "Nona." She didn't respond. I leaned back. The pillows felt lumpy.

I didn't sleep again until light seeped into the sky and through the drawn blinds. Two hours later, I woke believing I was drowning in James's blood. I sat up with a start, painfully pulling on tubes in my arms. Sweat drenched my hospital gown. I was staring straight ahead at the white wall opposite me, breathing hard, when I felt another presence in the room. My mother sat in the chair by my bed watching me.

"Are you OK?" she asked. It took me a minute to realize she was real and not some sick twist in my dream.

"Hi," I said. She smiled and looked down at her hands, which were folded on top of her floral-printed skirt. I leaned back on the pillow and closed my eyes, steeling myself for the conversation ahead. It'd been almost a year since my mother and I last spoke.

"It's good to see you," she told me. I thought about our last conversation, its escalation into a screaming match, the hurt and anger I'd felt then. Funny how I used to think that was hard.

"James is dead, Mom."

"I know that." She began to twist the simple gold band on her wedding finger.

"Is Bill here?"

"He took our things to the hotel. I came straight here. He's just heartbroken about this whole thing."

"Did you see Nona?" I asked.

"Yes, she went home for a little while."

"Did you see Hugh?"

Her lips pursed. "Yes, he was arriving at the same time I was."

"I hope you didn't say anything cruel."

She opened her mouth wide to show me her shock. "I don't know what you think of me, but I would never. That young man, as confused as he may be, is in pain, and I would not want to do anything to injure him further."

"He's not confused, Mom. You are." She stood up and walked over to the window.

"Nice view."

"James left a will."

"I know." She didn't turn to look at me.

"Hugh told me he had provisions in it about his funeral." She nodded. "I want you to promise me you won't try and interfere with that." She didn't answer me. "Mom?"

"Bill says that--"

"Fuck Bill. I don't give a shit what that asshole thinks or says."

She turned on me. "He is your father," she said with all the fierceness of a stray kitten's hiss.

"No, Dad's dead. Bill is just who you married. He's warped your mind against your own children. Can't you see that?"

"James and you have turned against God, don't you understand?" She came to my bedside. "Jesus is your only hope for salvation." Her eyes filled with tears. "I just wish that James could have understood that before he--" Her voice faded away.

"Before he was murdered, Mom. Murdered." I had started to cry without noticing. "You think he's in hell, don't you?" She looked at the ground with wet eyes. "He didn't go to hell. No one as good as him, as true as him, could go to hell."

"I feel like this is all my fault. If I hadn't let the devil rule our lives for so long," she wrung her hands and watched the linoleum floor, "then you two might understand how important Jesus's love is."

"Jesus Christ, shut up. I don't need this shit right now." My tears evaporated. "Our childhood was fine until you started drinking. And even then it was better than this bullshit." I waved a hand at her bad haircut, her thick shoulder pads, her gold cross necklace and the pamphlets about Jesus I knew to be in her ridiculous purse.

"Now you can say what you want about me, but taking the Lord's name in vain--really, Joy." She pulled herself up tall. I hung my head, which she took to mean an admittance of defeat instead of the pure fatigue it really was. "Now Joy, I think that your brother, sitting from where he is now, would appreciate a service that glorifies God." I looked up at her. Her eyes were glowing the way only religious fervor can make eyes glow.

"No."

She exhaled. "I'm your mother."

"That doesn't give you the right to deny James's entire life."

"I don't deny his life." She leaned over and took my hand. "I just think it's important for you to realize God did this for a reason."

"Did what?" A burning started in my chest.

"Called him to Him."

"Killed him?" She nodded. "You think James was murdered because he was gay?"

"The Lord works right here on Earth." I pulled my hand away.

"He was your son," I told her.

"We are all God's children," she rebutted.

"You are so cold."

She reached for my hand again, but I recoiled from her. "Don't you understand? I am filled with God's love."

"Mom, if you try and make this funeral about God instead of James, I will never speak to you again, do you understand me?"

"Joy, my path is clear."

"Please."

"I'm going to do what I feel is best for my own son. Now, let's talk about something else."

"You can't. He had a will."

"There's a police officer who wants to see you. I've already spoken to him."

"Mom."

"It's important that he speak to you, and I told him that I would call him as soon as you were awake. I'll be right back." She leaned in to try and kiss me, but I dodged her. She looked at me and said, "I hope one day, before it's too late, you will come to understand." She pursed her lips and looked at me with eyes full of something I didn't understand. "Why won't you just let Jesus share some of your burden?"

"Because I don't need him. I can take responsibility for myself. My success and my failures are mine and mine alone."

"That's what you are, Joy. Alone." She stared down at me. "Your whole life you've been alone."

"I've never been alone." I sat up and felt shooting pains in all sort of places. "I always had James. When you were drunk and destroying our lives, when Dad was dying, when you were getting sober and finding God, I had James. And even now, when he's dead, I still have him. I feel bad for you that you never got to know him."

"He was my son."

"And you never knew him. You never understood him, and you never tried. Just get out." She reached a hand toward me, her eyes wet. I slapped it away, too angry to find compassion, even for my own mother. She held the slapped hand to her chest, opened her mouth to say something, thought better of it and walked to the door. She opened it and then turned to me. "Joy, the devil is at your doorstep." Her voice quivered. "If you invite him in--" Her fear at my fate stopped the words in her throat. My eyes burned, and I turned away from her. The door closed.

Hugh walked in minutes later. "She is an unbelievable bitch," I told him before the door had a chance to swing shut.

"What?"

"She believes that from where James is now, he would want his funeral to glorify God."

"No." The blood was quickly draining from Hugh's face.

"She thinks you guys were confused. She thinks we're all God's children."

"It's OK. He had a will."

"Oh, she'll get all her ridiculous God-loving buddies down here and they'll sue or protest or something. 'Bill says', 'Bill says.'" I did a lousy impression of my mother. "Calm down. It'll be all right." Hugh sat down on the edge of my bed. "No matter what she does she can't ruin our memories. Even if Jesus himself protests, we'll know. Right?"

"No wonder my brother loved you." He smiled. "What does his will actually say about his funeral?"

"Well, he wanted to be cremated and have his ashes thrown off the Brooklyn Bridge."

"That's beautiful."

"And totally illegal. So I figure we'll do it at night and then just run like crazy."

I laughed. "How James is that?"

"I know. Nona has offered to host a service at her place first, then we can walk in a procession to the bridge. I figure there's strength in numbers. If the cops try to arrest us, we can always just scatter."

"Hugh, it's hard to scatter on a bridge."

"Don't be such a defeatist," he smiled.

"Sorry."

"There's something else."

"Yeah."

"James had life insurance."

"He did?"

"It was a $100,000 policy."

"Wow."

"And he left it all to you."

"To me?"

Hugh nodded. I didn't know what to say. "You look tired."

"Hmm?"

"You want to watch TV for a little while?"

"Yeah, sure." I couldn't believe that my brother, my best friend, had a $100,000 life insurance policy. "Why didn't he tell me?" I asked Hugh, who was flipping through the stations on the little TV hanging on the wall.

"I don't know." He turned to look at me. "He just wanted to make sure that if something happened to him, you would be OK. I mean, he knew you would be OK, but he just thought this would make it easier."

I looked up at the TV in time to watch the channel change from Judge Joe Brown to New York One. The mayor's wife stood before an audience in front of a new building. "I know my husband would love to be here today. This shelter behind me means as much to him as it does to me. But even the mayor of New York gets the flu." A smattering of laughter rose from the crowd. "This new building will provide respite for the thousands of homeless mothers and children on the streets of New York. But beyond that, it will also offer educational opportunities that we hope will allow them to get off the streets and stay off them." The crowd clapped with enthusiasm. The first lady of New York smiled a perfect smile. On her ears glinted large gold earrings.

As the news cut to a commercial, Declan Doyle knocked on the door. Hugh excused himself as I clicked off the TV. Declan sat on the chair next to my bed and reached out to hold my hand. I found it hard to look at him. "How are you?" he asked softly.

"Not good."

"What happened?"

"The mayor killed my brother and tried to kill me and my dog," I blurted out. Declan dropped my hand.

"Shit. Have you told anyone else?"

Relief washed over me. He believed me. It felt amazing to have it off my chest. "I have not talked to anyone else. I didn't know what to do."

"All right," Doyle stood up and crossed to the window. "I'll get you some money and you can get out of here."

"What?"

"You've got to go Joy, you've got to run." He looked back at me, his brow was creased, and he frowned. "I'm sorry, but it's the way it's got to be."

"What, and let him get away with it?" I sat up in bed, pushing the covers back.

"What?" Declan laughed. "You think you're going to take him down? *You're* going to stop Kurt Jessup."

"Well--"

"Joy, he will be taken care of, I'm sure."

"What do you mean?"

"Karma, sweetheart." He smiled at me.

"You're joking. My brother's been murdered and you're joking with me right now. Are you fucking mad?"

"I'm not the one claiming that the mayor is a killer. You sound crazy Joy, and that's how everyone will treat you."

"Get out," I said.

"Look, I know you're upset, but I'm trying to help you."

"Really, because it sounds like you're trying to help the murdering bastard who killed my brother!"

"Joy, calm down."

"Get the fuck out of this room before I make you." I picked up my glass of water and threw it at him. It fell short, spilling all over the floor.

Declan looked down at it. "Joy, listen to me. I really like you. You're a hell of a girl. That's why I'm telling you that if you want to live, get your shit together and leave New York City." He looked up from the floor and caught my eyes with his. "If you're not gone by the end of the month I won't be able to help you after that."

"What does that mean?"

But Doyle didn't answer me. He stepped over the spilled water and walked out the door.

I do not think of myself as the type of person to learn something from my dreams, but while I was sleeping I figured out what I had to tell the police. It was a vivid and nasty dream, but it solved a problem. I called Mulberry to tell him about it.

"Wait, why are you going to lie to the police? Why make up a story? Don't you want them to catch whoever did this to you?"

I squeezed my eyes shut. Was everyone an idiot? "Have you really not figured it out yet?" I asked him. There was silence. "Get this, the mayor is not dead--yet." I hung up.

Detective Heart showed up as I clicked down the receiver. He had a friendly smile that implied he could be trusted. Detective Heart, who insisted I call him John, sat down in the only chair in the room.

"Joy--can I call you Joy?"

"Sure."

"Joy, I know this is hard for you. You've been through more than I can imagine." His empathy meant more when contrasted with my mother's reaction. His big, warm eyes and soft voice made me sad that I would have to lie to him. "I can only guess at how much you want your brother's killer caught. But let me tell you that I want it very much." He leaned toward me, earnest.

"I appreciate that."

"I need you to help me."

I wanted to. I really did. I wanted to tell John Heart everything. I wanted to lay all the weight of the thing on him, but I knew I couldn't do that. He would never believe me. "I wish I could help you, but I just don't remember anything about that night," I said.

"Tell me what you do remember."

"I walked into my apartment, and then I woke up here."

"What about the night before your brother was killed?"

"I remember it."

"Nona said you were attacked in the park?" I nodded. "Where did you sleep that night?"

"At Detective Mulberry's place, of the 67th Precinct." John didn't seem surprised.

"Why?"

"I ran into him in the park right after it happened."

"Why didn't you file a complaint with him?"

"I really just wanted to sleep somewhere I felt safe. I promised I would go to the station with him in the morning if he would just let me stay at his place."

"Wasn't he recently thrown off a murder investigation and placed on suspension because it was suspected that he had mistreated you?"

"That wasn't true."

"Why would someone think that?"

"I don't know."

"Why didn't you clear his name?"

"No one asked me."

"Are you sleeping together?" That caught me off guard for no good reason. "No. No."

"But you're close?"

"Sort of. It's not like he's been to visit me."

"You said he made you feel safe."

"He's a cop."

"Cops are often scary, especially to people your age."

"Not him."

"What about this attack in the park. Can you tell me about it?"

"Yes." He waited for me to continue. "I was walking through the park, and as I was passing the Peter Pan statue, a man grabbed me from behind. He threw me into the bushes. He punched me and told me he was going to rape me." John was watching my face. I looked down at my hands and tried really hard to believe my lie. "He unzipped his pants. I kicked at him, and he punched me again. I struggled and he wrapped his hands around my throat." A tear dropped onto the sheets. "I thought I was going to die. But just as I was about to black out, I managed to buck him off me and climb out of the bushes. I ran blindly through the park, but I don't think he followed. I ran right into Mulberry. He made me walk back and show him where it had happened and look around for the guy, but he was gone."

"So he didn't radio for a search?"

"I really just wanted to go somewhere safe." I looked up at John again.

He pulled out a small, black, spiral-bound notebook and a knobby pencil from inside his suit jacket. He licked the pencil, flipped open the book, and wrote something down. Then he looked back at me. "Could you recognize the man who attacked you in the park?"

"Maybe. It's all such a blur."

"Do you think it was someone you knew?

"No." The question made me nervous.

"Did you know that Marcus Nygel has been seen around your building?"

"We used to date," I said stupidly.

He smiled. "Yes, I know. I think it's possible that he is a little obsessed with you." I didn't know what was happening all of a sudden. My lies were choking me. "Do you think that's possible?"

"I'm sure that it wasn't him."

"Sometimes it's hard to think something like this about someone you cared for, but it's more likely that you knew the killer of your brother than that you didn't."

"I would know if it was him. I mean, I was with him for a while," I protested.

"Just think about it. Try to think about how he's been acting since the breakup."

"Not like a stalker." John stood up to leave. "Wait. I really think you have the wrong idea here. Marcus didn't do this. He wouldn't."

"I've got a lot of leads to follow up on. If you can remember anything--stuff might come back to you over the next few days--call me. Anytime." He placed a card on the bedside table.

"I--" I couldn't think of anything else to say.

"Just think about it." And he was gone.

CHAPTER THIRTY

THE BATTLE BEGINS

I FLITTED in and out of sleep unsure of what time or day it was. My father, who died in a hospital when I was a child, became very paranoid toward the end of his life. He told my mother that they were trying to kill him because at night, in the dark, he would try and pull out the tube that ran down his nose to feed him, and the staff restrained him to save him. He mistook this as attempted murder.

Me, I was right that someone was trying to kill me when I woke up in the night, in the dark, to find my face covered by a pillow. Strong hands pushed down on my nose and mouth. I thrashed under the pressure and knocked my arm into one of the metal gates on the side of my bed meant to keep me from inadvertently tumbling to the ground. I reached through it and felt blindly at a man's leg. My lungs felt on the verge of explosion when I found his balls.

He screamed, the sound muffled by the pillow, when I dug my nails into the soft, sensitive flesh that is woman's most trusted weapon against man. He let go of my face and grabbed at my hand, but I'm not one to let go. I sat up, knocking the pillow off my face and punched the asshole right in the throat with my free hand. He staggered back struggling for breath. I swung my legs off the bed to stand up and continue the fight, but instead I became incredibly nauseous. I wavered on the edge, gripping at the mattress, watching my attacker regain his breath.

Anger bloomed across his face as the pain subsided. I knew if I didn't do something soon I was fucked. He came at me, his fist clenched, and when he was about to strike I puked. It hurt like hell, my whole body ached from the effort and my throat burned worse than ever. He jumped back, covered in my vomit, looking down at his soiled scrubs disgusted.

The overhead light flickered on, and I could see the man for the first time. He was medium- sized with brown hair and no distinguishing features. Dressed like all the other nurses on the ward he was the kind of guy no one would notice. The perfect hit man, I thought. "Holy shit," I heard Hugh say behind me. I turned, ignoring the searing pain in my neck, to see him in the doorway, his hand still resting on the light switch. "What's going on?" he asked.

Before I could speak, my attacker did. "I came in to give her a fresh pillow, and she attacked me!"

"What! That is bullshit. He was trying to kill me." My voice was weak, and it hurt to speak. I suddenly felt exhausted. The stink of my vomit filled the room, and it was all I could do not to retch again. Hugh looked from me to the hit man and then back. I followed his eyes and saw that from his viewpoint we looked like a nurse and a patient. To be honest the patient looked nuts. "He did," I said, but my conviction was lost to fatigue. "Hugh?"

"I think you should go," Hugh said to the man. As he began to leave, Hugh said, "And can you send someone in to clean this up."

"Sure."

"He won't send anyone," I said, "because he's not a real nurse. He's a hit man." My heart was racing, but my body and mind were moving in slow motion. I knew it wasn't safe to stay in that room, but I didn't have the strength to get out of there.

"All right," Hugh said, "How about I find you a nice clean gown?" I looked down at myself and nodded. Hugh was helping me change when a nurse wearing scrubs covered in pictures of teddy bears came in.

"Oh honey," she said, "You shouldn't try and get up." She swung my legs back into the bed smiling at me. "You've got trauma girl." For some

reason her calling me girl sounded nice. I smiled at her. "Any fast movement will make you puke."

"Who was that guy?" Hugh asked her.

"Who?" the nurse asked as she readjusted the pillow behind my head.
"The nurse who told you to come in here, that she'd puked."

The nurse was holding up my head, putting the pillow under it,
when she replied, "I don't know what you're talking about, sweetie. I'm
just doing my rounds. No one came to tell me anything."

I was so tired all I could say was, "Hugh, please don't leave me. I
don't want to die." I felt him take my hand and squeeze it before I drifted
off to sleep.

I checked myself out of the hospital the next day. The doctor explained
to me that my body had experienced a severe trauma and that they could
help me. That without them it was going to be--and then his pager went
off, and he didn't finish his sentence.

A nurse wheeled me out of my room, down a long hallway with
white, scuff-marked walls and fluorescent lighting. Her shoes squeaked
on the green linoleum that was graying with age. We rode an elevator
two floors down, then maneuvered around a moaning figure on a
stretcher to get out the front door.

It was hot, and I was sick. As Hugh helped me into a cab, I wondered
how crazy I really was.

The next morning I went to pick up milk at the bodega. I looked
down and thought I was standing in a puddle of thick, red blood. I
picked up my foot, and it stuck to it like gum. Before I began to scream,
it was just the floor again. The woman behind the counter with the long
nails was shocked by my face. "My God," she said. "What happened?"

"I'm fine," I told her.

"Your boyfriend beat you up?"

"No, nothing like that. I was in a car accident."

"Oh yeah, that happens."

I kept waking in the middle of the night hearing James calling my name. Cars backfired and I freaked. I eyed every average-looking person, as nondescript as my last assassin. I thought they were going to kill me.

I was staying at Nona's because my apartment was a crime scene. My mother called me every day, and we fought for custody of James's corpse. Reporters called, too. They wanted to know who killed my brother. Why I couldn't remember? Were Mulberry and I "an item"? Did he murder James? Did I have a comment? If they would just shut up!

I picked up Blue from the veterinary hospital. He was different. He was always on guard, watching out for me. A large white bandage covered his left shoulder. I changed it twice a day, marveling at how quickly his body was healing itself.

I thought for sure my dog-walking route would be gone until I checked my messages and heard Elaine telling me that she and the girls would cover it for me as long as I needed. Their generosity made me break down and cry. Blue rushed to my side and put his head on my knee.

Hugh and I called all of James's friends, the same crowd that had gathered only two weeks earlier for the house-warming party. My mother invited her friends and planned to petition for James's body.

"We should just steal it, burn it, and toss it off the bridge," Hugh said as we sat on Nona's couch planning our defense.

"We can't steal it," I told him. Hugh huffed and took a sip of the coffee Nona placed in front of him.

"I think you have to appeal to your mother in some way," Nona suggested.

"Maybe a decapitated horse head in her bed would do it," Hugh suggested, only partly joking. Nona and I laughed. Hugh grimaced. He had lost weight, enough for me to notice.

"Hugh, you all right?" I asked him.

"Stupid question, Joy." He leaned back on the couch and rubbed his temples.

"Sorry."

He looked over at me. "No, I'm sorry. I just haven't been sleeping."

"I'm sorry. You're right. It was a dumb question. Neither of us is OK. It will take a long time before we are."

He gave me a weary smile and squeezed my arm. "You've lost some weight."

"Funny, I was going to say the same to you."

"I can solve that," Nona said as she disappeared into the kitchen.

"Maybe Nona's right. Maybe you should go to your mother and try and talk to her," Hugh said.

"How? She's insane."

"Either you persuade her not to do this, or we're going to have to fight her in court and in the media for James's body." Hugh's voice broke. I put a hand on his knee.

"I'll try," I told him.

"We just have to figure out how to appeal to her," Hugh said. Nona walked back in and put two slices of dark chocolate-chip cake in front of us and smiled broadly.

"Now, eat up. It's good for you."

CHAPTER THIRTY-ONE

BLACKMAIL?

BILL AND APRIL Madden were staying at the Luxor. As I rang the bell to their room I had to resist the urge to make some sort of comment about how well God paid. Bill answered the door holding a glass of Scotch and wearing a hotel robe. Ice clinked when he turned to yell to my mother that I was there. He turned back to me, with more clinking, and smiled, his lips sliding over his teeth.

"Good to see you, Joy," he told me, starting at my feet and ending at my breasts. I swallowed my revulsion.

"Bill." I gave him a tight-lipped smile. A large gold cross hung around his neck, nestled in his graying chest hair. I remembered when that hair was jet black, and he'd wanted me to sit on his lap. My mother came out of the bathroom, her makeup freshly applied.

"Hi, Mom."

"Hi." She smiled. Her foundation cracked, making her instantly older.

"Can I talk to you alone?" I asked over Bill's hulking figure.

"Anything you need to say to her you can say in front of me," Bill interjected, rocking back on his heels and puffing out his chest. He didn't even look at my mother. He kept his eyes locked just south of mine.

"This is a mother-daughter thing, Bill," I told him with a very fake smile on my face. "Woman-talk." I tried to sound cheerful.

His gaze moved to his feet, and he thought for a moment. "I guess you two could go downstairs," he finally came up with.

"OK, Mom?"

"Sure," she said. We rode the elevator in silence. I rehearsed my speech in my head. Nona, Hugh, and I had worked on it for hours. We hoped it would persuade her to let James have his dignity. When I looked over at her, she was watching the numbers light up one at a time. She didn't look as though she had been sleeping well. Even under all that paint, I could see dark circles around her eyes. I hoped it was because she missed her son and not because she was worried that he was burning in hell.

The elevator dinged, and we stepped out into the gilded lobby. There was an overpriced coffee shop with several people sitting around with luggage waiting either for a room or a ride. We took a table away from everyone else and silently read our menus. I ordered chamomile tea, and my mother a glass of water. We looked out the window at the Manhattan street as people with umbrellas hurried by in the rain. We watched as a woman in a navy suit fought with an inside-out umbrella, eventually taming it and then continuing on her way. I scanned the passing pedestrians, looking for anyone who might want to hurt me.

Our water and tea arrived, the waitress walked away, and I began, "Mom, I'm here to beg you one last time to let James have the funeral he wanted."

She sipped her water, not taking her eyes off the street. "I can't do that."

"But why not?"

"Bill and I have sworn to spend our lives fighting for God. I am God's soldier."

"This is your own son. He didn't want this. Can't you respect other people's wishes? Not even other people. Can't you respect your own son's wishes?"

"He didn't know what was best for him, and I couldn't help him in life."

"Do you think doing this will in any way change his fate?"

"It's the right thing to do." She looked back at me. Her eyelids, colored crayon-blue, hung heavy.

"Mom, I love you. James loved you. But if you do this you will have lost not only your son but also your daughter."

"I have to do what is right." She looked down at her water.

"I didn't want to have to do this."

"What?"

I took a deep breath before continuing. "I will tell the world that Bill molested me when I was a teenager." My mother gasped.

"He never did such a thing," she said, her eyes wide, her mouth gaping.

"Doesn't mean I won't say he did."

"But no one will believe you."

"Yes, they will. Why wouldn't they?"

"Because he is a man of God."

"Even if only a couple of people believe me, it will be enough. I can ruin him and you. I will do it if I have to." She couldn't believe what I was saying. "I'm serious, Mom. In fact, I think I would even enjoy it a little."

"This is blackmail."

"Maybe."

"You can't do this."

"I just did." I stood up to leave. "Talk it over with Bill." I turned and walked away.

"Joy!" she yelled after me. I turned to look at her. She was so small, and so silly-looking it almost broke my heart. "Please," she said. The other people in the shop were watching us, and the waitress was getting nervous. I walked away.

Later that night, I got a call from Bill. He screamed at me that I was going to hell, and I almost believed him. Then my mother got on the phone and begged for me not to do this. Eventually she told me I could do whatever I wanted with James. I tried to remind her that it was what *he* wanted, not I, but she had already hung up. Hugh was as happy as one can be about earning the right to give the love of your life the send-off he wanted.

I got a call from Mulberry the morning of the funeral. It was a stormy Saturday. The trees outside Nona's window bent in the wind, exposing the silver-green of the leaves' underbellies. "How have you been?" he asked.

"Never been worse," I told him.

"Can we talk in person?"

"Not today."

"This isn't over."

"Oh. I know."

"Call me when you're ready."

"I will."

The worst of the storm proceeded east, spreading its turmoil to the ocean. Waves whipped white and lightning crackled. New York City's streets shone black and wet, dotted with green leaves recently ripped from branches. Occasional gusts of wind caught in the maze of buildings whooshed down streets, splattering resting raindrops violently to the ground. People started arriving at Nona's soon after the sun set. Nona, then me, then Hugh, then an ice-cold martini, greeted each guest.

We drank for a while at the apartment. Everyone told stories of James's compassion, his sense of humor, and his vibrant life. I felt like there should be something cathartic about the funeral. Standing with the people who loved James, shouldn't I feel that some of my grief rested on their shoulders? Even if only for a moment, I wanted to breathe. But their loss only compounded mine. It was all my fault.

The mood turned sober as we walked toward the bridge. We must have looked strange, 30-some-odd people dressed for a funeral walking in a pack through the streets of Brooklyn. Pedestrians moved out of our way instinctively. Hugh held James's ashes. We walked with our heads held high.

My mother did not show. I wondered where she was as we reached the edge of the bridge. Was she already on her way back home to continue her work? Was she crying at the hotel knowing that she was missing her only son's funeral because her mind couldn't wrap itself around something simply different? Would she regret this for the rest of her life, or would she feel righteous and hateful forever?

The wind on the bridge whipped my hair around. My skirt and those of the other women pressed against one side of us. Men's suit jackets flapped. But we pushed on toward the bright lights of the city.

Hugh stopped us in the middle of the bridge. "Can everyone hear me?" he yelled over the rushing wind. People nodded. "This is totally illegal, so after we open the canister and we watch the ashes fall, we really ought to run. Those of you in the back should run back to Brooklyn and those of us in the front will run to Manhattan." More nods. "Before we go, I'd like to thank you all for coming. I know James would have loved this." People smiled sadly, and I felt a clench in my chest. Hugh turned to me. "Ready?"

"As much as I'll ever be." We leaned over the edge. Hugh removed the lid of the urn and tilted it toward the turbulent black water below. A gust of wind shot up just then and took James's ashes. They poured out of the urn and twisted up into the light-polluted clouds. The wind stopped, and James remained suspended right in front of us for just a moment. Then the gust continued on its way. Up, up, and away. Hugh wrapped his hand into mine, and we ran.

I woke up on Nona's couch with Blue on top of me. He was crushing my legs, and I tried to push him off me. He warbled with his eyes closed, pretending to be asleep. I couldn't help but laugh. Nona came into the room and smiled at my predicament.

"Tea?" she asked.

"Please." I pushed Blue onto the floor and made my way into the bathroom. I turned on the tap and started brushing my teeth. Since the funeral, everyone I talked to kept saying that now my life would get back to normal. The suggestion being that James's death was something I, like most victims of violent crime, would recover from, that one day it would no longer sit on top of my brain affecting every single fucking second of my life.

The people who thought my life could be normal again didn't know shit. Someone tried to kill me, and it was only a matter of time before they came back and tried again. I was so scared that I actually left fear behind--like when it gets so hot that you stop feeling the heat, and everything is just in slow motion.

The bruising on my face was still a brilliant yellow with patches of green. The finger marks on my neck were already gone. The cuts stayed hidden under bandages, which I pulled off as a part of my morning routine. I applied fresh Vaseline, then new white cotton pads. I knew that within the week the stitches would dissolve and I'd be left with just white scar lines. I thought it was possible I might miss the pain, the constant tending to the wounds. They were this very real, easy reminder of how much I hurt.

"You want toast?" Nona asked through the door.

"Yeah," I said. The doorbell rang. When I walked out of the bathroom, my mother was standing on the threshold. She looked uncomfortable and tired. Her face was bare, her skin sagging on the bones. I recognized James's and my gray eyes.

"How about I take Blue out for his walk?" Nona suggested, slipping into a pair of clogs. "Come on, boy." Blue bounded over to her, holding his leash in his mouth. "What a good boy," Nona cooed. They left, and I was alone with my mother.

"You can come in," I told her, my voice hard and defensive. She took small steps into the hall, and I closed the door behind her. I gestured for her to continue into the living room. We sat down on Nona's couch after I pushed my bedding to one side. "What do you want?"

"I just wanted to come and say good-bye. Bill and I are leaving now."

"Good-bye." She twisted her wedding ring and looked at me with wide eyes. "You have something to say?"

"I'm worried about you."

I smiled. "Don't be."

"Are you OK for money?"

"Yes."

"Where will you live?"

"I don't know."

She looked out the window. "I remember when your grandparents first moved here."

"Yeah."

"We were close then, you know?"

"I know."

"We were so young--" She looked back at me and didn't finish her thought.

"I know, Ma. I know."

"I wish--I wish I could be a better mother to you."

"So do I."

Her eyes filled with tears. "I love you very much." Her chin shook uncontrollably. Tears dripped down her face and onto that stupid wedding ring that she just kept turning round and round.

"I love you too, Mom." I didn't want to cry, but she grasped at me. She pulled me into her, and she still smelled like my mother--like the woman who made my lunches, walked me to the school bus, who had laughed at all my Dad's jokes. She still smelled like she was supposed to. So I cried, too. We cried together because James was dead, because we didn't even know each other, because there was nothing left to do but sob.

She wiped the tears off my face with the hem of her awful skirt, and I smiled at her. "I wish you had come to the funeral, Mom."

"I should have," she said, a hint of defiance in her voice.

"Was it Bill?" She looked back down at her wedding ring.

"He has very high expectations of me," she told me. I didn't want to argue, so I left it at that. "I want to give you something," my mom said after a moment of silence. She reached for her white leather purse, opened the giant brass clasp, and pulled out an envelope. "This is from Bill and me, to help you get back on your feet." She pushed it into my hands and stood up quickly. I could tell it was money.

"Mom, I don't want this." She was already moving toward the door, and I followed her quickly. "I don't need this." She opened the door and was going to leave. I grabbed her wrist. "I'm not taking it."

"Oh, please, please do."

"I don't want this money. It's dirty." She was about to start to cry again.

"Please. I want you to have it," she said.

"Do the people who donated it want me to have it?" She pulled herself free from me and fled down the hall. I started to follow her but gave up before I'd even begun the chase. Her skirt swished behind her as she disappeared down the stairs. I stayed staring at that empty hall for a long time, trembling.

CHAPTER THIRTY-TWO

SOME DREAMS DO COME TRUE

AS I WALKED from the subway east toward the river, my stomach clenched, flipped, and threatened to empty itself. When I was last here, James was alive. He was walking around talking to people. And now he was a million little pieces in the air, all around me, everywhere.

Snowball jumped up in her cage, pushing her small pink paws through the bars when she saw me. At the dog run, I got a bunch of hugs, some sorrowful nods, and all the gossip. It was good to just sit there and let them talk. I heard about the new doorman at one of Fiona's buildings and the puppy a young couple had bought. "Having trouble with house-training," Marcia told me.

"They should be here soon," Fiona said, looking around.

"It's funny," Elaine whispered to me.

"They are so desperate to praise him for going outside they scare him," Marcia said.

"They've read too much," Fiona decided.

"Have you guys heard anything about Julen?" They all looked away from me. "What?" Marcia glanced at my face and then at a nearby tree. "Guys, what's going on?"

"He killed himself," Marcia mustered the courage to tell me.

"No." I felt a sinking inside me.

"I'm afraid so. His testimony is what got Mrs. Saperstein indicted and after that--in fact that same night, he cut his wrists." I couldn't speak. Poor Julen. He had been caught in the middle of something so not to do with him, and it killed him. I wondered if he'd killed himself or been murdered. But it didn't matter whether by his own hand or someone else's--this was all Kurt Jessup's fault. And poor Mrs. Saperstein was going through hell because her husband had wanted to run away with his lover.

"This is horrible," I said.

"At least that Jacquelyn is getting what she deserves," Fiona said. "If it weren't for her, Julen would still be alive."

"Not to mention her husband," Marcia added.

"You guys really think she did it?" I asked.

"Isn't it obvious? I mean Julen admitted that she wasn't with him. She was the only one who had access to that toupee; she matches the description of the woman seen leaving the scene of the crime."

"But isn't that all circumstantial? I mean, is there any physical evidence?" I asked.

"Her fingerprints are on the toupee," Fiona told me.

"But Toby chewed on it. How could there be prints?" I defended her.

"If it wasn't her leaving the scene of the crime, who was it?" Elaine asked, her face the picture of innocence. The other women nodded.

"I don't know," I admitted.

I walked into Snaffles' house and discovered Cecelia asleep on the couch, a picture of her younger, accused sister, held to her breast. I listened to the gentle purring she made as she slept and had an over-whelming urge to protect her--to stop all the pain she had ever known, to solve all of her problems. But that was stupid. So instead I took the dog for a walk.

Although the day was warm, I felt chilled. A strong wind blew off the river and raised goose bumps on my skin. I felt someone watching me. Turning quickly around, I saw him--the hulking stranger, the man with the hot breath. He was walking behind me, following me.

At first I thought he was there to kill me, but he just watched. I decided to call the large man following me Bob. Bob followed me all day. At first Bob tried to hide himself, but soon he realized (I waved at him) that I knew he was there. Whether behind a tree, around the corner, riding in a different elevator, I knew Bob was with me. He watched Snaffles and I go around the block; he meandered through the park as Toby and I walked in it. Bob stood outside Charlene's building when I went to see Oscar. But Oscar was gone. The apartment was empty. I hoped Charlene had come for him, but an open window worried me. I filled his food and water, just in case he decided to come home.

After my work was done, Bob followed me to the subway and observed me get on a train headed for Brooklyn. I don't know why Bob didn't kill me. Maybe the mayor was saving that for himself. Or maybe, just maybe, he was afraid of me. I'd proved myself pretty hard to kill, I thought, as the train passed over the Manhattan Bridge, and I looked out into the darkening skyline. Maybe I made Kurt Jessup nervous, and just maybe he didn't know what to do about me.

I went to Nona's, picked up Blue, and went walking. I headed deeper into Brooklyn. Blue followed me, not bothering to pull over for whiffs of trees or sniffs of trash cans. He stayed directly behind my left leg; we moved in unison.

I wasn't looking for answers or a solution or anything, I was just walking. I was a little surprised when I found a gun shop. "You ever used one of these before?" the greasy man on the other side of the counter asked me. I didn't answer him.

"I want one that holds a lot of bullets." I paused. "And I need a silencer." The man's yellowed tongue shot out and flicked at his chapped lips.

"You need a permit for that kind of thing, you know."

"Show me that one." I pointed through the glass at a nice-sized silver gun. He placed it in front of me. "Can I get a silencer for this?" He turned around, opened a drawer, and came back with a black silencer. He screwed it onto the end. "I'll take it," I told him. He put the gun down in front of me.

"It takes a couple of days. You can't just walk out of here with a gun."

I pulled out my mother's envelope of guilt money and laid hundred-dollar bills on the counter until the gun was in its box, in an unmarked bag. I held a bill in the air and asked, "Bullets?" He dropped a box into the bag. I placed the bill on the top of the stack, picked up my purchases, and left. The weight of the bag filled me with a deep and satisfying pleasure.

That night on Nona's couch, I dreamed I was on top of the mayor, pushing on his eyes. But this time I didn't pussy out. This time I pushed his eyes into his head. Blood exploded out the back of his skull, and he laughed and laughed.

I decided to take the gun to work with me the next day. It is illegal to carry a gun in New York City, let alone one you don't have a permit for, but I didn't care. If anything, I liked the element of danger the gun brought to my daily life. I liked the weight of it in my purse but decided that I wanted a shoulder strap just like the good guys on TV--or maybe a garter holder. Wouldn't that be sexy?

A large woman sat across from me on the subway as I pictured the perfect place to put my pistol. She was not just wide but also tall. She sat in the middle of two seats, on the rise meant to separate them. She had long red hair with white roots, yellow teeth, and an under bite. Her tank top revealed soft arms with hairy pits. Her eyes were a clear, focused blue.

She was listening to an iPod that she held in one of her large, manly hands. "Ya'll gonna make me lose my cool," she half sang, half said out loud. "Take some shit," she bobbed her head. "All was his pain, they say we could play the game." On the chorus, "X is gonna give it to you, X is gonna give it to you," she bounced with the music, first to the left and then to the right.

At the Brooklyn Bridge stop, a mariachi band boarded the train in costume. The beaded jackets and sombreros sparkled under the florescence. They began to play a sweet and sad song. The men swayed with the motion of the train and just managed to be heard over its squeaking and wheezing. The woman across from me continued to bounce and announce that X would indeed get us all. The mariachis sang a song I didn't understand but guessed was about a love first found and then lost. One or two of the other riders glanced up to look at the brightly dressed men and then returned their gaze to whatever they had brought to look at. No one looked at the woman across from me.

My phone beeped to let me know I had a message as I stepped out of the dark subway into another sun-filled July day. "Hi, Joy. This is John Heart. Give me a call back when you get a chance." I called him back.

"Joy, I wanted to let you know that we're going to be able to let you back into your apartment this week."

"I'm moving."

"I can understand. The thing is, it's a rental, right?"

"Yeah."

"That means you're responsible for the cleanup." I couldn't hear for a second as a bus barreled past me.

"Cleanup?" I asked.

"There are specialists who clean up crime scenes."

"Specialists?" Here was something I had never thought about.

"Yes. They're like house cleaners. I mean, they are house cleaners, but they just clean up after crime scenes. You know, spackle bullet holes, rip up stained carpet and replace it. Or in the case of hardwood floors they-- I'm sorry."

"That's OK." I thought about the stains that James had left in my house, about the bullet I fired into my molding.

"I talked to someone about taking care of it for you, and he's willing to do it for $1,000. You should be able to recoup most the cost from the Crime Victims Reparations Agency."

"OK."

"Would you like me to arrange it?"

"Please."

"All right, I'll call you back with some details."

"John?"

"Yeah?"

"Do you know anything yet? Do you know who did it?" I held the phone hard against my ear and watched traffic fight forward.

"Not yet. We're following some strong leads, though. I'll let you know."

"OK." I hung up and put the phone in my bag, next to my gun, which I squeezed.

Snowball and I did not go directly to the dog run. Instead, we made a circle around Gracie Mansion. I tried to look in through the windows, but the reflection in combination with curtains prevented me from seeing anything. I wanted to see the mayor. I wanted to see what I'd done to his face. Snowball wanted to chase pigeons--a true waste of time.

I gave up on the mansion and headed over to the dog run. Bob joined me, a cup of coffee in his meaty fist. We walked along the river. I looked out at Hell's Gate, its waters churning dangerously. A ship sank in those waters in 1780 and now, over 200 years later, people were dying because of it. How much treasure had the mayor found? How much treasure does it take to murder a man? I thought back to my own inability to kill and assured myself that it would not happen again.

Later that day, Snaffles and I walked into The Excelsior, a hotel on 80th Street between Second and Third Avenues. The Excelsior was built in the '70s and preserved. The lobby floor was covered in shag carpeting. A bizarre, faux crystal installation, reminiscent of Superman's fortress of solitude, covered one wall. Snaffles sniffed with interest at a dark red stain. Bob waited outside, attempting to see through the tinted glass front door.

"Do you have suites?" The bored-looking man lounging behind the wood-paneled front desk nodded. He was the first person since the fight not to stare at my wounds.

"I'd like to see one." He motioned to an eager young bellboy to come over. The boy half-ran, half-walked, in a way that made him look like a duck in a hurry. The guy behind the desk handed the bellboy a key and motioned for us to go with a flip of his wrist.

The elevator stuttered on its way up to the fifth floor. The bellboy smiled at me wildly and then stared stonily at the elevator floor. Then the big smile again. The hallway we walked down was dark, not only because of the deep-brown carpeting and burgundy walls, but also because most of the lightbulbs in the fixtures that lined the corridor were burned out.

"Nice lighting," I joked. The bellboy smiled back at me as he led the way to room 523. It was a shit hole. The brown carpeting from the hall continued into the living room of the suite. The walls, originally painted white, through years of smoking were stained the same yellow as old men's fingers.

The couch was the same rough material of airport waiting seats. The coffee table, dotted with burns and scratches, wobbled. "Joanie loves Chachi" was markered onto the bathroom wall along with the news that Harriet was a slut.

Beige carpet with cloud-like water stains covered the walls of the bedroom. The bed, large and lumpy, took up most of the floor space. The bellboy smiled at me shyly and pointed to the ceiling. It had a mirror on it.

"I'll take it," I told the man downstairs. "I'll pay for two weeks now, and I want a discount. There is no way in hell I'm paying $250 a night for that shit hole." He feigned surprise but got bored halfway through.

"One fifty," he suggested.

"A hundred bucks a night." I put $1,400 in cash on the counter between us. He shrugged, swept it up, and handed me the key. "One more thing." I laid another $200 on the counter. "Anyone asks, I'm staying in room 784. You get me?" The man smiled and slid the money off the counter.

Marcus phoned while I was returning Snaffles to his empty house. "That cop thinks I killed James, that I was stalking you," he opened with.

"I told him it wasn't you."

"You need to tell him again. I can't work. I can't sleep. They keep coming to talk to me."

"That must be real hard for you."

"It is. Joy, I'm scared," he squeaked.

"Nothing is going to happen to you. You didn't do it."

"But," he whined, "this is really hard."

"Marcus. Who do you think this is harder on? You or me?" Silence. "How 'bout you try watching your brother die, and then tell me about what's hard, you prick." I slammed the phone shut. It rang again almost immediately. Without checking the caller I.D., I started yelling. "Don't call me anymore!"

"Whoa, whoa, whoa," came a voice I didn't recognize across the line.

"Hello?"

"Hi, this is Marty Schwartman, James Humbolt's lawyer. Is this his sister, Joy?"

"I'm sorry. I thought you were someone else."

He laughed easily. "I figured that one out. I've been trying to reach you but I think I had the wrong number."

"Oh?"

"We need to talk about your brother's assets. I've already spoken with Hugh Defry, the only other beneficiary."

"OK."

"Where do you work? I could come by on your lunch hour."

"I'm a dog-walker on the Upper East Side."

"Great. I'm in East Midtown. Where would you like to meet?"

"The Excelsior Hotel, room 523."

There was a pause on the other line, just long enough for me to notice but not long enough to be rude. "Tomorrow, about 1?" he suggested.

"Sounds good."

Bob once again left me at the train station. I went back to Nona's. She wasn't there, so I wrote her a note thanking her for taking such good care of me and left my new address at the Excelsior. I packed the few items of clothing I had and put a leash on Blue. I picked up a bottle of tequila at the liquor store and then hopped on the subway acting like it was legal to bring a giant dog on the train.

Halfway there I opened the bottle of tequila and took a painful swig. A child watched me with big, glistening eyes. Her mother, without looking at me, distracted him with a colorful stuffed toy that had lots of legs.

I stumbled on the steps on my way out of the subway, scraping my knee on the filthy cement. Blue whined and licked my face. I picked myself up and walked to the Excelsior. The man behind the desk didn't move as I walked by him to the elevator.

Once in my room I placed the bottle of tequila on the coffee table. I pulled my gun out of my bag and put it next to the tequila. I found my bullets and spilled them onto the coffee table. A couple of them rolled onto the floor. They were gold and pretty looking. I ran my hands over their smooth surfaces, pushing them around.

The next morning I woke up naked in bed with a big hangover. I walked barefoot into the living room and grabbed a $7 beer out of the mini bar and opened it on the bottle opener attached to my bathroom wall. I didn't look in the mirror.

When I got to the dog run about a half-hour later, Marcia took one look at me and told me to go home. I started to protest, but when I saw that even Elaine was looking at me with pity, I put Snowball's leash into Fiona's outstretched hand and walked back to the Excelsior.

I took a nap on my face, on the couch. I woke up with drool on my cheek and a cramp in my back. Someone was knocking on the door. I stumbled on my shoes, then opened the door to a short, sweaty man wearing a suit and thick glasses. "Joy, I assume? Call me Marty." He handed me a card that had his name on it followed by "Esq."

"Come in." Blue sniffed him intently before letting him pass. Marty took it well. I threw myself back down on the couch. Marty perched on the edge of the coffee table, ignoring that it was covered in bullets and spilled tequila.

"I've actually been working on this thing for a while. Like I told you, I couldn't get ahold of you." He opened his briefcase and pulled out a file. "Your brother made you the beneficiary of his life insurance." I nodded. He rifled through the folder. "So here is your check."

"What?" I sat up too fast, and for a second my vision swarmed with black dots. He handed me the check. It had my name on it, and it was for $100,000.

"What do I do with it?" I asked stupidly.

"Whatever you want. It's all yours."

"Oh." He stood up.

"All right, Ms. Humbolt. I'm happy we got this sorted out. Good luck to you." I stayed seated on the couch, and he let himself out.

"Thank you," I said long after the door had clicked shut.

CHAPTER THIRTY-THREE

A PROPOSITION

HOURS LATER, after the sunset, and the street lights turned on, Blue and I went out looking for food. Bob was asleep on one of the couches in the lobby. His face looked almost sweet in sleep. Bob had not shaved in a day or two. He was working on a nice set of crow's feet. Bob's hair was thinning, running away from his face. He didn't look so big or so mean.

I got us a pizza covered in sausage. I was going to offer Bob a slice, but he was gone when we returned to the Excelsior. Blue ate his half quickly and loudly. I had a slice-and-a-half and then turned back to beer. Three beers later, Blue and I went out and got another bottle of tequila.

When I got back to my room, Mulberry was sitting on my couch. "That's a fancy trick," I said, trying to act as though I wasn't surprised.

"You look like you're healing well," Mulberry stood and approached me. He reached a hand out to touch my face, and I backed away. "We need to talk," he said.

I smiled, then grabbed two beers out of the fridge and headed into the bathroom to open them.

"So what's going on?" Mulberry asked from the other room.

I handed Mulberry his beer and then leaned against the window still. "You figured any of it out yet?"

"A bit."

"Like what?"

Mulberry sat back down and took a slug of his beer. "There are tunnels leading from Gracie Mansion to the basement of Eighty-Eight East End, among other places." I nodded. "I talked to a friend in City Planning, and, apparently, the rumor is the first passageways were discovered during the O'Dwyer administration. They decided to upgrade them and use them for security."

"What else do you know?"

"The mayor, Kurt Jessup, right?"

"Yeah."

"He killed Joseph and Tate because of something having to do with the coins Charlene had."

"What do you know about the gold?" I looked out the window. Several stories down, industrial fans hummed.

"It's old, British, and valuable."

"It is from the H.M.S. Hussar, a very famous shipwreck, a long sought-after shipwreck. It sank in Hell's Gate in 1780 with not only the British payroll but also pirated treasure. Then some 200 years later, the mayor found it."

"He found the Hussar?"

I nodded. "He and Tate. Joseph knew about it and was helping them to cover the sale of the treasure, but then he got greedy." Mulberry was paying close attention. "He got horny and greedy. He wanted to run off with Charlene and the treasure."

"That's why he was killed?"

"That's why the mayor killed him. Why did he set up his wife?" Mulberry shook his head. "Because he thought it was really all her fault. If she had kept her man interested, he would never have tried to run off with Charlene and the gold."

Mulberry sat back and took a long swig. I pulled the bottle of tequila out of my bag, running my hand over the gun on my way. I thanked Jesus that I had cleaned up the bullets before Mulberry broke in.

"Shot?" I asked. Mulberry's eyes focused on the bottle. He shook his head. I opened the tequila, savoring the sound of the plastic safety seal breaking. I poured a large shot into a glass and drank it back, then shivered. "Kurt Jessup is not a good guy." I leaned back, getting comfortable in my story. "He's a bad egg."

"Did the mayor bleed at your place at all?" Mulberry asked.

I smiled. "I tore the shit out of his face. That's why he's had the 'flu'." I made my fingers into quotation marks.

"So that means his DNA is in the apartment. We should be able to nail him." A look came over Mulberry. He could see the glory he was gonna get for cracking this case.

"No."

"Of course I can! He's totally fucked." Mulberry laughed.

"Oh, he's fucked, but you're not the one who's gonna fuck him."

Mulberry looked at me, his eyes narrowed. "What?" he asked.

"I'm going to kill him and steal his treasure."

"Joy, you're talking crazy." Mulberry said.

"It's going to be the stealing of the treasure that's hard," I said ignoring Mulberry's judgment on my mental state. "I'm not sure how I'll carry all that weight."

Mulberry stood up. "You can't do this, Joy. You'll go to jail for the rest of your life."

"Only if I get caught, which I don't think I will."

"You're not a killer."

"Mulberry, you of all people should know that everyone is capable of murder." He finished his beer and grabbed another out of the fridge without asking, stepping into the bathroom to open it. "I want you to help me," I said quietly.

"What?" He asked stepping back into the room, beer bubbling over the lip of his bottle.

"You could use the money," I said. "I don't even want it. I just want to take it. But you could use it. Think of the things you could do."

"What?"

I stood up, and he took a step back. "You could help me plan it. Help me carry the treasure. Don't worry. You won't have to kill anyone. I'll take care of that." I took a step toward him. He backed away.

"You've lost your mind."

"Mulberry what are you sticking around here for?" I waved my arm at the room surrounding us. "You're on suspension for trying to solve a case. People think you're corrupt. No one trusts you. When was the last time you woke up in the morning and felt like any of it was worth it?" He was pressed against the wall, and I was talking directly into his face. "Come on. Join me. Let's steal some treasure."

"You're crazy."

A flash of anger ran through me. "You're a loser," I shot back.

Mulberry's jaw tightened, and I turned back into the room. I plopped onto the couch, leaned my head back and let my mind drift over images of pirate booty and murderous revenge. I thought I heard Mulberry crying, but when I turned to check he was looking at me with clear eyes.

"Do you even know where the treasure is?" he asked.

I smiled. "Not yet."

"How are you going to find out?"

"With your help."

"You're nuts and I'm leaving." He walked out the door, taking his beer and bad attitude with him.

It was raining when he came back. It always is in these dramatic situations, like the sky knows that someone's life is changing--a change best symbolized by thunder, lightning, and rain. "Another beer?" I asked as Mulberry dripped on my carpet.

"I've been thinking." He pushed his hand through his hair. It stayed flattened to his scalp.

"I figured."

"I've been a cop for my entire adult life. My father was a cop. A good man." I nodded. "I think you're right that we'll never get Kurt Jessup through regular channels of justice." He paused, and a drop of water dripped off his nose. Mulberry bit his lip in concentration. Lightning crackled. "I just don't know that it works." He paused. "I guess I've felt this way for a while, maybe always." He laughed, even though it wasn't funny. "I just don't know."

The lights dimmed then brightened again.

"So you'll join me."

He flopped onto my couch, a smile across his face. "I guess I'm in. As insane as this is, I'm in."

I handed him a beer, clinked mine against it and said, "Welcome to this side of the 'in it' line."

In the morning I went to the bank closest to the Excelsior and told the woman behind the bulletproof glass that I wanted to turn my check into cash as soon as possible. She looked down her nose at me, which was impressive, since she was sitting and I was standing, until she noticed the amount on the check. Then she turned polite.

"Are you sure you wouldn't prefer to open an account with us? We have many ways to grow your money."

"That's all right; it's plenty. I just want it to be cash."

"You're going to have to open an account, deposit it, wait for it to clear, and then withdraw it."

"How long will that take?"

"With a check this large, it could take up to five business days."

"Fine."

I called Hugh and told him I wanted to take him out to dinner. He agreed to meet me at 7:30 at the Métrazur in Grand Central.

I called Elaine and told her she could have my route; I was quitting. She asked why and then remembered that it was a stupid question. "I'll see you around," I told her.

"I hope so."

John Heart left me a message about getting my apartment cleaned that I ignored. I didn't care about those stains.

I had lunch in front of Gracie Mansion. The mayor still had the "flu" and hadn't made any public appearances since we last met. I wondered if he was thinking about me, if he wanted me the way I wanted him. I wondered what Bob had told him. What they were planning. Bob sat several benches down. I thought about asking him, then changed my mind.

I was ten minutes early to meet Hugh. The maître d' at the Métrazur seated me in the mezzanine, Grand Central spread out below. The clock in the center of the marble floor marked each minute that passed. The ceiling, an unreal green blue with the constellations painted in thin gold lines, curved above me.

I ordered a gin martini and watched people hurrying below. There was a family, clearly from somewhere else, trying to figure something out. The father was smacking a schedule with the back of his hand while his wife rolled her eyes. Their daughter leaned on her Barbie suitcase and looked up at her parents bickering, bored.

I sipped and shuddered as the cold liquid filled my mouth and burned my tongue. Hugh arrived moments later and ordered a martini for himself and a dozen oysters to split. He smiled at me. I could tell he hadn't been sleeping. "How've you been?" I asked.

"As good as can be expected."

"Same here."

"We both look like shit, huh?" Hugh smiled through chapped lips.

I smiled back. "Yeah. But we'll be OK," I said.

He shrugged. "I hope. I don't know if I can do it on my own."

"What do you mean?"

"I've been thinking about seeing someone."

"I think that's a great idea." His martini arrived, and he sipped it deeply.

"I think people always think it's a good idea for other people to see a therapist," Hugh said. I laughed. "What about you? Don't you think you could use some help dealing with this?"

"I'm all right. I've decided to leave."

"New York?"

"Yeah, I don't want to be here anymore." I looked out at the crowd below us. The family was gone. Bob read a magazine near the information booth.

"Where will you go?" Hugh asked.

"I don't know. Just not here."

"I didn't think you would ever leave New York."

"Neither did I."

"When did you decide this?" Our oysters arrived. Twelve mollusks from the Atlantic Ocean, split open, laid on a bed of crushed ice and served to us. I picked up a shell, squeezed lemon onto the grey, slimy creature inside and then tipped it toward my mouth. The shucker had separated the oyster from his shell for me, so it slid easily. I chewed, feeling the life, the insides, burst against my cheeks.

"Very recently. That's why I called you. I wanted to tell you I was leaving," I said. "I hope you'll visit me wherever I go."

"Of course Joy." He looked at me for a moment and then continued. "Please don't make yourself invisible."

"What do you mean?"

"Joy," he massaged his temples. "We both know how easy it is to disappear. Just don't, please."

"Hugh, I--"

"You're all I have left of him, okay. You're the only thing left of him alive, don't you dare fucking disappear." His eyes were suddenly hot with anger.

"I promise, Hugh. I won't disappear on you."

I paid the bill with the last of the money from the envelope my mother dropped on me.

CHAPTER THIRTY-FOUR

SOON, VERY SOON

MULBERRY'S KNOCK woke me up the next morning. "I think I know where the treasure is," he said, pushing his way into my room.

"Good morning," I said, my eyes only half open.

"When we did a search of the basement of Eighty-Eight East End, we found a lot of really strange stuff," Mulberry started. I looked in the mini fridge for a beer, but they were all gone. "I've been going over it in my mind, and I think that some of it is stuff used for underwater excavation." I was trying to wrap my mind around my lack of beer. "It wasn't all in one room, mind you. It was spread out so that no one would think 'hey, here's a room full of underwater excavation equipment'. I mean you wouldn't have even noticed it unless you knew you were looking for underwater excavation equipment."

I held up a hand to stop him. "Stop saying underwater excavation equipment or I'm going to throw up." I walked into the bathroom and closed the door.

"Don't you understand what I'm saying?" Mulberry called through the door. I turned on the tap and started brushing my teeth, ignoring him. I washed my face and looked at myself as the water dripped off my chin. I looked like I hadn't slept, that I had drunk instead. My head was large, fuzzy, and in need of a beer.

When I came out of the bathroom, Mulberry was waiting for me. "The point is that if they left the equipment down there, then they might have been launching it from there." I walked right past him into the bedroom and closed the door. "I bet there is a passage to the river. They could launch the equipment from the old marina and then bring the treasure back to the basement. They could have false rooms, or they could be bringing it out slowly. I don't know." He was breathing hard when I came back out, dressed and ready for a drink. I picked up my keys, clipped Blue to a leash and walked out the door. Mulberry followed me into the hall.

"See, what I'm thinking is we should explore that basement. You said we could get in through the drainage. I think we should wait till it's dark. There's no reason to risk anyone seeing us." The elevator opened, and we stepped in. "Once inside we can search the rooms. I mean, we're not in a rush, right? We can take our time. Find all the treasure. We might even be able to remove it without killing anyone." The doors opened on the ground floor. I pushed the door-close button. Mulberry turned to look at me. "What are you doing?"

"Mulberry."

"Yeah?"

"Shut up." I pushed the door-open button and walked out, waving at the guy behind the desk. He didn't wave back. Mulberry followed me silently. I walked to the bodega, directly to the cooler holding the beer and picked up a six-pack.

"What are you doing?" Mulberry asked.

"Breakfast." He blocked my path.

"No way." Blue growled at Mulberry. "This is bullshit."

"Excuse me?"

"What you need is coffee and eggs and sausage. Not beer."

"I'll take beer, thank you very much." I tried to push past him but the aisle was too narrow. "Come on."

"You don't even want that."

"Yes, I do."

"No. You're faking it."

"What?"

"Cut the crap." Mulberry leaned toward my face. "You're not an alcoholic. You don't need that, you don't want it, and I'm not gonna let you drink it." I pushed up against him. He was made of stone.

"Fine," I exhaled loudly, too tired to argue. Hell, maybe he was right.

"Coffee?" he said. "I'm buying."

"Fine." We walked to a diner nearby that had outdoor seating. Blue climbed under the table, his nose and tail sticking out from either end.

"Coffee for two and two hungry-man breakfasts."

"That's gross," I said once the waitress had left.

"You need it. You look like all you've been doing is drinking."

"And plotting my revenge." I smiled at him.

"This isn't a joke."

"Hey, you're the one who showed up at my doorstep acting like a kid at Christmas, talking all loud about treasure and," I lowered my voice, "killing people." Mulberry waved his hand at me to shut up. "That's all I'm saying."

"What do you think about my idea?"

"I think you're right. I saw wet suits down there and a really powerful flashlight. The Expedition something." Our coffee arrived and I slurped at mine.

"Exactly," Mulberry said. Our hungry-men arrived: sausage, bacon, ham, pancakes, French toast, and two eggs. After the first bite I realized how hungry I was. Neither of us spoke again until the plates were cleared away. "Mulberry, I want us to be clear on one thing before we go any further with this." He nodded. "I'm going to kill him." Mulberry nodded again. "For me, the treasure is secondary. Do you understand?"

"Yeah. But don't you think that taking the treasure is punishment enough? I mean, don't you think leaving him alive to realize that his treasure is gone is better than killing him? Also, then we don't face any legal repercussions. He's not going to call the police and report it missing."

"Mulberry I'm going to kill him. That's it. There's nothing else to talk about here."

"Fine." Mulberry frowned and looked away.

"You don't have to be there," I said gently. "We'll get the treasure out, and then I'll go and take care of him myself. You'll be long gone by the time he's dead." He nodded, frowning. "So, back to this theory of yours," I said. "If Tate and Kurt were accessing the river via the basement, then so could we." Mulberry nodded again. "Theoretically we could carry it out the same way they carried it in."

"Right."

"The question is, how do we turn the treasure into money?"

"I think I know a guy who can help with that."

"Yeah?"

"I've got a meeting with him tonight."

"Can I come?"

The waitress came over and refilled our coffees. After she left Mulberry said, "No."

"Why not?"

"He's a very private man."

"It's a man, then."

"Shut up."

"Fine, talk to your man." I stood up. Blue hurried out from under the table and stood next to me.

Mulberry stood up, too. "Where you going?" he asked.

"I'll call you." I started to walk away from the table. Mulberry tried to follow but a manager--a big, hairy man--asked him how he would like to pay for his check. Blue and I kept walking while Mulberry struggled to pull his wallet out.

I led Blue around the corner and out of Mulberry's sight. I turned into a building. The lobby was empty except for a security guard standing next to a bank of elevators. He watched as Blue and I stood up against the wall.

"Can I help you?" the guard asked.

"No. I'm fine," I said as I watched Mulberry come rushing around the corner. He looked up and down the street. I watched the frustration set into the lines on his face.

"Ma'am, is everything OK?" the security guard asked, eyeing the lingering bruising on my face. The bandages were gone, but the scars looked fresh, pink, and scary.

"Yes. Thank you. I'll leave in just a second."

"Are you hiding from someone?"

I smiled at him. "Of course not." Mulberry turned back toward the restaurant. I waited a few more minutes, watching people walk by.

"Is that the guy you're hiding from?" the security officer asked, pointing across the street at the bus stop. Bob stood large and conspicuous, surrounded by tired women holding plastic bags. "I think he knows you're in here."

"Yeah." Bob was looking right at us. "Looks that way," I said.

Stepping outside, I waved to Bob. He nodded. Then I headed over to Jackie Saperstein's house. I wanted to talk to her. I had a feeling she knew something she hadn't told anyone that she was just dying to tell me.

Cecelia opened the door. "Joy, this is a surprise. Elaine told us you were no longer walking dogs."

"That's true, but I want to talk to Jackie."

"Come in." She closed the door behind me. "I heard about what happened to your brother, and I wanted to tell you how sorry I am."

"Thanks." I didn't want to talk about it, and she dropped it. Jackie and Mildred sat across from each other at the small kitchen table. Snaffles waited for me at the gate, his tail wagging.

"Joy," Jackie said. "This is a surprise."

"Hi, how are you?"

"I'm all right. How are you?"

"I've been better, but I'll be OK. Mildred." I nodded at Mildred. She nodded back. "Could I speak to you alone?" I asked Jackie.

Cecelia took Jackie's place across from Mildred, and we went into the living room. Almost blinding sunlight filled the room. Jackie closed the curtains. "It gets really hot in here if I let the sun come in all day," she explained. The sun struggled through the dark-blue drapes, and the room took on a somber tone.

"I wanted to talk to you about something your husband was involved in."

She sat down on the couch and motioned for me to sit next to her. "What kind of involvement?"

"It has to do with treasure." Surprise was all that registered on her face. "The basement of Eighty-Eight East End." Her surprise was tainted by guilt. "What do you know about the basement?"

"Nothing."

"I think it was you."

"What?"

"I think it was you seen leaving the emergency exit."

"But--"

"I don't think you killed your husband. In fact, I know you didn't. I think you were there, though."

Her eyes, large and frightened, stared at me. "How?" she asked in barely a whisper.

"I want you to tell me what happened. I won't tell the police or anyone else, ever. I give you my word of honor."

"Why do you want to know?"

"Will you tell me?" I could see that she wanted to. Her story pulsed inside her.

"I followed him," she started.

"From here?"

"Yes. I was here when he came back from his jog."

"He came back here? Why didn't Michael see him?"

"I don't know. He was probably looking at himself in the mirror. Or maybe he went out for coffee. I don't know why."

"OK. So, he came back here."

"He was here when I came in. I sneaked in the delivery entrance after leaving Julen. Joseph was packing a bag. He was wearing his jogging outfit and his stupid toupee, and he was packing a bag." Her words spilled out of her, angry and desperate. "When he saw me standing in the doorway, he jumped. He was obviously scared. I asked him what was wrong, but he wouldn't tell me anything. He brushed past me like I was the maid. But I was his wife. I followed him into the hall, and I grabbed

his toupee off his head. He tried to take it back, but I didn't let him." I
had an image of Mrs. Saperstein standing on the couch, the toupee held
high above her head as the late Mr. Saperstein tried to claw up her body
to get it back.

"It was so stupid, so childish of me. I told him he couldn't leave me,
that I loved him, that I wanted to save our marriage." She looked at her
hands where they fidgeted in her lap. "He looked at me with such
disgust--like I was nothing. I don't know how it got to that." She paused.
"We were really in love once, you know. We," she smiled sadly, "thought
we would be happy together forever." She looked up at me and shrugged.
"He gave up trying to take the toupee. He told me I would hear from his
lawyer and stormed out."

"Then what happened?" I asked.

"That's it."

"Come on, finish it." Her eyes glistened. She appeared to be
drowning on the inside.

"I took his toupee and I followed him," she whispered, "I took the
stairs, and I followed him out of the building. He didn't turn around
even once. He walked straight to this hatch in the ground in the park,
near the cherry trees." She looked to see if I knew the hatch she was
talking about. I nodded that I did. "Joseph opened it and then looked
around to see if anyone was watching, but he didn't see me and he went
down. I followed him. He had started wearing this awful cologne. A gift
from his girlfriend, I guess. I could smell it. Isn't that crazy? I tracked
him through the halls by his smell, like a dog." She was waiting for me
to say something.

"I think it's impressive you were able to track him so cleverly."

"Sure," she laughed, the sound was tinged by tears. "clever, not
psychotic. Whichever it was, I followed him. I saw him go into a room,
and then I heard him inside the room. He was apologizing, and I heard a
man tell him it was too late. I ran around the corner and hid. They came
out of the room and walked in the opposite direction. I went after them.
They went through the emergency exit. I was about to follow when I
heard a bang." She paused. "I thought it was a truck backfiring. How
silly." A tear escaped and rolled down her cheek, leaving a track in her

makeup. "I opened the door and saw Joseph on the ground." her breath shuddered and I put a hand on her shoulder. "I don't remember doing it," she continued, "but I must have dropped the toupee." She choked on a sob.

"It's OK. You can stop now."

"No. I want to finish. I saw him lying there. He had no face."

"I know."

"And he was in his own blood. I was standing in the doorway looking at him when I heard Chamers yell to me. I ran. I ran blindly through the halls. Somehow I found myself back at the room that Joseph came out of, and I went into it."

"What was in it?"

"It was so strange. It was just a bunch of wooden crates marked fragile." Her eyes were unfocused, staring into the gloomy light coming through the curtains. "I keep going back there, but I still don't understand."

"That's how Snaffles ate the rat poison?" I asked.

"Yes, I took him with me for the company." We sat in silence for a moment. "You won't tell anyone?" she begged and questioned in the same breath.

"Not a soul," I promised. "Have you figured out what your husband went down there for?"

"No." She smiled without her eyes. "I haven't a clue. The boxes are all empty. I don't understand it."

"Thank you for telling me." She looked at me but didn't say anything. "I've got to go," I said breaking eye contact. I stood up; she followed.

"Do you know why he went down there?"

"I think so."

"Will you tell me?"

"Later." She reached for my hand and held it lightly.

"Please, tell me. I can't sleep."

"The answer won't help you."

"Please."

"I can't tell you now. I promise you that I will explain it all soon." I took my hand away from her. She reached toward me. "I promise, soon."

Bob was waiting for me outside. He followed me back to the Excelsior where I sat in my room until the sun set. Mulberry called. I told him to come over. He arrived with Chinese food.

"You trying to fatten me up?" I asked.

"Someone's got to do it." He pulled out General Tso's, moo shoo pork and spring rolls. We ate directly out of the cartons. I didn't have any plates or bowls.

"I did some research today after you ran off," Mulberry said, a piece of shredded pork hanging from his chin. I motioned to it. He tried to get it with his tongue.

"Lower," I told him. He stretched his tongue as far as it would go. I laughed.

"Did I get it?"

"No." He took his hand and wiped just below it. I laughed harder.

"Shut up." Mulberry reached into the bag, found a napkin, and vigorously wiped the wrong side of his face. "Hmm?" I shook my head, laughing. Mulberry got angry. "Just get it off me." I took the napkin from him and was about to grab it when I burst out laughing and had to slap my knee. "Joy!" he yelled. "Come on." He thrust his chin out toward me. I leaned over and wiped at the pork with the napkin.

We were just inches away from each other. Mulberry made eye contact, and the air grew thick for a moment. We both turned away quickly.

The detective grunted. "Like I said, I did some research today," he started. I smiled at him, laughter playing with my lips. "Don't look at me like that," he said.

"What?" I asked.

"I'm not cute."

I laughed. "You are when you have moo shoo on your chin."

"Listen to me, OK?"

"OK, sorry," I said.

"There is a drainage system underneath Eighty-Eight that flows into the river. It goes under the highway." Mulberry unfolded a map onto the

coffee table and ran his finger over one of the dotted lines. "This one," he said. "We can take it right under the building and out to the open water.
"

"We just have to find how to get into it?" I asked.

"Exactly."

"I found some stuff out today, too."

"Yeah?"

"I know what room Joseph Saperstein walked into in Eighty-Eight right before he was murdered." Mulberry's jaw dropped. I savored his surprise for a second before I continued. "It was the room with all the empty fragile boxes."

"I know what you're talking about," Mulberry said.

I popped the last bite of spring roll into my mouth. "I think we should check it out tonight," I said, my mouth full. Mulberry looked at me. I swallowed. "What?"

He cleared his throat. "Nothing, nothing. Let's check it out tonight."

"There's one thing."

"Yeah?"

"We're going to have to evade Bob."

"Who?"

"That's what I call my tail."

"Are you on something?" Mulberry asked.

"No, really. There's a guy who's been following me. I call him Bob." Mulberry just stared. "He works for the mayor. He's the same guy who threatened me on the subway."

"And he's been following you?"

"Yeah, but he doesn't really seem to be that into it."

"What?"

"I mean, I see him all the time. He nods at me when I wave."

"You wave?"

"Yeah, I think he's bored. But I don't think we should let him follow us tonight."

"OK?"

"We can go out the back."

"OK."

CHAPTER THIRTY-FIVE

THIS IS IT

GOING out the back meant taking the elevator down to the basement and following exit signs till we were standing behind the hotel. Mulberry and I found our way onto 79th Street and headed for the park. Armed with police-issued flashlights, we made our way to the hatch in the bushes. Even though I'd told Mulberry that the drainage hatch led to a secret passage, he was still surprised when I pulled on the sprinkler and the door rose.

"Ladies first," Mulberry said, looking down into the darkness. I clicked on my flashlight and pointed it at the steps below.

"Scared?" I asked.

"Just cautious," he said. I led the way. Smelling the river, I wondered if I would really be using it to escape New York. The hatch closed, and I felt Mulberry stiffen.

"The lights will come on soon," I said.

"I'm not worried," he told me. The lights went on as promised.

"Ready?" I asked when we reached the door. Mulberry nodded. I opened the door and led him through the closet to the next door. He pushed past me and led the way to the room with the boxes marked fragile. Our flashlights cast white circles of light on the strange, empty wooden crates. I found a light switch and flicked it. The single bulb in the ceiling splashed light over the room.

Mulberry pulled a crowbar out of his bag and approached the first box. It was an inch or two taller than me, sealed with nails all the way around. Mulberry huffed and puffed, cracking wood to open the case.

"Nothing," he said, peering into the hole he'd made. I shone my flashlight in and saw the inside of an empty box. The next one was the same and so was the one after that; the next three were just as treasureless. Mulberry was red-faced and panting by the time the last box was opened. "What the fuck?" he said.

"They sounded empty," I reminded him.

"Crap!"

"Not so loud!" He turned away from me. I let out a breath of air, letting it vibrate my lips so he would know that I was exasperated by him.

"Shit!" he yelled again and punched the box. It tipped over and Mulberry cradled his fist.

"That's what you get for--" I smelled the river. Looking down, I saw water rushing below the floor. "What the--?" Mulberry looked over at the hole that the box had been concealing.

"It's the drain."

"The drain?" I asked.

"This is it. This is how they were getting in and out."

"Where's the treasure?" Mulberry walked over to another box. He put his weight against it, and the thing tipped over revealing another hole. This one had a net suspended over it in which rested a trunk. Water hummed below. Mulberry and I stared. He reached in and lifted the trunk's lid. It was filled with gold coins. The gold glowed in a way that made it hard to swallow.

"Holy shit," Mulberry finally said. He walked over and knocked down the next box-- another chest. I knocked over the box closest to me. Inside a net was a velvet bag. I pulled it up and opened it. Diamond necklaces and pearl earrings lay tangled together inside the pouch. I looked over and saw Mulberry holding a matching bag, his face dotted with white facets of light.

"Diamonds?" I asked. He nodded. A smile spread across Mulberry's face--the smile of a very rich man.

After putting the room back together the best we could, Mulberry and I headed back. "We've got to get a boat that can either handle a heavy load--" Mulberry said as we walked through the park, "Or a couple of boats that we could tie together. Ones that we could inflate once we got down there."

"Good idea," I said. We walked out of the park toward the Excelsior.

"I think we have to get it out in one go or he'll notice it's disappearing--and we should do it soon," Mulberry said.

"I can get some boats in the next couple of days," I said as we walked to the back of the building.

"I'll talk to my man about price. We might want to hold on to some of it and sell it slowly," Mulberry said in the elevator.

"That sounds smart." I opened the door to my room. Blue greeted us warmly. Mulberry sat down on the couch. I passed him a can of beer. I opened mine, he opened his, and we clinked them together.

"To treasure," Mulberry said, his beer in the air.

"To treasure." We took long sips, watching each other over the edge of our cans.

Two days later I went to the bank and withdrew my one hundred grand. It was in four envelopes. I put them in my purse next to my gun and walked over to 60th and 2nd to an army surplus store.

"Hi, I called a couple of days ago about some boats."

The woman behind the counter was sitting on a stool, and when I say sitting I mean swallowing with her ass.

"You didn't talk to me," she said

"I spoke to a man."

"What was his name?" She rolled her eyes just to make sure I understood she hated not only her job but also me.

"Joe."

"He's not in today."

"Do you think you could help me?"

"What do you want?"

"Boats. Joe said that he had some boats that could be inflated using a pump and that they would be able to hold the weight of three to four average-size people, approximately a thousand pounds total. He said they were good for whitewater rafting, something about them being easy to navigate in rough currents."

"I don't know." I waited for her to continue, but she just looked down at her nails.

"Is there someone here who could help me?" I asked with a really nice smile on my face.

She found a hangnail and pulled at it with her teeth. "I'm the only person here," she told me as the skin ripped.

I couldn't help but grimace. "OK. When is Joe going to be in?"

"Not today."

"That part I got. Look, I just want to get these boats. Are you sure you can't help me?"

She rolled her eyes again and then turned around to look at some papers on the desk behind her. "Boats, right?" she asked.

"That's right."

"Joe left a note." I waited. She didn't turn around.

"And?"

"I'm reading it." She swiveled back on her stool and tried to give me an evil look, but the fat around her beady little eyes made her just look constipated. I tried not to hate her. Anyone as miserable as she was deserved my compassion. She looked back down at the note. "Says here he's got it all set up to have them sent over to you if you just pay." She looked back up at me. "It's a lot of money."

"I know how much it is." I pulled one of the envelopes out of my bag and began to count.

"You paying cash?" she asked.

"Yes." I answered looking up from the cash I was in the midst of counting.

"What do you need the boats for?" she asked right before popping a taffy into her mouth. I looked up at her. She was working her jaw hard, and I could just make out the muscles through the fat of her cheeks.

"Taking 20 girl scouts whitewater rafting in the Catskills."

"That what happened to your face? Was it a rafting accident?" I didn't answer her. "Seems suspicious to me you buying these boats with cash," she said through the taffy. I ignored her. "I said it seems to me that you wouldn't want to walk around with that much cash."

I ignored her again. She gave up, and I listened to her cheeks smacking together as I finished counting. I laid it on the counter but kept my hand on it. "I'd like a receipt, please."

She rolled her eyes again. "Fine." She reached for a receipt pad, but it was too far away. She was going to have to get off her stool. I realized it before she did. She kept reaching with her thick arm, her round fingers straining to extend.

"I don't think you can reach it," I said.

Her head whipped around to look at me. "I think I know how to do my own job." She went back to reaching for the pad. I did a terrible job stifling a laugh and snorted. She looked back at me, her face red with effort.

"Did you just make a piggy noise at me?"

"Excuse me?"

She eased herself off her stool. "People like you think you're so great." She muttered as she picked up the pad. It took her a minute, and both hands, to climb back up on the stool. She took her time writing out the receipt.

"Name?" she asked.

"Just write down the product I'm buying, the amount paid, and the date. You could put a note about the delivery if you wanted." She glared at me.

"I know how to do it."

"Then you know you don't need my name." She wrote out the rest of the receipt in silence. She ripped it off the pad, handed it to me, and gathered the money up.

"When can I expect the boats to be delivered?" I asked.

"Sometime today."

"Can you be more specific?"

"No." She smiled, pleased with how unhelpful she was.

On my walk home I decided it was time to talk to Bob. He was walking a block behind me. I stopped. He stopped. I walked toward him. He walked away. "Bob!" I called to him. "Bob, wait up!" He looked over his shoulder and stopped. He waited on the curb, out of the way of pedestrian traffic. "Bob, I'm glad you're here. I need to talk to you." He glanced around, probably looking for Bob. "I want this to be over. I've come into some money. I want to leave town. I want to make it out of this alive." He didn't say anything. "Look, tell Kurt," Bob flinched at my use of the mayor's first name, "that I'm going to get the gold from Charlene, and I will bring it to him on Tuesday night." Bob nodded. "Tell him I'll meet him in his office at eight, OK?"

"Ok," Bob said.

I went back to my room and wrote a letter to Jackie. I explained why her husband died and why she was being blamed. I told her about James and what really happened. I wrote that I was sorry and hoped that this letter would do something to ease her pain. I signed it and dropped it in a mailbox.

The boats showed up at 5:30pm. I'd told the man downstairs that a delivery for room 1864 was coming to the front desk, and he should call me when it did. He had smiled and nodded. When I went to pick them up, he was smiling at me. "Your delivery." He waved at the three boxes stacked next to the desk.

"Can I borrow a pushcart to take them up?" I asked.

He put a hand on the top box. "We don't usually accept packages in this manner. I mean for rooms that don't exist." I pulled out a fifty and laid it on the desk. He smiled, slid the bill into his pocket, and then went to get me a pushcart. He even helped me bring the stuff to my room. The boxes were heavier than I had anticipated, and I worried that Mulberry and I would have trouble carrying them. Blue could carry one, but that left two. I just hoped that Mulberry could handle two.

I ripped open the boxes and unfolded one of the boats. Made of reinforced rubber, it took seven minutes to blow up with a high-powered pump. The pump had a rugged, all-steel cylinder base with a six-foot hose curling off one end and a power cord off the other. "Speeds deflating too!" I read off the box. Blue sniffed at the boat spread out flat on the floor.

Mulberry showed up around six and stood over the boat with a big nervous smile on his face.

"Can Blue carry one?" he asked. Blue wagged his tail at the sound of his name. It thunked against the air pump.

"That's what I was thinking," I said.

"How much weight can they handle?"

"A thousand pounds each."

Mulberry circled the boat. "What about currents?"

"We should be able to make it."

"How do we attach them?" I showed him where the end of the boat had thick plastic loops to run rope through, then I showed him the rope we would run through it. "You ever used a boat like this before?" he asked.

"No. Have you?"

"No." We both stood staring down at the boat.

"Do you think you can take two of them with two things of gold, if I take the third boat with the jewelry, the other chest of gold, and Blue?"

Mulberry scratched at his stubble-covered chin. "I should be able to," he said.

We spent some more time looking at the boat. "I got us life vests," I told him.

"Great." I found them in the box with the rope and pulled them out. They were black and sturdy looking. "This is insane," Mulberry said.

"I know," I said.

"Are you sure you want to do this?" he asked.

"Are you?" I countered.

"Yes."

"So am I."

Blue's tail wagged wildly as we walked toward the park. He was carrying one of the boats on his back in a pack I bought for him at "The Canine Camper", a store for dogs who camp. Mulberry carried a boat, the air pump, rope, and his life vest in his backpack. Mine held one of the boats, a life vest, and extra bullets. The straps hung heavy over my shoulders, pulling me back. Mulberry and I each carried an oar.

My gun was tucked into a holster Mulberry had lent me. He'd taught me how to load the gun and persuaded me to buy an extra clip and fill that with bullets, too. He didn't like the idea of letting me march into the mayor's office to blow his brains out, especially since my experience with guns began and ended with when I shot my molding.

But I didn't care. I knew that I could do it. I had this sick and unnatural confidence in my trigger finger. "Just squeeze it," Mulberry told me, "don't pull it." I repeated this to myself as we walked. Just squeeze it. The night was hot, and sweat pooled between me and my pack. We had the streets to ourselves. Everyone was at home with the air conditioning humming.

Mulberry had trouble getting into the drainage hatch with his bag on, and we shared a moment of suppressed laughter when he got stuck. Blue wagged his tail and barked. Mulberry and I both told him to shut up. Blue smiled at us and thunked his tail through the air.

Once inside, we moved quickly to the room with our booty. I dropped my pack next to Mulberry's and pulled my gun out. I put the extra clip in my back pocket. I closed my eyes and took a deep breath.

"You don't have to do this," Mulberry told me. I opened my eyes and saw him watching me. "Taking the gold and gems is enough."

"It'll be OK. Just leave me a boat." Mulberry nodded, and I turned to go. Blue tried to follow me. "No boy. Stay here." I closed the door in his face. I heard him whimpering softly as I moved toward the room with the paisley couch.

I was surprised by how fast the memories rushed back at me when I opened the door. The place was in shambles. A splattering of blood arched across the floor from when the mayor had hit me with the sign. I tried not to think about how much I had lost since then. I turned the sprinkler and began to drop.

Lots of people kill other people every day. People get drunk and drive into other people. Men kill their wives; wives kill their husbands. Sons kill their mothers; daughters are killed by their fathers. Strangers kill other strangers for sexual satisfaction. Doctors kill patients because their hands slip. Humans are constantly dying because another human fucked up, or got angry, or horny, or bored, or drank too much.

Before that summer I had experienced one death--my father's. He died of cancer. First, he got so thin you could see his skull in his face and then he died. At his funeral, James held my hand and told me that it would be OK. He told me that our father was in a better place, which after watching the cancer eat him from the inside out was easy to believe, especially for a 7-year-old. Our father was gone. We would never hear his voice again or smell his smell. But he also would never yell at us. He wouldn't be around to be disappointed in us when we got to be teenagers. He would never tell us he didn't like our lifestyle or our deci- sion-making. My father remains the father of little children. We never had a fight about curfews or grades. He pushed us on swings and helped us build sand castles. That's what happens when you die. You stop.

And now I was about to stop someone. Kurt Jessup's wife would never hold her husband's hand and feel him squeeze back. His mother was going to be forced to attend the funeral of her child. I was going to do this. I was going to make this happen. I knew that he deserved it, but what I wasn't so sure about was whether his mother did or his wife or his best friend, whoever that may be. Did he have a sister? Did it matter?

I pushed against the wall in the little room and felt it give. I walked down the long hall to the elevator and pushed the button. I held my gun in my right hand. I checked to make sure my extra clip was in my back pocket. My stomach churned. The elevator doors opened. This was it. I stepped inside, the doors closed behind me, and I began to rise.

I raised the gun at the doors that would open into the mayor's study. The elevator stopped. I heard the bookcases slide apart, and then the silver doors in front of me parted. The mayor was at his desk, his eyes were open, his mouth slack. I stepped into the room. He didn't move. I fired.

The first bullet hit his shoulder with a silent, sickening tear. His body twisted with the force, but he did not make a sound. I squeezed again, and this one thunked into a pile of papers on his desk, spitting out shreds into the air. The third shot struck him in the neck. A round, red wound slowly poured blood onto his chest. His eyes looked the same as a freshly caught fish--clear and dead.

I took a step into the room. It was very quiet. I looked at him and saw that there was blood on his left temple. He'd already been shot. The fucker was dead, but I wasn't the one that killed him. Shit.

I turned back to the elevator as it began to close. Sticking my foot out, I made it open. I heard voices on the other side of the mayor's door. I pushed myself up against the side of the elevator, letting it block me from view. The door burst open, I heard yelling, and then someone was firing bullets into the elevator as it closed.

Three bullets smashed into the back wall, leaving deep dimples in the metal. The doors closed, and the lift descended. Racing down the hall toward the small anteroom, I was breathing hard and thinking clearly. I jumped on the couch and climbed into the room above. The sign the mayor had used to mash my face lay on its side. I ran it under the couch. It stretched across the platform, and I hoped it would prevent it from lowering.

I barreled through the door of the treasure room. Blue was waiting for me, standing next to the hole in the floor that led to my escape. But there was no boat. I stopped breathing, and the room swam around me. There was no boat. Mulberry, that bastard, had taken all the treasure and all the boats and left.

I heard a loud banging, clicking, and then whirring sound coming from way too close. They were coming for me. They would catch me. They would kill me.

Blue whined and shifted on his paws nervously next to the hole. "Fuck," I said out loud. I walked over to him and rested my hand on his head. Glancing into the hole I saw my boat, floating on liquid black. In the boat sat three sacks and one oar.

I lowered myself into the hole. Loud banging came from down the hall. My feet hit the boat. It wobbled until I crouched into it. I motioned for Blue to join me, but he just stood at the edge, looking down at me, whining.

"Get in here," I hissed at him. He didn't move, so I grabbed his front paws and dragged him down. He fell, all legs, into the boat. I fought with the knot holding us to the building. The lights went out. For a moment all sound stopped. The power was gone. I fumbled in the darkness, trying to free us from Eighty-Eight East End Avenue. The building's generator whirred, and the bulb above my head flickered back to life. The knot gave, and the current took us. We headed into an impossible blackness. I stayed low, holding onto Blue, trusting that Mulberry was right. That this would end with the river.

We spent an immeasurable amount of time in that damp darkness. Blue whined softly. I listened to the gentle splashing of water against the hull. When I thought that we would drift in the depths of the city's drainage system forever, I saw a glow. We moved toward it quickly, and in a rush the sky was above us, Queens was to our right, Manhattan to our left. The East River was carrying us through the city, shrouded in darkness. Sirens screamed, and I heard the distant sounds of people yelling and horns honking--the excitement and mayhem of a blackout.

The wind blew steadily, and the waves carried us up and down. Water splashed against the boat, spraying over its sides, coating us in a fine, briny mist. The moon reflected against the black water, and we were gone. Into the night. Into the future.

EPILOGUE

SYDNEY RYE

THE SUN FLIRTED with the horizon, reflecting off the Sea of Cortez. I dug my feet into the sand past the warmed top layer down into the moist, heavy stuff. A plate of oysters and an unmarked bottle of tequila sat on the table next to me. Blue slept under the table, his nose and tail sticking out of either end

"How've you been?" asked a voice behind me. Blue lifted his head to turn and look. I kept watching the sea. I knew the voice, and I knew there was nothing to hurry about. The sun was getting ready to make a plunge, and I didn't want to miss it.

"Have a seat," I motioned to a chair. Mulberry sat, his weight pushing the plastic legs deep into the sand. "You've gained weight," I said.

He laughed, his round belly shaking softly. "I know," he said. "I know."

We sat for a while, in silence, watching the sun splash the clouds with gold and pink and purple. The ocean changed too. The sky's personal mirror reflected the sun's work, distorting it only slightly to make it more dramatic. The dark blue crept up behind us and started over our heads, invading the sky, forcing the sun to retreat. I turned to my oysters, splashed one with tequila and sucked it into my mouth.

"You want one?" I asked Mulberry, looking him in the eyes. He looked happy, I thought.

"You look like shit. Something haunting you?" Mulberry asked.

I soaked another oyster and slid it down my throat before answering him. "No."

He laughed again. It was filled with ease and comfort. "You're right where I left you," he said. "Wasting away down here." I didn't answer him. "What's your plan--sit on this beach for the rest of your life, eat oysters from a dirty fucking shack?" He waved at the shack behind us where I'd bought my oysters from a slow-moving man named Ramone. I still didn't answer him. I had nothing to say. He sat back in his chair. "I want you to come work for me. I've got a business I set up with some people. I could use you."

"I'm happily unemployed." I skipped the oyster this time, going straight for tequila.

Mulberry was smiling. I spent every day nauseous and afraid and every night sweating and hoping it would just stop. And Mulberry was smiling at me.

"You're down here making yourself miserable for no reason." He picked up one of my oysters, and splashed some tequila on it.

"I'm fine."

"The only problem is your name."

I turned back to the sea. Thanks to Jacqueline Saperstein, Mayor Kurt Jessup was exposed for the killer he was. Jackie took my letter and ran with it. She kept pushing until the city was forced to acknowledge the truth. Jackie called me a hero. Others called me a cold-blooded killer. The police called me wanted. I considered myself a failure.

I hadn't told anyone that Kurt was dead when I got there. And no one mentioned that there was more than one type of bullet imbedded in the corpse. Recently promoted Detective Declan Doyle named me the killer, and only I was the wiser. Declan did tell me that Kurt would reap what he sowed. Karma is what he'd called it. Murder is what most people would.

I guessed my Karma would come around someday soon. It turned out the mayor was right about one thing: He owed people, and they came a calling. I was still testing his theory about treasure making you free.

Mulberry laughed. "Don't tell me it's guilt about James." The name stabbed me in the gut, and Mulberry saw it. "Jesus, you think that's what he wants? You think he wants his only sister down here moping away into the sunset because a psycho killed him?"

"He would have never died if it hadn't been for me."

Mulberry laughed and threw his hands in the air. "Of course he would have died. Everyone dies."

"I mean not so soon."

"Not so soon. Who cares when it happened? It happened. He's dead, and guess what? You're not. No matter how much you try and make out like you are, you're not. So what do you say? Join me?" He was smiling at me, all confidence. I turned back to the sun. It sat on the horizon, wavering between sky and sea, glowing gold and gorgeous.

"I'm a fugitive," I said.

Mulberry pulled out a passport, as dark blue as the sky creeping up on us, and threw it onto the table.

"What's that?"

"Open it." Inside was a picture of me, the new me with the scars, next to the name Sydney Rye. I looked at Mulberry. He was smiling. "Sydney, you've got talent."

"Talent?" I hissed. "I got my brother killed, myself exiled--what are you talking about, talent?" I spit the word at him.

He just smiled, so relaxed and unwound. "Join me."

"I can't." I put the passport down and stared back out at the darkening sky.

Mulberry sighed. "However you want it." He pushed on the table to help himself stand. It wobbled under his weight. He stood over me. "You're never going to be happy here. You're never going to be happy again until you get off your ass and do something right." I looked up. His eyes were locked onto mine. "Dammit, Joy." He slammed his fist down on the table, knocking over the bottle of tequila and making the oysters quiver in their shells.

"What do you want from me?" I yelled back at him.

"I want you to work for me. I want you to get off your ass and do what's right. I want you to be Sydney Rye."

"I don't think I can." I felt my face grow hot and tears well in my eyes. Mulberry grabbed the collar of my shirt and hauled me out of my seat. Blue stood up from under the table and growled.

"Don't give me that bullshit," Mulberry said, his face close to mine. I pulled at his hand, but although his belly had softened, his arms were still made of boulders. "You know what you are. There's nothing else you can be. Do you get that? You don't have a choice. You're stuck, as stuck as me." I looked up at him and realized he was right. "You're a detective, God help you. You're Sydney Rye, private investigator now, and you better stop crying and start thanking me for saving your sorry ass." He dropped me back into my chair, turned, and started to walk up the beach.

I sat for a moment, regaining my breath. He was right, I thought. I wasn't Joy anymore. I hadn't been for a long time. Somewhere between the beginning of this story and the end, without even trying or knowing or wanting to, I became Sydney mother-fucking Rye.

The last glint of the sun dropped into the sea leaving the sky streaked with violet, soft-pink, and pale baby blue. I looked at Mulberry's retreating figure and yelled, "Wait!" Mulberry didn't turn. "Wait!" I hauled my sorry ass out of that chair and ran down the beach after him, Blue on my heel.

Turn the page to read an excerpt from
Death in the Dark, A Sydney Rye Mystery Book 2, or purchase it now and continue reading Sydney's next adventure: emilykimelman.com/DDwb

Sign up for my newsletter and stay up to date on new releases, free books, and giveaways:
emilykimelman.com/SRnews

SNEAK PEEK

DEATH IN THE DARK, SYDNEY RYE MYSTERY BOOK 2

I woke up with my hands over my head, the joints at my shoulder aching. It was hot in the small space, and I tried to scratch an itch on my nose but couldn't move my arm. I blinked my eyes open.

There was a man sitting on the end of my bed. Instantly I was awake and nauseous with fear. I yanked at my arms but instead of moving them down to me, I moved myself up to them. Sitting on the bed, my feet underneath me I could see that my hands were tied and stuck to the headboard with what looked like a giant nail. My ankles were bound with a thick rope that itched once I saw its rough fibers rubbing my skin red.

The man was small in stature, thin, with black hair that curled in tight ringlets almost to his waist. His skin was tan and his eyes deep brown. His eye lashes curled up, long and thick, like a cow's. He watched me without comment.

"Who are you?" I asked, my voice rough.

He smiled, a wide grin that showed off big teeth with even, thick spaces between them. "I'm Merl."

"What are you doing in my bed?"

He reached out a hand and that's when I saw the dogs. There were three Doberman pinschers patiently panting. Two on his left and one on his right. Blue sat next to the last, his pant in sync with theirs. Merl reached into his belt and pulled out a knife.

I breathed deeply, trying to slow my heart which was in the process of filling me with so much adrenaline that my teeth began to chatter uncontrollably. I clenched my jaw to shut them up and felt my stomach threatening to empty.

"Cat got your tongue?" Merl asked and then laughed, showing off his wide-set teeth again. The knife glinted in his hand. Merl reached toward me with the knife. When his head was close enough, I reared back mine and tried to slam it into his skull. But Merl was much too quick for me and I threw myself through the air, flipping off the bed.

Getting my bound feet underneath me I faced him, my teeth grinding and my heart about to explode.

"You're even better than Mulberry said," Merl told me from the end of the bed. *How did he get all the way down there?*

"What?" I asked.

"Mulberry sent me," he said.

"Mulberry sent you to tie me to my bed and threaten me with a knife?" He shook his head. "You're the trainer?" I asked, the fact dawning on me.

Merl nodded. "And I brought help." He pointed to the three dogs. "Thunder, the oldest and most faithful of my companions." The first dog stood and barked. His slick black coat shone in the dull light that filtered through the RV's small windows. There was a sprinkle of grey on his formidable muzzle. "Michael, the largest of my friends." The middle dog stood and barked a welcome, his tongue lolling out of his head. He was a giant, not as tall or thick as Blue, but it looked like he was carved from pure black granite. "And Lucy, the smartest dog that ever crossed my path." Lucy stood and wagged a small nubbins, the remainder of her cropped tail. She was not as big as Michael or as wise as Thunder but there was something in the dog's eyes that made me think she might be the most dangerous of the three.

"I see you've met Blue," I said, still standing in my underwear and torn T-shirt with my wrists and ankles bound.

"If I let you free do you promise not to try to headbutt me?" Merl said, his eyes all smiles.

"Ok, but I think you should realize that was a pretty normal reaction." Merl laughed as he came around the bed. He leaned across my pillows and cut the rope on my wrists. There were soft red lines but nothing permanent. "I think there were a couple of factors that made me think you were here to hurt me. Like the binding and the knife."

Merl leaned over the bed and cut the rope around my ankles. I stepped away quickly and pulled a pair of pants out of my closet. I slipped into the oversized jeans and pulled the belt tight.

"You know you kind of dress like a hobo?" Merl said and cocked his head. I looked over at the four dogs and their heads were all cocked too.

"That's a compliment coming from a guy dressed like one of the Columbine shooters."

Merl laughed heartily at that. He was wearing a black T-shirt tucked into black jeans and I just bet there was a matching trench coat somewhere in his car or tossed over the couch in my living room.

Now that I was no longer in mortal danger I could feel that I was hungover. My head was banging and the nausea I'd experienced was not subsiding. "I need a glass of water," I said pushing past all the fucking dogs into my living room. The place was a mess. I hadn't done any dishes since Mulberry's arrival and he hadn't done any either. Another reason the two of us living in an RV together hadn't worked out.

I pulled out a bottle of water from the fridge and took a long slug. The small space smelled like dogs panting. I pushed open the door and stepped out into a cloud-covered day. A cool breeze was blowing off the sea and I walked toward it. Blue leapt out after me and ran toward the beach. He jumped into the small surf and turned to me, his ears and tail high with anticipation.

The other three dogs followed Merl out. They flanked him like tigers in a circus show. "Free," Merl said, and the dogs took off, black streaks of speed against the beige sand. They barreled toward Blue and soon it was a just a mess of dogs in the surf, rearing up against each other, teeth to neck fun time.

"You like to play like your dogs," I said, then took another sip of the cold water.

"What do you mean?"

"Playing at killing each other."

Merl laughed. "Very well put, Sydney. Very well."

He was the first person to call me Sydney without ever calling me Joy.

"Let's get some food," Merl suggested. "Do they serve breakfast here?"

I nodded and we walked over and sat down at one of the plastic tables. Ramon came out and waved to me. "Huevos, por favor," I called. He held up two fingers, I nodded. Ramon went back in the house.

"Interesting set up you have here," Merl said.

"It's been working."

"But not anymore?"

I took another sip of my water. "Maybe."

Click to download and continue reading
Death in the Dark, **Sydney Rye Mystery Book 2:**
emilykimelman.com/DDwb

A NOTE FROM EMILY

Thank you for reading my novel, *Unleashed*. I'm excited that you made it through my whole bio right here to my note. I'm guessing that means you enjoyed my story. If so, would you please write a review for *Unleashed*? You have no idea how much it warms my heart to get a new review. And this isn't just for me, mind you. Think of all the people out there who need reviews to make decisions. The children who need to be told this book is not for them. And the people about to go away on vacation who could have so much fun reading this on the plane. Consider it an act of kindness to me, to the children, to humanity.

Let people know what you thought about *Unleashed* on BookBub, Goodreads, and your favorite ebook retailer.

Thank you,

Emily

ABOUT THE AUTHOR

Emily Kimelman not only writes adventure, she lives it every day. Embodying the true meaning of wanderlust, she's written her Sydney Rye mysteries from all over the world. From the jungles of Costa Rica to the mountains of Spain, she finds inspiration for her stories in her own life.

Sign up for Emily's newsletter and
never miss a new release or sale:
emilykimelman.com/SRnews

Emily now has an exclusive Facebook group just for her readers! Join *Emily Kimelman's Insatiable Readers* to stay up to date on sales and releases, have EXCLUSIVE giveaways, and hang out with your fellow book addicts: emilykimelman.com/EKIR.

If you've read Emily's work and want to get in touch please do! She loves hearing from readers.
www.emilykimelman.com
emily@emilykimelman.com

facebook.com/EmilyKimelman
instagram.com/emilykimelman

EMILY'S BOOKSHELF

Visit www.emilykimelman.com for a complete list.

EMILY KIMELMAN

MYSTERIES & THRILLERS

Sydney Rye Mysteries

Unleashed

Death in the Dark

Insatiable

Strings of Glass

The Devil's Breath

Inviting Fire

Shadow Harvest

The Girl with the Gun

In Sheep's Clothing

Flock of Wolves

Betray the Lie

Savage Grace

Blind Vigilance

Fatal Breach

Coming Early 2021

Starstruck Thrillers

A Spy is Born

EMILY REED

ROMANCES

The Kiss Chronicles

Lost Secret

Dark Secret

Stolen Secret

Buried Secret

(Coming 2021)

The Scorch Series

co-written with Toby Neal

Scorch Road

Cinder Road

Smoke Road

Burnt Road

Flame Road

Smolder Road

CPSIA information can be obtained
at www.ICGtesting.com
Printed in the USA
LVHW090335080421
683817LV00011B/367